THE
GLORIOUS
PRODIGAL
★

BOOKS BY GILBERT MORRIS

Through a Glass Darkly

THE HOUSE OF WINSLOW SERIES

1. *The Honorable Imposter*
2. *The Captive Bride*
3. *The Indentured Heart*
4. *The Gentle Rebel*
5. *The Saintly Buccaneer*
6. *The Holy Warrior*
7. *The Reluctant Bridegroom*
8. *The Last Confederate*
9. *The Dixie Widow*
10. *The Wounded Yankee*
11. *The Union Belle*
12. *The Final Adversary*
13. *The Crossed Sabres*
14. *The Valiant Gunman*
15. *The Gallant Outlaw*
16. *The Jeweled Spur*
17. *The Yukon Queen*
18. *The Rough Rider*
19. *The Iron Lady*
20. *The Silver Star*
21. *The Shadow Portrait*
22. *The White Hunter*
23. *The Flying Cavalier*
24. *The Glorious Prodigal*

THE LIBERTY BELL

1. *Sound the Trumpet*
2. *Song in a Strange Land*
3. *Tread Upon the Lion*
4. *Arrow of the Almighty*
5. *Wind From the Wilderness*
6. *The Right Hand of God*
7. *Command the Sun*

CHENEY DUVALL, M.D.
(with Lynn Morris)

1. *The Stars for a Light*
2. *Shadow of the Mountains*
3. *A City Not Forsaken*
4. *Toward the Sunrising*
5. *Secret Place of Thunder*
6. *In the Twilight, in the Evening*
7. *Island of the Innocent*
8. *Driven With the Wind*

THE SPIRIT OF APPALACHIA
(with Aaron McCarver)

1. *Over the Misty Mountains*
2. *Beyond the Quiet Hills*
3. *Among the King's Soldiers*
4. *Beneath the Mockingbird's Wings*

TIME NAVIGATORS
(for Young Teens)

1. *Dangerous Voyage*
2. *Vanishing Clues*

THE GLORIOUS PRODIGAL

★

GILBERT MORRIS

BETHANY HOUSE
PUBLISHERS
MINNEAPOLIS, MINNESOTA

The Glorious Prodigal
Copyright © 2000
Gilbert Morris

Cover illustration by Chris Cocozza
Cover design by Dan Thornberg

Published by Bethany House Publishers
A Ministry of Bethany Fellowship International
11400 Hampshire Avenue South
Minneapolis, Minnesota 55438
www.bethanyhouse.com

Printed in the United States of America by
Bethany Press International, Minneapolis, Minnesota 55438

Library of Congress Cataloging-in-Publication Data.

Morris, Gilbert.
    The glorious prodigal / by Gilbert Morris.
        p. cm. — (The House of Winslow ; bk. 24)
    ISBN 0–7642–2116–7
    1. Winslow family (Fictitious characters)—Fiction. 2. Ex-convicts—
Fiction. I. Title.
    PS3563.O8742   G58   2000
    813'.54—dc21
                                          00–010797

To

Esther Gardner, my Canadian friend—

We all need companions on our pilgrim way,
and your friendship has been a blessing to me.

GILBERT MORRIS spent ten years as a pastor before becoming Professor of English at Ouachita Baptist University in Arkansas and earning a Ph.D. at the University of Arkansas. During the summers of 1984 and 1985, he did postgraduate work at the University of London. A prolific writer, he has had over 25 scholarly articles and 200 poems published in various periodicals, and over the past years has had more than 70 novels published. His family includes three grown children, and he and his wife live in Alabama.

CONTENTS

PART FOUR
1917

THE HOUSE OF WINSLOW

★ ★ ★ ★

THE HOUSE OF WINSLOW

★ ★ ★ ★

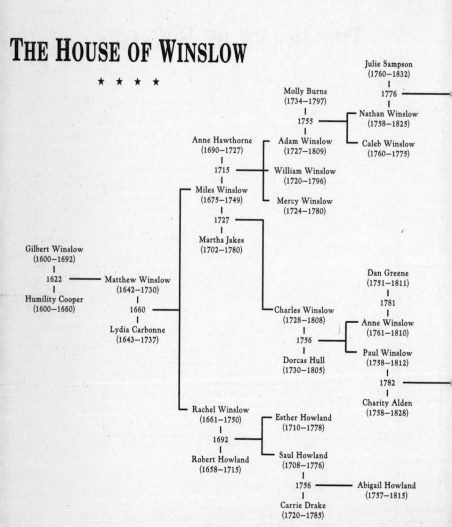

Gilbert Winslow (1600–1692)
1622 — Matthew Winslow (1642–1730)
Humility Cooper (1600–1660)
1660
Lydia Carbonne (1643–1737)

Miles Winslow (1675–1749)
Anne Hawthorne (1690–1727)
1715
Martha Jakes (1702–1780)
1727

Adam Winslow (1727–1809)
Molly Burns (1734–1797)
1755
William Winslow (1720–1796)
Mercy Winslow (1724–1780)

Nathan Winslow (1758–1825)
Julie Sampson (1760–1832)
1776 ——
Caleb Winslow (1760–1775)

Charles Winslow (1728–1808)
1756
Dorcas Hull (1730–1805)

Dan Greene (1751–1811)
1781
Anne Winslow (1761–1810)
Paul Winslow (1758–1812)
1782 ——
Charity Alden (1758–1828)

Rachel Winslow (1661–1750)
1692
Robert Howland (1658–1715)

Esther Howland (1710–1778)
Saul Howland (1708–1776)
1756 —— Abigail Howland (1757–1815)
Carrie Drake (1720–1785)

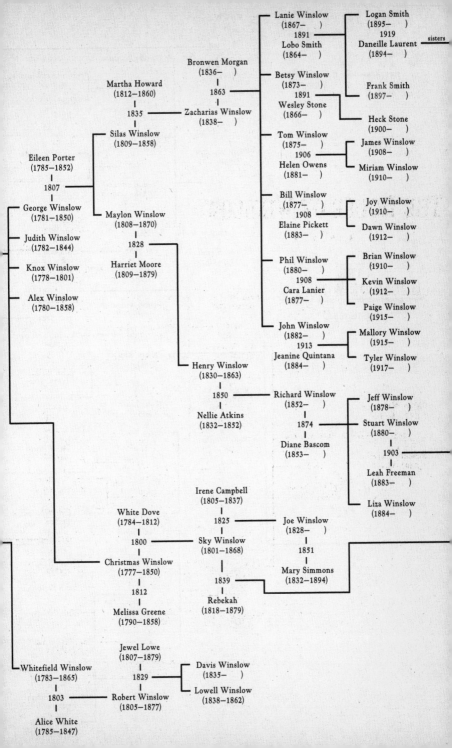

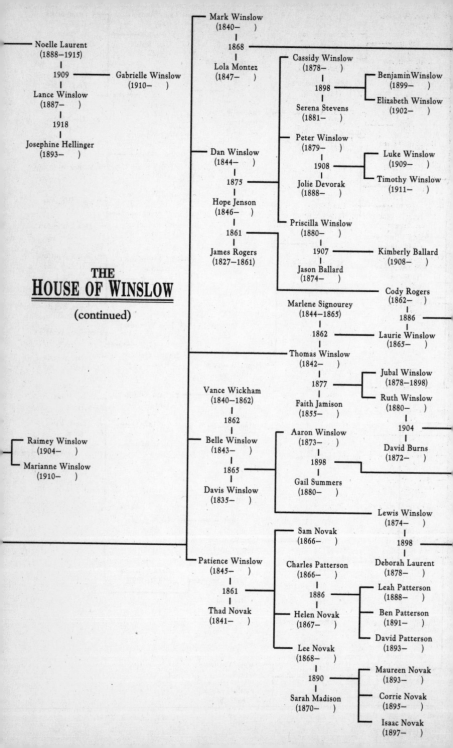

THE
HOUSE OF WINSLOW

(continued)

Noelle Laurent
(1888–1915)

1909 — Gabrielle Winslow
(1910–)

Lance Winslow
(1887–)

1918

Josephine Hellinger
(1893–)

Raimey Winslow
(1904–)

Marianne Winslow
(1910–)

Mark Winslow
(1840–)

1868

Lola Montez
(1847–)

Dan Winslow
(1844–)

1875

Hope Jenson
(1846–)

1861

James Rogers
(1827–1861)

Cassidy Winslow
(1878–)

1898

Serena Stevens
(1881–)

Peter Winslow
(1879–)

1908

Jolie Devorak
(1888–)

Priscilla Winslow
(1880–)

1907 — Kimberly Ballard
(1908–)

Jason Ballard
(1874–)

Benjamin Winslow
(1899–)

Elizabeth Winslow
(1902–)

Luke Winslow
(1909–)

Timothy Winslow
(1911–)

Cody Rogers
(1862–)

1886

Laurie Winslow
(1865–)

Marlene Signourey
(1844–1865)

1862

Thomas Winslow
(1842–)

1877

Faith Jamison
(1855–)

Jubal Winslow
(1878–1898)

Ruth Winslow
(1880–)

1904

David Burns
(1872–)

Vance Wickham
(1840–1862)

1862

Belle Winslow
(1843–)

1865

Davis Winslow
(1835–)

Aaron Winslow
(1873–)

1898

Gail Summers
(1880–)

Lewis Winslow
(1874–)

1898

Deborah Laurent
(1878–)

Patience Winslow
(1845–)

1861

Thad Novak
(1841–)

Sam Novak
(1866–)

Charles Patterson
(1866–)

1886

Helen Novak
(1867–)

Lee Novak
(1868–)

1890

Sarah Madison
(1870–)

Leah Patterson
(1888–)

Ben Patterson
(1891–)

David Patterson
(1893–)

Maureen Novak
(1893–)

Corrie Novak
(1895–)

Isaac Novak
(1897–)

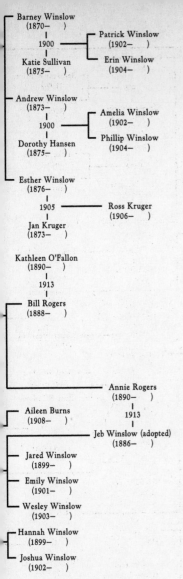

Barney Winslow
(1870–   )
|
1900 ———— Patrick Winslow
| (1902–   )
Katie Sullivan
(1875–   )   Erin Winslow
             (1904–   )

Andrew Winslow
(1873–   )
|
1900 ———— Amelia Winslow
| (1902–   )
Dorothy Hansen   Phillip Winslow
(1875–   )   (1904–   )

Esther Winslow
(1876–   )
|
1905 ———— Ross Kruger
| (1906–   )
Jan Kruger
(1873–   )

Kathleen O'Fallon
(1890–   )
|
1913
|
Bill Rogers
(1888–   )

Annie Rogers
(1890–   )
|
1913
|
Aileen Burns   Jeb Winslow (adopted)
(1908–   )   (1886–   )

Jared Winslow
(1899–   )

Emily Winslow
(1901–   )

Wesley Winslow
(1903–   )

Hannah Winslow
(1899–   )

Joshua Winslow
(1902–   )

PART ONE

1903–1912

★ ★ ★ ★

CHAPTER ONE

AFTER THE BALL IS OVER

★ ★ ★ ★

Directly overhead the sun sent down blistering waves of heat on the backyard where two young women had exited from a white two-story house. The scorching heat waves had burned all the crops to a crisp and seared the Ozarks, turning everything green-gray and dead. Summer was at its height, and July brought only more dry weather. It had not rained in weeks, and now the small Arkansas town of Lewisville was gasping for relief.

"It's hot enough to melt the brass hinges off the door!" said Ellie Mason, a young woman with a florid complexion and expressive blue eyes. Her face was flushed with the heat as she turned to her companion. "I don't know if it's worth all this trouble getting ready just for a dance."

Leah Freeman smiled at her friend's remark. "You know you wouldn't miss a Fourth of July dance for anything, Ellie. Now let's wash our hair."

"I'll bake out here in this heat. You don't sunburn like I do."

"We can sit in the shade of the tree," Leah said. "You bring some chairs out while I get the water." Moving over to a wooden forty-gallon barrel that sat just under the eaves, Leah lifted the lid and peered carefully down into the interior. The water from the well was hard and would not work up a lather at all, so she was grateful for the rainwater that was carefully stored for washing. Dipping the galvanized bucket into the water, she noticed the water was warm, as if it had been heated on the stove. It was that hot a day. Moving back to the table under the towering apple tree, she carefully filled a large basin and then set the bucket down.

"I'll do you first," Ellie said, plopping two cane-bottomed chairs on the ground. Leah sat down and Ellie placed the wealth of hair in the basin supported by a low table. Removing the wrapper from a bar of soap, Ellie chatted as she worked up a lather. "I ordered this new soap from Sears. It's called Ricco Toilet Soap." Looking at the wrapper, she read, " 'A nicely perfumed soap for complexion and hair.' It seems they could make a soap just for hair, don't it, Leah?"

"You'd think so."

"Well, I got it at a bargain. Seven cents a cake," she said as she lathered Leah's hair, which was the color of dark honey with reddish glints. "I bought some perfume, too. Rose geranium in a stoppered bottle. It cost twenty-five cents. I hated to pay that much."

"You ought to stop spending all your money on mail-order houses."

Ellie dug her fingertips into Leah's scalp, ignoring the young woman's protests. "You're a fine one to talk! I hear you spent a week's pay, or maybe two, on that outfit you're wearing to the dance tonight."

The two young women spoke amiably, laughing at times, as they spoke of the Fourth of July dance to be held at the armory. The two had become friends quickly, for both of them were rather lonely. They roomed at Mrs. Helen Gates's boardinghouse. Neither had family in the area, so they spent a great deal of time together. Ellie did most of the talking as she rinsed Leah's hair twice. Then Leah rose and wrapped the towel around her head, saying, "Now let me do you."

The process was repeated, and when Ellie's hair was done, the two sat down on chairs and spread their hair out to dry. As Leah had said, there was no point in sitting out in the direct rays, for the stifling heat was enough to dry their hair even as they sat in the shade.

They both had grown drowsy when suddenly an explosion

practically under their chairs brought them up, screaming.

"I see you, Billy Funderberg!" Ellie yelled. "I'm going to tell your mother on you!"

A young boy no more than ten with a freckled face and a broad grin laughed. He lit another firecracker and threw it toward the two women. It fizzled and went off with a resounding *bang*, and then Ellie ran after him. She returned after he had disappeared and plumped herself down in the chair, muttering, "Kids are incorrigible these days."

"I expect they're about the same as we were," Leah said.

"I was never a rotten kid like that Billy Funderberg."

The two settled down, and finally Ellie felt her hair. "I'm almost dry. Hey, are you excited about your beau? I would be. He's some catch."

"Mott's all right," Leah said casually as she ran her hand over her hair. "I'm about dry, too. I guess we can go in now."

She thought briefly of Mott Castleton, whom she had known only for two weeks. He was a lawyer with a practice in Fort Smith, which was only a short drive from Lewisville. Leah had met him when he had visited the office of her employer on a legal matter and she had accepted his invitation for a date. The dance tonight would be their third date, and she smiled at Ellie's obvious envy. "Maybe we ought to trade dates tonight."

"In a flat minute!"

"I thought you liked Ace."

"Sure I like Ace. Everybody likes him. Tell you what," she said, rising and beginning to gather up the towels and soap. "You'd better turn on the old charm, kiddo, if you want to snag yourself a husband."

"You know I won't do that. I hardly know him yet."

"You'd better!" Ellie stopped and leaned forward, her eyes intense. "A girl's got to think about herself these days. All this stuff about a woman having a career—that's ridiculous. Men run the world, and we've got to run them if we're going to get anywhere. Grab him while you can, Leah. What with him being a lawyer, he's a real catch!"

"Don't be silly!"

Ellie had gathered all the materials up in her right hand and picked up the chair with her left. She was a strong and active young woman, but rather cynical. Her blue eyes reflected this as she said with some vigor, "You know what your trouble is? You're too romantic. Mott Castleton's not exciting enough for you. What you want is some white knight to come charging up on a white horse to save you from a dragon. You've been reading too many romances."

"Don't be foolish, Ellie!" Leah flushed slightly and, picking up the other chair, said, "Come on. Let's go inside."

As they walked back toward the boardinghouse, Leah asked, "What about you and Ace?"

"Why, he's a lot of fun. But he's not the marrying kind." Ellie laughed as they mounted the steps. "Better say a prayer for me that he doesn't get me drunk and ruin me."

"That's easy. Don't drink."

"At a Fourth of July dance! Who are you kidding?" As they entered the boardinghouse, Ellie changed the subject, as she often did. "Say, tomorrow let's get our fellas to take us to that new motion picture. There's a new one out called *The Great Train Robbery*. I hear it's great. It lasts a whole ten minutes!"

★   ★   ★   ★

The chief reason why Leah had chosen Mrs. Gates's boardinghouse over two others was the upstairs bathroom. The house was old, and the room had originally been a large bedroom, some twelve feet square, but Mrs. Gates's husband had converted it into a bathroom and installed all the plumbing himself. Two large windows admitted sunlight and a breeze. The wallpaper was beige with tiny blue violets, and directly over the huge bathtub with the claw feet was a calendar, a gift from Brown's Funeral Parlor. The picture revealed two small children being prevented from stepping to their death by a radiant angel. As Leah settled herself down into the tepid water, she smiled, thinking of how Mrs. Gates must have garnered an armful of the calendars, for she had put one in every room of the boardinghouse. The date on the calendar was small—1903—and Leah studied the two angelic-looking children. "I don't think there were ever two children that sweet," Leah said, smiling.

The bath was a luxury, and although the water was hard, she had managed to work up a lather. She had been amazed at the size of the tub, for it was over six feet long. During the mountain winters she knew it would be freezing to the touch. From outside she could hear the sounds coming from the ball field only a few blocks away. The local team, the Blue Jays, had taken on a semi-professional team, and it seemed that everyone in the county had come to watch. She heard a roar and knew a hometown favorite must have done something marvelous to the baseball—perhaps a home run.

Finally she sat up, rinsed off, and pulled the plug. She watched the water swirl around in a miniature maelstrom, then disappear. As the water drained, she took a sponge and carefully wiped the bathtub, cleaning it thoroughly. Five other young women occupied rooms at Mrs. Gates's, and by common consensus they all kept the bathroom as clean as possible. Mrs. Gates had said firmly, "There'll be no men here. I had one man to take care of, and I'd rather take care of six women any day of the week!"

Stepping out of the bathtub, Leah dried off on a light blue fluffy towel, then put on a brown bathrobe, slipped her feet into a pair of floppy slippers, and left. As she stepped outside into the hall, she saw Ellie leaning against the wall.

"Well, you ought to be clean enough," Ellie said.

"Sorry to be so long, Ellie."

"Won't take me that long. I can hardly wait for tonight. I'm ready to start dancing right now."

As Leah stepped into her room, she glanced at the gilt clock that perched on top of the shelf. It had been her grandmother's and was one of the family heirlooms she had kept when she and her mother had broken up their home in Fort Smith. It chimed six times now with a silvery note, and she quickly moved over toward the bed, thinking of how her life had changed recently.

As she removed her robe and tossed it across a straight-backed chair, a brief memory of her life up until six months ago came to her. She had lived in the same house all of her life on the outskirts of Fort Smith, Arkansas, a frontierlike town in the northwest corner of Arkansas tucked in among the foothills of the Ozarks. She had led a happy enough childhood, but her father had died three years earlier, which had been a great sadness to Leah, for they had been very close. She and her mother had lived alone. Her brother and sister were much older than she, and both were married and had families of their own in Georgia. Her mother had grieved over the loss of her husband, but two and a half years ago she had met a well-to-do merchant from St. Louis. The two had gotten along well, and Leah had not been surprised when her mother had informed her that she was marrying George Stephens and moving to St. Louis.

Leah had visited her stepfather's home for two months but was unhappy there. She did not like St. Louis—or any big city for that matter—and had taken a course on operating the new typing machines. She seemed to have a natural talent for it and became certified as a "typewriter" before moving back to Arkansas. She took a job in Lewisville because it paid more, and she liked the small town very much. At times she felt sad at how alone she was in the world, but she was a sturdy woman with an inner strength and was determined to make the best of it.

Leah's eyes brightened as she looked at the clothing laid out on the bed and began to dress. She had, indeed, ordered a complete new outfit for the dance tonight, and now she slipped into a pair of crinkled crepe drawers, then donned a corset made especially for a slender figure. She had paid seventy-nine cents for it from Perry Dame and Company, a New York mail-order house where she had gotten her new clothes. She fastened the corset, which tucked tightly around her waist, then slipped on a pair of fine-gauge silk stockings with silk embroidered clocks at both sides. Fastening them to the garters, she stepped into the high black patent-leather boots and, using a buttonhook, quickly snapped the buttons into the openings.

Finally she slipped into a corset cover and then picked up the dress she had spent much time in choosing. Carefully she slipped it over her head.

When it was in place, she moved across to stand at the mirror and study the full effect. What she saw was a rather tall young woman, five feet eight inches, full-figured, and strongly formed. Gray eyes looked back at her from the mirror, which at times, she knew, would become green. They were large, almond-shaped, and shaded by thick dark brown lashes. A round face, a firm chin, and a long, composed mouth with lips glinting and curving in an attractive line stared back from the mirror. Her complexion was fair and rosy, but now a summer tan shaded her features slightly.

The dress was rose colored with a close-fitting bodice. It was cut rather low and off the shoulders, which troubled her somewhat, and had balloon sleeves. The skirt was full and decorated with lace-trim side panels.

Reaching up, she touched her hair, which was brushed back high on the forehead in the popular Greek style, exposing her delicate ears. Still studying her reflection, she suddenly made an impatient gesture with her hand, then turned and walked over to the window. Several young boys were setting off squibs, which people were beginning to call *firecrackers* now, and she watched them curiously. Mrs. Gates had put a large American flag up in the front yard, and it stirred in the slight breeze that swept across the street.

I wonder if Mott is serious about me. The thought had come before, and now Leah paused to consider it. Mott Castleton, as Ellie had said, was considered a catch among the young women of Lewisville and Fort Smith. She wondered why she did not feel more pleased over his attentions to her. Mott Castleton was not handsome, but that shouldn't matter, as Leah often told herself. He was pleasant enough and could converse on many things, but still there was something lacking in him, and the thought disturbed Leah. *Am I too fussy?* she thought as she turned from the window and paced the floor, wondering about her own feelings. He had kissed her once, and she had not been stirred deeply by it. He was not a man who was demanding in that way, for which she was grateful. Still, as she moved across the carpet, causing tiny dust motes to rise in the yellow sunlight that lay in bars streaming from the window, she remembered Ellie's question. *"Would you want to spend the next fifty years of your life waking up beside him? That's the test of a husband."*

The thought troubled Leah, and she put it out of her mind. *There's no need to think about that now!* she told herself firmly, then moved out of the room to see how Ellie was doing with her new outfit.

* * * *

Leah had just finished brushing her hair and had sprayed on some perfume from the new atomizer she had bought when a knock sounded at her door. She knew it was Mrs. Gates and said, "Come in."

The door opened. "Your young man is here," Mrs. Gates announced.

"I know. I heard him drive up."

"My, don't you look pretty!" Mrs. Gates declared. Out of all the girls that boarded with her, Leah was her favorite, and she came over now and reached up to adjust a curl that had slipped over Leah's forehead. "You go now and have a good time, but I wish Mr. Castleton drove a buggy. I hate those nasty new automobiles. They're good for nothing but scaring horses, and they'll be killing people one day. You'll see."

Leah laughed and patted Mrs. Gates's shoulder. "I'm a bit nervous about them myself. As a matter of fact, I've never ridden in one."

"Well, if you'll take my advice, you'll have him park that thing outside and you two walk to the dance."

"Oh no. I wouldn't miss it," Leah said.

"You come in early now." Mrs. Gates was a motherly woman and spent considerable time worrying about her young ladies. "And you watch out. You know how these dances are."

"I'll be very careful, Mrs. Gates. Don't worry."

Leah went downstairs, opened the door, and found Mott waiting for her. He turned to face her. A tall man, six feet two with blond hair and hazel eyes, he was wearing a linen double-breasted suit with a matching cap. His face was puffy with the heat, and as he nodded, he said, "I'll sure be glad when it cools off. You ready?"

"Yes, I am."

Mott led her outside toward his new vehicle and said, "How do you like it?"

Leah eyed the contraption skeptically. "To tell the truth, I've never ridden in an auto."

"You haven't? Well, you'll like this one. A fella named Henry Ford built it. Here, let me help you in."

Leah mounted the single seat and sat down and then watched as Mott cranked the engine. As soon as it was running, he leaped into the seat beside her. "Sure would be nice," he said, panting, "if we could start these things from the inside instead of cranking them. That'll come someday."

Moving the levers on the gearshift, the small automobile jerked and then moved out noisily. The armory was only ten blocks away, but they managed to scare several horses along the way. One of them pulling a buggy reared up and ran away, careening madly down the street.

"That's too bad," Leah remarked.

"Yes, it is, but horses will get used to them in time. As a matter of fact, horses are on their way out."

Leah preferred horses herself. She had always loved the animals and had a horse of her own back in Fort Smith, but she was realistic enough to know that Mott was probably right.

"You look very nice," Mott said, taking his eyes off the road for a moment. He was wearing a pair of goggles and nodded firmly. "I like that dress."

"Thank you, Mott. I'm looking forward to the dance."

"Me too. There'll be a lot of drinking and carousing going on. There always is at these things."

"Well, we don't have to join in."

"No, we don't. Can't think of anything more foolish than drinking your health away."

★   ★   ★   ★

The armory was an old red brick building three stories high. It had seen plenty of use over the years, for it had been an armory during the Civil War. It was the largest building in Lewisville, and the second floor had been converted into a meeting hall. When the chairs were removed, it served as a ballroom for those rather rare occasions when Lewisville citizens came together for such an event as the Fourth of July dance.

As Leah crested the stairs and looked around, she was surprised at the size of the crowd. The place was packed, and she murmured, "I don't think there's going to be room to dance, Mott."

"Sure there will. Here, let's move around for a bit."

Mott was, Leah knew, a politician at heart, and she followed him as he greeted people, whispering to her from time to time the pertinent facts about each one. "He's the judge. A good man to know. I'm going to ask him to support me when I run for office."

High above them, red, white, and blue festoons were strung across the ceiling. The late afternoon sun, along with the large crystal chandeliers, threw a blazing light over the dancers. The bright colors of the women's dresses caught the rays from the chandeliers—green, red, blue, purple—and the sound of many people talking and laughing made a pleasant, though rather loud, noise throughout the decorated armory.

Leah danced with Mott, and then he surrendered her to a friend of his, Luke Garrison. Mott had laughed and said, "Luke is the sheriff, Leah. I'll trust him to take care of you."

Garrison, a short man built like a wrestler, had cool gray eyes and was soft-spoken. He danced well enough but shrugged, saying, "I'm no dancer, Miss Freeman."

"Why, you do very well, Sheriff."

"I understand your fella's going to be running for office soon."

"Well, he's not really my fella, Sheriff. I think you're right about his running, though. He's very interested in politics."

A gloomy light touched the sheriff's eyes. "I'd just as soon be out of it," he said. "I should have been a farmer like my dad. Less trouble."

"I thought law-enforcement officers led exciting lives."

The two were doing a two-step, and Garrison concentrated on the intricacies of the dance for a moment. "Well, you're mistaken about that. I spend most of my time locking up pitiful drunks and trying to get votes for the next election."

"You make it sound terrible. I've read about Wyatt Earp and Bat Masterson and all the famous lawmen of the Old West."

"I don't think they were quite what the books make them out to be. Earp was all right, but Masterson was nothing but a cheap crook. Some of those fellows just happened to be on the right side of the law. They could have been outlaws and desperadoes just as easy."

Leah found the sheriff interesting, but then he surrendered her to Ace Devainy, who had come looking for her deliberately.

"Where's Ellie?"

"She's dancing with the mayor." Ace was a homely and gangly man with yellow hair and light blue eyes. For all his homeliness, the mothers of the town feared him, for young women had a failing for him that was hard to understand.

Leah found Devainy an entertaining man. He enjoyed his dance with her, paying her close attention. When the band started to play a cakewalk tune, Leah protested. "I can't do that dance!"

"Sure you can, honey. Nothin' to it." Ace grinned. The cakewalk dance, originally done by southern blacks, featured prancing struts, shuffling feet, and exaggerated sways. The white version was somewhat different. The couples formed a square with the men on the inside, high strutting to a sprightly tune as they paraded imaginatively around the figure. It had a rather frenetic rhythm and a rollicking melody that was becoming known as ragtime.

Leah was a good dancer and quickly caught on, and by the time the cakewalk was over, her eyes were sparkling, and she said to Ace, "It's fun, but I don't think it's very respectable."

"Oh, I think it is. All my friends do it, and my friends are all respectable."

"That's not what I've heard, Mr. Devainy."

"You've been listenin' to the wrong people." Ace then said, "Whoops, I've got to get back to the bandstand. Come along. I'll take you over to the refreshment table."

Leah allowed herself to be guided to the refreshment table and watched as Ace made his way back to the bandstand. She was soon joined by Ellie, who was laughing.

"I saw you carryin' on with my fella. You tryin' to steal him?"

"No. I don't think so. He's a lot of fun, though."

Mott came over to join them, and the three stood there as the master of ceremonies called for quiet. As soon as everyone settled down, he said, "We have a real treat now. Stuart Winslow's going to play and sing a brand-new song. You all know Stuart. His song is 'Won't You Come Home Bill Bailey?'"

Leah's eyes were on the bandstand when a strongly built man stepped forward with a violin in his hand. He had the blackest hair she had ever seen, with brows to match, and his dark blue eyes looked almost black. Tucking the instrument loosely under his chin, he began to play and tap his foot and sing. He was handsomely dressed in a pair of fawn-colored trousers, a snow-white shirt with a string tie, and a pair of shiny leather half boots.

Leah listened as Winslow sang the racy song, accompanying his own singing with impressive fiddling skills. When he had finished, she said, "What a wonderful voice!"

Ellie nudged her with an elbow. "Better stay away from him. He's worse of a woman chaser than Ace. They're best friends, you know."

The crowd applauded, and then Stuart held the violin in one hand and nodded to the band. They began a slow melody, and the piano player picked out the notes in a very slow fashion. Lifting his voice, Stuart Winslow began to sing, "Because you come to me, I'll cherish thee. . . ."

The song was one of Leah's favorites. She had heard it sung at many weddings, and it never ceased to touch her emotions. As the singer's smooth voice filled the hall easily, Leah could sense the pathos in it, and suddenly she discovered that his eyes were fixed on her. She knew that oftentimes some entertainers had the ability to make everyone in the hall think they were singing or speaking directly to them—but this was no illusion. Their eyes locked, and as Stuart Winslow sang the words, Leah found herself unable to turn away.

As soon as the last note of the song ended, she saw Winslow put his violin down and come straight across the room. Walking right up to her, he smiled and said, "Our dance, isn't it?"

"Why don't you keep on playing, Stuart," Mott said.

"Why, Mott, I don't mind," Leah said. It was the first time she had seen Mott angry, but it would be rude to refuse the man's invitation. "You don't mind, do you?" she asked gently.

"I suppose not."

"Thanks, Mott."

Turning to Leah, Stuart said, "Come along. This is one of my favorites."

It was a waltz, and Leah found herself moving easily across the floor. As she had suspected, Stuart Winslow was a marvelous dancer. She followed his lead effortlessly.

"I'm Stuart Winslow."

"Yes, I know. My name is Leah Freeman."

"I hate to begin a relationship like this, but I must tell you, Miss Freeman, that you're the most beautiful woman in the room."

Leah laughed. "That sounds like something your friend Ace might say."

"Ace has no taste in women, but I do. Do you live here? What about your family?"

As they danced Leah spoke of herself and what she did. "I'm a typewriter," she said.

"Oh, you're a smart young lady to learn that." They spun around the room, and he asked abruptly, "Do you have a regular beau?"

Leah hesitated, then shook her head. "Not really."

And then Stuart Winslow smiled. He had an olive complexion, and his teeth were very white against his skin. She saw a small cleft in his chin, and he wore a small neat mustache.

"Well, I'm available," he said and laughed softly, "and this is your lucky day, Miss Freeman."

"Well, there's no modesty about you."

"Oh, I've got all kinds of modesty. But I've got a feeling about the two of us, Miss Leah, if I may call you that."

Leah listened as he spoke and enjoyed the dance tremendously. Stuart Winslow had a way with women, she knew, but somehow she felt he was half serious beneath his light bantering.

Mott came up immediately after the dance and nodded curtly. "Our dance, I think, Leah."

"I've got to play awhile, Miss Leah," Stuart grinned, "but save another dance for me."

"Of course."

Leah turned to Mott and they began a two-step. Mott did not speak, but he was obviously not pleased. "What's the matter, Mott? Have you had trouble with him before? Don't you like him?" Leah asked as they moved across the ballroom.

"Nothing to like about him."

"What's wrong with him?" she asked curiously.

"He's a wastrel. Comes from a fine family. His father is one of the leading citizens here in Lewisville, and his mother's a fine woman. Richard Winslow and his wife, Diane. I think a great deal of them."

"What does he do?"

"He owns two stores—one here and one in Fort Smith—and is thinking about opening a third, I understand. He's a good businessman."

"I thought Stuart was very attractive."

"All women think that. I hate to talk about a man behind his back, but young women aren't safe with him, Leah."

Leah did not answer. Somehow she knew there was truth in Mott's words, and yet as she continued to dance, she kept thinking of the words Stuart had said: *This is your lucky day. . . .*

"Hey, Ace, we've got a little job to do."

Ace Devainy looked over at Stuart and grinned. "You've got trouble in your eyes, boy. I know it. What are you up to now?"

"Have you met Leah Freeman?"

"That young woman with Mott? Sure. She deserves better than him."

"Well, she's going to get better." A light of deviltry flashed in Stuart Winslow's eyes, and then his lips curved upward in a smile. "You want to do me a favor?"

"Why not. Anything for a friend."

"Go out there to that automobile he's so proud of and drain the gasoline out of it. I don't want it to start when it's time for them to leave."

Ace laughed. "I can take care of that. You got your eye on Leah Freeman?"

"Prettiest thing I've ever seen."

"You got that right. I'll take care of the gasoline."

★　★　★　★

"What's wrong with it, Mott?"

"I don't know. Sometimes it just won't start. They haven't got these things perfected yet." Mott had cranked until he was sweaty. The dance had ended and it was after midnight. Now Mott came around from the front of the auto and shook his head.

"You wait here, Leah. I'm going to go get Fred Jefferson. He can always get these things started."

"All right."

Leah sat there as Mott disappeared. The stars overhead were brilliant dots against a sable sky, and she sat quietly thinking of the dance. It had been an exciting time for her. She had danced twice more with Stuart Winslow, knowing that it displeased Mott but not caring a great deal. As she sat there waiting, she remembered Ellie's words. *"Don't be a fool!"* she had hissed. *"Hang on to Mott!"*

Not long after Mott had left, she heard the sound of a buggy approaching, and she was suddenly aware that it had drawn up beside her.

"Well, you'd better come with me, Miss Leah."

Leah blinked and saw by the full moon overhead that Stuart Winslow had pulled up beside her.

"I'm waiting for Mott. He's gone to get a repairman."

"I know, but he'll not find Fred. That's who he always goes for when this contraption breaks down. I think you'd better let me take you on home."

"No. That wouldn't be right. I'll wait for Mott."

Leah watched as Winslow jumped out of the buggy and came over to stand beside her. "It's not really safe for a young woman to be out alone this late. Look, you just leave a note for Mott. Tell him I'm driving you home, and he won't worry about you."

The argument went on only for a few moments, and then Leah surrendered. "All right, but I'll have to leave him a note."

She looked in her purse, pulled out a piece of paper and a pencil, wrote a note, and pinned it to the steering wheel with a hairpin. "He can't miss that," she said.

"Right. Now you come on. It's getting late."

As Leah got in Stuart's buggy, she smiled. "Do you often worry about keeping young women up too late?"

"Always." Stuart grinned. "Come along."

Leah was amused. She suddenly had a thought and said, "Did you have anything to do with that car not starting, Stuart?"

"Me? Not a thing," he said innocently. "I don't know a thing about cars. How could I do that?"

Leah laughed. "I don't believe a word you say." A few moments later she looked around suddenly and said, "You're going the wrong way."

"Well, you didn't tell me where you lived."

"I'm staying at Mrs. Gates's boardinghouse."

"Oh . . . well, you'll have to direct me."

Leah tried to tell him where to go, but he persisted in making wrong turns. Finally she found herself out beside the small river that circled Lewisville. The moonlight turned it into a silver track, and as she protested, he suddenly handed her the reins. "Here. You drive yourself."

Leah was a good driver, and she laughed, saying, "Why should I drive you?"

"I've got other things to do." He reached behind the seat and pulled out his violin. Tucking it under his chin, he began to play, and Leah was entranced.

"You play beautifully," she said.

He did not answer but continued to play. Finally he played and sang "After the Ball Is Over." It had been a hit for about ten years, but somehow he did something different with it. As she silently sang the words in her mind, they evoked a pathos in her. She had always felt it was a sad song, but now Stuart's clear, tender voice brought out some things in it she had never heard:

After the ball is over
After the break of morn
After the dancers leaving,
After the stars are gone.
Many a heart is aching,
If you could read them all;
Many the hopes that have vanished,
After the ball.

"That's a beautiful song," she whispered, touched by it.

"It was written by a fellow named Charles Harris back in 1892. He spotted a young couple quarreling after a dance and wrote it. It got to be real popular," Stuart said.

The only sound was the clopping of the horses' hooves and the chirping of crickets as they moved along the road beside the river.

He turned to her suddenly, put the violin back, then took the reins. "I've always thought the moon was the most beautiful thing," he said and put his arm around her, "but now I don't think that anymore."

Leah was amused, and the pressure of his arm around her shoulders was pleasant enough. "How many times have you said that to young women?"

"Oh, I've taken a few girls out for a buggy ride."

"I've heard that."

"But you're different."

"How original!" she laughed.

He did not speak for a moment but turned the horse back toward town. She was surprised, for she had expected him to try to kiss her. He did not speak again until they drew up in front of the boardinghouse. The lights were all dark except for the one in the foyer, and she said, "I've got to go in."

"Wait a minute," he said and turned to her. "I know I've got a bad reputation, but a man's got to change sometime. He's got to settle down."

Leah felt he was trying to be sincere, although she had no justification for believing it. "I think it might be good for you to do that."

When she started to move, he turned and put his arm around her and drew her to him. Her face was a mirror that reflected her feelings as they changed, and as he pulled her forward, he noticed the delicate curve of her mouth.

As for Leah, she did not know why, but she permitted him to hold her tight. When his lips touched hers, she did not pull away but waited until he finally released her. "I've got to go in," she said.

He reached out, took her hand, and said quietly, "I wish at a time like this that I hadn't led the life I had."

"It's never too late to change."

At that moment, perhaps for the first time in her life, Leah felt something more than a mild interest in a man. As she kept her eyes fixed on Stuart's face, she saw in him something that she had been seeking for, for a long time. One part of her was aware of that side of Stuart Winslow that was not what a woman would want, but she could see in his eyes a fire and a zest for living that drew her to him. Without meaning to, she put out her hand and laid it on his cheek. "It's never too late to change," she said again. "All of us have to—"

Leah never finished her statement, for the silence of the moonlit night was broken by the increasing roar of an automobile. Quickly Leah turned to see Mott Castleton's vehicle appear. A wave of guilt washed over her, and she cast a quick glance at Stuart. He simply stood there, turning to face Castleton as he stopped the car and strode toward them. Castleton's face was taut with anger, and even by the faint light, Leah could see that his body was stiff with rage.

"Stuart, get out of here!"

Quickly Leah stepped forward, for she saw that Mott's fists were clenched and she did not want the two men to get into a fight. "It was my fault."

"No. It was my fault," Stuart said. He stood straight and faced the larger man, his own body tense. He was, however, not ready for what happened next. Mott suddenly struck out, catching Stuart high on the forehead and driving him backward.

"You're a rotter, Stuart! You don't know a decent woman from the trash you run around with! Never come around Leah again! Do you hear me?"

Stuart jumped to his feet, and for one terrible moment, Leah thought he was about to throw himself forward. She stepped between them and put a hand on each man's chest. "Please," she begged, "don't fight."

Stuart Winslow was struggling inside to control himself. He was handy with his fists, and although Mott Castleton was larger, there was no doubt in his mind that he could whip him. But Leah's eyes pleaded with him, and he released a ragged breath. "All right, Leah." His eyes came around to Mott, and he said, "I don't want any trouble."

"Get out of here and stay away from Leah!"

Without a word, Stuart walked to his buggy, got in, and spoke to the horse, which moved forward.

"There was nothing wrong, Mott," Leah said. "He was afraid to leave me in the automobile by myself. He was just giving me a ride home."

"That wasn't what he wanted. He's not worried about your safety. He's never worried about any woman. Don't you know that, Leah? You don't know the kind of man he is."

Leah knew there was truth in Mott's words, but she could not answer him, except to say, "I know, but anyone can change."

Mott Castleton twisted his head to stare at the disappearing buggy. When he turned his head back, his eyes still held a cold glint of anger. "Not him," he said. And then he put out his hand, and took hers. "I was worried about you, Leah. You don't know how to handle that kind of man. Other women thought they knew him, and they wound up disgraced."

Leah remained silent, pondering the truth she felt in Mott's words. Then she said quickly, "I've got to go in, Mott." He held her hand for a moment, not allowing her to leave, and she looked up at him, surprised. She saw genuine concern in his eyes, and she whispered, "Don't worry about it, Mott. You're right. I should have stayed in the automobile and waited for you."

He pulled her forward then and kissed her. When she pulled away, he said, "Good night, Leah. I'll see you tomorrow."

Leah went inside and moved at once toward her bedroom. She crossed the room in the darkness and looked out the window. Moonlight flooded the street, and she watched as Mott drove the noisy automobile away. For a long time she stood quietly. Then finally she murmured, "He could change. I could help him. . . ."

CHAPTER TWO

"WHAT WE HAVE IS FOREVER!"

★ ★ ★ ★

"I think Stuart's doing much better, don't you, Richard?"

Diane Bascom Winslow had turned from the dressing table where she had finished doing her hair. She was of no more than average height and not a beauty in the classic sense, but at the age of fifty, she possessed a graceful elegance, and her spirit shone out of her fine light brown eyes. Her hair was also brown with tints of red. She was a quiet woman but given to flashes of humor. Now, however, she seemed concerned and came over to stand beside the large man who stood staring out of the window. "Don't you think so, Richard?"

Over six feet tall and strongly built, Richard Winslow's black hair had some gray in it now at the age of fifty-one. He had intense dark blue eyes, heavy eyebrows, and there was strength carved into his features. His chin was rather blunt, and he tended to shove it forward aggressively. Even the gestures he made with his hand as he turned to answer his wife demonstrated a certain power. "No. I don't think so!" he said, and the glumness made its mark on his face.

"But he's doing so well out on the farm."

"He'd do better to pay more attention to the business. That's where the money is. If it weren't for Jeff, I wouldn't have any hope at all."

"Jeff's a little older, and he's more given to business, Richard."

The two had been over this many times before. Winslow owned two large general merchandise stores, one in Lewisville, another in Fort Smith, and he was thinking of opening up a third. He had also bought up land, and the only part of the small empire he had created that interested Stuart was the farm, mostly because of the fast horses that the family bred there.

"He's more interested in dances, fast horses, and parties than he is in a profession," Richard said shortly.

"He's young. He just hasn't found his way yet."

"You always make excuses for him, don't you, Diane?" Richard Winslow was truly known by one person, and that was this woman who stood before him. Now he came over and put his arm around her and said, "I hate to be an old bear all the time."

"I know you love Stuart," Diane said quietly. She put her hand on his cheek. He had muttonchop whiskers that she had hated at first but had grown to like over the years. She stroked them now, trying to soothe his irritation. Always, she was the one who had to stand between her husband and the headstrong son who, in many ways, was so much like his father. "He has been coming to church some lately."

"Yes. I'll give him that."

"I think that's because of Brother Fields. He always liked Charles, and he's had a good influence on him." They spoke of Reverend Charles Fields, the pastor of the Baptist church. Richard was a deacon there and had been instrumental in getting the church to issue a call to a young man whom he admired greatly. Charles Fields had grown up almost as a member of the Winslow family, and now Richard Winslow took satisfaction in the fact that the entire church was united behind the young pastor. "He's been good for Stuart, but Stuart's got to take his own life in hand."

"I'm sure he will. We've just got to encourage him."

"What about this young woman he's been seeing? Do you know anything about her?"

"She's very respectable, I think. Stuart introduced me to her after church. Her name is Leah Freeman. You were having a meeting with the deacons. I think she's a fine young woman."

Richard Winslow had grown a bit cynical over the years that

his youngest son would ever come around and settle down and lead a normal life. Stuart had given him a hard education in parenting, and now Richard said noncommittally, "I hope so. He needs someone to help him. Well, come along. Let's go meet her."

★ ★ ★ ★

As Ellie came in, she laughed at once, saying, "Where did you get that thing?" She walked over and picked up a small brown bear with bright buttons for eyes and moveable arms. She twisted them around and said, "This is cute. Where did you get it?"

"Stuart gave it to me. It's called a teddy bear."

"Why do they call it that?"

"Stuart said it's named after the president."

"After President Roosevelt? Why would a toy bear be named after a president?"

Leah turned and put down her brush. "He said that President Roosevelt was visiting Mississippi, and he went bear hunting there. They gave him an easy shot at a cub—the photographers, that is—but he wouldn't shoot at a helpless target. Then Stuart said there was a man named Morris Michtom who had a toy store and had read about the story, so he made this toy cub bear and named it Teddy."

"It seems to me that that would be against the law."

"Well, you know what the president's like. He gave his permission, and now everyone wants one." She went over and picked up the bear and held it to her cheek. "Isn't he lovely? I thought it was sweet of Stuart."

Ellie Mason stood for a moment, her eyes fixed on her friend who held the bear, and she shook her head. She was a worldly-wise young woman, much more so than Leah Freeman, and now a sudden thought came to her. It expressed itself by a grin in her eyes, and, as usual, she came out with it rather bluntly. No one had ever accused Ellie Mason of having any tact.

"Has Stuart ever—you know—acted ungentlemanly toward you when you were alone?"

"Ellie!" Leah's face flushed, and she gave her friend an indignant look. "What a rude thing to say!"

Ellie laughed. "I see he has. Well, he wouldn't be Stuart Winslow if he hadn't tried something like that."

"I don't want to talk about that, Ellie."

"You may not want to, but you know what's on Stuart's mind."

The flush deepened on Leah's face, for Stuart had indeed attempted improprieties she had been forced to fight off quite stringently. It had come to the point where she had threatened to never go out with him again if he didn't behave as a gentleman should. Now she could not think of an answer to make, and she saw that Ellie was watching her with a cynical look. "He's . . . just not . . ."

Seeing Leah's inability to find words to put Stuart Winslow in a little box, Ellie sobered. "You're serious about him, aren't you?"

"I like him a lot, Ellie. I really do."

Ellie came over and looked directly into Leah Freeman's eyes. "Let me give you some advice. Don't be swayed by his charms until you've got him tied down."

"Tied down?"

"Yes, and I don't mean simply an engagement ring. Stuart has convinced more than one young woman that he meant to marry her."

"How do you know all this?"

"It's common knowledge, but I got it from Ace. As a matter of fact, he's kind of worried about you, too."

"Ace is? Why, have you two been talking about me?"

"Of course we have." Now it was Ellie's turn to hesitate. She gave a defiant look at Leah and then shrugged. "I've not been as good as I should have with Ace, but I don't want it to happen to you."

"Ellie, you shouldn't have!"

"Don't preach at me, Leah. I am what I am, and that's why I'm telling you I know what Stuart Winslow is like. He's been spoiled to the bone by his good looks and his money. He can sing and play, and women have always fallen over themselves with him. Don't let it happen to you. Get him tied down—get him all the way to the altar. That's the only way with a man like him."

Leah felt there was something wrong in even talking about such a thing, and she stood silently as Ellie continued. Inwardly she knew there was some truth to her friend's words, for they were similar to the warning Mott had given her, but she had become much fonder of Stuart Winslow than she had ever imagined she would.

"And I'll tell you something else," Ellie said firmly. "If you do marry him, it's not over."

"What does that mean? It's not over."

"I mean Stuart's going to look at other women. He's handsome as mortal sin, and women have become a game to him. There'll be plenty around to give him anything he wants."

"I don't believe that! If I did marry Stuart, he'd change."

Ellie knew then how serious her friend was. "When I hear that kind of talk," she said, "I know there's real trouble right around the corner." She chewed her lip for a moment, then shook her head and walked out of the room without another word. As she closed the door, her brow was furrowed. "I've got to convince her," she muttered. "She doesn't understand what kind of man Stuart is."

★   ★   ★   ★

Leah was impressed by the decor of the dining room at the home of Stuart's parents as they sat down to dinner. It was a medium-sized room with an oak floor. The walls were papered in gold, blues, and greens, and there was a large marble fireplace to one side. A massive oak table with eight chairs upholstered in green fabric sat in the middle of the room on a large Persian area rug, and a sideboard was filled with silver tureens and platters.

The table was set with china and sparkling crystal, for Diane Winslow was a fine hostess. She did keep a servant who helped her, but Diane had taken great care in all the preparation for this meal.

"This is a lovely house you have," Leah murmured.

"Richard designed every bit of it," Diane said proudly. "He asked me what I wanted, I told him, and here it is."

"That's wonderful, Mr. Winslow." Leah had been somewhat intimidated by Stuart's father, but now she began to relax when he smiled at her compliment.

"Thank you, Miss Freeman. I don't think I ever enjoyed anything quite as much as building this house for Diane. We had to wait a few years, and the first house we had was rather small.

But I always told her I'd build her the house she wanted, and this is it."

"I believe Dad could build the Taj Mahal if he put his mind to it," Stuart remarked. "He's always been able to accomplish anything he's set his mind to."

"Not quite," Richard said.

His eyes were fastened on Stuart, and for one awful moment, his wife thought he was about to launch into one of the arguments that frequently occurred between the two men. Quickly she said, "Tell me how you became a typewriter, Leah."

Leah sensed the immediate tension that filled the room. She glanced over at Jeff Winslow, who was twenty-five, two years older than Stuart. He was no more than medium height, lean with dark hair, and had mild blue eyes. She sensed a steadiness and reliability about him and liked him very much already. Her eyes shifted to Liza, Stuart's nineteen-year-old sister. Leah felt that the girl did not approve of her, although she could not think of why. "Well," Leah said, "when Mother moved away to St. Louis, I had to do something. I didn't like it there at all. It was too big for me. . . ."

Richard Winslow listened as the girl talked, and he found himself liking her very much. *She's not at all like the floozies Stuart usually runs with, or so I'm told. This girl's got character.* Finally, he said, "I'm glad you visited our church."

"Yes. You have a very fine pastor. I like his sermons very much."

"What church did you belong to in Fort Smith?"

"The First Baptist there. I belonged to it all my life," Leah said.

"I know the pastor very well," Richard said. He mentioned his name, saying, "He's a fine preacher."

The talk went on for some time, and when the meal was finally over, the men moved away toward the parlor. Jeff stopped long enough to whisper to her, "Glad to have you here, Miss Freeman." He winked at her and said insistently, "Maybe you can make a man out of Stuart."

This statement startled Leah, but she had no time to respond. She helped carry the dishes into the kitchen and chatted amiably with Stuart's mother.

"You're a wonderful cook, Mrs. Winslow."

"Do you like to cook, Leah?"

"Oh yes, Mrs. Winslow. My mother began teaching me when I was very young."

Diane began cutting and dishing out the cake she planned to have in the parlor. "And you don't have any family at all left in Fort Smith? Is that right?"

"Yes. I only had my mother and my brother and sister. But they all live far away."

"Well, that's sad. You must get very lonely at times," Liza said as she helped her mother arrange the dessert on trays.

"Yes, I do, but I try to make the best of it. It's nice living at Mrs. Gates's boardinghouse. She's almost been like a mother to us girls."

Mrs. Winslow left the room, and as soon as she did, Liza said quickly, "I'm glad you came to visit, Miss Freeman, but I wanted to say one thing." She hesitated, then shook her head. "I hate to speak against Stuart. He's my brother and I love him . . . but be careful."

Leah was more startled by this second warning. First from the brother and now from the sister. "What do you mean, Liza?"

"Stuart is—well, he has no morals where women are concerned."

Leah did not know how to answer Liza. Indeed, she had no time, for right then Diane came back and asked her to help carry the tea service into the parlor. The Winslows were all musical, and she enjoyed a pleasant hour singing with all of them. Something about the family's closeness appealed to her greatly, and never having had such a close family as the Winslows, Leah felt somewhat envious.

They talked at length about current affairs, and it was Leah who said, "I read in the paper yesterday that the Wright brothers are still working on that airplane of theirs. Do you think it'll ever fly?"

"I sure do," Jeff said. "I wish I could work with them. I'd like to go up in one of those things."

"Not me," Richard said. "Besides, it'll never amount to anything."

"Well, it's a beginning, Dad," Stuart said. "Everything has to begin small."

"That's true enough, I suppose." Richard gave Stuart a direct look and said, "Have you given any more thought to giving your time to the business instead of running around playing that violin of yours at dances?"

Instantly the atmosphere changed, and Leah could sense it. It was thick, and she saw the father and son locked in some sort of struggle. Neither of them spoke for a moment.

Finally Richard said heavily, "I see you haven't. I hate to see a man waste his life with things like that."

It was an embarrassing moment, and only Diane Winslow's tact saved it. She immediately went over to the piano and began playing "In the Good Old Summertime" and other popular melodies.

★　★　★　★

"Well, you won the family over."

Stuart had driven down beside the river, and he pulled the horse to a stop. "I knew you would. You could win anybody over, Leah."

"You have a wonderful family, Stuart. You must be very proud of them."

"I am." He hesitated and then laughed shortly. "Of course, not all of them are so proud of me. As a matter of fact, I guess I'm one of the lesser Winslows."

"Lesser! In what way?"

"Pretty much every way, I guess. I don't have Dad's drive for business. Jeff's got that. Nobody's like Mom. And Liza's got much more talent than I do."

"I don't think they feel that way about it."

They sat there and enjoyed the unusually cool evening air for a while. August had been a hot month, and now Leah said, "Let's walk a little bit. Could we?"

"Sure." Stuart leaped out, tied the horse to the fence, and then turned to Leah. "It's a pleasant night."

"Yes, it is."

The two of them walked along the river and admired the

moon as it reflected on the ripples broken up into a thousand silver-crested waves.

"I used to swim in this river when I was a young boy. Jeff and I would come down and spend hours here. There's a hole down there under a bridge that's twelve feet deep. It was a big day in my life when I was able to go down all the way and touch the bottom."

"How old were you?"

"Oh, I don't know. Maybe ten."

The two stopped at a bend in the river and listened as the river made sibilant whispers around their feet. Neither of them spoke for a while, but finally Stuart turned and examined her face. She was surprised at his intense scrutiny and said, "What is it, Stuart? Why are you looking at me like that?"

"I think I'm working up to tell you how much I've come to admire you, Leah." He put his hands out gently and drew her forward. "I want to marry you, Leah." He pulled her close and kissed her. She was not a girl to give way, for he knew she was stronger than that. She was, in fact, the strongest woman he'd ever met, and now as he held her, he felt the half-giving, half-refusing strength of her body. A wild sweetness came to him, and when she drew back, he was shocked at the power she had to stir him. "Marry me, Leah," he whispered.

Leah found herself trembling, for she had already been warned about the wild side of Stuart Winslow. He had a force of will and an attractiveness beyond most men. She drew a quick breath, then put her hands on his chest. "I can't do that, Stuart."

"Why not? Don't you care for me at all?"

"I . . . I do care for you, but I could never marry a man who wasn't a Christian. You know that, don't you?"

"But you could help me with it, Leah. I could find my way if I had you to help me!"

Leah felt a wild impulse to accept his proposal right then, but she forced herself to say, "I can't give you an answer." She turned and walked quickly back to the buggy, knowing that it was not Stuart Winslow she was fleeing—but her own heart!

★ ★ ★ ★

Reverend Charles Fields looked up at the knock at his door,

then rose from his desk. He had been working on his sermon and had reached some difficult points, so he was glad for an interruption. He opened the door and blinked with surprise. "Why, Miss Freeman!" he said. "It's good to see you. Come in."

Stepping back, Fields waited until the young woman had entered. "Here, sit down."

"I don't want to interrupt you, Pastor," Leah protested, but she took the seat at once.

Fields laughed. "I'm never unhappy to be interrupted when I'm working on sermons. I like to preach, but getting something to say is hard for me." Fields was a small man with a pair of clear, steady gray eyes. He was not handsome, but there was a winsomeness about him, and he had a wonderful voice. He was not a married man, and all the young women—and their mothers—of the congregation were very much aware that he was an eligible and willing bachelor.

Fields saw that Leah Freeman was tense, and although he was a young pastor, he had learned to recognize certain signs, and now he said quickly, "I've been wanting to talk to you. You've done a wonderful job with your Sunday school class. When Mrs. Evans got sick, I didn't know what we'd do, but you stepped in, and all the girls love you. I'm very grateful for what you've done to help out."

"Oh, that was nothing! It's something I love to do." Leah had taken over a class of junior girls and for the past month had met with them faithfully. It was something she had done before in her church in Fort Smith, and it was not difficult for her.

The two sat there talking about the Sunday school and about church business. All the time Fields was aware that the tension in Leah was getting worse. He finally slowed down the pace of the talk, and as he knew would happen, she soon came out with what was really on her mind.

"I . . . I'd like to talk with you about a problem, Pastor."

"Certainly. As you know, nothing that I speak with people about ever goes out that door."

Leah struggled for a moment, bit her lip, and then she said quickly and nervously, "Stuart Winslow has asked me to marry him. He's not a Christian man, but I love him, Brother Fields. And I've come to ask for your advice."

Fields was not taken completely off guard by her announcement. He was a good friend to Stuart and to all the Winslow family, and he was an astute young man. He had noted that Stuart had recently started coming to church with Leah, something he himself had not been able to persuade the young man to do. He had also had a brief talk with Mrs. Winslow, who had some inkling of the situation.

Fields glanced out the window for a moment and studied a squirrel that was perched on the limb of the oak tree out in the yard. He prayed for wisdom, for he felt he was treading on very dangerous ground himself.

"Miss Leah, I'm going to be very honest with you. You know, of course, that Stuart and I are good friends. Indeed, the Winslows practically helped raise me. I'm very close to the entire family."

"Yes, I know that, Pastor."

"As to your question," Fields said carefully. "Usually I try to be very nondirective. When people ask me what to do, I hem and haw around and pretty much tell them to pray and ask God what to do." He turned his compassionate eyes upon Leah and said, "Miss Leah, please take this the right way. I'd . . . hate to see you marry Stuart."

Leah dropped her eyes, and her lips began to tremble. A brief moment passed before she was able to respond. "Why do you say that, Pastor?"

"He's too young, and he hasn't found himself yet. Certainly you must see that."

"But he can change." Leah lifted her head, and there was pleading in her fine eyes. "Anybody can change, can't they?"

"I've heard so many young women say that," Fields said. He shook his head sorrowfully. "They think that if they just marry a man who's wild, they can be a good influence. But I've never seen it work out. Not one time."

A silence fell across the room then. Fields knew he had not given the counsel the young woman had wanted, but he felt it was the right thing. "Wait awhile. He is young, and we'll pray for him, as his family has been doing for years. But he's not ready for marriage yet, Miss Freeman. I tell you that honestly."

Leah rose and her voice was trembling. "Thank you, Pastor, for your time."

Fields saw her to the door, and when she left, he closed it. He leaned back against it and thought, *Most people don't want advice. They want you to agree with what they've already decided to do. She's decided to marry him, and she'll try to change him, but unless Stuart finds God, he'll break her heart exactly as he's broken his parents' hearts!*

★   ★   ★   ★

Leah smiled up at Stuart. "You're going to like this preacher," she said confidently. "I heard him once before. He's such a wonderful speaker."

Stuart glanced down and smiled at Leah. "I never thought I'd drive fifty miles to hear a preacher, but you could make me do anything, Leah."

Since he had first spoken of marriage three months earlier, he had thought of little else, and his life had changed since. It had been encouraging for his family to see him throw himself into the work of the farm and even help out with the general store. He had been faithful at attending church, and even Richard had hope for this prodigal son of his.

The two of them had come to Little Rock to hear the famous evangelist Gypsy Smith, who was holding a large tent meeting on the outskirts of town. As Stuart and Leah made their way toward the enormous tent, Stuart said, "That's not his real name, is it—Gypsy?"

"No. His name is Rodney Smith, but he's a real gypsy. He was born in a gypsy tent in England," Leah said. "He couldn't read or write. I heard him tell all this in his testimony at another service. Maybe he'll give it again tonight."

The two found seats midway to the front. A layer of sawdust covered the floor, and the lighting threw its brilliance over the crowd. It was a noisy gathering, and Stuart looked around curiously. His coming here was more a matter of wanting to be with Leah than to hear a preacher, but he was impressed at the size of the crowd. "Is that him up on the platform?"

"Yes. He looks like a gypsy, doesn't he?"

"Yes, he does."

"He joined the Salvation Army after he was converted. General William Booth heard him sing and pray, and soon after that he became an evangelist for the Army. Everywhere he's gone since then, God has blessed him."

The two sat there and finally the singing began. Gypsy Smith himself led it. He was no more than medium height, rather stocky, with a swarthy complexion. He had a brilliant smile that was so full it even shone from his soulful brown eyes. He played the accordion well and had a powerful voice that reached to every corner of the tent.

"Well, he sure can sing. I'll say that for him," Stuart said.

"Wait until you hear him preach. He stirs your heart."

Stuart had a clinical interest, for he had heard a great deal about Gypsy Smith from Leah. When the evangelist finally rose to preach, Stuart noted that he had a marvelous speaking voice as well. Being a singer himself, Stuart admired the man's clear baritone. He soon found out that the gypsy from England was also a gifted preacher.

The sermon was on the subject of the blood of Christ, and over and over again the evangelist would say, "The blood of Jesus Christ, His Son, cleanses us from all sins." He went on to talk about himself and how he had needed so desperately to be cleansed from sin. Then he raised his voice and said, "All have sinned and come short of the glory of God. Every one of you sitting out there. If you are not under the blood of Jesus, you are under the condemnation of hell."

Stuart began feeling uncomfortable. He had heard preaching all of his life, but had never been moved by it. But there was something about this sermon he could not ignore. He began to shift uncomfortably in his chair and was aware that something was happening deep down inside of him.

Leah also felt the power of the sermon. When Smith spoke of the death of Jesus, it brought tears to her eyes, as it always did. She was aware that beside her Stuart was sitting ramrod straight. A glance at his face showed that he was tense, and all of the frivolity was gone. She prayed silently, *Oh, God, let him hear your voice and let him get saved tonight.*

Finally, Gypsy Smith said, "It's time for you to come to the cross. There's no other place for you if you're lost. Only Jesus can save you. I want you to come forward now. We'll pray for you, and you'll be on your way to heaven before you leave this tent."

Stuart stood there, his head bowed, looking unseeingly at the sawdust-covered floor. He was amazed at how many people of all ages were going down to the front of the tent, and an almost irresistible urge came to him to go forward as well. But he fought it off.

"Would you like to go down, Stuart? I'll go with you."

Stuart shook his head, shutting off the soft voice. "I can't go now."

The service was soon over, and Leah's heart broke at Stuart's reluctance. She had felt that tonight was the one chance he might have had, and he had turned down God's invitation.

They said nothing until they reached the hotel where they both had taken rooms, and when he took her to the door, he said, "I've got to talk to you, Leah."

"You can't come into my room, Stuart."

Desperately, he said, "All right. We'll talk here. I'm a lost cause if you don't help me, Leah. I should have gone forward tonight, but I just couldn't. But if we were married, you could help me."

It was the old plea that had touched her heart before, and Leah found herself responding to it.

He stood there pleading, and she felt her resistance breaking away. When he put his arms around her, she felt him trembling.

He's so close to the kingdom. I can help him. If we were married, I know I could show him the way. The certainty she felt in her heart strengthened her resolve, and at that moment she made up her mind.

"All right, Stuart. I'll marry you whenever you say."

"Tomorrow?"

"Yes, but you must promise me one thing."

"Anything!"

"You must seek after God. Jesus is the only hope of our having any kind of a marriage."

"I promise," he said. He put his arms around her, and they clung together.

Then she stepped back and said, "Tomorrow I'll marry you."

* * * *

The two of them were married the next day by the pastor of the small church. She had not understood how Stuart had managed to obtain the license, but he had been gone all day, and they had been married at four o'clock. He had taken her out to the finest restaurant in the city, and now they had come back to the honeymoon suite he had insisted on.

Stuart had stepped outside for a moment, and Leah still couldn't believe she was now actually Mrs. Stuart Winslow as she unpacked her small carpetbag. A few minutes later the door opened, closed, and Stuart stood before her. He had his violin case in his hand, and he flashed her a quick grin.

"Mrs. Winslow, I have a special wedding present for you."

His cheerful expression relieved her. She sat down on the bed and waited.

Stuart winked at her and said, "A wedding present for my new wife." He took the violin out, tucked it under his chin, and began to play. He played so softly that no one in the next room could have heard it. It was such a beautiful tune. There was a poignancy and power to its lilting melody that warmed Leah's heart. Somehow as she listened, Leah could not keep the tears from her eyes. When he put the violin back in the case, he came over and sat down beside her for a moment. "I just wrote it today," he said. "It's for you."

"What's the name of it?" Leah asked, brushing the tears from her eyes.

"Leah's Song."

"Oh, Stuart, how beautiful!"

Stuart rose, put out the light, and took her in his arms. "I haven't written the words to the song yet, but I'll write them as we live together."

As he kissed her, Leah could hardly believe the happiness that flooded her heart as she held on to him fiercely.

"By the time we've been married fifty years," he whispered, "it'll be a very long song."

As she nestled into his strong arms, she heard herself crying out, "Never leave me, Stuart."

And then his voice came to her. "I never will. What we have is forever."

Leah felt more tears gather in her eyes, but she turned and whispered, "Yes—it'll be forever!"

CHAPTER THREE

FIRST ANNIVERSARY

★ ★ ★ ★

Thanksgiving had always been a special holiday for Leah. Some of her earliest memories were of those times when she was little more than a toddler, following her mother around in the kitchen. She always associated the season with the smell of turkey roasting in the oven, spicy pumpkin pies, and the bustle of getting everything ready at the same time.

Now Thanksgiving had come again, the end of her first year of marriage, and she had risen from bed determined to cook a Thanksgiving dinner that Stuart would never forget—their first together as husband and wife. She moved carefully, for the baby she carried was only a month away from entering the world. She was swollen and her face was puffy, but she ignored the discomfort as she moved around the kitchen, then reached up to get a large mixing bowl from a top shelf. The effort, slight as it was, brought a grimace to her face. Her pregnancy had been difficult. She had not complained, but she had felt guilty. She knew all too well how little patience Stuart had with any kind of distress she might speak of.

Getting the eggs out of the icebox, she cracked four of them and then beat them with a fork until they were light yellow. She added the pumpkin that Annie had cleaned and put it in a bowl and then stirred it with a wooden mixing spoon. From time to time she added cinnamon, ginger, and allspice as she continued to stir. Finally she poured half a cup of molasses and a cup of milk into the bowl. She was just getting it all mixed together when a voice behind her said, "Now, whut you think you're doin'?"

Guiltily Leah held up the spoon and said defensively, "I'm making pumpkin pudding for dinner."

The black face of Annie Waters was a study in disgust. She was a large woman—not overweight, just big—in her middle thirties. She came quickly across the room and snatched the spoon away from Leah. "I done told you you ain't cookin' today! I reckon I'm able to do all the cookin' around dis here place!"

"But, Annie—"

"Don't you 'But, Annie' me! Dr. Morton done tol' you to do nothin' but lay in dat bed!"

"But I get so tired of the bed, Annie."

"Then you go set down in the parlor in that big easy chair. You hear me?"

"All right, Annie, but bring the pecans in. I can crack them for the pecan pie."

"I ain't studyin' no pecan pie! You just get in there and do what I tells you!"

Subdued, Leah moved slowly into the parlor. She had become very fond of Annie Waters and her husband, Merle, who had been on the farm for five years. Merle, a big bruising man and strong as a bull, did the outside work, and Annie did a great deal of it, too. During Leah's pregnancy, however, Annie had become housecleaner, nursemaid, cook, and all other things. *I don't know what I would have done without Annie*, Leah thought as she made her way into the living room. She sat down slowly and carefully in the overstuffed chair and propped her feet up on the hassock with a sigh of relief. She stared down at her legs, which were swollen, and a moment of fear came to her. Dr. Morton had called on her daily during the pregnancy, and often he had waved his thick forefinger in her face, saying, "If you want to keep this baby, you'll stay in bed. Let Stuart and Annie take care of you."

Picking up the composition book that she used for a journal, she took her pen and began to write.

November 20, 1904: I had a bad night. Stuart was not home. He went to play for the opening of a new bridge over in Clayton County. He told me he might not be home, but I hoped he would.

For a moment she paused, and a quick memory came to her. She knew if she looked back over her entries for the past year, since the day she and Stuart got married, she would find many similar entries. *Stuart gone to play for a wedding. . . . Stuart gone to play for the opening of a new building. . . . Stuart invited to play for the inauguration of the governor.*

She sighed at the remembrance of so many nights alone and continued to write:

I try not to feel bad about his being gone so much, but it does get lonesome, especially with the baby coming so soon. I must be patient with him. How many prayers have I prayed, and I pray again. I'll never quit. I remember reading that George Mueller prayed for two men for over sixty years, and neither of them were saved during his ministry, but they were converted two months after he died. The Lord is good and He will hear my prayers. I know the church is praying for him, and as for Diane, I don't know of a mother who prays for her son more than she prays for Stuart.

She continued writing for some time. It was a means for her to express her deep feelings, since Stuart was away so much. These past three months she had been a very lonely woman. The first few months of her marriage had been nothing but constant joy. Stuart had stayed with her, and they had enjoyed doing everything together. He had turned down hundreds of invitations, it seemed, to go away and play, but then something had happened between them, and she could not understand what it was. At first he accepted a few invitations to play, and soon he was away more and more.

She flexed her fingers and then wrote:

I don't want to complain, for I love Stuart and I know he loves me. I had thought he would be saved by this time. He came so close a year ago at that tent meeting with Gypsy Smith, but now he seems to be drifting far away. As for me, I don't know where I am. I was so happy during the first months of our marriage—and I believe I will be again after the baby is born. But right now I feel like I'm standing in the middle of a bridge and I can't see either end of it. All I can do is look down at the water and wonder what to do next.

★　★　★　★

Annie turned at the sound of the door slamming and watched as Merle clomped across the floor and dumped an enormous armload of wood into the woodbox.

"Well, is that all the noise you can make?" she said sharply.

"I don't know how you expect me to put wood in a box without makin' no noise." He came over suddenly, and her back was to him. He put his arms around her and squeezed as he lifted her clear off the floor.

"Put me down, you silly man!" she said sharply, but he held her there until she began to giggle. "You hear what I tells you? Now you put me down!"

"Woman, you just get sweeter every year."

Merle was an enormous man, six feet four and weighing over two hundred fifty pounds. His strength was proverbial in the Lewisville area. He picked up loads no other man could even think of lifting. Once, he picked up a whole bale of cotton and carried it twenty steps just to win a bet. His skin was a glowing ebony and his hair nappy, and a deep inner peace glowed through his warm brown eyes.

"How Miss Leah doin'?"

"She ain't doin' no good."

"Ain't that too bad. I glad we's had our chilluns easy."

"*We* had our chilluns! Where do you get that *we*?"

"Well, you had 'em easy, then. Does that make you feel better?"

Merle stood over her, watching as she cooked the Thanksgiving meal, and finally she turned and said, "Where's Mistah Stuart?"

"Why you ask me that? It ain't none of my business. Why you always jumpin' on me for somethin' I never done?" Merle was peeved, but he saw that Annie was perturbed. "I know," he said. "It's bad, ain't it?"

"She don't really know what Mr. Stuart's doin'."

Merle shook his head sadly. "I guess it's best she don't know about his carryin' on."

"Well, this is Thanksgivin', and it's their weddin' anniversary. I want you to go find him and bring him home."

"Me! How am I gonna bring him home if he don't wanna come? He's the boss."

"Knock him on the head and bring him home."

"I can't do that!"

"You're big enough."

"Where we gonna go after he throws us out?"

"He ain't gonna do that. He's guilty as a sheep-killin' dog." Annie was filled with indignation. She had grown to love Leah Winslow with a motherly affection, and now she reached out and grabbed Merle's arm. "We gotta do somethin'," she said. "You know how he is. He won't even think about comin' home until he's dead drunk. Now you go fetch 'im."

"I don't know where he is."

"You go find Mr. Ace. He keeps up with him, and you bring him back. You hear me? Don't you come back without him."

"I'll do the best I can, but how you expect a black man to boss a white man around is more than I kin see."

"If you can't do nothin' else, you go to his mama. She'll figure out some way."

"She already done got her heart broke over that man."

"Well, it'll just have to be broke a little bit more, 'cause I ain't havin' my baby in there without her husband on their first anniversary. Now git!"

★ ★ ★ ★

The sun was high in the sky, almost at the zenith, as Ace Devainy caught sight of the beginnings of Mapleton. He was whistling a tune, as usual, but he stopped abruptly as the first shacks on the outskirts of town came into view. The air had a sharp bite to it, for it was a cold Thanksgiving. "I expect we might get some snow," Ace muttered aloud. He sat loosely on the seat of the wagon, clucking occasionally at the matched team of bays that paced in a sprightly fashion down the rutted roads. A late rain had come and churned the roads into a red gumbo, and then the cold weather had frozen it again. The frozen ruts caused the wagon to bounce along in time, making Ace swear softly as his teeth clicked together.

Unhappiness scored Devainy's homely face as he slowed the team down. He pulled his soft wide-brimmed hat off and ran his hand through his yellow hair. His stormy blue eyes reflected the agitation he felt inside, and he muttered once, "I'd rather do most anything than try to drag Stuart away from his fun."

He sat up straighter as a memory flashed across his mind of the massive form of Merle Waters, who had come to his room earlier. Merle's black face was embarrassed, but his eyes were determined as he had explained his mission. "Mr. Stuart needs to be home, Mr. Ace. Annie done sent me to get you and to find out where he is. I got to try to bring him home."

Ace had understood the black man's own agitation. Merle was certainly big enough to simply put most men under his arm and walk away, but it wouldn't do in the south for a black man to behave like that.

"I'll fetch him back, Merle. You go tell Annie that I'll have him there before dark."

"He might not want to come, suh."

"He's comin' whether he wants to or not."

Now as Ace guided the wagon down the single main street of Mapleton, his jaw hardened and he nodded, speaking to himself, "He's comin' all right, whether he likes it or not. Why does he have to act like this?"

He had a fairly good idea of where to find Stuart, so he drew up in front of a saloon on a side street, tied the horses, and went inside. He was greeted at once by an old friend of his, Betty Marrs.

"Well, Ace, look at you!" Marrs was a hefty woman, and she wore more cosmetics than necessary. She came over to give Ace a hug. "Sit down and have a drink."

"Before noon? I reckon not."

Marrs laughed. "I've seen the time when the hour of day wouldn't matter to you, Ace. You're gettin' old."

"Reckon you've got somethin' there. A man's got to grow up sometime."

The words seemed to disturb Betty Marrs. She heaved a big

breath and said, "I guess you're right, Ace. What are you doing over here?"

"Looking for Stuart."

"He's down at Cora's house."

"I thought he might be. I hoped I'd catch him here."

"He's been in and out, but mostly he's with Cora. You know what's going on between those two?"

"None of my business, Betty. I'll see you later."

Leaving the dingy saloon, Ace climbed up into the wagon and drove it slowly down the street until he pulled up on the east outskirts of town in front of a freshly painted frame house. "Whoa," he said, and when the horses stopped, he sat quietly, wondering how he should handle the situation. "I wish it could be easy," he murmured. "But with Stuart I doubt it. He never did like to be bossed around." Reaching under the wagon seat, he pulled out a box and opened it. Inside was a .44, a box of shells, and a leather-covered blackjack. Ace had bought the revolver and the shells, but he had taken the blackjack away from a gambler who wanted to argue about the call of a card in a poker game. He had seldom thought of it and never carried it, but now he slipped it into the back pocket of his overalls. Pulling his hat down, he stepped out of the wagon, tied the horses, and walked up to the front steps. He knocked loudly, and for a long time, it seemed no one was there. He banged vigorously on the door and said, "Cora, open the door!"

After another long pause the door opened just half a crack, and a woman's pale face appeared. "What do you want, Ace?"

"Let me in, Cora."

"It's too early. Go away."

Ace Devainy wasted no time. He shoved at the door, forcing the woman to step backward. She was wearing a pink robe, and her face was rosy with agitation, though puffy with sleep. "You can't come busting into my house like this! I'll have the law on you!"

"Sure. You go call the sheriff, Cora," Ace said easily. He had known Cora Langley for a long time. She had been the most attractive woman in the county. She was still beautiful, but her reputation was not good.

"What do you want?"

"Where's Stuart?"

Cora's face seemed to harden. "None of your business! Get out of here, Ace, if you don't want trouble."

Ignoring her, Ace simply brushed her aside and walked down the hall. He opened one door and saw a bedroom with the bed made up. He was conscious that Cora was pulling at his arm, but he ignored her. Opening a door on the opposite side, he paused and then stepped inside and stared down at the man in the bed. "Get up, Stuart!" he said loudly.

Cora shoved herself past Ace and turned to face him. "What are you doing here, Ace? What Stuart does is none of your business!"

Stuart heard this last statement, for he had been half awakened by the knock at the door. Now he sat up and shook his head for a moment. His black hair hung down in his eyes, and his mouth had a sour pucker to it. "What are you doing here, Ace?" He was wearing a linen undershirt, and he shook himself and seemed to come more awake. "What's the matter? Somebody sick?"

Ace had decided on his trip over that there would be no point in reasoning with Stuart. Now he simply stared at him and said coldly, "Get out of the bed."

"What are you talking about?"

"You heard me, Stuart. Get out of the bed. You're going home."

Anger flared in Stuart Winslow's eyes. He was a man who hated to be controlled, and he glared at Devainy's tall, lanky form. "Get out of here, Ace! I don't want to hear any more."

"You can go easy or you can go hard," Ace said. "Make up your mind. But you're going one way or the other."

Anger flashed in Stuart's dark eyes then. He threw back the covers and stood up, swaying for a moment, for he had a pounding headache. Still he advanced toward Ace and put his hand out and shoved against his chest. "Get out of here before I hurt you!"

Ace knew full well that he was no match for Stuart in a fight. He was tough enough himself, but Stuart's blows were quick as a striking snake, and he had the muscle to put a man down with one blow.

"It's time for you to go home to your wife."

Guilt washed across Stuart's face, and he shot a quick glance at Cora, who was standing back against the wall, her eyes wide. Perhaps because of that guilt Stuart was spurred to action. He yelled, "Get out of here, Ace! I'll take care of my own family!" He reached forward and gave another shove, which drove Devainy backward, but his reaction times were slower than he had known. Quickly Ace pulled the blackjack out of his pocket before Stuart started swinging with those quick fists of his.

Stuart yelled, "Hey," and raised his hand, but it was too late. The leather-covered weight struck him in the temple, and he knew nothing else.

"Stuart!" Cora screamed and came over to kneel beside him.

"If you want to help," Ace said, "help me get his clothes on him."

Cora began to curse him, but Ace paid her no more attention. As he struggled to get Stuart's clothes on, he turned to Cora and said, "If you were a man," he said, "I'd punch you out, Cora. Stuart's got a good wife."

"That's his business and mine. Not yours."

"Well, I'm making it mine today. Stay away from him. I thought you were going to marry Carter."

"Maybe I am. Maybe I'm not."

Knowing that there was no point arguing with the woman, Ace Devainy simply reached over and pulled Stuart's legs fully off the bed, then he straightened him up to a sitting position. Taking a deep breath, he stooped, pulled the limp body forward, lifted it over his shoulder, and rose suddenly. He turned toward the door with Stuart's limp body dangling and left the house only vaguely aware of Cora's voice screaming at him from what seemed to be a far distance. When he reached the wagon, he simply dumped the limp form of Winslow inside and was not overly concerned when he heard his friend's head thump the bottom of the wagon. Climbing into the seat, he spoke to the horses, "Get up, Babe! Get up, Hector!" and the two wheeled around, careened sharply, and then moved along practically at a gallop.

As soon as he had cleared the outskirts of Mapleton and was heading back toward Lewisville, Ace slowed the horses down to a brisk trot and held himself against the jolting of the frozen ruts. He was disturbed at what he had done, for he and Stuart had been friends since boyhood. He knew that this could end all that, and a deep regret washed through him. But he shrugged his shoulders and shook himself, saying, "A man's got to grow up sometime, but it looks like Stuart won't ever make it."

★ ★ ★ ★

The sun was three-quarters of the way across the sky when Devainy glanced back to see Winslow struggling to gain his feet. He had reached as far as his hands and knees and was shaking his head, which had a considerable-sized knot on it. "Whoa, up there, boys! Whoa, up there!" Ace commanded. When the wagon came to a halt, he turned and said, "You want to get in the front seat?"

Stuart slowly rose and stood for a moment in the bed of the wagon. He reached up and touched his head and then winced and looked at his fingers. His eyes were bloodshot as he stared at Devainy.

"All right," he grunted. Moving carefully, he stepped over the seat and plunked himself down beside Ace.

"Get up!" Ace commanded, but he kept the horses to a fast walk. Out of the corner of his eye he watched as Stuart sat there saying nothing for what seemed a long time. Finally he said, "Are you all right, Stuart?"

"I guess so."

Stuart Winslow was having a hard time. He had trouble for a few moments remembering what had brought him to this place, and then he turned and said, "You hit me with something."

"Blackjack."

"What did you do that for, Ace?"

"Because you wouldn't listen to reason."

A dull flush rose on Stuart's neck, and he could not meet Ace's eyes. He turned his head forward and saw that they were almost at his farm. "Did she send you to get me, Ace?" he asked in a subdued tone.

"Merle came. I couldn't let him get into trouble dragging you away from Cora's house."

Winslow had no answer for this. A deep feeling of shame flooded him, and he clamped his lips together and held on to the seat. His temples were beating as if someone were driving spikes through them, and he dreaded having to face Leah.

"You ought to know better than to fool around with Carter Simms's woman."

A hot answer leaped to Stuart's lips, but he knew there was no proper response. As he sat there hanging on to the seat, the bile rising in his throat, he thought he was going to be sick and vomit, so he said nothing. Finally the wagon stopped in front of his door, and he caught a quick glimpse of Annie at the window looking out. She disappeared, and he finally managed to say, "Thanks, Ace."

"Go see your wife. And it's your anniversary, which you obviously don't remember."

"I . . . I guess it slipped up on me. I didn't get her anything."

Ace reached down beneath the seat and handed him a package. "Here. Give her this. I bought it for Ellie. You're a sorry specimen, Stuart Winslow."

Stuart turned to face Ace, and the man's light blue eyes seemed to bore deep down into the cavern of his own depravity. He swallowed hard, then nodded and without another word got out. He swayed for a moment, clutching the package, and looked down at his soiled, wrinkled clothes. He did not turn, but he heard Devainy's wagon drive away. Everything in him wanted to turn and run, but there was no running from his shame.

Moving slowly and carefully, Stuart mounted the steps and paused for one moment with his hand on the doorknob. *Why did I do it?* he thought. *Ace should have shot me. I'd have deserved it.* Everything within him hated to have to face not only Leah but also Annie, whom he had seen glowering from the window. He had gone through this many times before; promising himself to behave, to stay away from Cora and other women, to stop drinking, to be a better husband to Leah. He thought of the child to come, and guilt and shame washed over him. Taking a deep breath, he gritted his teeth and opened the door. Annie stood in the hallway, her eyes fixed on him, her mouth turned down in a scowl. Avoiding her eyes, he moved down the hall and glanced to the left. He went to the bedroom. Closing the door, he turned to face Leah, who was in bed sitting up with a pillow bracing her. She was reading by the fading light that came through the window, and she closed the Bible and put it down by her side.

"Hello, Stuart," she said quietly.

Stuart swallowed hard. His throat seemed as dry as dust, and the silence in the room was thick, almost palpable. From far away a rooster crowed, and then he heard the monotonous ticking of the clock. His tongue was thick, and his head was splitting open, but he moved over and pulled the rocking chair up and sat down beside his wife. "Sorry to be late, Leah," he managed to get out as he put the package on the bed.

"What is it?" she asked.

Stuart realized with some confusion that he had no idea what was in the package. "Just a little gift," he said. "Nothing much."

Leah opened the package. She recognized the haggard look on Stuart's face. He had been drinking again, and he smelled of stale perfume, and she knew he had been with some woman. Her fingers felt numb, and there was no joy in her as she removed the wrapping from the package. She saw a brooch with gold trim and a green stone inside and knew instantly that it was not a gift that he had picked out for her.

"Thank you, Stuart," she said evenly.

Suddenly Stuart saw the tawdriness that he had allowed to creep into his life, and he could not keep silent. "I was drunk and Ace came to get me. He made me come home. That brooch was one he bought for Ellie."

Leah looked into Stuart's face and could still see the handsomeness that had stirred her a year ago, but now she saw a certain weakness that had left its mark. Perhaps it had always been there, but she had never recognized it until now. God had given him great gifts, a strong body, handsome features, but something was missing from him. *Perhaps it was what was missing from all men*, she thought suddenly. She looked into his tired face and saw his haunted eyes and quietly reached out and took his hand.

The touch of Leah's hand on his seemed to hit Stuart Winslow like a blow. He was as guilty as a man could possibly be, and never in his life had he felt so low and worthless. He looked up with pure misery in his dark eyes and said, "I'm sorry, Leah."

Leah tried to control the emotions that churned inside, but she did not want to confront him on their anniversary, so she said, "It's all right, Stuart."

"No, it's not." Stuart lowered his head and stared at the wedding band on her hand and then at the one on his own finger. "I feel like a ticket that someone's bought and then lost on," he said bitterly. "I'm a loser. You should never have married me, Leah."

"It'll be different, Stuart. When the baby comes, it'll be different."

Suddenly Stuart leaned forward, and she took his head and held it against her breast. "Things are going to change," she whispered, "when the baby comes." She tried to believe her own words as she felt the shaking of his shoulders, and a ray of hope sprang up. She had never seen him broken like this before, and she cried out, "Oh, Lord, make him different!"

CHAPTER FOUR

CRACKS IN A MARRIAGE

★ ★ ★ ★

"There's a good boy!"

Leah laughed aloud as Raimey splashed vigorously, holding his fat fists clutched tightly together. He sent the soapy water in the large dishpan everywhere, and Leah turned her face to avoid getting soap in her eyes. "You are a water bug! That's what you are."

Raimey, at the age of five months, was fat and pink and lively. His dark blue eyes, so much like those of Stuart, looked up at her. He clutched his right fist even more tightly and struck himself in the face with it. "Yah!" he said in shocked surprise.

"That's what you get when you hit yourself in the face, Raimey."

Giving her baby a bath was one of the pleasures of motherhood for Leah. She had had a difficult pregnancy and an even more difficult delivery, but since the arrival of her new son, Leah had bloomed. Motherhood agreed with her, for even in the five-month period she had regained her figure almost completely and was healthier than she had ever been in her life, or so it seemed to her. Now as she soaked the baby's silky skin while he splashed and chortled and grinned toothlessly, a thought came to Leah.

I'm like a beggar who only has a few things and is afraid to put them down for fear someone will steal them. The thought startled her, and her smile disappeared as her mind continued to work.

It was a fanciful thought and a sobering one for Leah Winslow. Her treasures, she knew full well, were not jewelry or clothes or a house, but a husband, a child, and a family. And now as she began to work up a lather on Raimey's hair, already as dark as his father's, she thought of those aspects of her marriage that she could cherish. Since Stuart's last escapade on their first anniversary, he had made an effort to change his ways, and she was grateful for that. But it seemed as though five months were as long as he could manage to stay sober. Even now he was beginning to be drawn away more and more to his old ways. And so Leah reminisced over the good memories and shoved the bad ones off into a dark corner of her mind. Some memories pleased her—the times Stuart was kind and thoughtful and loving. Indeed, there had been many moments like that which had made her happy and joyful after she had recovered from Raimey's birth. It had been a time of joy for Leah such as she had never dreamed. Her cheeks had glowed, her eyes had sparkled, and everyone in the house and all of Stuart's family and her friends at church had remarked at how wonderful it was that Stuart Winslow had at last grown up.

But Leah had known that deep down something was missing in Stuart. True enough he loved her and had been more thoughtful, but for the last two months she had sensed a drawing away, and she dreaded the thought that he was falling back into his old life-style.

Annie interrupted her thoughts. "You let me take care of that young'un. You go get yourself ready."

"All right, Annie. Be sure you powder him good."

"You teach your grandmaw to suck eggs?" Annie said with sprightly disdain. "I reckon I knows how to take care of a young'un, since I got four of my own."

"I know. I was just teasing, Annie." Leah hugged Annie and then left the room, saying, "Put on his blue suit. He looks so good in that."

Going into the bathroom, she quickly bathed her face and fixed her hair. Then going to her bedroom, she took off the worn brown dress that was so comfortable and slipped into the new one she had worn only twice. It was an expensive dress, a gift from her mother-in-law, made of fine dotted voile. It had a deep collar and cuffs of sheer organdy, and the colors were a light delicate green with gold checks within. She was admiring herself in the mirror when the door opened and Stuart came in.

He grunted, "I got Merle hitchin' up the team." He stopped suddenly and said, "I don't feel up to going to eat with the folks. You take Raimey and go on."

Leah's heart sank and she turned to him, studying his face. His eyes were bloodshot, for he hadn't returned until three in the morning after a late-night engagement with a band in Fort Smith.

"Stuart, you've got to go," she said. "Everyone's expecting you."

Stuart rubbed his stubby cheeks and shook his head, saying with irritation, "I wouldn't be good company."

"You'll feel better. You go shave, and I'll fix you a snack to eat."

Stuart's jaw set stubbornly. "I don't feel like having Dad preach at me. That's all I ever hear out of him. 'Why don't you straighten up?' What does he want out of me, anyway?"

"Things have been going better lately. He's proud of the way you've taken hold here at the farm."

"He's always at me to come into the business. I can't stand there selling beans and horse collars to a bunch of farmers all day long every day. That may be all right for Jeff, but I'm not cut out for it."

It was an old argument, for Richard Winslow could not give up his dream of having both of his sons in the business with him. Already Jeff had taken over as manager of the store in Fort Smith, which was growing rapidly. He boarded there now but came home on the weekends and as often as he could. This left Richard to run the store in Lewisville, and he was struggling to open another one over at Twin Oaks. He was having trouble finding someone to operate it, and he had had several vociferous arguments with Stuart about it.

"Have you thought about just taking over the new store for a while? Just until you can get things under way."

"I can't do it. It's just not for me."

Stuart stared defiantly at Leah and listened as she pleaded with him. Finally he growled, "All right! I'll go. But it won't be any pleasure for me or anybody else."

"Well, at least you'll get to meet Jeff's fiancée. She's a fine young woman from what I hear."

Stuart did not answer but left without another word to shave and get ready.

By the time they were both dressed and ready to leave, Annie had dressed Raimey in the new blue suit that his grandfather had picked out for him from the store stock. "Oh, he looks wonderful, doesn't he, Stuart!"

"Good-lookin' boy," Stuart said, smiling as he picked up Raimey.

And at that moment Leah knew a quick surge of pride. "He looks just like you, Stuart. He's going to be big like you, too. He's got big bones."

Annie was watching all this, getting Raimey's gear together, and her thought was, *I hope he's a better man than his daddy is. Good looks ain't nothin' in this world without a good heart to go with 'em.* When the family had gone off in the Oldsmobile Stuart had recently bought, her heart was heavy, and she turned back into the house, saying aloud, "He ain't no fit man for Miss Leah. No, indeed he ain't. The Lord's gonna have to deal with him!"

★　★　★　★

The dinner was a success, except for Stuart's withdrawn attitude. Hillary Devoe, Jeff's fiancée, was an attractive, tall young woman of twenty-two with blond hair and sparkling blue eyes. She hit it off at once with the family, who were all intensely proud of Jeff's choice.

The meal was wonderful, as it always was when Diane Winslow set her mind to it, and she hovered longer over Stuart than over any of the others, urging him to eat more.

"Mom, you'll have me fat as a pig."

"You've lost weight, Stuart," Diane said. She reached out and touched the hollow spot in his chin. "You've been doing too much."

Richard glanced up quickly and opened his mouth to protest, but one look at his wife silenced him. He shook his head and went on eating.

"How's the new store coming over in Twin Oaks, Dad?" Jeff

asked. He was happy with his new fiancée, satisfied in his work, and his life was going well, and he showed it.

"Not good. I had to let Blevins go."

"What was wrong with him?"

"He was stealing and he was lazy. Half the time he would open the store an hour late."

It was Hillary who made the mistake of saying, "Twin Oaks isn't too far for you, is it, Stuart? It looks like a perfect opportunity for you to develop it."

Stuart turned his eyes on the young woman and said in a hard tone, "Everybody else tries to run my life in this family, Miss Devoe. I don't think they need any extra help."

An embarrassed silence ran around the table, broken only by the faint cry of the baby in the next room. "I'll see to Raimey," Diane said. She got up and left the room and was joined by Leah. Picking up Raimey, Diane turned her eyes toward her daughter-in-law. "I wish Hillary hadn't said that," she murmured.

"So do I."

Diane cuddled the baby and planted a kiss on his smooth cheek. "He'll find his way, Leah," she said gently. "It's just taking him more time than any of us would like."

"I know. I pray for him every day, and I know you do, too."

Back at the table Jeff had started talking quickly to cover the embarrassed silence, but the fellowship had been destroyed. Stuart said nothing for the rest of the evening, and his father kept a tight rein on his own remarks. It was after they went to bed that Diane said tentatively, "I'm sorry it turned out so badly, Richard."

"Why can't he see what everyone else sees, Diane?"

"I don't know. He's different from Jeff."

"He certainly is!"

Diane reached over and took Richard's hand. "You must be patient, dear," she said.

"I think I've been patient for a long time, but he's got to wake up. He's not a child now. He's got a wife and a baby. It's time for him to take control of his life and be responsible."

Diane did not have an answer for her husband's valid concerns. She lay silently and, as always, went to sleep praying for her son who had given them all such grief.

★ ★ ★ ★

Without question, the summer wedding of Carter Simms to Cora Langley was the most extravagant event to ever take place in Lewisville. Reverend Charles Fields performed the service, and the church was packed. Everyone had followed the stormy courtship of the pair, and several bets had been made as to the outcome of it.

Stuart Winslow was one of the few unhappy spectators. He had sat beside Leah and after the ceremony had attended the reception in a large hall nearby. A tense moment came when Leah approached Cora to wish her well. Her cheeks were slightly pale, for she well knew what she had never voiced to Stuart. She said quietly, "I hope you have a happy marriage, Cora." Then she turned quickly to Carter. She was almost as tall as he was, and she noted the strain around the edges of his eyes. "Congratulations, Mr. Simms," she said. "I hope you have a happy marriage."

"Thank you, Mrs. Winslow." His eyes did not remain on her but darted quickly to his bride.

His expression changed as he saw Winslow lean forward and kiss Cora on the cheek. He did not speak, but he heard Stuart say, "Congratulations, Cora."

Neither man offered to shake hands, and Winslow nodded and said coolly, "I wish you a happy marriage."

"Thank you."

The tension between Carter and Stuart was evident, and everyone watching knew that the two men had clashed before. Lewisville loved its drama, and here was Carter Simms marrying Cora Langley—a woman who had never been denied by any man she chose to put her eyes on. The other actor in the drama was Stuart Winslow, who had pursued Cora avidly—many said he had captured her heart—but the moment passed quickly.

Ace Devainy later encountered Simms, who had deliberately come over to stand beside him. "Congratulations, Carter," he said. "Hope you'll have a long and happy marriage."

Simms nodded briefly and murmured a word of thanks. His eyes went across the crowd to Cora, and then he said, "Your friend Winslow's a dashing fellow."

Ace hesitated, not knowing how to answer. "I guess so," he

said finally. "He's had his troubles, but he's settling down now."

Simms turned to him, and there was a cold light in his hazel eyes. "You can pass the word along that he won't be welcome at my home. Cora won't be receiving any of her old friends, at least not him."

The threat was not even veiled. As plainly as if Carter had shouted the warning, Ace understood that Simms would not tolerate any advances at all on the part of Stuart Winslow. He nodded and murmured, his voice soft as the summer breeze, "I'll pass the word along, Carter."

"Make it clear."

Carter left Devainy and went over to stand by Cora. He possessively put a hand on her arm, and she turned and smiled up at him, then reached up and patted his cheek. Devainy watched all this and then glanced at Stuart. He saw that his friend's eyes were on Cora, and a sense of foreboding came over him. He knew he would never pass the warning along, for Stuart was just the sort of fellow who would take it as a challenge.

I hope he shows a bit of good sense for once, Ace thought. Then he turned to Ellie, who was coming to him to take his arm.

"Wasn't it a wonderful wedding?" she said.

"Yes. Makes a fellow want to get married himself."

Ellie blinked with surprise. "That's strange coming from you."

For some time Ace Devainy had felt the futility of his life. Now he said abruptly, "What about me, Ellie? Will you have me?"

Tears came into Ellie Mason's eyes. She dropped her head, and her shoulders began to shake.

"Here, Ellie. Don't carry on so," Ace said quickly. He put his arm around her, and suddenly she embraced him.

From across the room Leah was watching them. Her heart warmed suddenly as she turned to Stuart. "Look," she said. "Isn't that sweet?"

"It's about time those two got hitched," Stuart said. "Come on. Let's go see if we can't shove them into a marriage."

★ ★ ★ ★

"Looks like a man ought to be able to do something other than build fences."

Merle Waters looked up with surprise at Stuart's remark. They had been working on a stretch of fence that would hold in the new group of colts that had come. With winter approaching, they needed to get the post-holes dug before the ground froze. "Why, I guess somebody has to build fences, Mr. Stuart," he said. "Them new colts gotta have a place to grow up. They're mighty fine. You's gonna have a good herd. They be mighty good stock for you."

He leaned on the post-hole digger, his eyes thoughtful. For several months he had observed how Stuart Winslow had thrown himself into the work. To Merle it had been somewhat alarming, and he had told Annie, "That man needs to have some fun."

"Don't argufy with him, Merle," Annie said. "It's about time he worked."

"I know, but he done cut off all his playin', and all he do now is work like a crazy man."

"I think he's trying to show his family he can work iffen he have a mind to."

"Works fine, but he gotta have some other life."

Now as Merle studied Winslow, he saw a restlessness he had seen before from time to time. *He's like one of them there volcanoes just waitin' to blow off*, he thought.

The two worked on for another hour. Finally Stuart looked at Merle, and his mouth turned downward. "I've dug enough post holes," he announced.

"Yes, sir, boss. You go back to the house. I'll finish up."

Without another word Stuart left the field. His back was straight as he stalked toward the house, and Merle shook his head. There was an ancient wisdom in the black man, and he said, "Looks like that volcano's gonna blow mighty soon."

Leah was in the kitchen cooking supper with Annie. She heard the door slam and said, "I guess that's Stuart. He came in early."

"You go get ready. If you folks are going to that camp meeting, you'll have to prettify yourself up. You don't worry none about Raimey. I'll take care of him."

"We can take him with us."

"There ain't no need of that. He's too young to enjoy preachin'. He ain't even a year old yet."

"He will be next month."

Leah removed her apron and headed toward the bedroom. As she passed the bathroom, she heard Stuart splashing in the tub and went at once into the bedroom. She sat down and wrote in her journal for a few moments.

> *Stuart has worked so hard the past few months. Too hard really. I'm going to try to get him to take a vacation. Maybe he and Raimey and I could go to St. Louis and visit Mother.*

She hesitated for a few moments and then added:

> *He seems so tense, and I worry about him. But at least he hasn't been playing at dances in a while. He won't even play his violin around the house, which grieves me. He loves music so much. He's got to find some kind of balance.*

She heard Stuart's footsteps and quickly closed the journal and put it back under some clothes in her armoire. For some reason she did not want him to know that she even kept a journal, though she suspected he did.

"Well, I'm glad you quit early," she said. "Let me go take my bath, and then we'll get an early start."

"I'm not going to the meeting."

Leah blinked with surprise. "Not going! I thought you said—"

"I know what I said," Stuart said. Stuart's voice had a hard edge, and he turned to face her. His jaw was set in that stubborn way, and his eyes were troubled. "Look, Leah, I made a mule out of myself working for the last few months."

"I know you have. You're working too hard. Let's take a vacation. I've been thinking we could take off and go to St. Louis. We could take Raimey and go visit Mother. She's longing to see him."

"I'm not going to St. Louis. I'm going to stay here, but I'm not going to be tied down anymore."

"Tied down! What do you mean?"

"You pin a man down too much, Leah. You and the rest of

my family. You want to make a puppet out of me."

"Well, Stuart, I've never—"

"Maybe you don't mean to, Leah. I don't guess you do. But you try to make me into something that I'm not." Angrily Stuart threw his arms out in a gesture that was almost violent. "I'm going to work this farm and raise horses, but I'm also going to do some of the things that I want to do."

Instantly Leah knew exactly what Stuart meant. "You're going back to playing for dances, aren't you?"

"Yes! It's the thing I like best in life, and there's nothing wrong with it!"

"Not for a young single man, but you've got a family now."

Stuart turned to her and said, "There! You see? You're pinning me down again. I know several fellows who are married men, and they travel around and play. It doesn't hurt them."

"Yes, it does, Stuart. You know it does. How many of those men who play in that band are happy? How many of their wives are happy with them gone so much?"

Stuart felt like a trapped animal and began to lose control. He bit his lip for a moment to gain it back and then said, "You're pinning me down, Leah."

Anger suddenly swept across Leah. "Pin you down! That's what marriage is! It's two people giving up a part of themselves for another."

"I don't see it that way. I don't try to tell you what to do with your life."

"That's because you know I'm here for you, and I live for you and Raimey. But if you go out again playing, you know exactly what will happen. You'll start drinking and you'll start seeing other women."

"That's your problem, isn't it! You're jealous!"

"Should I be, Stuart?"

Leah saw the guilt that flashed into Stuart's eyes and swept across his face. He dropped his head for a moment, and then finally he lifted his eyes to her. "No point arguing about it. I'm going to have a life of my own."

The argument went on for some time, and finally Leah felt a weariness and exhaustion and a sorrow that she had never imagined. Quietly she stood there as he put on his coat and prepared to leave. She said something she had never thought she would hear herself say.

"You never loved me, Stuart."

"Of course I love you, but a man has to do some things."

"No. You never loved anyone but yourself. Did you think I didn't know about Cora Langley and your women?"

The words were too much for Stuart. He grabbed his hat and his violin case. Turning back toward her as he reached the door, he said, "I'll be back. We'll talk about it."

But Leah knew as she heard the door slam that talk would not change this wall that had come between her and her husband. She went to the window and watched as he started the car, got into it, and drove off. He did not even look back toward the house, she noticed. As she bowed her head, her shoulders began to shake, and she wept bitterly.

CHAPTER FIVE

"THE WALLS CAME TUMBLING DOWN"

★ ★ ★ ★

Sitting in the bow of the cypress johnboat, Stuart was conscious of the August sun beating down on his neck, of the mushy, earthy smell of the black dirt soaked with summer rains—but most of all of his four-year-old son who sat opposite him. *It's hard to believe*, he thought, *that he'll be five in a few months. Time's gone by so fast, and he seems to grow up every day more and more.* He studied the summer tan that covered Raimey with a golden glow, and as the boy pulled his straw hat off, Stuart noted that the hair, long over his ears and neck now, was the same intense black as his own.

A strange feeling came to Stuart Winslow then. As he watched his son, he suddenly was jolted back in some sort of time machine, for the few pictures that existed of him revealed that Raimey was an exact copy of himself at that age. The same squarish face, close-set ears, a broad mouth, and above all, the incredibly dark blue eyes—so dark that they seemed at times to be almost black, especially when he grew angry. Stuart had been told many times that his eyes were often a danger signal. Ace had once warned a man at a dance who was looking for trouble, "When Winslow's eyes turn black, look out!"

"I got a bite, Dad!" Raimey yelled.

"Let him take it. You've got to give him a chance to hook himself."

"What do you think it is?"

"A crappie. If it had been a bass, he would have run off with it. See how the cork moves away real slowly? Hang on now." Stuart grinned at the excitement that kept Raimey's hand white around the cane pole. When the cork moved slightly underwater, he said, "All right. Don't jerk. Just lift him up slowly. He's got a tender mouth. You'll yank the hook out if you pull too hard."

Raimey lifted the pole, and a shiny, flashing fish cleared the water. It struggled to free itself as Raimey carefully lifted it up and swung it over to where Stuart sat. Grasping the fish, Stuart removed the hook and put the fish in a tow sack that kept their catch underwater. Peering into the sack, he said, "We've got at least ten or twelve nice crappies. You ready to go in?"

"No, Dad. Let's catch some more."

"All right. What do you say we try for a bass?"

"Good. Let's try for a bass."

Stuart grinned, for he noticed that Raimey had the habit of repeating things he said to him word for word. He knew that the boy did not do that with everyone, and it pleased him. Indeed, Raimey was the most pleasant thing in his life at this period, and as he picked up the paddle and began moving the johnboat along the edge of the lake, he asked, "What do you want for your birthday this year?"

"What can I have?"

Stuart laughed aloud, his eyes merry. "That's coming right out with it. Well, you can't have a full-grown horse."

"Can I have a forty-five pistol?"

"No, you can't have a forty-five pistol!"

"Oh, Dad, I can shoot it! You let me shoot it one time. Remember?"

"Yes, and I was holding on to it all the time. You'd probably shoot Merle or Thunder or one of the horses."

"Can I have a pet?"

"What kind of a pet?"

"A dog."

"Well, that might be in order. What kind of a dog were you thinking of, Raimey?"

"A big dog that could hunt rabbits and bears."

"Well, we don't have any bears around here, but a good rabbit dog wouldn't be hard. Won't be long before you'll be having your own gun."

"When?" Raimey demanded instantly.

He was that kind of a youngster, always alert and conscious of time. Tomorrow never came soon enough, and this trait amused Stuart. "We'll have to talk to your mother about that. She doesn't like guns too much."

"Did you have a dog when you were my age?"

"I had a cat."

"A cat! Cats are for girls!"

"This one wasn't. He was the biggest cat I ever saw, a big brindle. Must have weighed twenty pounds. He could whip every dog in the neighborhood." Easing the boat into a small cove practically covered with lily pads, Stuart put the paddle in the bottom and thought back to when he was a boy, and the memories softened his features. "He was a big tomcat," he said softly. "He and I did everything together. He would come when you'd whistle for him just like a dog."

"Sure."

"He went hunting with me, too. Every time I'd leave the house, he'd go right along. When I came home from school I'd plunk down, and that big cat would jump right up in my lap and we'd talk. I'd say, 'Moose, what have you been doing all day?' And he would talk back to me."

"Ah, Dad, he couldn't really talk!"

"Sure he could. Cat talk, of course, but I understood him. He'd tell me how many mice he'd caught and how he almost caught the mockingbird that came to our front yard every day. And I'd tell him the fights I had, about my girlfriends, and, oh . . . we had all kinds of conversations."

Raimey's tanned face grew solemn. "Could you get me a cat like that?"

"I don't think so. I don't think there are any more like that. You see that spot over there where there aren't any lily pads? The clear place."

"Yes."

"I want you to put your minnow right in there. Just plop it down. Here. I'll put the minnow on." Picking up Raimey's hook, he hooked a minnow through the tail right behind the fin and held it up. "All right. Easy now."

Raimey swung the pole around and dropped the line into the open space. The red-and-white cork rolled on the small ripples of waves that came, and Raimey became very still. It never ceased to amaze Stuart how such an active boy could sit so quietly for long periods of time. He did not remember doing that when he was a boy. It was something Raimey had gotten from his mother.

Five minutes passed by and neither spoke. Stuart felt the tension flowing out of him and wished briefly that he could do nothing but fish with Raimey. Over the past four years, the relationship between him and Leah had become more difficult, and he knew deep in his heart that it was all his fault. Something in him would not let him live the placid, easy life that Leah so desired for him. He also knew that he had been running from God, and even as the thought came to him, he shoved it away, which had become habitual with him.

Suddenly the cork disappeared with a *PLOP*!

"Pull on it hard, Raimey. You've got a big one!"

Raimey came to his feet and would have fallen over if Stuart had not leaped forward and grabbed him by the back of his overalls. "He's a big one! Keep the tension in the line! He'll shake that hook out if you let him."

Raimey's face was fixed on the taut line, and his eyes were enormous as he struggled with the fish. It was indeed a large fish for such a small boy, and a full five minutes went by with the fish zinging the line in circles as it tried to tangle it in the snags of the shallows. Unobtrusively, Stuart helped the boy without appearing to do so. Finally, when the exhausted fish was drawn to the side of the boat, Stuart reached down, jammed his thumb into the mouth of the bass, and lifted it up. When the fish cleared the side of the boat and Stuart held it up, he grinned at Raimey's expression. "Biggest fish you ever caught. Must weigh at least six or seven pounds."

"He's a big one, isn't he, Dad?"

"He sure is."

Raimey reached out and ran his hands along the fish's shiny scales, and Stuart Winslow knew at that moment that when he was an old man, this picture would still be in his mind as fresh and clear and brilliant as was the sight itself. Raimey, his eyes enormous, stroked the side of the large bass. Stuart smiled at all the pleasure and joy and excitement of youth pictured in Raimey's face. He enjoyed the simple pleasure of just being alive and sharing the joy of this good experience for the first time with his son.

Stuart reached out and ran his hand over Raimey's black hair. "I'll tell you what," he said. "How about if we don't eat this fellow. We'll keep him alive, and I'll take him into Fort Smith and have him mounted on a board. We'll have a brass plaque put on there with your name and the date. Would you like that?"

"Sure, Dad. I'd like it a lot."

"All right. We'll head in now. Anything after this would be an anticlimax."

"What does that mean?"

"It means nothing that we could do today will be more fun than catching this fish."

They pulled in their lines, secured the fish carefully, and then started back.

"I'll tell you what. When I get rich, Raimey, we'll go down to the Gulf. I'll take you out on a big boat, and you'll catch a fish as big as this boat we're in right now."

"Really, Dad?"

"Really. It's just a matter of time. You'll see."

★   ★   ★   ★

On their way home from the lake, Raimey chattered like a magpie. He was more excited over catching his big bass than Stuart had ever seen him. Inwardly, Stuart made a resolution. *I've got to do this more often. He's growing up so fast, and all I'll have left will be a few memories.* He had resolved this before and had always broken such vows, but now as they rode behind the chestnut team that pulled the wagon along at a fast clip, Stuart made a decision to spend more time with Raimey. He knew that a wall had risen between him and Leah, but he did not want the same to happen between him and Raimey, so he determined to get close to his son.

Raimey looked up and said, "There's Mrs. Simms, Dad. Stop and let me show her my fish."

Momentarily Stuart hesitated, and then he drew over to the side of the road and saw that Cora Simms had done the same. He got out and went to the back of the wagon and pulled out the bass that was already getting stiff. Handing it to Raimey, he said, "You carry it and show it to Miss Cora."

Stuart followed behind as Raimey ran quickly to where Cora sat in the wagon and thought, *I shouldn't be doing this. I ought to know better.*

"My, what a big fish! Did you catch him yourself, Raimey?"

Cora Simms was even more striking, if that were possible, than she had been four years earlier. Her auburn hair was done up in the most fashionable mode, her green eyes sparkled, and she still had the same perfect complexion and attractive figure that had captivated Stuart before his marriage. She had shaken off much of her earlier shady reputation because she and Carter spent much of their time traveling. Simms's business ventures had blossomed, and they had money enough to do whatever they chose. Taking off his hat, he said, "Hello, Cora."

"Well, hello, Stuart." Cora's eyes fixed on the dark handsomeness of Stuart Winslow's face, and something stirred in her. He was wearing a thin white shirt, and the smooth muscles of his shoulders and his deep chest were obvious. "Give me a smile, Stuart. You are so solemn these days. I always loved it when you smiled. Your eyes disappear. Do Raimey's do that? Give me a smile, Raimey."

She chatted on mostly with Raimey, but her eyes kept coming back to Stuart.

As for Stuart himself, whenever he was around Cora, he felt drawn to her as steel is drawn to a huge magnet. She had some power over him that he could not explain, and though he had fought against it every time she came home from one of the long travels with her husband, he somehow knew it even before he was told. Memory rushed over him and brought a dark flush to his face. *I must be the weakest man in creation! Here I am with a wife and a son and flirting with another man's wife. . . .*

Finally he said, "Better put the fish back, son."

"All right, Dad."

As soon as Raimey was gone, Cora leaned over, reached out, and put her hand on Stuart's cheek. It was cooling and warm at the same time, and the very touch sent something like an electric current through Stuart. He stood there willing himself to move away and was aware that she could sense his struggle. It seemed to amuse her.

She lowered her voice and said in a husky whisper, "Carter has gone to Pine Bluff for two days. Come tonight."

For some reason Stuart had a sudden impression that he was much like the fish Raimey had caught. That fish had struggled with all of its might but had been drawn into its doom. Now Stuart hoarsely said, "I told you. It's all over, Cora." He shook his head, pulled away from her touch, and turned.

"You'll be there." Her whisper floated to him.

Stuart shook his head slightly and without turning back went to the wagon. Raimey had gotten the fish back into the sack, and he lifted it over and put it into the pail of water. The two of them climbed into the wagon, and Stuart kept his eyes fixed firmly on the road ahead while Raimey turned and waved at Cora. "She's a pretty lady."

"Yes, she is," Stuart answered tersely. He did not say another word on the rest of the trip home, but his face was red, as if he had been burned by her touch.

★　★　★　★

All afternoon, after they had gotten back from their fishing trip, Stuart worked with Merle and his oldest son, Wash. They were building a new barn, and Stuart was not a particularly good carpenter. Merle was, though, and his boy Wash, at eighteen, knew how to handle a hammer and nails, as well. Wash was a strapping young man, excellent with horses, so that he and Stuart always had plenty to talk about. As they were nailing on the decking that would take the roofing, Merle spoke of the horses that he so fondly loved even more than Stuart, if that were possible. Both of them loved fine racing horses, although they also raised mules for sale to the surrounding farmers. The quality animals that came from the Winslow place were always in high demand.

"Mr. Stuart, you know what I think?"

Stuart carefully nailed on another board and said, "What's that, Wash?"

"I been thinkin' if you would breed Princess to Thunder—my, that would be a fine colt!"

Stuart hit his thumb with a hammer, swore, and stuck it in his mouth. "Oh, that hurts!" he said. "Don't you ever hit your finger?"

"No. I hits the nail, boss. That's what hammers are for."

Stuart scowled at him. "You always do have a smart answer."

"Yes, sir, but I'm tellin' you. That would be one fast hoss if we could just get a good colt out of Princess and Thunder."

"I been thinkin' the same thing. You're a pretty smart fellow, Wash."

"I learned a lot about hosses from you, Mr. Stuart. You know more about hosses than anybody I know of."

The praise felt good to Stuart, and he continued working on the roof, trying not to hit his finger again. The two talked more about breeding and future colts until finally Annie appeared from the house.

"Supper's ready! Come and get it."

"I'm ready. I'm not much of a carpenter," Stuart said, setting his hammer down.

"You do all right, boss, but you do better with hosses and playin' that music. My, I wish I could play like you can!"

"You're doing well with the guitar. We'll have another lesson after supper tonight." Stuart had been teaching Wash how to play and had discovered that the young man had the potential to be a fine picker. "Maybe come Christmas we'll get you a really good instrument. That makes all the difference, you know."

The two men came down the ladder and went to wash up. By the time Stuart got inside, Annie had already left to go feed her family.

When Stuart sat down he found Raimey was still talking about the fish. Stuart listened with amusement and finally said, "That fish is gettin' bigger every time you tell it. By the time we get him mounted, he'll be as big as this dinner table."

Leah had been pleased that Stuart and Raimey had enjoyed the fishing trip so much. She had duly admired the fish and had seen to it that it was frozen with ice left over in the icehouse. Whenever the river froze over, they always kept ice covered with sawdust and buried deep in the ground. They all liked tea with ice in it, but she had sacrificed enough to keep the fish fresh until it could be stuffed.

Sitting down now, Leah bowed her head and asked the blessing without comment. There was never any question about this. Stuart never argued, but he also never could be persuaded to ask the blessing himself. He had said to her when she had once requested it, "I'm not a man of God, Leah. It wouldn't be right."

Leah saw something wrong with his answer, and she had said quietly, "But you must be thankful for something, Stuart. Someday you'll know God, but you can be thankful even now."

She had never brought it up again, but her words had stayed in Stuart's mind for a long time. He thought of it even now as he looked over the table. Pushing the thought aside, as he often did with matters concerning God, he said, "It's a fine supper."

It was a fine supper indeed—baked country ham, candied yams, beet salad, and pecan pie for dessert.

As Raimey was working on his pie, Stuart asked, "How do you feel, Leah?"

"Very good. It's much easier than last time."

"The last time what?" Raimey demanded. He had a considerable amount of his supper on his shirt, for he ate rapidly and often spilled some.

"The last time I had a baby—which was you."

"Why is this one easier?"

"I don't know, Raimey. I guess maybe the first child's always hard for a woman."

Raimey considered that thoughtfully. He had a way, Leah saw, of thinking things over and knew that this trait came from her. Stuart was impulsive, but her own habit of meditation and thoughtfulness had been passed along to this dark-haired son of theirs.

"Can I have a brother?"

Leah laughed suddenly. She had a good laugh, and then she shook her head. "That's not up to me. God decides that."

"Maybe you could have two babies—a boy and a girl."

"Maybe, but I don't think so. At least your grandmother says I'm not. She says it'll be a girl."

"How does she know?" Raimey demanded after a moment's silence.

"Your grandmother's a very wise woman. You ought to listen to her more."

Raimey continued to eat his pie, and finally he turned to Leah and said, "Dad says that when we're rich we're gonna go to the Gulf and catch a fish that's big as a boat."

"I'd like to see that, but it would sure be hard to clean, wouldn't it?"

The idea amused Raimey and he grinned, his dark eyes glowing. "I wouldn't care," he boasted. "I'd clean it myself."

For a while the three sat there, the adults listening to Raimey as he had to tell his mother again exactly how he had caught the fish. As he spoke, Leah felt a pang of sadness. Times like this were all too rare for the three of them. More and more over the past years Stuart had pulled away from her and from their son. She hoped their little fishing trip would be the beginning of more special times.

Stuart had become one of the most popular musicians in the county and even beyond. Invitations to play arrived constantly, and Leah knew Stuart found his real contentment in playing for people. Anymore, the horses were the only part of the farm that interested him.

It was different with Leah, for she loved her home and everything about it. But now as she looked silently across the table at Stuart, she knew there was a gap between them that was growing wider every day.

★　★　★　★

Stuart left the house after supper and walked down to the stock pond. The August days were long, so that even at seven-thirty the sun was not yet down. He walked around the pond, watching the small circles that appeared where the brim rose to take the insects that came too near the surface. Once a bass broke the surface, splashing the water and shattering the stillness of the evening air. He had put that bass in himself when it had weighed no more than a pound, and now he guessed it probably would be as large as the one Raimey had caught. He had stocked the pond so that Raimey could catch it one day. Now as he circled the pond, he smiled as he thought of the boy's pleasure.

Sitting down on the stump of an old cedar tree that had fallen the previous year in a storm, Stuart still smelled the aromatic, pungent odor of the cedar oil. The heat of the day was passing away from the earth, and he sat for a long time simply soaking in the sight of the sun slowly dipping behind the hills, leaving the golden glow in the heavens. The longer he sat there, the more aware he became of his surroundings. At his feet a tiny green snake slithered in the grass. He did not move but watched the strange grace of the reptile as it moved away. Overhead a hawk was circling in the last vestiges of daylight, and Stuart felt a moment's envy for the freedom of the raptor.

A dissatisfaction for the emptiness of his life came to him, and he could not shake it off. This part of his being he could never understand. The day had been a good one. He had enjoyed it as he had few other days in the past months. It was a joy for him to be around Raimey, and one thing he knew for certain. The love he had for this boy of his was stronger in him than he had ever dreamed possible. Once again the resolution came. *I've got to do more with Raimey. I've got to be a real dad to him. He deserves that.*

But another thought rose from deep within him and surfaced, and he fought it off. It was the memory of Cora. She was intoxicating and seemed to possess a power over him he could not define. Vainly he struggled to put the thought of her out of his mind.

He got up, kicked angrily at a stone, and sent it spinning into the pond. He turned and walked rapidly, gritting his teeth. *I've got to shake her. I can't go on this way*, he thought. *I won't go.*

He went at once to the house that he had helped Annie and Merle build and found them sitting on the porch with Wash, watching their three younger children playing a game of tag in the yard. "I'd like to try that new idea for a shoe we were talking about, Wash," Stuart said abruptly.

"Why, yes, sir! Yes, Mr. Stuart, we'll work on that. I'll get the forge fired up right now," Wash said.

Annie watched the two go off and shook her head. "That Stuart ain't got no peace and no contentment."

"No, he ain't. It's like somethin' on the inside is fightin' him all the time," Merle said sadly. "He's got the world by the tail and everything a man could want, but it ain't enough for him."

The two sat there quietly, both disturbed in their minds, and soon they heard the sound of the hammers striking on steel, and they knew that it would go on until Stuart Winslow exhausted himself.

★   ★   ★   ★

Leah lay in bed running her hand over her swollen abdomen. The baby was beginning to move, and always she was awed by the life that was growing within her. She lay there thinking of the child to come in a few months until Stuart slipped into bed beside her, and then she waited for him to speak. He had stayed out at the forge until almost eleven o'clock, and she had gone to bed, too tired to stay up. Her thoughts troubled her, and she whispered, "Stuart."

"Yes. What is it?"

"The baby's moving. Here. Feel it."

Her hand tugged at him, and he rolled over slowly and put his hand on her abdomen. He could feel the quick movement of the baby, and he, too, was struck with a sense of awe. "I hope it's a girl," he said.

"I thought you wanted another son."

"A girl would be more company for you."

Leah laid her hand on Stuart's and said, "I do get lonely, Stuart. You're gone so much."

Quickly he pulled his hand away. "I have to do it. I don't know why."

Leah felt a sense of pain and anger. For years she had been losing this man, and now it all seemed to rise within her, and she said, "A woman needs a man, Stuart. You're my husband and I'm losing you."

"You're not losing me."

"You think I don't know about what you do? You come in smelling of perfume and whiskey. It's Cora, isn't it? Why don't you just go to her?"

As soon as she had spoken the words, Leah could have bitten her tongue. She had vowed she would not be a shrew, that she would never bring up such an accusation. She had known about Stuart's old affair with Cora, and she knew he was still infatuated with her, yet she had vowed never to say a word. But now it had slipped out.

Stuart went rigid, and then with a violent gesture he came to his feet. "All right. I will!"

"Stuart, I didn't mean it."

Stuart did not hear her, for a mixture of anger and old attractions filled him as he threw on his clothes. "I'm going to Fayetteville," he said. "I'll be playing there for three nights."

As soon as he was dressed, he picked up his suitcase, threw some clothes in, and then moved toward the door.

For Leah it seemed to be the end of the world. The truth about Cora was out in the open now between them. She got up and fixed her eyes on him. She stood between Stuart and the door and said, "Stuart, don't go."

"Don't try to stop me, Leah. I'm going."

And then Leah said in a voice that was not her own, "If you go, don't bother to come back!"

"Maybe I won't!" he said, then shouldered past her.

She heard the door slam. Stiffly she moved over to the chair beside the bed and sat down in it. All her strength seemed to drain out of her, and she cried out, "Oh, God, what's happening? I'm losing everything."

★   ★   ★   ★

Stuart Winslow hooked up the chestnut stallion to the buggy, threw his things in it, and drove through the night. It was dark overhead, so dark that he could barely see the road, but he knew it well enough.

As he traveled along, he came to a familiar fork in the road. The right branch led to the Simms's place, the other to town and on to Fayetteville. For one moment he drew up and held the reins so tightly that his fingers cramped. He felt like a man on the razor's edge, and then with wild abandon he pulled the line. "Go on, Tony. Giddyup!" He took the road to the Simms's place.

Ten minutes later he was approaching the house. He saw a

light in the upstairs window and could see Cora moving about the room in her dressing gown. He picked up a small stone and threw it so that it struck the glass.

Moving over to the door, he waited until it opened. When he saw Cora in front of him, all the attractions and thoughts about her he had tried to fight off came flooding back. For a fleeting moment he thought about the argument he had just had with Leah. Then he took her in his arms and held her, saying, "I'm a rotten dog, Cora."

A moment's silence passed, and then she took a deep breath. "Sure you are, Stuart, but that makes two of us. I've been waiting for you. I knew you'd come."

★   ★   ★   ★

Leah was mixing biscuit dough when she heard the sound of a buggy approaching. She had slept very little that night, and dark circles were under her eyes. A hope suddenly rose within her. *He's come back!* she thought and moved over to the window. Her heart sank when she saw that it was not Stuart but Luke Garrison, the sheriff.

She saw him get out of the buggy and went to the front door. "Hello, Luke," she said. "You're out early."

"Hello, Leah."

"Come in for some coffee."

Garrison hesitated. He shrugged his muscular shoulders, and his eyes had an odd expression. "I have some bad news."

Instantly, fear washed over Leah.

"Something's happened to Stuart. Has he had an accident?"

Garrison looked down at the floor. He had removed his hat and twisted it awkwardly and nervously in his strong square hands. When his eyes came up there was compassion in them, and he said, "I don't know any easy way to say this, Leah."

"What is it, Luke?"

"Your husband killed Carter Simms last night."

For one moment the room seemed to reel, and for the first time in her life Leah knew she was fainting.

Seeing her stagger, Garrison leaped forward, put his arm around her, and led her down the hall to a couch. He helped her sit down and said, "Maybe I should have had somebody else come to tell you, but I thought—"

"It's all right, Luke. Tell me what happened."

Garrison reached up and tugged at his droopy mustache and said, "Well, I don't know how long it's been going on, but it looks like your husband's been seeing Cora."

"I know about it, Luke."

"Well, Carter was supposed to be gone for two days. He came in early last night and he caught your husband with Cora."

The pain had become a dull ache in Leah's broken heart, and she listened without looking at the sheriff. "What happened?"

"It looks like Carter had a gun, and he started shooting. He hit Cora, but he didn't kill her. Then Stuart jumped up, and they started struggling for the gun. It went off and Carter took a bullet right in the heart."

The silence in the room was heavy. Luke Garrison wished that he were anywhere else in the world. Like others in the community, he had a great sympathy for Leah Winslow. He had known of Stuart's infidelity, as he knew most things that happened in the county. Now he sat there helpless, knowing that the agony for this woman was just beginning.

"What will happen to him, Luke?"

"He'll have to stand trial."

"But it was an accident, wasn't it?"

Garrison knew his politics, and he understood how unlikely it was that this shooting would be called an accident. "It depends on the jury," he said carefully. Then honesty compelled him to say, "It's serious. He could hang for it, Leah. Have your father-in-law get the best lawyer he can. Stuart's going to need it."

Leah sat there with her hand on her stomach, the child inside of her moving rapidly as a wave of nausea came over her. A deadness seemed to settle on her spirit, and she could not think clearly. She was aware that Luke Garrison was watching her carefully, but she could not frame a single word.

She remembered a spiritual that Annie sang a lot, but the only words she could remember clearly were, "And the walls came tumbling down."

CHAPTER SIX

THE VERDICT

★ ★ ★ ★

Leonard Stokes stood looking out of his office window. Fall had come, and now the red, gold, and yellow leaves of the sweet gum tree were dropping to the ground, making a multicolored carpet on the dry, dead grass. Somehow autumn always brought a sense of fatalism to Stokes, for he was a man sensitive to moods and to those about him. It was a trait that had served him well as a lawyer. He was only thirty-five, but already he was the rising star in the firmament of the state judicial system. A tall, lean man with sharp gray eyes, Stokes had been the hottest defense lawyer available, and many had been shocked when he had left a lucrative practice in order to become district attorney for a rather minimal salary. What those people did not understand was that Stokes intended to move up in the world, and a record as a crusading district attorney would get him a good start on the governor's chair. After that there was always the Senate, and beyond that, who knew where his political ambitions would lead?

Turning from the window, Stokes moved back to his desk, sat down, and stared at the elderly man who was seated across from him. "You're not looking too well, Mordecai."

Mordecai Frasier indeed did not look well. He was in his eighties and had been a legend for many years, both as a lawyer and finally as the chief justice of the State Supreme Court. He could have risen to greater heights but had chosen to remain in his native state of Arkansas and had served his people admirably all of his life.

"I'm doing very well for an old man." Frasier's voice was thin now. He had lost his trumpet voice, which had been powerful enough to fill any courtroom in the state, making many lawyers realize they had met their match. His eyes were faded, and his hands trembled, so he quickly folded them in front of him. "I think we need to do some more talking about the Winslow case."

"I can't see that there's a lot to talk about, Mordecai."

"Well, after all, it wasn't premeditated, and there was no malice intended."

"You can't change one fact, I'm afraid. Carter Simms is dead and buried, robbed of his life, and Stuart pulled the trigger."

"That's not been proven yet."

"It can be easily proven that Winslow was with Simms's wife. Carter had every right to defend his home from an intruder. You know that as well as I do."

Anger washed across the face of Mordecai Frasier, and a touch of the old fire glowed in his eyes. "You and I know that if every adulterer were shot, there wouldn't be enough men left in the state even to elect you governor. And that's what you're after, isn't it?"

Stokes suddenly grinned. He liked Mordecai Frasier and admired him greatly. He had patterned much of his own practice and tactics on this old man's life and career, but when Stokes went into the courtroom, everything else went out—friendship, family, money—nothing meant anything except winning.

"What do you have on your mind?" Stokes asked. He already knew what the elderly man had on his mind, but it had to be said. As he watched Frasier try to put his thoughts together, he felt a sharp stab of pity. *Twenty years ago he would have cut me to pieces in a courtroom. I wouldn't have stood a chance. But now he's a poor choice for a lawyer. He may be a good friend of Richard Winslow, but that's not enough. His memory's gone and he's a sick man.* Stokes well knew that Frasier had come out of retirement to take on the case as a personal favor to Richard Winslow. He also knew that it was not a wise move on Richard's part. *He should have gotten a young, tough, sharp fellow wanting to make a reputation for himself, but he didn't.*

"I'm thinking of accidental death."

"Come on, Mordecai. You know that won't do."

Indeed, it was merely an opening gambit for Frasier. He shrugged his thin shoulders. "Well, manslaughter, then."

The conversation did not last long, and finally Frasier got up and nodded. "Think about it, Leonard. This is a young man we're talking about. Stuart Winslow has great potential."

Stokes did not respond to this. "Take care of yourself, Mordecai. This case may be too much for you." He ventured to hint at something that he would not have bothered with if it had been any other man. "Why don't you take on a young assistant and let him do the hard work and the hollering in court?"

The suggestion offended Frasier. His pride was still there, and he said, "I think I can handle myself in court, Leonard."

As soon as Frasier left, Jim Johnson came into the room. He was only twenty-five, but Stokes had picked him to work with because he was just the type of aggressive attorney he wanted.

"What did you give him?" Johnson asked.

"What did I give him? Nothing."

Slumping back in his chair, Leonard Stokes had a prophetic moment. He saw himself as a tired old man, still struggling, as he knew he would be someday. "I gave him sympathy." Underneath his competitive bravado, Stokes could at times be compassionate, especially at moments like this when he saw his own human frailty. It was a trait he kept well hidden, however, for in the eyes of many, it would not do for the district attorney to be perceived as kind. Now he looked at Johnson and said, "Richard Winslow made a bad mistake retaining Mordecai."

"Yes, he did. What are you going to do? Go for the jugular with first degree?"

Stokes's gray eyes grew hard, and he murmured, "I always do, don't I? That's what I get paid for."

* * * *

Frasier had long since given up his office, so he met with Richard and Diane and Leah Winslow in a bare, unadorned room in the courthouse. There were pictures on the wall of Washington and Lincoln and a calendar advertising Lydia Pinkham's tonic for women. The only furniture was a table and five chairs, dented and marred from years of wear. One window opened up to the outside world and admitted a yellow shaft of sunlight that struck Mordecai Frasier's face, accentuating his pallid complexion. He was obviously troubled as he looked over at the couple, then shifted his glance to Leah Winslow.

They're all looking at me to help them. They think the law is some kind of a magic act—that I can pull a rabbit out of a hat and everything will be well. He was disturbed by the notion, and the light of expectancy in all of their eyes troubled him even more.

"I don't have very good news," he said finally. "I talked with the district attorney."

"What did he say?" Richard Winslow demanded. The two months since the killing of Simms had aged him considerably. He had lost weight, and the muscles of his face had begun to sag. He had always been a strong man, but this blow to the family had brought him very low indeed.

"I've tried to get Stokes to go for second degree, but I don't think he will. I wish we could get him to agree to a trial for manslaughter."

"What's the difference between manslaughter and murder?"

Frasier leaned forward and began to speak. He knew there were two times in a person's life when fear was liable to get out of hand. One was when facing a doctor who had bad news. The other was at a moment like this when someone's freedom or even his life was in danger. He had been through this many times and knew that for most people the complexity of the law was like a dark forest in which one could stay lost continually. He had seen the hopelessness in so many faces, and he hated to see the same look of despair in this family, for he had been a good friend to Richard and Diane Winslow for many years. Directing his gaze at Leah, he said, "Basically speaking, Mrs. Winslow, manslaughter is the unlawful killing of another human being without malice, either expressed or implied." He fell into the pattern of speech that had been his habit throughout his years on the bench and as a teacher of law. "It implies a killing without deliberation in the sudden heat of passion."

"But what is murder, then?" Leah asked as she twisted her hands.

"The distinction between manslaughter and murder rests on one thing. That is *malice*. In manslaughter, though the act that occasioned the death was unlawful, no malice is involved. But malice is the very essence of murder."

"You mean if someone is angry and bitter and expresses it and says so and then kills someone, that becomes murder?"

"Yes, although we call it homicide in the court. There are three kinds of homicides—justifiable, excusable, or felonious."

"I don't understand any of that," Richard muttered.

"Justifiable homicide is the taking of a human life with justification, such as self-defense. Excusable homicide, well, that's the killing of someone by misadventure, such as when you accidentally strike them with a moving vehicle. Felonious homicide is the wrongful killing of a human being without justification."

"What's the difference between first degree and second degree?"

Mordecai shook his head. "That's not even clear to many lawyers and judges, but basically first-degree homicide is the thing you want to stay away from. When a jury gives any judge that verdict, he will always hand down the stiffest sentence at his command."

Leah listened for some time as Frasier continued to explain the labyrinthine ways of the law. Finally she said, "What if he's found guilty?"

For a moment Frasier hesitated, then he said, "Judges have a great deal of latitude. For murder in the first degree it could be the maximum sentence."

"You mean he could be hanged?" Leah whispered.

"We'll hope for better things than that. If it comes to a prison sentence, it's all in the hands of the judge. Judges have been known to give a sentence and then suspend it upon condition of good behavior. That's what I'm hoping for in Stuart's case."

"What about the judge? Who'll be conducting the trial?" Diane Winslow asked.

All three of the Winslows saw the expression that crossed the face of the old man, and they all knew that something was wrong.

"What is it, Mr. Frasier?" Leah whispered.

"Well, the judge will be Marcus Broz." He hesitated for a second and then shook his head. "His nickname is the 'Killer Judge.'" He passed his hand over his face, and the hand trembled visibly as he whispered, "He's the worst man we could have had."

★ ★ ★ ★

Leah lowered herself into the chair carefully. She was uncomfortable and knew that all of the strain of this ordeal had affected her pregnancy. All the ease was gone now, and she had not slept a full night since Stuart had been arrested. She sat in the small room with the worn furniture and listened until she heard the sound of approaching footsteps. The door slowly opened and a guard entered. He stepped aside to admit Stuart, who was wearing leg-irons and handcuffs.

"Just knock on the door when you're through," the guard said.

Leah watched him as he waited for a moment before leaving them alone. He was a small, burly man with a callous face. This was just a day's work to him, and Leah wondered what a man could be like who so constantly observed the fear of men that he had become immune to it.

"How are you?" she asked as Stuart lowered himself into a chair.

He ignored the question, put his hands on the desk, and stared at the steel handcuffs. His face was thinner and he had lost weight. There was a twitch in his lips that had not been there before, and finally he said, "All right. How's Raimey?"

"He's . . . all right."

"What does he say about having a father on trial for murder?"

"He doesn't talk about it."

Stuart's head came up. "He *must* talk about it. What does he say?"

Leah had not wanted to talk about Raimey, but she saw that it was necessary. "He's afraid, Stuart. He's heard talk from other children, and he's so *quick* to catch on to what's happening. I've tried to keep the truth from him, but it's been on the front page

of the newspaper for days. Even your picture. I found him looking at it the other night."

"Does he say anything?" Stuart's voice was forced, and there
was agony in his eyes as he waited on her answer.

"He won't say anything. I think he's put it out of his mind.
It's like he thinks if he just ignores it, it'll go away."

Stuart suddenly laughed hoarsely. "That sounds like something I'd do."

Leah could not think of anything to say except, "I'm sorry. I
wish I could do something."

The silence grew between them, and finally he said, "I read a
book once about trapping beavers out west. It said that sometimes a beaver will get his foot caught in a trap, and then he'll
gnaw it off himself just to get away. I wish I could do that . . .
whatever it cost just to get away."

Leah sat in silence, and the awkward gulf between them
deepened with each passing second. It was as if she had been in
a coma ever since her world had collapsed. She had tried to pray
but could not. Everything seemed dark and bleak. It was not that
she doubted God, but she did not know how to handle such a
problem. She knew all of the Scriptures and read them over and
over, trying to go on with some ray of hope. She had dutifully
sat and listened to the pastor and to her mother-in-law and to
Annie whenever they tried to comfort her, but it was as if she
were locked inside her own prison and could not get out.

Stuart studied her face, and finally he said, "Can we ever get
over this, Leah? I mean if I don't have to go to prison, can we
start over?"

It was a question Leah had asked herself many times, and
now she merely shook her head mutely.

"Is it all over?" Stuart said. "Have I ruined it all?"

When she still did not answer, Stuart slumped. "It's all gone,
then? We can't start over."

Still something inside Leah urged her to reach out to offer
comfort and love and assurance, but it was no use. The years of
loneliness and betrayal had left deep wounds in her soul. She
merely shook her head and whispered, "I don't think so." She
felt bound by a coldness in her heart that tightened its grip. And
struggle as she might, she could no longer summon love from a

broken heart. And so the two of them sat there until finally Stuart rose and knocked on the door. He disappeared, escorted by the guard, and Leah sat there quietly unable to move, unable to think, unable to pray.

★   ★   ★   ★

"Come on! You can ride better than that, Raimey!" Merle had strapped a saddle on an ancient sorrel mare and lifted Raimey up into the saddle. Usually the young boy enjoyed riding, but there was no happiness in him today. He held the reins obediently and went around but had not a word to say.

Finally, after half an hour, Merle said, "I reckon that's about enough." He pulled the boy down, unsaddled the mare, and then removed the bridle.

When he returned from putting the mare into the pasture, he saw Raimey standing there. The forlorn look on the boy's face wrenched the black man's heart.

"Mr. Merle, what's gonna happen to my dad?"

"Why, he's gonna be all right, Raimey." Merle put his huge hand on the boy's head and brushed his black hair back. "You just gotta trust the good Lord."

Merle wanted to say more to try to comfort the boy, but he could think of nothing. He took Raimey back to the house, then turned and walked slowly to his own house. When he entered the kitchen, he found Annie peeling apples.

"That's good," she said, "giving Raimey a ride."

"He didn't take no joy out of it. He's all worried about his daddy."

Annie looked up, her eyes filled with grief. "That boy's gonna be a mess if his daddy goes to jail."

"Well, maybe he ain't goin'."

"Don't talk foolish. He's goin' all right. Mr. Ace say he ain't got a chance."

"When you talkin' to Mr. Ace?"

"Everybody knows it. That judge, they call him the 'Killer Judge.' Mr. Ace said he ain't never let a man off, and he always give 'em the most years he can think of."

She looked up suddenly and squinted. "There comes Miss Ellie. Maybe she can cheer Miss Leah up."

★ ★ ★ ★

"Come in, Ellie," Leah said. "My, that girl's growing every day!"

Mattie, Ellie and Ace's two-year-old blond daughter, began to clamor to be put down. Ellie set her down just as Raimey came into the room. Ellie saw the forlorn look on his face and quickly said, "I left some candy out in the wagon. Raimey, why don't you go get it and share it with Mattie? Don't make yourself sick, now."

"Yes, ma'am."

The two women watched as the two children went outside, and Ellie said, "I could stand a cup of coffee."

"It's on the stove." Leah moved slowly and carefully, following Ellie to the kitchen.

"You sit down," Ellie said. "I'll fix the coffee." She poured two mugs of coffee, laced her own with sugar, then sat down and said, "Are you all right?"

"Yes. This baby's no trouble. I just wish it were here."

The conversation went on aimlessly for a while, although both women were aware that they were dodging the subject. Finally Ellie said, "How's Stuart?"

"Ellie, I don't know. When I go to see him, we don't have anything to say." Leah's face was tense and her lips trembled. "I know I ought to encourage him, but it's like I'm all . . . well, I'm all frozen inside! I can't pray. I can't even think." Tears suddenly began to roll down her face.

"I know it's hard, honey. I know it is."

"No, you don't know, Ellie. I can't hold my head up."

"It's not your fault, Leah."

"I think it is." And then Leah spoke the thought that had lain heavily on her heart, not just recently but for years. "If I had been the right kind of wife, I'd have kept my husband at home. I didn't have whatever it is a woman has to have to hold on to a man."

"Why, that's foolishness! You can't talk like that." Ellie continued to speak for over half an hour, but she saw that it was hopeless. She had never seen Leah so despondent before. She and Ace had been terribly worried about her. Now she said, "Maybe he'll get off and you can start over." She saw something pass over Leah's features, and she said, "Don't you think so?"

Leah shook her head. "I don't know. I don't really think I can."

Ellie reached over and took Leah's hand. "Honey, I know he ain't done right. I ain't no Christian myself, but I know the Bible says something about forgiving folks. Especially a husband."

Ellie's words cut into Leah's heart, and tears began to stream down her face. "I know it, Ellie, but somehow . . . I just can't!"

★ ★ ★ ★

Charles Fields stepped up beside Leah and took her arm. "Let me help you up these steps, Leah," he said. The minister kept a firm grip on Leah's arm and asked, "Who's taking care of Raimey?"

"Annie." Suddenly she turned and whispered, "I don't know what's wrong with me, Brother Fields. I can't seem to pray anymore. It's as if a part of me has died."

"You're not the first to have that happen, Leah. Some of the most courageous and best of God's saints have gone through it. The old church fathers called it 'the dark night of the soul.' I've had a little of it myself, and I know how bitter it is. It's as though God has died, or He's shut you off and refuses to listen."

Leah bit her lip as they reached the top of the steps to the church. "I feel like I'm totally lost."

"You mustn't feel like that. Come on. Let's go in."

Fields could see how hard the trial had been on Leah. It was taking its toll on the whole family, but it was affecting Leah's faith. He escorted her to the front, where she took her seat beside the Winslows, then he took a seat and began to pray for her and for the outcome of the trial. He had faithfully gone every day and sat in the back of the courtroom and prayed silently for the entire Winslow family. As the trial progressed, he, as well as the rest of the town, was amazed at how Mordecai Frasier had somehow found new life and had made a spirited defense for Stuart, but Fields remembered how in the eyes of the jury it seemed to have had little effect. When the time for the closing arguments had come, Fields had listened as the two men dueled in front of the courtroom, each trying to sway the jury. At the time, Fields had thought, *Richard should have gotten another lawyer. I have a bad feeling about this.* He could still picture Stuart sitting at the table with Frasier. At one point Stuart had turned and looked at Leah. Field's gaze had shifted to Leah, and he saw her drop her head and slump her shoulders, and he knew that something was terribly wrong.

Right then the music started, and Fields shook the sad memory from his mind and reached for his sermon notes. He offered a silent prayer, for this week he had chosen to speak on God's boundless love and His unfathomable mercy.

★ ★ ★ ★

"You'll pull out of this all right." Ace Devainy was sitting beside Stuart in the small room off the main courtroom. The final arguments had been made, the defense and the prosecution rested, and the judge had charged the jury to deliberate behind closed doors and reach a verdict. Now there was nothing to do but wait. Devainy had pressured the sheriff and had been given permission to sit with Stuart as he waited. Ace looked over and saw that his friend's face was pale.

"Ace, what will happen to Leah and Raimey and to the new baby? That's what's eating me alive."

"Well, maybe the jury will see it was self-defense and let you off."

"Have you been watching them, Ace? You know better."

Devainy knew that Stuart was right. Leonard Stokes had outmaneuvered his opponent quite skillfully, for the jury was stacked with solid citizens, all handpicked by Stokes.

It would have been better, Ace thought, *if the jury had been a bunch of sorry rascals. Some people that could come in and understand a man's weakness. They look like a bunch of Pharisees up there.*

The bailiff stepped inside and said, "The jury's comin' in, Stuart."

Stuart Winslow rose to his feet, and Ace watched him leave. *I'm afraid he's in for it. I hope he can take it,* Ace thought, then he quickly joined the others in the courtroom awaiting the verdict.

★ ★ ★ ★

Richard Winslow reached over and took his wife's hand. His

own hand was unsteady, and he had to struggle with his feelings against his own son. For years he had carried on a running battle with Stuart, about the way his son lived, and now all this had almost wrecked him. He had slept very little over the past few months, and his health had been affected. He turned to Diane and knew, however, that she was worse off than he was. He squeezed her hand and she turned to look at him. Then both of them turned to watch as the jury filed in. Richard was a man who knew people, and from the blank expressions on their faces, he drew no hope.

Judge Broz asked, "Have you reached a verdict, gentlemen of the jury?"

"We have, Your Honor."

"How do you find the defendant?"

The foreman of the jury, a wealthy farmer dressed in a black suit, held a slip of paper in his hand. He looked directly at Stuart Winslow and said, "We find the defendant guilty of murder in the second degree."

Everyone turned to look at Stuart, but his face seemed to be frozen, and he did not say a word.

Judge Broz studied the tall figure of Stuart Winslow. Though he was a hard man, he was just, or so he felt. He was dedicated to the courts and the system of law, believing strongly that they were ordained by God to keep anarchy away from the people. And now as he sat examining the prisoner, his eyes drifted to Stuart's wife and his parents. He felt compassion for the family, and at times such as this, he wished himself in another profession. Still it was a question he had settled long ago.

"This country was built on contracts. A contract of a man or a woman with their country. If a man signs up to be a soldier, he contracts to obey his superiors. If he violates that contract, he must pay the consequences. This country was also built on the contract of marriage, and you, Stuart Winslow, have violated your own marriage vows. You have debauched the wife of another man. You killed that man when he discovered you with his wife." He hesitated only briefly, then he said in a level tone, "There are times when leniency is in order, but you have not shown any remorse. I sentence you to the state penitentiary for a term of twenty years. Remove the prisoner."

A murmur ran through the courtroom after the sentencing, but Leah seemed locked in a trance. Though she heard the words and saw all the commotion all around her, it didn't seem real. But then she saw Stuart, who turned and gave her one unfathomable look—and then he was taken away.

And it was at that moment Leah Winslow knew that she herself had been sentenced along with her husband, Stuart Winslow.

CHAPTER SEVEN

NUMBER 6736

★　★　★　★

Stumbling off the police wagon that stopped in front of the rising, cold walls of the Tucker State Penitentiary, Stuart stepped down and took his place in a ragged line of miserable men. Two armed guards watched them with bored faces, one of them muttering impatiently, "Come along—step out there!"

Leg chains jingled as the eleven men hobbled forward, and Stuart lifted his eyes to the grim structure that was to be his home for the next twenty years. Ever since the trial he had been in a mental and emotional coma. He could barely remember the good-byes of his friends and loved ones before he was taken away. His mother had clung to him and whispered, "God won't forget you, Stuart, so don't you forget Him!"

But God seemed very far away, even nonexistent, as Stuart entered the gates that swung back to admit him. Behind him one of the men uttered a choking sob, but Stuart simply narrowed his eyes and looked around the yard, where men in stripes were gathered in small groups. They were smoking and joking, and if the clothing had been different, he could have pictured the same kind of men gathered outside a rodeo or a ball game. But despite the almost friendly sounds of voices and laughter, a chill ran up Stuart's spine. He saw that some of the inmates had lined up and were calling out, "Fresh fish! How do you like your new home? Tucker Farm ain't so bad. Be good boys now and you'll be all right." The shouting became more raucous and cruel, the remarks cruder, as the new inmates were forced to shuffle past. The guards ignored the regular prisoners as they marched their new ones through another set of barred doors guarded by a man with a shotgun held firmly in his hands.

Concrete and steel loomed everywhere, and guards with shotguns stood all around, giving the place a cold, clammy air of gloom. These new dismal pictures soaked into Stuart's numbed mind, and he kept his lips firmly clamped together, determined not to let any emotion show on his face.

"All right. Line up here!" The guards who had escorted them now formed them into a ragged line and ordered them to face front. They were standing shoulder to shoulder, miserable and frightened, when a steel door opened and a short, sturdy man briskly entered. He had iron gray hair with a slight curl and a pair of penetrating blue eyes that looked as hard as nails.

"My name is George Armstrong. I'm the warden." Armstrong's voice was not loud, but it carried well. He walked up and down looking the men over, then stepped back in front of them and took a deep breath. "I don't have a long speech for you. You men have all broken the law, and you are here to serve your sentences. You'll hear it said that I'm a hard man." Warden Armstrong paused, and his eyes fastened onto those of the men standing closest to him. His glare had made many a man feel that he was being searched, tried in the balances, and found wanting. "Maybe I am. Maybe I have to be. I hope I'm a fair man, however, and there's one verse of Scripture that I want to leave with you without preaching to you. 'Whatsoever a man soweth, that shall he also reap.' That's the rule here. You behave yourselves, and you'll be all right. But don't try my patience, or you'll find yourself in a worse condition than you'd ever dream possible." He turned and said, "All right, Mr. Munger." Wheeling on his heels he left the room, and silence reigned.

The man the warden had addressed as Mr. Munger came forward. He was six feet tall and appeared to be as hard as the concrete prison walls. His eyes were hazel, his hair a light brown, and there was an implacable air about him as he stalked back and forth, staring at the line of fledgling inmates. "Which one of you is Moore?"

"Here. I'm Moore."

Munger's head swiveled, and he went at once to the middle-aged man who had answered. The prisoner was a meek-looking fellow, undersized and with a fearful expression.

Without warning, Munger raised his stick and, with one swift, practiced motion, drove the blunt end of it into the pit of Moore's stomach. Moore's breath exploded as he doubled over and fell to the floor gasping for breath. Munger stood looking down at him with a cold, sadistic expression. "I'm Mr. Munger, *sir*!" he said. He reached down, jerked the man to his feet, and shoved him into line. "Moore, I've been looking over your records. I look over the records of all new cons." He grinned suddenly, but there was no humor in it. "I see that you've got five years to serve for embezzlement. I can't stand an embezzler, Moore! Don't think you're going to get any time off for good behavior. I'll see to it that you don't."

Moore's face turned a sickly pale color, and he expelled and inhaled air as if he were drowning. Trembling like a man in a stiff breeze, he opened his mouth as if to say something, but all that came out was a faint whisper. "Yes, sir, Mr. Munger."

Munger nodded, then turned his head. "Winslow! Where are you?"

"Here, sir!"

Stuart stood straight, his eyes locked onto those of Munger. Winslow had never seen such eyes before. They were glassy like a cat's—with nothing beneath them, a total lack of emotion.

"Well, Mr. Murphy, we have a killer here with us. He got caught with another man's lady and shot the poor fellow when he tried to protect what was rightfully his. Is that right, Winslow?"

Stuart knew there was no use in denying what a jury had convicted him of, so he nodded. "Yes, sir."

"We'll just call you Lover Boy, then. Will that be all right, Lover Boy?" Munger waited for Stuart to answer, and when no response was forthcoming, he reversed his stick and drove it into Stuart's stomach.

Stuart had seen the blow coming and tensed his muscles. He did not move; nor did his eyes flicker.

"Oh, a tough one! Lover Boy's a tough one, Mr. Murphy,"

Munger said to one of his subordinates standing nearby. Then with one quick motion, the chief guard swung his stick and caught Stuart in the head.

The unexpected blow drove Winslow to the ground, and the world seemed to be made of flashing lights. From far away Stuart could hear a voice saying, "Why didn't you toughen your head muscles against that, like you did your stomach muscles? Come on, get to your feet, Lover Boy."

Stuart came slowly to his feet, the room reeling. He squeezed his eyes and shook his head, and Munger's face came slowly into focus inches from his own.

"Oh, we're going to have lots of fun, Lover Boy! I've had plenty of guys here before who thought they were tough, but they were jelly when I got finished with them. I never saw a woman chaser who wasn't yellow." Turning to the middle-aged guard who was watching all this without expression, he said, "Mr. Murphy, as soon as the men get their clothes, put Lover Boy on the new unit. Have him push a barrow. That ought to take some of the starch out of him." He turned again and stared into Stuart's face. "I hate a womanizer," he said between clenched teeth. "But you won't be doing any of that again for twenty years, Winslow. That's all over for you. You'll be pushing a wheelbarrow until you're an old man!"

★   ★   ★   ★

Stuart had the number 6736 displayed prominently on the back and front of his black-and-gray striped uniform. When the other new prisoners were taken to their cells, the guard named Murphy took him at once to the construction site.

"A new unit's being built, Winslow," the guard said as they approached a big mixer churning the wet concrete. A line of inmates stood with their filled wheelbarrows, waiting to push them up a steep incline. "This is a new unit. It's going to be three stories high. You ought to have some gloves, but you're on the bad side of Mr. Munger, and he won't permit it." Murphy studied Winslow's face and shook his head. "Don't give him any trouble. If you bow down and don't get his back up, he'll forget about you soon enough and move on to someone else. But if you're stubborn about it, life will be even more miserable for you here than it oughta be."

Stuart had arrived at the construction site slightly after one. For the next five hours he pushed the wheelbarrow up and down the incline. At first it was bearable enough, for he was stronger than most men, but his hands were in screaming agony by the time the construction superintendent said, "All right. That's it for today."

As Stuart picked up the handles of the wheelbarrow, he felt a sticky moistness. Looking down at the grips, he saw that they were stained scarlet with blood. His hands were torn to pieces, blistered, and then the blisters destroyed. Twice during the long day, Felix Munger had come by to watch with sadistic pleasure in his eyes as Stuart pushed the wheelbarrow up the incline. Each time Stuart had let nothing show on his face, making Munger laugh.

"You're a tough one, all right, Lover Boy. We're going to have a lot of fun, you and me."

Stuart stood there for a moment trying to flex his hands. He turned to fall in line with the inmates who were heading across the yard back toward the main gate, but a double shadow loomed in front of him. He looked up to see Munger and Murphy blocking his path.

"Well, did you have a pleasant day, Lover Boy?"

Determined to do nothing deliberately to anger the chief of guards, Stuart said tightly, "Yes, sir."

"Well, now, I see this killer's learned some manners, Mr. Murphy." A slight triumph lit Munger's glassy eyes, and he looked down at Stuart's hands. "Oh, you got some blisters! Too bad." He turned to the other guard. "Mr. Murphy, I think we ought to show a little kindness to Lover Boy. Take him to the infirmary and get those hands fixed up. Then to the mess hall and see that he gets a good supper. Now"—Munger grinned—"say, 'Thank you, Mr. Munger.'"

Stuart considered complying with Munger's order, but something rose in his throat. He looked full into the man's eyes, then clamped his lips tightly together. Stuart knew full well that his own stubbornness would lead him to disaster, yet he remained silent, waiting for the consequences of refusing to play Munger's game.

"Oh, you still haven't learned anything, Lover Boy! Well then, take him to the hole, Mr. Murphy. Throw him in tonight with nothing but water. That'll teach Winslow here a few manners."

"Come along, Winslow," Murphy said, leading Stuart away.

Neither man said anything as they entered the main gates and headed toward the dispensary. An inmate on infirmary duty was tilting back in a chair reading the *Police Gazette*. He got up and said, "What's this, Murphy?"

"Guy's got some bad hands. Do what you can, Charlie."

"Sure. Here, sit down. What's your name?"

"Stuart Winslow."

The attendant looked at the hands and whistled, "Boy, you *did* tear your paws up, didn't you? Let's get somethin' on 'em and some bandages."

The inmate quickly washed off the blood, applied some yellow salve, and then carefully wrapped each palm. "Better do this every day and take it easy now, will ya? You're cut to the bone."

"No advice, Charlie. Just do your job," Murphy said.

The inmate's eyes came up quickly, and he studied the guard until something passed between them. He said no more but shook his head, then went back to his chair, picked up the paper, and began reading it while Murphy led Stuart from the room.

"Come along, Winslow."

Stuart was ravenously hungry. He had had nothing since breakfast, and that had been only a bowl of oatmeal, two pieces of toast, and a chunk of salt bacon. He followed Murphy through the labyrinth of corridors, passing through doors that were carefully guarded by men with shotguns and side arms. They went down two flights to an underground level where the dank air was cold and miserable.

Murphy passed by a guard and asked, "Which hole is empty?"

"All of 'em right now. Been an easy time, Jerry."

"This is Winslow. Put him in number one overnight."

"Just one night? He's lucky. Come on, Winslow."

For a fleeting moment Stuart caught a glimpse of compassion in Jerry Murphy's eyes as he handed the prisoner over. The other guard pushed Winslow down a corridor lined with six solid-steel doors, each with a small steel flap to allow the guards to slip in food and water.

The guard opened the last door and pointed with his gun. "In there."

Stuart stumbled inside, and for one moment, the dirty yellow bulb in the hallway cast dim light into the cell. It was nothing but a cubicle, seven feet square and no more than seven feet tall. The gritty concrete floor was empty, with no bed, nor even a pad to sleep on. He faced the door as it closed and all light was shut out. Total darkness enveloped him, and he stood, unable to move. He had never liked closed spaces, and now the pitch blackness seemed to enter into his very spirit. Weariness from the hard work all day wore on him, and the pain of his hands was almost unbearable. He sat down on the cold floor, hugged himself, and shut his eyes. He found it was no darker with them shut than with them open.

Time ceased to have meaning for him. He had no watch, of course. There was no sun, no moon or stars—nothing but the cold, frigid darkness. He finally dozed but then woke with a jolt, terrified and not knowing where he was. Then it came back to him, and he rose swiftly. He was trembling, and his teeth were chattering. He walked in a tiny circle on the damp, cold concrete for what seemed like hours until he finally slumped down again and tried to sleep.

Sleep came only in brief snatches. He had no way of knowing how long he slept each time. His memory, however, was the one part of him that was functioning well. He could think of Leah and Raimey without difficulty. He thought of the trial and the judge's face when he had sentenced him to twenty years. He thought of what a fool he had been, and he finally bowed his head and gritted his teeth, determined to block those thoughts out of his mind. The night seemed to last forever, but finally when the door clanged open, he woke with a start. Getting to his feet, he blinked his eyes in the dim light.

"Come on out of there, Winslow."

He had to grope, reaching for the walls, as he blindly stumbled forward. Finally a voice he recognized came to him. It was Jerry Murphy's.

"I'd like to give you breakfast, but Mr. Munger said no. You'll have to work today with no breakfast. Show some sense, Winslow! Just say what he wants."

As he was led out of the building across the yard, Stuart could only see through slits, for the sunlight was blinding. He could hear comments from the inmates. "That's Winslow. He won't make it. Munger's down on him. I give him a week before he hangs himself."

"Don't pay no attention to those guys," Murphy whispered. "Just last through today and say, 'Thank you, Mr. Munger.' That's all you have to do. Then you'll get out of this."

The day began, but it never seemed to end. With each trip up and down the ramp pushing the wheelbarrow full of wet concrete, his body cried out from weariness and his back muscles wrenched in spasms from the heavy loads. The day droned on and on. At noon everyone went to lunch except Winslow. While the others filed to the mess hall, Felix Munger confronted him.

"Well, you've put in a good morning, Winslow. I'd like to see you go have some lunch." Munger waited and his voice dropped. "Just say, 'Thank you, Mr. Munger.'"

Stuart's body cried out for rest and food, and he told himself he was insane for resisting Munger. This man could kill him if he wanted to. But something in him refused to answer. He stood there without speaking a word and stared straight into Munger's eyes.

"All right, tough guy. You'll go back in the hole tonight. Nothin' but bread and water until you learn how to be polite. I like tough guys." He smiled, then turned to Murphy and said, "Every day he goes back in the hole with bread and water. That's all."

"Yes, Mr. Munger."

Munger left and Jerry Murphy stood beside Stuart. "You're a fool, Winslow," he said. "He'll kill you. All you have to do is say that one thing—'Thank you, Mr. Munger.'"

Stuart did not reply.

"All right, it's your funeral," Murphy said and turned and walked away.

★　★　★　★

The only sound in the room was the shuffling of papers as Warden Armstrong sorted through the new inmate files on his desk. Pete Jennings was cleaning the warden's office, keeping as quiet as possible, for he knew the warden did not like to be disturbed. Jennings was a lifer and one who had learned to survive the rigors of prison life. A quiet man of fifty with scanty gray hair and careful brown eyes, he had been the warden's personal servant for some time. Being good with his hands, he kept the warden's Studebaker running like a watch. Now he moved around the office quietly, dusting and arranging the books as he knew the warden liked them.

Warden Armstrong closed the file in front of him and stared at Jennings. "This man Winslow. You met him, Pete?"

"No, sir. He's been in the hole every night. Works on the new unit all day."

"So he's working on bread and water. He must be pretty tough and a pretty bad one." Armstrong motioned to Jennings and said, "Come here, Pete."

"Yes, sir." Pete came over and stood in front of the warden's desk, his eyes alert.

"What's going on, Pete? Something's wrong here." The warden's finger tapped the file on top of the pile. "He came in the first day and didn't even get assigned to a cell before he was thrown in the hole and put on the hardest job in the prison." The warden's eyes penetrated Pete Jennings. "What's going on?"

Jennings hesitated for a moment. "Well, he got on the wrong side of Mr. Munger."

"A lot of people are on the wrong side of Mr. Munger."

"Yes, sir, but most of us learn to bend. I don't think Winslow's learned that yet."

"What did he do?"

"Nothing really, Warden. Just that—well, Mr. Munger wants him to say something, and Winslow won't say it."

Warden Armstrong's eyes glinted. "*Say* something! What does Munger want him to say?"

"The way I hear it, all Winslow has to do is say, 'Thank you, Mr. Munger,' and he'll lay off him. But Winslow just won't say it."

The warden opened Winslow's file again and stared down at

it. Pete Jennings knew exactly what the warden was thinking. The warden was a smart man, and he knew that Munger had a sadistic nature that made him hard beyond belief. It took a hard man to run a prison, but more than once Pete had picked up something from Armstrong. He knew the warden was troubled when a guard's pride caused him to cross the line into cruelty. The inmate stood waiting.

Finally Armstrong looked up and said briefly, "Thanks, Pete."

"Sure, Warden."

As Pete gathered his cleaning gear and turned to leave the room, he heard Armstrong say to a guard, "Taylor, have this new man Winslow come in to talk with me."

★ ★ ★ ★

There were still three hours of work time left, and Munger had come over to make one of his periodic visits to torment Stuart Winslow. Winslow put his wheelbarrow down and turned to face him.

"Having an enjoyable day, Winslow?"

"Yes, sir."

"Be pretty nice to get those hands seen to again. They're looking pretty ugly. You been actin' a fool for a week now. Are you feebleminded as well as being a woman chaser?"

"I suppose I must be, Mr. Munger."

"Look"—Munger's face grew red—"all you have to do is say, 'Thank you, Mr. Munger,' and then you can get out of this." He waited but saw there would be no surrender in the face of the tall man across from him. "You think you're tough, but I'm tougher than you are, and I've got you where you can't cry. It won't do you any good. One last chance. Say, 'Thank you, Mr. Munger.' "

Stuart stared at Munger and said, "When you do something for me, I'll be glad to say, 'Thank you, Mr. Munger,' but until you do, you won't hear that from me."

Munger's face flushed with anger, and he raised his stick, but at that moment a voice said, "Munger, the warden wants to see Winslow."

Munger turned quickly. "What's that you say, Taylor?"

The guard, a tall thin man with black eyes and hair to match, said, "The warden . . . he wants to see Winslow."

"What for?"

"I wouldn't know, Munger. But he doesn't like to be kept waiting."

"All right, Winslow. You go see the warden, then you come right back."

Stuart did not answer. He silently followed the tall guard away from the construction site to the warden's office. His mind was so bleary and stunned with the manual labor and the lack of food that he could barely think. He stumbled along, intent on not falling, until he found himself inside an office with a rug and a huge walnut desk in the middle of the room. The man behind it rose and said, "I'm Warden Armstrong."

"Yes, sir."

Stuart wondered what the warden was doing as he came around the desk and approached him.

"Let's see your hands." The warden studied the bloodstained bandages, then said, "What's the trouble, Winslow? It seems you've gotten off to a bad start." Stuart merely shook his head.

"Look, we get tough ones up here all the time, but there's no point in making things harder on yourself than they have to be." He waited for an answer and got none. "I have a letter from Reverend Charles Fields. We get lots of letters asking us to make things easier for prisoners, mostly from females. Quite frankly, I don't usually pay much attention to them, but my brother was in school with Charles Fields. I met him a couple of times. He's a fine man."

Stuart nodded. "Yes, sir, he is one of the best I ever met."

"You're a Christian, then?"

"No, sir, I'm not."

Warden Armstrong stood silently studying the face of the man before him. It was a handsome face, but worn, and the eyes were sunk back into the sockets. The hands had appalled him, and he remembered once what his brother had said: *If Charles Fields tells you something, George, you can go to the bank with it.* The letter had been simple enough. Fields had stated that although Winslow was guilty, there was something in him that he felt God would use someday. He had asked the warden to watch out for Stuart and help him find his way back. He had asked no other favors, which had impressed the warden. Now Armstrong said briefly, "I'm assigning you to a new job. You'll be working with Pete Jennings. He'll be your new cellmate."

Stuart blinked with surprise. A faint ray of hope came to him, and he said, "What about Mr. Munger?"

"I'll take care of him. You're a musician, I understand."

"Yes, sir. A little." Stuart looked down at his hands. "I used to be, but now I'm nothing."

"Whose fault is it that you're in here, Winslow?"

"Mine, Warden. All mine."

"All right. I'm going to go over the head of one of my guards. It's only about the third time I've ever done that in my ten years here. See that you don't make me sorry for it. I'd like to see you do better."

During the past week, Stuart Winslow had given up on men, on kindness, and on generosity. To him the world had become a place of cruelty, but now he said, "Thank you, Warden." The words came hard, but he knew this man that stood before him was fair.

"All right. You put yourself into a bad situation, Winslow. Don't let it sour you."

A knock sounded gently on the door, and the warden said, "Come in."

When the door opened, Taylor stuck his head inside and said, "Mr. Munger's here, sir."

"Send him in." The warden waited until Munger came in. With a blunt tone, he said, "Mr. Munger, I'm reassigning Winslow. He'll be a cellmate to Pete Jennings, and he'll work on the janitorial detail."

A flush of anger suffused Felix Munger's face. He started to protest, but one look at the warden's face, and he choked it back. "Yes, sir," he muttered.

"Mr. Munger, I'll expect you to follow my wishes in this."

Munger knew he was being told to keep his hands and his stick away from this inmate. He swallowed hard and nodded. "Yes, sir."

"You can take Winslow to his cell now."

Without another word, Munger walked to the door. He opened it and stood back to let Winslow pass.

Instead of walking out the door, Stuart turned and faced Munger. The warden watched this carefully, expecting trouble, but Winslow suddenly smiled.

"Thank you, Mr. Munger," he said quietly, then turned and walked away.

Warden Armstrong waited until the door was closed, and then a smile broke across his face. He had been seeking some way to put Felix Munger in his place for some time. Now it seemed that it had been taken care of better than if he had planned it himself. He sat down, stared at the papers before him, then nodded, as if making a decision.

Without a word, Munger stepped outside the warden's office, then turned to a guard and said stiffly, "Take Winslow to Pete Jennings' cell."

"Yes, Mr. Munger."

Sullenly, Munger stalked away while Stuart followed the new guard out of the administration building. It seemed like a long walk, and they had to pass through many checkpoints, but finally he stood before a cell and the door slid open.

"Pete, this is your new cellmate," the guard said.

Winslow stepped in and found a slight man lying on the lower bunk, reading a book. He sat up and swung his feet around.

"Hello. I'm Pete Jennings."

"Stuart Winslow."

"Maybe you'd like the bottom bunk?"

"No. The top's fine." Exhausted, Stuart climbed up into the top bunk and, without even taking off his shoes, fell into a deep sleep.

He was awakened when a voice said, "Time for chow, Stuart."

"No. I just want to sleep."

"Come on now. You can go back to sleep afterward, but you've got to be hungry."

Stuart knew Jennings was right. He came down off of the top bunk slowly and joined a line that went down the cold gray corridors. The men made not a sound as they marched lockstep toward the chow hall, but once inside, Jennings guided him through the dinner line to pick up their food, then to a table.

"Right over here."

Stuart found himself sitting at a long table with eight other men. He had had nothing but bread and water for a week, but now, strangely enough, he was not hungry. While the other men fell on their food like famished wolves, he simply toyed with his. Then he felt a nudge from Jennings.

"Come on, Stuart, put it down. I went through this once. Bread and water for a week. You've forgotten how to eat, but you need to get your strength back."

A tall, burly man with a bald head across from Winslow was staring at him. He looked like a brute, but there was a lively expression in his green eyes. "Hey, I hear you put Munger down. Good for you, guy."

Stuart looked up and down the table and saw that everyone was watching him—even from the adjoining tables. *I've become some kind of a celebrity*, he thought wryly. *If I'd let him kill me, I guess they would have made a martyr out of me.* He said nothing but shrugged and began eating the food. The act of eating made him suddenly ravenous and he downed everything on his plate. All around him men were talking, but he himself said nothing.

★   ★   ★   ★

Prison life improved for Stuart with Pete Jennings as a cell-mate. Jennings was a kind and compassionate man, and he knew all about prison life. He gladly taught Winslow what he needed to know about surviving at Tucker Farm without getting himself in trouble. He also talked to him about God.

Stuart was thankful that Jennings did not disturb him with incessant talking, and he grew to like him very much. But at times the man's jubilant spirit got on his nerves. Stuart could not begin to fathom how a man could seem so happy in a place like this. Though Munger was no longer a problem for Winslow, the other guards could be cruel at times, too. Every day was filled with backbreaking labor, and worse, the ever-present aching loneliness of serving out his twenty years for a crime he now deeply regretted.

Seasons came and went, though Stuart barely noticed their passing. Even the summer sunshine that pleasantly warmed him during his breaks in the yard or on outdoor work detail could not brighten his mood. The constant gray and cold of his concrete surroundings reflected the growing despair in his heart as day after day dragged by, one indistinguishable from another.

His family and friends had long since deserted him. He never had visitors, and even his mother had stopped writing within a week of his incarceration. It was probably easier to forget he existed than to live with the shame of having a criminal for a son, he figured.

He went through periods of terrible depression, believing that he was surely doomed to an eternity of hopelessness, even after his earthly sentence was satisfied. But Pete Jennings kept him alive through such despair. He was extremely patient, often urging him to read the Bible and believe that God loved him and had not forgotten him. Sometimes Pete's preaching got the better of him and Stuart would lash out, but deep down he knew that Jennings truly cared, and some part of him did not want to lose the friendship he had come to cherish. Warden Armstrong talked to him from time to time as well, also urging him to read the Bible and get his life focused on God, instead of on his own troubles.

Three long years dragged by in this way for Stuart Winslow. The thought of seventeen more of the same made him want to kill himself. Twice he tried, and twice he failed, with the result that he was put on a constant suicide watch. At those times Pete redoubled his efforts to persuade Stuart that his life could be better if he would simply stop running from God.

Somehow Stuart survived those years with the help of Pete Jennings and Warden Armstrong.

★ ★ ★ ★

One Sunday Stuart was lying on his bunk reading a western for the third time when Jennings said, "Hey, what do you say we go to chapel, Stuart?"

"Not me, Pete. You know that."

"Oh, come on. It's better than lying in the bunk," Jennings insisted. "Some of the singin' is pretty good sometimes. The guys keep asking if you'd play. The warden found an old guitar for us to use, but no one knows how to play."

"I said no. I'm never going to be able to play again anyway. I'll just stay here, Pete."

Jennings hesitated, then finally left.

Stuart lay there for a while, regretting his decision. Pete had asked him many times before if he'd consider playing for the men in chapel if they could find him an instrument and he always refused, but today seemed different. He did miss his music and began to wonder if he could indeed still play the guitar or fiddle after so many years of neglect. Not wanting to deal with the thought, he closed his eyes, locked his fingers under his head, and dozed. After a time he came to a half-conscious state, and the thought that often drove him to a state of despair came to him like a voice out of hell: *Twenty years, Winslow. Your folks will be dead. They don't care about you anyway. You'll be a worn-out old convict.*

The walls seemed to close in on him, and he resisted the impulse to rise and beat his head against the concrete. The temptation to give in to the despair had been constant these last three years, yet it was growing less severe lately, thanks to Pete Jennings' gentle encouragement.

"By the time I get out," he muttered aloud, "Raimey will be twenty-four years old, and I won't ever have seen my other child."

The image of Leah suddenly came to him as vividly as if he were looking at a portrait. He had not thought about her so clearly when he had been with her, but now something in him seemed to cry out, *I've lost her. I've lost her forever!*

Stuart Winslow had been a tough enough man in the outside world, but the hopelessness of spending seventeen more years in this desolate place had broken him—not outwardly, for he let no one see the anguish he fought against in his heart. But now as he lay there alone in the cold prison cell, he suddenly realized that tears were rolling down his cheeks. Before prison, he had never been afraid of anything, but now he was afraid—afraid of *time*. It was going to crush him and leave him, and he would have nothing left. With a desperate motion he rolled over and pushed his face into the pillow, and his body began to shake.

★　★　★　★

As soon as Pete Jennings reentered his cell after the chapel service, he saw instantly that something had happened to his new friend. From the day of his arrival, Stuart Winslow had shown almost nothing of what went on inside his spirit. Pete knew he had had a hard time with Munger that first week at Tucker, yet Stuart's face had been almost frozen in a fixed expression. Even after becoming his cellmate, Jennings felt as though he just couldn't reach the man. It was as if Winslow had buried all his feelings behind a cold wall—and *nobody* was going to get at them!

But one look at Winslow's face now and Jennings understood that something had broken. Winslow was sitting on his bunk, his hands clasped together, and when he turned, Jennings thought, *I've never seen such misery in a human being!*

"Stuart, what's wrong?"

At first Stuart Winslow appeared not to hear the question. His cheeks were drawn and his mouth stretched into a thin white line. But it was his eyes that caught Jennings' attention, for they were fixed in a terrible stare—as if Winslow were looking at something dreadful.

Jennings sat down and put his arm around Winslow's shoulders. His voice was gentle as he said, "I see it's caught up with you, Stuart, and I'm glad."

"What . . . what's caught up with me?"

"Everything," Jennings responded. He was a man who was intensely sensitive to people, especially the men in prison he'd come to know over the years. He'd been down a hard road of his own, which had landed him at Tucker Farm. Now as he gripped Stuart Winslow with his arm, he said, "Most everybody learns to bury things, Stuart, things we don't want anyone to see . . . things we're ashamed of. I had a cemetery of my own, and all the rotten things I didn't want anyone to know about, I buried them there. It was a pretty crowded place, Stuart, because I was a bad guy."

Winslow's eyes flickered with recognition, as if Pete's words were a familiar story to him. He said nothing but focused on the face of his fellow prisoner, who continued to speak in a soft voice. He was acutely conscious of the pressure of Jennings' arm as it pressed against his shoulder. At one time he would have shaken it off, but now he welcomed the gesture.

"So I buried all my bad stuff in that cemetery, but I knew it was there. At night I'd dream about it . . . and wake up in a cold sweat. What if somebody found out about all that junk? What would my wife say? Or my mother and father? It got to be pretty bad, Stuart. In fact, it got so bad I couldn't stand it."

"What did you do, Pete?" Winslow's voice was slightly above a whisper, and a tortured expression twisted his face.

"I did all the wrong things. I tried to drink enough whiskey to blot all that stuff out. That didn't work, of course. It never does. Then I tried to reform. That made sense to me—for a while. I quit drinking and gambling, and I even started going to church. Oh, I put on a pretty good front." Jennings smiled and shook his head as if amused somehow by the memory. "But it was no good."

"Why not?"

"Because I found out pretty soon that changing the outside didn't do anything about what I was. All the bad things I did— why, they weren't the problem!"

"I can't see that."

"Sure you can, Stuart, if you'll think about it. Why did I do all those things? Because I was messed up *inside*. See that? If a guy gets his heart right, then the things that come out of him will be good. But if he's got a rotten heart, that'll come out sooner or later. Like the preacher says, you can take a hog and wash him and polish his hooves and put a pink ribbon on him and douse him in cologne, but the first mudhole he sees—why, he'll jump right in and wallow in the mire! Because he's still a hog, no matter how good you make him look and smell!"

Jennings paused, then suddenly rose and moved to the small table beside his bunk. Picking up his Bible, he sat down and opened it. "You need one thing, Stuart, and just one. Get that one thing right, and all the other things will straighten themselves out."

Stuart Winslow had heard Pete tell him these things many times, and he had heard many sermons in his life, but somehow they always seemed unrelated to him. Even if the preacher was eloquent, he'd really felt no compunction for the way he had been. But he felt something now—for the first time—and it frightened him. He felt like a man on a cliff, dangling over an awful height. He felt a pressure to escape, but he didn't know how.

"I've ruined my life, Pete," he whispered. "It's too late for me!"

"No, it's not!" Jennings turned several pages rapidly, saying, "I want you to listen to one verse from Isaiah chapter fifty-three, the sixth verse." He read slowly, following the words on the worn page with his finger: " 'All we like sheep have gone astray; we have turned everyone to his own way. . . .' " Pete smiled, but tears stood in his eyes. "I guess that sums it up for both of us, Stuart. Nothing more stupid than a sheep! It'll wander off and die if left to itself." He shook his shoulders suddenly. "But listen to the last part of this verse—and listen close. It's what helped me to find Jesus." He read the last phrase of the verse with triumph in his voice: " 'And the Lord hath laid on him the iniquity of us all.' "

Jennings' hand closed hard on Winslow's shoulder. "Ain't that great? Ain't it wonderful!"

"I . . . I don't understand—"

"Why, the whole gospel is right there! We're all sinners, but God took all our sins and put them on Jesus! I don't have that cemetery anymore—it's all gone!"

Winslow listened as Jennings began to read from the Bible. The small man moved from the Old Testament to the New Testament, like a man showing a house, with pride in every room. His eyes shone, and his voice was filled with joy as he ended by saying, "Go back here to Isaiah fifty-three, verse eleven." He thumbed the pages and directed Winslow's gaze to the page. "Read out loud, Stuart—that part I've got underlined."

Stuart licked his lips, then read the verse in a faltering voice. " 'He shall see the travail of his soul, and shall be satisfied: by his knowledge shall my righteous servant justify many; for he shall bear their iniquities.' "

"That's what finally won me, Stuart, when I read the first part of that verse—the part that says, 'He shall see the travail of his soul, *and shall be satisfied.*' " Jennings shook his head, and the tears ran down his thin cheeks. "God saw what Jesus did—and it satisfied Him. That's what you've got to believe, Stuart! Believe that your sins were on Jesus when He died on the cross."

Something was beginning to stir in the heart of Stuart Winslow. Deep down inside he felt a *swelling* such as he'd never known. It was impossible to describe in words, but as he sat on the bunk in the gloom of the cell, a tiny light began to come into his heart. He suddenly realized that he'd felt this before but had ignored it. Now he welcomed it, for the thought was growing in him: *I need something more than myself!*

As if he had heard the thought, Pete Jennings said, "You can't do it by yourself, Stuart. None of us can. But you don't have to. Jesus has already done all of it."

For the next hour the two men talked, their voices swallowed up by the steel and concrete walls. Neither of them heard the sounds of the prison, nor was either conscious of the passage of time. Time meant little to them, in any case, and Pete Jennings loved the soul of this man with all his heart.

Finally Jennings said, "Stuart, Jesus loved you and died for you. But you have to open your heart to Him. If you do, He'll come in—I know it! He'll give you a new heart, and the whole world will be different. But you have to invite Him inside."

Winslow was trembling, but he whispered, "Tell me what to do, Pete! I want to know God!"

"Let's kneel right here and pray."

At once Stuart came off the bunk. He was trembling almost violently, and he could not seem to think clearly. One thing, however, was absolutely clear—the Spirit of God was calling him!

Jennings was not a man of eloquence. He prayed fervently but directly, speaking as he might to a dear friend. "Dear Lord, Stuart here is in a bad way, but you can help him. I know you can, Lord, for you helped me. He needs Jesus, and I'm asking you to draw him to yourself right now!"

Stuart Winslow began to weep great gasping sobs that wracked his body. He was conscious of Pete praying, but could not make out the words, for he was calling out as a drowning man might cry for help. He had no hope that he could ever find his way alone, but he was aware that One greater than himself was in the cell with the two of them. He did not know how to pray, but he knew how to cry out!

And cry out he did—not so much with his voice as with his spirit. He knew that he was whispering, "Jesus! Jesus! Help me!" over and over. He was vaguely aware of Jennings holding his arm. But he was lost in a fight that he knew he had to win—and he knew at the same time that he was helpless.

Later he was never able to remember how long the two of them prayed, but finally it was over. He came to himself, sitting on the floor, with Jennings beside him. He felt drained and enervated, powerless to do such a simple thing as rise from the floor.

But he *knew* something was different. He knew it!

Slowly he turned to his companion, and his voice was suddenly strong as he said, "I'll never understand it, Pete, but something has changed." He lifted his hands and raised them in a gesture of victory, and his expression was aglow as he whispered fiercely, "Thank you, God, for forgiveness! Thank you, Lord Jesus, for coming to me!"

Pete Jennings could do nothing but weep. Here in the dank, poisoned air of a foul prison, he'd seen the mighty God once again perform His ageless miracle!

PART TWO

1916–1917

★ ★ ★ ★

CHAPTER EIGHT

AN OLD DEBT

★ ★ ★ ★

"I wish you would just look at this, Lobo! I never thought I'd live to see such a thing in my born days!"

Lobo Smith had been gazing out of the window at his Missouri farm, but he turned now and put his one good eye on his father-in-law, Zachariah Winslow. At the age of fifty-two, Lobo Smith could have passed for a much younger man. He was no more than five ten, but there was a roundness to his arms revealed by the tan shirt that he wore. He had a deep chest and carried an aura of strength about him. His hair was curly and brown, and he was roughly handsome, but the most striking aspect was the black patch he wore over his left eye. It gave him the look of a bandit or a pirate. His good eye was an unusual shade of indigo that seemed to gleam against his dark golden tan.

"What's that, Zach?" Lobo said, coming over to look at the paper the old man was reading.

"Right there! Look at her."

Lobo scanned the picture and the caption of the *Springfield Herald* that read, *Bobbed Hair Craze Sweeping America and Britain.* "Well, she does look like she's shorn pretty close."

"It's indecent," Zach sputtered. "That's the trouble with the world these days. Bobbed hair and bossy wives!"

"Oh, come on now, Zach! I don't think that's really the trouble with the world, do you?"

Zach Winslow threw himself back in his chair and stared at his piratical-looking son-in-law. He was seventy-eight now, his hair was silver, and there was little to remind Lobo of the strong man that Zach Winslow had once been. Zach had been somewhat of a gunman, a prizefighter, a soldier in the Civil War, and a rancher, but now the years had caught up with him. He seemed frail, and liver spots covered the back of his bony hands. Yet even at his age, his eyes were still clear and his mind sharp.

"You're right about that, Lobo." Slipping the paper over, he thumped the front of it and said, "This here war across the water is gettin' plum out of hand. Look at that headline."

Lobo stared down at the headline dated November 9, 1916, and read aloud, "Casualties Mount as Battle of the Somme Enters Fourth Month."

"It's a pretty bad one from what I hear. Millions of good men are getting killed."

"I been reading about it, Lobo. Men are dying like flies over there. "

"Well, when you got three million men lined up against each other," Lobo observed, "all armed with machine guns and cannons and bombs, men are going to get killed." He sauntered over toward the cane-bottomed chair on the front porch and sat down on it, tilting it back. His eye looked out across the horizon, taking in the cattle grazing in the short distance, the corrals filled with thoroughbreds, and a feeling of pride surged through him. He had married Zach Winslow's daughter, Lanie, as a young man, and now a part of these thousands of acres would be his one day. He cared little for possessions. Indeed, he cared much more for the old man who sat rocking beside him. Although November, the sun of a late Indian summer shone down brightly, and Lobo sat there listening as Zach read items from the paper.

"I see this fellow Pancho Villa made a raid down in Columbus, New Mexico."

"Yeah," Lobo said, "but I hear the army's after him."

Zach laughed harshly. "Yeah, a fellow they call General Pershing. They won't catch Villa, though, not down in Mexico."

"I don't reckon so. That army stays all bunched up together, but those Mexican bandits will divide out and take fifty different trails. I don't reckon they'll catch 'em."

Lobo suddenly said, "I got a letter from Logan. He got his twenty-ninth kill."

Logan Smith, who was a son of Lobo and Lanie, had left America and joined the Foreign Legion, and then transferred into the Royal Air Corps. He was such a skilled pilot that he soon had become an ace.

"He'll do," Lobo said briefly. He could not hide the pride that shone in his one indigo eye.

"What are you two doing out here? Swapping lies as usual?" Lanie Smith came out on the porch carrying a tray with three cups of hot tea. She was a tall woman with only a few silver hairs among her rich auburn crown, and her brilliant green eyes that came from her Welsh mother glowed with humor as she studied the two men. She was concerned about her father, for he had been failing lately, and she eyed him carefully as he sat there. "Are you warm enough out here, Dad?" she said.

"Warm enough!" Zach snorted. "Why it's about as hot as any summer day today. Did I ever tell you about the time when we was fightin' down in Arkansas at Pea Ridge? It was spring but hot in them hills, let me tell you—"

"Now, Dad, I didn't ask for another one of your lying war stories," Lanie said. She put the tray down, stirred a generous spoonful of sugar into one of the cups, and handed it to her father with a smile. "If it gets too cold, you come in the house."

"Come in the house—come in the house!" Zach muttered. "That's all I get. Orders around here."

Lanie sat down on a chair and sipped on her tea as the men enjoyed theirs. "The reunion plans are going fine."

"Is everybody coming?" Lobo asked. He was looking forward to the reunion, which had been Lanie's idea. She was afraid that Zach might not last another year, and she wanted to get all the family possible together and had worked hard at it.

"John and Jeanine will be leaving Africa in time to be here."

"A mighty long way to come for a party," Zach said. Nevertheless, he was pleased, for John Winslow had been such a wild young man. Now, however, he had settled down and married a fine woman named Jeanine Quintana. They were serving as missionaries in Africa. "Be good to see them and that granddaughter of mine, Mallory. Never laid eyes on her. Ain't right a man should have a grandchild and not lay eyes on her."

"What about Phil and Cara?" Lobo asked. "They going to be able to make it?"

"Yes. Phil's doing a show, but he's going to cut it short."

"Seems funny to have an artist as a son," Zach muttered. "All the rest of us Winslows were roughnecks."

"Will they bring all the kids with them?"

"Yes. All three." Then she added, "Bill and Elaine will be here with their kids. And, of course, Tom and Helen and Betsy and Wesley. They'll all be here except Logan, of course."

"I reckon he's got better things to do, like shootin' down enemy planes. I wish he'd shoot down that horrible Red Baron."

"That might take some doin'," Lobo said, stroking his chin thoughtfully.

"Look, there's the mail. I'll go get it," Lanie said.

"No, let me. You sit here and drink the rest of my tea." Lobo got up and strolled out to the mailbox, where Ernest Benegian pulled up in his Studebaker and leaned out.

"Here's the mail, Lobo. How you doin'?"

"Fine."

"Read about that boy of yours shootin' down half the German air force. Congratulations. That's some son you got there."

"We're right proud of him," Lobo said. He turned and walked back to the house carrying a handful of envelopes and gave them all to Zach, who sorted through them. He handed most of them back to Lanie.

"Mostly bills and advertisements for stuff we don't need," he muttered.

Lanie left soon to start dinner, and Lobo sat with the old man, listening as always. He respected Zach Winslow as he respected few others and knew that time was short. He looked up finally and said, "We got a visitor."

"Who is it? My eyes ain't as good as they used to be."

"Looks like Tom. Yeah, it is in that fancy car of his. What is it? A Stutz Bearcat. He's gonna get killed the way he drives that thing. Give me a horse and buggy any day."

"I guess we're kind of past that," Zach said sadly. But he cheered up as the automobile stopped with a loud explosion out front and Tom Winslow came sailing out. He was a tall man with astonishing red hair, for which he was teased unmercifully. His father often told him, "You ain't none of ours. We found you under a farkleberry bush!" But wherever it came from, it highlighted Tom's light blue eyes.

Lobo rose, saying, "Hello, Tom. I'll let you sit here and listen to some of your dad's lies. I've had about all I can take."

"Okay, Lobo." Tom plumped himself down, leaned over, and patted his father on the knee. "How are you, Dad?"

"Can't complain."

"You never do," Tom said. He sobered briefly as he noticed the lines of pain and marks of weariness on his father's face. He had a quick memory of Zach Winslow when he had been a younger man, full of strength. Now that day had passed, and Tom covered up his surprise at the toll the years had taken on his father.

The two men talked for a while, and Tom said, "I'm staying overnight if I can have my old room."

"Go get unpacked, and then maybe we'll go for a drive tonight. I'd like to look over the place."

"Sure, Dad."

Tom went inside, kissed his mother, then moved his things upstairs. When he had finished unpacking his few belongings for his overnight stay, he looked around the room and thought of the years he had spent growing up here. They had been good years. He and his brothers had learned to ride wild horses, they had hunted and fished and rodeoed together. Now they were all grown, and he felt a sudden nostalgia for the good old days. He was a successful lawyer in Springfield now with a fine wife and family, but as he stood in the midst of the old trophies tacked to the wall, he suddenly laughed.

"You can't go home again," he said. "I can't be sixteen years old anymore. I have to be what I am." Then he went downstairs and found his sister with a worried frown.

"Something's wrong with Dad," she said.

"It's not his heart, is it?" Tom demanded quickly.

"No. I don't mean physically. He got a letter. He didn't tell me what it was, but it bothered him. I could see that." Lanie was mixing up biscuits, and she stopped and wiped her hands on her apron. "I'm worried about him, Tom. Go out and talk to him. Maybe he'll tell you."

"Sure, Lanie."

Going back on the porch, Tom sat down and stretched his long legs out, but he was too good a lawyer to say anything. He saw immediately that Lanie had been right. Something was bothering Zach, but the old man would have to come out with it himself, which he finally did, but not right off. As was his way, Zach began talking about something else.

"Wish I could have known Gilbert Winslow," he said, giving a quick glance at his son. "Been studying the old genealogy and the journal he left."

"That's some journal," Tom said.

The journal of Gilbert Winslow, the first of the Winslows to come to America, was indeed a treasure. It revealed the heart of a man struggling with himself and finally finding God. It also revealed a love story. Gilbert Winslow fell in love with Humility Cooper.

Tom smiled and said, "I know that journal by heart. I wish there were a picture of him."

"There was one of his brother Edward, but do you know that's the only person who came on the *Mayflower* we have a picture of? Of course, Edward was a famous man, so he had commissioned more than one portrait of himself. Why, he became governor of the colony and all that. He was a fine-looking fellow with auburn hair. Not as bright as yours, but lots of Winslows have had it. Same kind of tapered face and light blue eyes. All Winslow men look pretty much alike."

The two talked about the Winslows for some time. Indeed, the Winslow family was most interesting. The extensive family line included judges, governors, hunters, prizefighters, and some missionaries. Most of them had left a good legacy, serving well, but as is common, there had been a few black sheep along the way.

Tom finally said, "I'd like to have a reunion and get as many of the Winslows together as we can. Not just our own family, but all the rest that are scattered out all over the country. I'd like to see Cass Winslow and Barney from over in Africa. Some of those who have really made a mark in the world and those who haven't, too. We can't all be heroes," he laughed.

Zach was silent for a time, and then finally he said, "You better have it soon, Tom. I won't be around to enjoy a get-together like that much longer."

"Oh, Dad—"

"I'm not complaining, Tom. I've had a good life. I've had a good family, and I'm anxious to see heaven."

"I hope it won't be for a long time, Dad."

"I got a letter that's brought me some grief," Zach said.

"What is it, Dad? Maybe I can help."

"Here. I want you to read it, but before you do, let me tell you a little about something you don't know about." Zach clasped his hands together, dropped his head, and was quiet for a moment. Then he shook his shoulders and handed the letter over. "It's from Diane Winslow."

"Who's she, Dad?"

"Well, go get that genealogy chart, and I'll show you. It's on my desk."

"All right, Dad." Tom went at once to the desk and came back with the chart that showed the extensive Winslow family tree in a diagram. He laid it out on Zach's lap, and the old man touched it with a thin finger.

"Right here. You look at this. My father, Silas, your grandfather, had a brother who was one year older. His name was Maylon. He married Harriett Moore in 1828. They had one son named Henry. He was my first cousin. He married his childhood sweetheart, Nellie Atkins, in 1850. Sadly, she died giving birth to their only child, named Richard. Maylon and Harriet raised Richard after Henry was killed fighting for the Union at Gettysburg."

From far off the sound of a coyote sounded. It was a sad, plaintive sound to Tom, who had never liked it. He saw his father look up for a moment, take in the sound, and then continue.

"When you were one year old, Tom—that was in 1876, of course—the bottom dropped out for me. Lanie was nine, Betsy was three, and I bought this place mostly on credit. I got into the worst financial mess you can ever imagine."

"I never knew that, Dad."

"Well, I ain't proud of it. I overextended on it. Bought too much land, but I wanted a big family, and I wanted to give all of you something when I left. Well, anyway, I was going down the drain. Then you got sick, Tom, real sick. Medical expenses were high, and it just about scared me witless."

"I remember Mom talking about that."

"She was scared, too. And then she got sick. It was the worst time in my life, Tom. Worse than anything that happened to me during the war. I was a believer, but my faith got shook pretty good. For a while it seemed as though God had forgotten me."

Tom listened carefully, his analytical mind clicking. "What happened, Dad?"

"Well, we just reached plum bottom, your mom and me. We had you three kids, and we were gonna lose this place. There wasn't any way out. I'd been to every banker... everybody I knew that might lend me money. No luck."

Tom saw that this moment from back in time was very real to his father. "What happened, Dad?" he asked quietly. "Obviously you didn't lose the place."

"Your mom never gave up. She was a praying woman, you know, and she kept telling me, sick as she was, that God was going to help us. Well, it was just four days until we were about to lose this place when all of a sudden a knock came at the door. Your mama was too sick to get out of bed, so I answered the door, and when I opened it, there stood my cousin Richard and his wife, Diane."

Tom smiled at the expression on his father's face. "What did they say?"

"Richard said, 'Cousin, I'm here to take over. You just sit back and I'll handle it.'"

"And you say you didn't know him all that well?"

"No. But Bronwen had been writing to his grandmother, Harriet Winslow, who was still alive at the time. They knew how bad off we were. I'm telling you they just took over, Tom! Richard had some money from his grandfather, Maylon, and he had a lot of business sense. They paid our bills and got us back on our feet. Richard somehow just handled it. And Diane nursed you and your mother back to health."

"That's a wonderful story, Dad. I'm glad you told me."

"Well, as you can imagine, Tom, I've never forgotten that. I paid Richard back the money he spent, of course, but that didn't change anything. I've never ceased to be grateful. Been one of the sad things in my life that I haven't been able to be with Richard and his family very much. Now read the letter."

Tom opened the letter and began to read.

My dear Zach,

    I have been hesitant to write this letter, but the Lord has been speaking to my heart. You know, of course, the trouble we had with our son Stuart.

Tom looked up and said, "What trouble did they have with Stuart?"

"He killed a man and got sent to the state penitentiary. That was about seven years ago, I think. Go on and read."

    As you can imagine, I've been praying for Stuart ever since he went to prison. We've had no contact with him these past seven years. We tried to write to him, but our letters were all returned unopened, and the prison officials told us Stuart wanted no visitors, so we know nothing of what has happened to him there. Lately God has put a vision of some kind into my heart. I can't explain it, but He keeps telling me to write to you. I have no idea why, Zach. I believe with all my heart that God is going to get my boy out of prison, but I realize that you are not in good health and can't imagine why God would have me put another burden on you. Please don't take this as a burden.

    Richard and I have always loved you and your family, and we ask you to pray for us and especially for Stuart.

                    Your loving cousin,
                    Diane Winslow

Tom read the letter again quickly and then looked up at his father. He saw the disturbance in his father's face and said, "This bothers you, doesn't it?"

"Yes, it does, Tom, and I can tell it's not going to get any better. Richard and Diane did everything for us. I don't know what would have become of us if they hadn't come."

"Do you know any of the details of their son's crime?"

"Not really. It was open and shut, I think. Probably he was guilty. If I remember correctly, he did shoot the man."

"That doesn't necessarily mean guilt," Tom said quickly.

Zach looked up and reached out. There was a surprising strength in his hand as he gripped Tom's wrist. "Tom, we Winslows have got to stick together. The world's falling apart. You've got a nephew that's putting his life on the line every day."

Tom put his hand on his father's hand. "What do you want me to do, Dad?"

"I want you to go and talk to Stuart, talk to his family, talk to the warden, talk to anybody you can. I know you're a busy man, but if you'd do this one thing for me, Tom, I'd consider it a personal favor."

Tom's eyes suddenly grew dim with tears. It was the first favor his father had ever asked of him. He did not even pause for one moment but shoved all of his busy engagements out of the way. "Of course I'll go, Dad. I'll leave tomorrow. I'll do what I can."

"Thank you, son." Zach looked fondly at this tall son of his and said, "Remember how in the book of Esther she had to take a chance and risk her life for her people, and Mordecai said, 'Maybe you've come to the kingdom for such a time as this.' Maybe, Tom, you've become a lawyer, a defense attorney, for just this one thing."

★　★　★　★

Tom left early the next morning. First he needed to go back to Springfield to see his wife, Helen, and children and get his appointment book cleared out at the office before he left for Little Rock. His father was not up yet, but he spoke to Lobo and Lanie about what he was planning to do. "It's the first thing Dad's ever asked me to do, and I've got to go."

"What about all your work?" Lobo asked.

"My partner will just have to take a double load. I'll make it up to him."

"Do you think you can do any good?"

"I have no idea legally, but I've got to give it my best. You two do the praying, and I'll do the lawyering."

Tom finished breakfast and left, and Lanie waited until her father was up. She gave him his breakfast and told him what Tom had said, then she came over and put her arms around him. "We're going to win this one, Dad, you'll see."

CHAPTER NINE

A TABLE IN THE WILDERNESS

★　★　★　★

Tom Winslow had always liked the early-morning hours. He sometimes called them the cobwebby hours of the day for no real reason that he could think of, except it seemed to fit. He had gotten up before dawn and left Springfield, heading for Tucker State Penitentiary outside of Little Rock. Now as he drove along the almost deserted two-lane road south, he watched the fall color sweep across the land. He always took pleasure in the vigor of the morning changes. For one moment it was almost pitch black with only the stars glittering overhead in the sky. Then over in the ebony east the horizon seemed to split, and a pale violet fissure divided earth and sky as long waves of light began to roll out from the east.

Draping his right hand over the wheel, he watched for the space of half an hour as the world came alive, bathed in morning freshness, but it was very cold. Yesterday's Indian summer warmth had soaked out of the earth, and fall's chill flowed over the land and lay in the still air, its thin edge cutting against Tom's face and hand. He had the habit of dramatizing scenes that he expected to happen, sometimes acting them out in his mind almost as if they were flashed on a screen at a movie theater. He did so now, imagining his interview with his relative he had never met, wondering what kind of man Stuart Winslow was. He had gotten little information from his father, for Zach had known little of Stuart, except what he had heard from Stuart's parents. His mind shifted abruptly as he took a big sweeping curve on the road, outlined by the skeletons of trees now devoid of their fall color that reached upward with bony arms. He thought of his interview he had arranged with Warden Armstrong, and like a good lawyer, he had tried to find something out about the man. "Tough but fair" was the word that he had been able to get from an associate who lived in Little Rock. This was little help, for it would apply to most wardens, at least the *tough* part.

After driving for four hours, he stopped at a small café and went in for a big breakfast. He ate a tall stack of pancakes drenched in maple syrup, three large sausage patties that were spicy and bit at his tongue, and a bowl of grits liberally laced with butter, salt, and pepper. With that meal filling his stomach, he wouldn't need to stop to eat again until he got to Little Rock late in the afternoon. He left the pretty young waitress a quarter tip, which brought a smile to her face, then went out and started the Hudson.

On his last leg toward the prison, he took pleasure in the automobile. It was a new Hudson Super Six, and the seventy-six horsepower engine was powerful enough to propel the vehicle along at a brisk fifty miles per hour with no trouble, provided he had open road in front of him. He passed most cars, swinging wide to the left, then cutting back in on the narrow two-lane road that was paved for the last part of his journey nearing the capital.

He found a hotel for the night, ate a hearty meal of fried catfish, turnip greens, and fried potatoes, followed by chess pie, and settled in for the night.

At ten o'clock the next morning he pulled up to the gates of the prison and was greeted by a guard with a square, hard face and a pair of suspicious gray eyes who demanded to know his purpose.

"I'm here to visit a prisoner, and I have an interview with Warden Armstrong at eleven o'clock."

The guard consulted a clipboard and reluctantly nodded. "Go on in. Visitors park over there."

"Thank you."

Pulling the Hudson over to a line of cars and trucks, Tom

shut the engine off and sat there for a moment. As was his habit before he began any sort of work or started any project, he bowed his head and prayed quickly. "Lord, give me favor with Warden Armstrong and open up the doors to this place in the name of Jesus."

Grabbing a large paper sack stuffed full of items he thought Stuart might appreciate, he jammed a notebook into his pocket and moved across the yard. He passed a group of inmates carrying shovels and noticed the old, lost faces. Their hardened features seemed to be closed doors that had shut out the world. He heard not one sound as the men trooped along, flanked on either side by guards carrying shotguns. A shiver ran through Tom Winslow, and he gave a quick prayer of thanks that he was not locked up here. Like most men, he had a fear of losing his freedom. As a lawyer, he had visited several prisons, and it always brought a mixture of fear and compassion for those who had brought themselves to such a place.

"I'm here to see Stuart Winslow," he said as he approached a guard standing just outside a door. The guard was a tall man with high cheekbones and a broad slash of a mouth.

"Do you know his number?"

"No, I don't."

"Go on inside." He stepped back, opened the door, and nodded. "That guard over there will take care of you."

"Thank you."

Stepping inside, Tom saw a long hallway that extended the length of the building. He went at once to an open door where a guard in a dark blue uniform sat at a desk. A wood stove glowed with a cherry red flame that sent off heat waves throughout the room. The guard looked up and nodded.

"What can I do for you, sir?"

"I have an appointment to see one of the inmates."

"What's his name?"

"Stuart Winslow."

The guard pulled out a notebook, opened it up, and said, "You're all cleared."

"I also have an appointment to see Warden Armstrong at eleven."

"You'll have to go to the administration building for that. Go out the front door and turn to your left. Just ask anyone."

"Thank you."

"I'll have someone take you down to the visitors' room." He called out, "Jenkins, take this gentleman down to see a prisoner."

Tom followed the guard, a short, stocky man wearing his cap pushed back on his head in a jaunty air. He was shown to a large room with tables scattered around, and the air was filled with the murmur of conversations.

"Have a seat over there. I'll get Winslow for you," the guard said.

As soon as the man left, Tom moved over to one of the vacant tables. A large stove took the chill off the air, and what appeared to be a husband and wife stood close to it, the man holding his hands out to catch the heat. All of the inmates wore a dull, striped uniform, roughly cut and ill fitting. Their hair was cut short, giving them a rather sinister appearance.

As Tom looked around the room, he felt a great pity for these men whose lives had now, more or less, ended. Many of the visitors were wives, he supposed—some young, some older—and most of them looked like poor, hardworking women. The majority of them wore cheap clothing, and their hands were red from the cold and hard work.

"You got family in here?"

Winslow turned quickly to see a woman seated at the next table. She was in her sixties, he supposed, a small woman wearing an imitation fox fur that had lost a great deal of its substance. Her hands, which she kept folded on the table, were rough and worn, and the backs were dotted with liver spots. She had a pleasant, sweet face but looked very tired.

"Yes. A distant relative," Tom said.

"Your first time here?"

"First time."

"My name's Violet Bijorski."

"I'm glad to know you, Mrs. Bijorski. I'm Tom Winslow." He hesitated, then said, "You're visiting a relative?"

"My son." She clasped her hands together and looked down at them, then looked up and smiled. Despite the obvious fatigue on her face, there was a look of peace about her. "He's been here a long time."

"How long, Mrs. Bijorski?"

"It'll be sixteen years next week. We lived in Alabama, but when he was put in here, I left my home and took a room in a little town not far away. It gets kind of lonesome, and I still miss my old friends."

"You come pretty often to see your son?"

"I've only missed one visitin' day in all that time."

The enormity of what the woman said struck Tom Winslow forcibly. To give up home and friends and everything else to move to a strange place just so she could faithfully visit this son of hers was a stunning example of love and commitment. He was about to speak when the door opened and an inmate entered. He was a small man with a sharp face, but Winslow saw the resemblance.

"Hello, son."

"Hello, Ma."

"This is Mr. Winslow. He's come to visit a relative. This is my son, Davey."

"I'm glad to know you," Tom said. He reached out and shook hands. The man had a weak, flabby handshake, and his eyes were dull and vacant.

He nodded at Winslow, then said to his mother, "Did you bring the stuff I asked you to?"

"Yes. I've got them here. They'll give them to you."

There was no word of thanks from the man, and Winslow sat listening as the woman chatted. Davey had almost nothing to say. He did not show any gratitude, and a slight flicker of anger touched Tom. Then he thought, *Who am I to judge? If I were in this place for twenty years, I don't think I'd have much of anything left.*

He sat there for ten minutes, and then the door opened. As soon as the man entered, Tom recognized Stuart Winslow. He had the Winslow look about him. He was strongly built and heavy in the shoulders, but he was thinned down so that the cheap uniform hung loosely on him. He was closely shaved, and his eyes swept the room looking for his visitor. Tom stood up and saw the eyes, so dark blue they were almost black, come to him. He moved across the room and put his hand out. "I'm Tom Winslow. I'm glad to meet you, Stuart."

"Good to see you," Stuart said quietly. He looked around and said, "We can get coffee if you'd like."

"That would be good."

The two moved over to the stove, where a huge coffeepot was kept warm on top. A guard stood with his back to the door and gave Stuart a couple of chipped cups. They filled them and then moved back across the room. When they sat down at a table, Tom Winslow sipped his coffee and said nothing. Stuart was studying his visitor carefully, and somehow the gaze made Tom a little uncomfortable. In a lawyerlike fashion, Tom summed up his relative with a quick analysis. He'd expected something different, a weaker man or, perhaps, a little streak of viciousness. He saw none of this, however. He knew that Stuart was now thirty-six years old, and except for a few lines around the corners of his eyes, his face was smooth. He did not have a prison pallor, which surprised Tom somewhat, but he expected that Stuart did some kind of outside work. What really surprised him was the steadiness of Winslow's gaze and the peace that he saw on the man's face. There was little of the lost despair that he'd seen on the faces of other inmates, and he could discern no anger whatsoever. If he had met Winslow outside, he would have said without hesitation that he was a well-founded individual. Stuart's steady eyes rested on him, and there was a patience and a calmness in him that came as somewhat of a surprise.

Maybe prison does that, Tom thought to himself. But aloud he said, "I don't think we've ever met, but I met your father and mother once when they came on a visit to my home."

"You're Zach Winslow's son," Stuart said. "My parents used to talk about your folks a lot. They think there's nobody like them."

"Well, it's mutual," Tom said. He hesitated, but time was short, and he had a great deal to say. "Stuart, my father got a letter from your mother. She didn't ask for help, but my father has asked me to come to see what I can do."

"Are you a lawyer?"

"Yes. A defense attorney."

Stuart smiled, and his white teeth showed against his olive complexion. "I could have used you a few years ago," he said. There was no bitterness in the remark, and he simply sat there for a while, his big hands holding the cup. He had long, strong fingers, and his hands looked powerful. "Why exactly are you here, Mr. Winslow?"

"Call me Tom. I'm going to look into your case. I don't know much about it, but sometimes things can be done in the law."

"You're going to try to get me a new trial?"

"That would be one option, but I'll have to know everything. We don't have a great deal of time. I have an appointment with the warden at eleven o'clock, so I'm going to ask you a lot of questions. I ask you one thing, Stuart. Just tell me the truth. No matter how bad you think the thing is that you did, just tell me the truth. Never lie to your lawyer."

"No point in that. What do you want to know?"

For the next hour Tom fired questions at Stuart. He listened carefully and wrote a great deal in the notebook that he had brought in with him. As he listened, he became more and more convinced that whatever this man had been seven years earlier, he was not a dangerous man now. There was a calm simplicity about Stuart Winslow that impressed him greatly. Finally he shut his notebook and said, "I've got to go now to see the warden." He grinned briefly and said, "I'll see what kind of a character reference he gives you."

"He's a good man. He's been a big help to me."

"I'll be going to Lewisville tomorrow. Do you have any message for your folks?"

Stuart Winslow hesitated, then said in a choked voice, "Tell them that I love them . . . and that, I'd like to hear from them. I don't blame them for ignoring me, but I need their forgiveness."

Tom Winslow could not understand why Stuart would say that his parents were ignoring him. Surely they had done all they could to keep in touch with him. Since Stuart was visibly shaken, he decided not to press the issue with him, but would ask the warden about this. He went on, "And I'll be seeing your wife and your family. What can I pass along?"

Stuart remained silent for several moments, turning his mug around in his hands and staring down into the remains of the coffee as if it held some great interest. When he finally looked up, Tom could see the pain in his eyes.

"Tell them I love them," he said, "and that I'm sorry."

Tom was very moved by the man's contrition over how much

he had hurt his family. He saw at once that these were not just words, but that the man was truly sorry. "I'll tell them that." He got up and said, "I didn't know what to bring, but I left a whole sackful of stuff—candy, gum, shaving cream. I just filled it up at the store. If you can't use it, give it to somebody else."

"That was thoughtful of you, Tom."

The two men stood there, and those who turned to them saw, somehow, a similarity. One man was wearing expensive clothes and had an obvious air of authority and determination. The other was a criminal dressed in the shoddy uniform provided by the state. Yet there was something about the two that marked them as relatives.

"Your mother hasn't given up, Stuart. I'm a pretty stubborn fellow myself. You know, there was a time when some of our people were in jail in Salem. Looked pretty grim for them."

"Yes. I've read about them. Great people."

"Well, we Winslows have to stick together." An impulse came to Tom then. He stepped forward and put his arm around Stuart's shoulder. They were about the same height, and he squeezed him, saying, "God's able to furnish a table in the wilderness and feed a million children with bread from heaven. I think He's able to get you out of this place, so don't give up."

A light flared suddenly in Stuart Winslow's eyes, and a glimmer of hope changed his expression. "I'm glad you believe that, Tom."

"I'll be seeing you again. Good-bye."

"Good-bye—and thanks for coming."

Leaving the visitors' room, Tom stepped outside, sought directions, and left the building. He found the administration building without any problem and told the attending guard that he had an appointment with the warden.

"Down that hall. His name's on the door on the right."

"Thank you."

Moving down the hall, Tom found the door marked Warden Armstrong and stepped inside. He found himself in an outer office, and an inmate was sitting there filing papers.

"Can I help you, sir?" he said. He was a small man with sharp features and coal black hair.

"I have an appointment to see Warden Armstrong at eleven o'clock."

The inmate glanced down at the paper on his desk. "Mr. Winslow?"

"Yes. Tom Winslow."

"He's expecting you. He said for you to come right in."

"Thanks." Tom knocked on the door, heard a voice, then opened it. He found a stockily built man with iron gray hair cut short sitting at his desk. "Warden Armstrong, I'm Tom Winslow."

"Glad to meet you, Mr. Winslow. Take that chair there." Armstrong waited until Tom was seated and then said, "You've come to see Stuart. I've got his record here. Is he a relative of yours?"

"A cousin, Warden. My father and mother are very close to his parents."

"I see."

The warden's eyes were sharp and brightly intelligent. They had seen much grief, yet the hardness that Tom had heard connected with him did not show in his features. Indeed, he had an interest that caught Tom's attention. "I know you're a busy man, Warden, so I'll put it all out on the table for you. I'm a lawyer. A defense attorney, really. My father's asked me to look into Stuart's trial."

"He feels that it wasn't fair?"

"He doesn't really know. Stuart's mother is a very lovely woman, so he says, and she wrote to him and asked him to pray for Stuart. My father's in bad health, so he couldn't come himself. I really don't know anything about the circumstances, but I came to visit Stuart, and I wanted to hear your opinion of him. I'll be going to Lewisville to rake up the old ashes to see if I can stir something up."

"I'm glad you came. A lot of men pass through here, Mr. Winslow. Most of them are pretty hard cases. Some of them are just scared and are beaten down. Stuart's different."

"Different in what way?"

"Well, it's hard to say. You know some men just impress you the first time you see them. When he came here he got off to a bad start."

"How was that?"

"Well, he got crossways with the chief of our guards here—Felix Munger. He's a hard man, and I learned that he was treating Stuart with unnecessary harshness. Within a week of Stuart's arrival, I reassigned him to another part of the prison so Munger could no longer bother him."

Tom listened as the warden described the difficulties that Stuart had encountered when he had first arrived at Tucker Penitentiary. "It would have broken most men," Armstrong said, "but not Stuart." The warden picked up a pen, turned it in his hand, then replaced it. "He had a lot of bitterness, Mr. Winslow, when he first came, but four years ago a dramatic change came into him. Up until that time he wouldn't talk to anybody except his roommate, Pete Jennings. He kept to himself, and I thought he would never pull out of it. I've seen that kind of bitterness rule in men before, but as I said, four years ago that all changed."

Tom leaned forward. "What happened, Warden?"

A smile touched the wide lips of Warden Armstrong, and his eyes brightened. "Pete Jennings is quite a fellow. He's in for life with no hope for parole. He committed a terrible crime, but he found God while he was here, and for three years he tried to talk to Stuart Winslow about God. Thankfully, he finally got through. Maybe Stuart will tell you more about it sometime. He has quite a testimony. Since then he's been a changed man. He's just one of the dozen or so that Jennings has been able to help. These last four years Stuart's been a model prisoner."

"Tell me all you can about him, Warden. I'm going to need everything I can get."

"Well, he just came out of himself, and the thing that has been different, besides his attitude, has been his music."

"His music? What do you mean?"

"Oh, he's a wonderful musician! Can play just about anything, and you've never heard such a voice. Nobody really knew it until he gave his heart to the Lord. But he started playing in the chapel services. We found an old guitar for him, then a banjo and a fiddle—he plays just about anything. About two years ago he came up with the idea of having a weekly concert, so I let him try it. Every Friday night he plays and sings. He organized some of the interested inmates into a choir. In fact, he's even teaching quite a few of them to play the guitar and other instruments. I tell you, it's been quite a thing. We have a pretty tough time in this place, Mr. Winslow, and anytime anyone can unify the prisoners into something like that, I say it's good."

Tom listened avidly, taking copious notes, and for a solid hour he pumped Warden Armstrong for every detail about Stuart's life. The warden was happy to supply any information he could, saying along toward noon, "Look, I don't know what use I can be. I'm pretty active in the politics of this state. You use my name if that's handy."

"That's very generous of you," Tom said. "Could I ask you just one more question, Warden?"

"Certainly."

"Stuart tells me that his family have ignored him these last seven years—not visiting or even sending letters. The letter from Diane Winslow indicated that Stuart himself refused all visitors and returned all his letters unopened. Stuart seems to think they've chosen to ignore him because they're ashamed of him, but from what I know of his parents, I find that hard to believe. Especially of his mother. Is there some reason he would not have been allowed any contact with his family?"

Warden Armstrong looked as if he had been struck in the face. He considered his words carefully before saying, "I know nothing about this, Mr. Winslow, but hearing this concerns me very much indeed. We have no such policy. Contact with home is a prisoner's lifeline. We would never discourage that. I'll look into it at once."

"Thank you, Mr. Armstrong."

"I've written a letter of commendation for Stuart. Here's a copy of it. Feel free to use it any way you see fit."

Tom took the letter and ran his eyes down it. "This is very fine!" he exclaimed. "I'm sure it will help."

"Well," Warden Armstrong said thoughtfully, "Stuart won't be eligible for parole for another five years."

Tom stood up and took a deep breath. "Warden," he said, "God is able. If He wants Stuart Winslow out of this prison, He'll open those steel doors."

Warden Armstrong had not seen many success stories, but somehow he felt that this tall young man before him would be hard to turn away. "Amen," he said. He put out his hand and grasped Tom Winslow's hand. "God bless you, and I'll pray with you that these doors will swing open for Stuart Winslow."

★   ★   ★   ★

As soon as Tom Winslow disappeared from the warden's office, George Armstrong sat back down with a heavy sigh. This news about Stuart not having any contact with home for seven years had shaken him, but a thought was forming in his mind that came clearer with each passing moment.

Munger! Could it be that the man had found his revenge in this way? When Armstrong had taken Stuart Winslow out of Munger's hands all those years ago, he should have known that the man wouldn't have accepted such a humiliation without a fight.

How could I have been so stupid?

"Taylor!" The warden called for the guard standing outside his door.

Taylor quickly opened the door and stuck his head in the warden's office. "Yes, sir?"

"Get me Felix Munger. Now!"

CHAPTER TEN

VALLEY OF DECISION

★ ★ ★ ★

Late-afternoon sunshine poured over Lewisville as Tom Winslow arrived and headed down the wide main street. He watched as some buggies and wagons still fought for their place among the automobiles and trucks. He took in the stores and shops—Smith's Drugs, Sanderson's General Store, Shultz's Laundry and Cleaner. The most opulent building was the courthouse, which sat in a square at the end of Main Street. Horses and buggies, wagons, cars, and trucks filled the parking spaces, and the courtyard was busy with people coming and going.

It was Wednesday, November 12, 1916, and Tom took his time studying the town and the faces of the people. Parking the Hudson, he got out and strolled down the street, impressed with the slow pace he observed in Lewisville. Fort Smith, he understood, was the "big town" where people went for important events. The weather had turned cold, and the women, with their skirts down to their shoes, were bundled up with wool coats, many of which had fake-fur collars. Most of the men were rough farmers and wore overalls and mackinaw jackets with corduroy caps with earflaps. The farm people were easy enough to differentiate from the townspeople, who wore more formal attire.

Finally Tom approached a man standing out in front of the bank and said, "I'm looking for a gentleman named Richard Winslow."

"Well, his office is right down the street, but I think he's already closed up."

"Can you direct me to his house?"

"Sure." The man spat an enormous glob of amber tobacco juice in a stream and wiped his mouth with the back of his hand. "You go right down this here street for two blocks. That's Magnolia. Turn right there and go until you see a big white house with pillars set out back from the road on the right. Got his name on the front by the mailbox. You a friend of his?"

"Distant relative."

"That so! What kin are you?"

Tom smiled and gave as little information as possible but thanked the man and returned to his car. He pulled out and dodged an overloaded log wagon that threatened to spill all over Main Street, then followed the directions. He spotted the house and pulled into the driveway. He was impressed with the beauty of the place. It reminded him a little bit of Mount Vernon on a much smaller scale. The house was two stories with four white pillars in front. The yard was carefully manicured, and he thought it must have been an impressive sight in the spring, for flower beds were carefully laid out everywhere. Getting out of the car, he walked up the four brick steps and rapped three times with the knocker. He tried to remember all that his parents had told him about Richard and Diane Winslow. When the door opened he said at once, "It's Mrs. Diane Winslow, isn't it?"

"Why, yes!"

"I'm Tom Winslow, Zach's son."

"Tom! Why, it's so good to see you."

Diane Winslow came forward, and Tom was surprised at the warmth of her welcome. He embraced her, took her kiss on his cheek, then she drew him into the foyer.

"I'm so glad you've come. Come into the parlor. Let me call Richard from the study."

Tom followed Diane into a tastefully decorated parlor. The walls were papered in a light blue-green color on the top half, and the bottom half was done in a solid green separated by a chair rail of dark oak. The pictures on the walls were all of well-dressed people, and by the faces of the subjects, Tom could see that they were Winslows. A large sofa in a dark green and gold damask was situated in front of a large marble and oak fireplace that was flanked on each side by two easy chairs upholstered in light blue and white material. Tables were covered with books and fancy crystal lamps, which caught the light of the day coming through floor-length windows on the east side of the home. It was a warm room, lived in, and Tom moved around, studying the pictures that decorated the bookshelves and the walls. He turned at the sound of footsteps and stepped forward at once. Richard Winslow looked older than he had expected, older than his sixty-four years. His hair was silver, and he had a weary look on his face.

He greeted Tom, saying, "I'm so glad to see you, my boy. Sit down. Let me poke up the fire. It's a little chilly in here."

Tom took a seat while Richard put another log on the open fire, which blazed up cheerfully. When Richard sat down beside Diane, he said at once, "Tell us about your dad."

"I wish I had a better report to give you," Tom said. "His health hasn't been good lately."

"I was afraid of that from his letters. He never complained, but he always talked about how much he hunted and about his fishing trips."

"That's pretty much behind him now, I'm afraid, Richard. If I may call you that."

"Certainly, Tom. Certainly."

Tom asked about their family. He learned that Jeff and Hillary had two children and that Liza had married and was expecting a child. Her husband, Dalton Burke, was managing the Winslow store in Twin Oaks. Richard and Diane did not mention Stuart. Tom went on to give the news of his family, and both Richard and Diane were quick to question him. They had kept up with all of Tom's brothers and sisters, and they were especially proud of Logan Smith.

"We kept a news clipping about his shooting down his twenty-fifth German," Richard said, his eyes warm.

Diane leaned forward and said, "Do you think we'll get into this war, Tom?"

"Bound to. President Wilson's kept us out so far, but the Germans have started their submarine attacks again. I thought surely we'd declare war after they sank the *Lusitania* with so many of our people on board. We can't put up with them killing Americans like that. It's just a matter of time."

"It's a terrible thing. I've been reading about the losses over in the Battle of the Somme. It's hard to imagine a million men dying, isn't it?" Richard said sadly. "All of them had lives of their own, families that cared for them. Many had wives and children. We can see one tragedy and be sorry for one person, but a million men dying in those trenches—how can a mind even take it in?"

"Some say this will be the war to end all wars," Diane said. "I pray it will be."

They talked for some time. Diane fixed coffee for Tom and Richard, tea for herself, and finally it was Richard who said, "What brings you to Lewisville, Tom? It's not on your way to anything, I'm sure."

"No. My dad sent me."

"He sent you?" Richard asked with a puzzled expression. "Sent you to do what?"

Knowing that he must be very careful, Tom hesitated, then said directly, "My dad has never forgotten what you two did for him years ago. I didn't know all of that until he told me just this week. He still feels in your debt."

"Why, he paid back every penny that I helped him with, Tom."

"It wasn't just the money. He knows that, but it was the fact that you cared. You and Diane came at a crucial time, and according to what he says, I might have died if you hadn't been there. My mother feels the same way," he said.

"We've always felt close to your parents, Tom," Richard said. "But you didn't come down here just to tell us that."

"No. As you know, I'm an attorney specializing in criminal cases. The Lord blessed me in my practice, and Dad asked me to come down and look into Stuart's trial."

Instantly something changed in Richard Winslow. Tom could not identify it at once. A tenseness seemed to stiffen the older man's body, and his eyes grew guarded.

"What good would that do?" he asked.

Diane Winslow said instantly, "It's an answer to prayer. I

didn't expect this, Tom. I hope your father didn't take my letter as a plea for help."

"No, he didn't. As a matter of fact, I read the letter, but this is what he wants to do." Quickly he said, "Now, it may be that I can do nothing. We have to be prepared for that."

"I don't think you can. He was convicted," Richard said heavily, "and that's all there is to it. He'll have to serve out his sentence. Until then, nothing can be done."

"I'm not sure that's true," Tom said. "Most trials are not as open and shut as this one seems to be. What I'm going to do is dig into all the court records and read all the stories in the papers. I suppose they've kept them all at the local newspaper office."

"Yes, they'd be there," Richard said grimly. "And people still talk about it."

Seeing that it was disturbing for Richard to talk about it all, Tom said, "It may be a little trouble for you, and I apologize for that. I'm going to have to go back and talk to all the witnesses, to the arresting officer, everybody."

"But what good will it do?" Richard asked, pain etched into his features. "He was guilty and he was sentenced."

"Well, there are different interpretations. I've seen too many cases where one man went to jail because a certain judge sat on the bench, whereas another man would have gone free. In any case, Dad hasn't asked me to do many things for him, but he wants me to do this. I want to help, sir."

"Thank God!" Diane said. "I know that He has sent you."

"Well, I think it's foolish," Richard said. "It can't do anything but cause more talk."

Instantly Tom knew that Richard had not forgiven his son for the shame he had brought to the family. Carefully he said, "There's no quiet way to handle this, I'm afraid, Uncle Richard. I'll be as circumspect as I can, but I'm going to push up some rocks to see what crawls out."

"And you'll stay with us while you're working on the case," Diane said. "We have plenty of room in this old house. Richard and I just rattle around. Go get your suitcase, and we'll get you settled in."

* ★ ★ ★

Leah pulled the mare up firmly and then reached down and patted the glistening neck. "That's a good girl," she said warmly. She stepped out of the saddle and handed the lines to Merle.

"Yes, ma'am. She sure is. Really the best of the line. I remember it was Wash that talked about breedin' Princess to Thunder, and he sure was right. This is a fine, fine mare. She's gonna give us some mighty fine colts."

"Walk her for a little bit. I gave her a pretty hard run, Merle."

"Yes, ma'am, I sure will."

Turning, Leah walked toward the house. She wore a pair of men's jeans, a short leather jacket with a wool lining, and a pair of black leather half-boots. The ride had brightened her cheeks and her eyes, and now as she moved toward the house, she heard voices. Skirting the house, she found Raimey swinging Merry in the tire swing that Wash had fixed for them in the huge walnut tree.

"Don't swing her so high, Raimey!"

"Oh, Mom, she likes it!"

Raimey turned and gave her a quick smile. For one moment a memory flashed over her. This son of hers was so much like Stuart that it was almost frightening. He was an exact copy of what Stuart must have been when he was nearly twelve: black hair, dark eyes, lean and strong. He was Stuart's son in more than looks, for he was also musically inclined. He could already play the harmonica and guitar by ear.

"Mama, it's fun," Merry said. Her name was Marianne, but the nickname had begun when she was in her cradle. At the age of six, she was a beautiful child with light blond hair and large clear blue eyes. She was cheerful, happy, loved dolls and animals, and had learned to read almost overnight, so it seemed. She was a creative youngster, making up stories and songs almost at will.

"You'll fall out and break your arm," Leah scolded. "Not so high."

"Aw, Mom, she'll be all right," Raimey said. He stopped the swing, and Merry popped out of it. Both were wearing warm coats, and their faces were red with the cold November breeze.

"Mom, can we go to the movie tonight in town?" Raimey asked quickly. "Charlie Chaplin's on."

"Yes. I like him," Merry put in. "He's so funny with his little cane and his funny hat. And he walks so funny."

"No. Mott's coming over to supper tonight."

"Aw, Mom, couldn't we all go?"

"It'll be too late. Maybe I'll take you later in the week. Now, you can play for another hour, and then you'll have to come in and get ready for supper."

Leah turned and walked into the house. She stepped inside, took off her coat, and hung it on the hall tree, then went at once to the kitchen, where she found Annie getting supper ready.

"What's for supper tonight, Annie?"

Annie Waters had grown heavy with the years but was still strong. Her hair was graying now, but she was as outspoken as ever. "We're gonna have catfish. Raimey caught 'em on the trotline. They just about the right size. About two pounds apiece."

"That sounds good. I'll come in and help you as soon as I do my bookwork."

"I ain't needin' no help! I take care of supper just like I always do. Ain't nothin' to it but bakin' some hush puppies and fried 'tatos, and we got some poke sallet. You go on and lie down now 'til suppertime."

"Can't do that. I have to work."

Annie watched as Leah left the room, and she picked up part of the corn-bread mixture and made a ball about two inches thick and plopped it down in a pan. "Always workin'. She don't look good. She gonna work herself to death," she fussed. She was a quick-minded woman and shook her head. Thoughts ran quickly through her, and she remembered what she had said to Merle. *She ought to marry Mr. Castleton. He's a state senator now and got lots of money. He'd take care of her and be a daddy to them kids.*

Now as she thought of it, the memory of Stuart and all the heartache he had caused came into her mind, and she shook her head. "He done lost his chance. Miss Leah's a young woman. She needs a man, and them kids need a daddy. That's all there is to it."

Leah was well aware of Annie's viewpoint. She herself was

troubled about Mott, and as she entered the study, she sat down at the desk and tried to put it out of her mind. For a while she worked on the books, which were becoming more difficult. Times were changing. The farm had been created mostly to breed mules and horses, but the automobile and the tractor had taken away much of that market and would take more. She knew something would have to change, but she did not know how to change it.

Finally she put the pen down, placed her hands flat on the desk, and pressed her forehead against it. She could not help thinking of Mott then, for he presented a challenge to her.

Mott had married, but his wife had died two years ago of influenza. He had deeply mourned her for a year and a half, but then he had begun seeing Leah at church and taking her home. Their relationship had suddenly changed, until finally Mott had shocked her two months earlier by asking her to marry him.

As she sat there, the conversation played itself again, as it had often, in her thoughts.

"Why, I can't do that, Mott! I'm already married."

"Stuart's in jail for twenty years. He'll be an old man when he gets out. Prison does that. He was no good for you, Leah, anyway. The kids need a dad and I need you. I was in love with you once, and now I am again."

"But I'm married."

"Get a divorce."

"I don't believe in divorce."

"I don't either ordinarily, but your situation is different. You'll have to bend your principles a little bit. You need a life, and we could have a good marriage and maybe even have our own children."

Mott had been persistent. He had changed over the years, mellowing somewhat, but he was convinced that Leah's marrying Stuart had been a grave mistake. Mott loved Raimey and Merry and would make a good father, which was a big factor.

Abruptly the sound of an automobile approaching came to Leah, and she straightened up and then rose to go to the window. She expected Mott, but she saw it was not his car. A tall man wearing a navy blue suit got out and came up toward the steps. She waited until Annie finally came to announce the visitor.

"There's a gentleman to see you. His name is Winslow. Must be your kinfolk."

"Where did you put him?"

"In the parlor."

Leah went to the parlor, and the man who faced her said at once, "My name is Tom Winslow. I'm a distant relative of your husband, Mrs. Winslow."

Leah was caught by surprise. "Is that right?" she said briefly. She did not ask him to sit down. "What can I do for you, Mr. Winslow?"

Tom saw instantly that there was something wrong. He expected to be welcomed, and, as usual, he had made up his mind how to approach Stuart's wife. He knew from his conversation with Stuart that the man was still in love with her and was grieved beyond belief over the way he had treated her. Tom had also heard much from Diane, so he knew the story of their difficult marriage. He had not expected, however, the hardness that he found in Leah Winslow.

"I'm here to do what I can to reopen your husband's case."

"What do you mean reopen it?"

"I'm hoping to prove that the sentence was not just. I would like to have the case retried."

Reluctantly, Leah said, "Well, sit down, Mr. Winslow, and tell me about it."

As Tom launched into his story, he was aware of the coolness in the woman's eyes. He was struck with her beauty, for at the age of thirty-three, she looked at least five years younger. She was wearing a pair of men's jeans, which was somewhat shocking, but he had heard that she worked with the horses a great deal, and it revealed a practical side to her.

Leah listened as her visitor spoke quickly, and finally she said, "You expect to get him out of prison?"

"That's my prayer. It's also his mother's prayer," Tom said. He hesitated and then said, "I don't want to pry, but I've talked to Stuart, and I've talked to his people. They both tell me that he was not a good husband."

"He was not."

The brevity and the coldness of Leah Winslow's reply made Tom pause for a moment. "I think he's changed, Mrs. Winslow."

"What makes you think so?"

She listened as Tom described his meeting with Stuart, and then he repeated what the warden had said. "He's convinced that he's had a change of heart."

"I would have to see it to believe it. I wish you well, but I must tell you this, Mr. Winslow. I hope you can get Stuart out of prison, but even if he does, I can't have him back. He's caused nothing but shame and disgrace." She hesitated, and her lips grew firm, and her eyes grew hard. "He has made it very difficult for my children. The other children are not kind, and they taunt them about having a jailbird for a father."

"I'm sorry to hear that, ma'am. A man can change, though."

Leah rose and said, "Thank you for coming by. I wish you well, and I wish Stuart well . . . but when you see him, you might tell him what I just told you."

Tom left the house feeling discouraged. She was an attractive woman and, from all accounts, a good mother and had been a good wife. He saw an adamant aspect to her character, and he shook his head, muttering aloud, "Stuart's going to have a hard time when he hears how she feels."

$$\star \quad \star \quad \star \quad \star$$

Mott arrived for dinner with a new pocketknife for Raimey and a doll carriage for Merry. They were both pleased with their gifts, as they always were, and Mott said to Leah, "I ought to bring you gifts."

"Don't do that, Mott," she said quickly.

They sat down to a dinner of delicious panfried catfish that Annie had prepared. Mott encouraged Raimey to tell how the fishing trip had gone and then said, "You and I'll have to go fishing for trout sometime. You'll have to use a different kind of pole."

"Could we, Mr. Castleton?"

"I don't see why not. Not now, of course, but in the spring we could go."

"Can I go, too?" Merry said.

"Why, of course. You and your mother and brother could get

a cabin up there on the river, and I could get another. We could have a real vacation there."

As the meal progressed, Leah was quieter than usual. She was wondering what it would be like to be married to Mott Castleton. She had never felt drawn to him as she had been to Stuart, but then, no other man had so captivated her heart as did Stuart Winslow that first time she saw him playing his violin and singing at the Fourth of July dance years ago. Nevertheless, watching as her children grew excited, she wondered, *Would it be worth it to have a father for Raimey and Merry?*

After the meal was over they moved to the parlor. Mott had brought a bunch of new records for the gramophone, mostly war records: "Keep the Home Fires Burning," "Pack Up Your Troubles in Your Old Kit Bag and Smile, Smile, Smile," "I Didn't Raise My Boy to Be a Soldier."

The war was on everyone's mind, and once Mott shook his head as he listened to the lyrics and said, "I've been wondering what I'll do when the war comes."

"Why, you wouldn't join the army, would you?" Leah asked with surprise.

"Well, I'm not too old. I couldn't pace with some of these young fellows, but maybe I could do something."

The thought troubled Leah, and she said, "There must be something you could do here at home. Going overseas to fight is for young men."

"You're probably right." After that he said, "Hawaii's big these days. I've got a couple of pretty cute records." He played one called, "They're Wearing Them Higher in Hawaii," and then "On the Beach at Waikiki."

Mott stayed until the children's bedtime, and then after they went to bed, he sat in front of the fire talking quietly. Leah found herself relaxed. She knew she liked Mott much better than when he had been a younger man. She also knew that he was in love with her.

When he got up to leave, suddenly he turned to her and said, "Marry me, Leah."

"I . . . I just don't know, Mott." She hesitated and then said, "I had a visitor today."

Mott listened as Leah told him about Tom Winslow's visit,

and then he shook his head. "He may be able to get him out. I don't know, but Stuart ruined your life once, Leah. Don't let him do it again." He put his arms around her suddenly, and she put her hands on his shoulders and looked up at him. "Let me be a dad to the kids and a husband to you."

He pulled her close, and Leah closed her eyes as he kissed her passionately. She tried to feel something in return, but all she knew was that she was confused.

Mott drew back and said, "Think about it. I know getting a divorce is a terrible thing, but it's terrible for youngsters to grow up without a dad. Or maybe even worse for Merry and Raimey to have a dad whose name everybody knows in the worst possible way."

Leah walked him to the porch and watched as he drove off; then she went back inside. She was more troubled than she had realized. Staring down into the yellow flames of the fire in the parlor, she had the feeling that time was passing her by. She was lonely, and although she did not feel for Mott what she had felt for Stuart, she knew that she once again longed to be a wife to someone who would love her and care for her children.

Finally she turned and pressed her hands against her eyes and whispered, "I made a terrible mistake once. I can't make another!"

CHAPTER ELEVEN

TOM WINSLOW GETS SOME ANSWERS

★　★　★　★

An iron gray sky cast a dull gloom over the land as Tom Winslow walked briskly along the side street. Dead leaves had piled up high, for towering oaks and elms had dropped their foliage earlier, and now the crackling sound that Tom's boots made broke the silence. Overhead, far to the east, a group of four buzzards circled, gliding effortlessly, and not for the first time Tom thought, *Strange that such an ugly bird can fly so beautifully. Like a lot of things, I guess they look better far off than they do up close.* His philosophy amused him, and he shook his head and turned in to a single-story white house that sat back off the street. Smoke curled upward for almost twenty feet, and then the wind caught it and bent it into what looked like a question mark. Mounting the steps, he rapped on the door and slapped his hands together, for a numbing cold was falling upon the earth. December was only three days away, and he could almost feel the snow that would soon be in the air.

The door opened and a tall, homely man stood there, his blue eyes fixed on Winslow. Almost instantly, he said, "Well, I wondered when you'd get around to me. It's Tom Winslow, isn't it?"

Surprised, Tom nodded. "That's right. I don't remember you, though."

"I'm Ace Devainy. We ain't met, but I figured we would. Come on in out of the cold."

Moving inside, Tom glanced around and saw a pleasant-looking house with a long central hall with several doors and leading to an outer door at the rear. Right then a small girl with reddish blond hair came sailing out of one of the rooms, stopping when she caught sight of the visitor.

"This is Mattie. This is Mr. Winslow, Mattie."

Mattie smiled and then turned and said, "Can I go outside and play?"

"What did your mother say?"

"I didn't ask her. She might say no, but you always say yes."

Ace Devainy laughed and said, "Okay, go ahead, sweetheart. We'll straighten it out with your ma later. Come on in by the fire. I just built it up."

Following the rawboned man into the parlor off to the right, Tom cast a glance around. It was a comfortable room filled with horsehide furniture, yellow curtains at the windows, and pine tables scattered everywhere covered with books and magazines.

"Have a seat by the fire there. I've got coffee on the stove. Do you take it black?"

"Black is fine." Tom grinned. He liked the way the man didn't ask him *if* he wanted coffee but simply assumed that he would.

Five minutes later the two men were sitting before the fire as it snapped, crackled, and sent a myriad of golden sparks up the chimney. "I like a good fire," Ace remarked. "I'd hate to live in a place so hot you couldn't have one." Without a pause, he said, "I guess you want to know about Stuart." He held the cup in his hand, turned it around, and then after taking a sip said, "What have you found out?"

"I didn't know my activities were so well known."

"In a small town like this? You don't know much about small towns, I take it. Every time a cat has a litter, everybody in the county knows about it. It gets on my nerves at times, but that's the way it is."

"I guess you already know that I'm trying to get a retrial or to do something to get Stuart out of prison."

Ace's eyes narrowed, and he ran his hand through his shaggy

yellow hair. "I'd be mighty grateful if you could do that. Do you think there's any chance?"

"In law there's nearly always a chance. You mind if I ask you a few questions?"

"Fly right at it, Tom. If I can call you that."

"Sure. Well, just start in talking and tell me about you and Stuart."

"We was always best friends. Grew up together, hunted together—deer and girls and everything else, I guess. . . ."

Winslow listened carefully, not taking notes, but soaking it all in. A picture had emerged of Stuart Winslow, and he had the feeling that this tall, homely man probably knew him as well as anyone. From what he had heard, the two had been quite the characters a few years back, raising all kinds of deviltry, playing together at dances, chasing women, drinking, and gambling. Now as he listened and noted the change in the man, Tom found himself liking Devainy very much.

"I'm a tame coon now," Ace shrugged. "Got a good wife and three young'uns. Twin boys. You'll get a look at 'em before you leave. I think they're gettin' their bath right now."

The grandfather clock ticked loudly as it gave a syncopated air to the room. Over the mantelpiece was a painting of Custer's Last Stand with the general dressed in yellow buckskin in the midst of the Battle at the Little Bighorn. Custer was shooting an Indian off a horse, but it was obvious that the general's doom was certain. Tom studied the picture for a moment and then said, "I need some advice, Ace. I don't know which way to go."

Ace started to answer, but at that moment a woman entered, and Ace said as the two men stood, "This is my wife, Ellie, and these are my boys, George and Henry."

"I'm glad to meet you, Mrs. Devainy." Tom smiled and stepped closer to peer into the twin faces that stared up owlishly at him. "Which is George and which is Henry?"

"It doesn't make any difference. They're just alike," Ace said, winking at Winslow.

"What a thing to say!" Ellie said. She had grown heavier, but there was a peace in her face that had not been there when she was a young woman. Marriage agreed with her, and having children even more so, and now she said quickly, "Take one of these lumps, Ace."

"Here, let me hold George," Tom said quickly.

"Do you have children of your own?"

"A boy eight and a girl six," Tom said. "Would like to have about half a dozen more, but Helen says I'm not quite ready for that yet. I'll talk her into it, though."

The three sat down, and Tom enjoyed balancing the baby on his knee. "He's a fine one," he said. "I know you're proud of your children."

Ellie shifted uncomfortably and said, "We've heard you're trying to get Stuart set free."

"That's right, Mrs. Devainy."

"I wish you well. But if you do get him out, make it clear to him that he needs to leave Leah alone. He's brought nothing but misery to her, and now she's got a chance to have something better."

"You ought not to talk like that, Ellie," Ace said uncomfortably.

"Why not? It's true enough! Mott Castleton wants to marry her. He's got money and could take care of her. He could be a good father to her kids, too."

Ace shook his head but argued no more. Tom sensed the discomfort between them and understood that these two differed strongly on the matter of Leah Winslow. He rose quickly and handed the baby back to Ellie, saying, "Thanks for your time. You've got fine children here."

"I'll see you out," Ace said.

The two men walked outside, and when they were clear of the house, standing by the picket fence that surrounded the yard, Ace said, "Me and Ellie don't quite agree on this thing. I don't know what's happened to Stuart in prison. It's like he just faded off the face of the earth. But I worry about him every day. Do what you can for him, Tom."

"I'll do that and thanks, Ace."

★　★　★　★

Sheriff Luke Garrison studied the young man across from

him and nodded. "Yes, I was the first one there after the shootin'."

"How did you know to come?"

"Stuart came in and got me. We picked up Doc Morton and went on out there."

"What did you find, Sheriff?"

Shrugging his beefy shoulders, Garrison said, "Well, Carter was dead, and Cora had taken a shot high in the shoulder. Stuart had bandaged it up and stopped the bleeding but wouldn't let her leave. It was fairly serious, and Doc had to give her something to let her sleep, so I didn't get to talk to her much. She was hysterical about it, anyway."

Tom leaned forward in his chair and considered what Garrison had told him. "What did you think, Sheriff? I mean it's all over now, but I guess everybody knows I'm tryin' to get Stuart another chance."

"I hope you can do it, Mr. Winslow. I always liked Stuart. He was wild, but he comes from a good family. I think he's got good stuff in him. I've heard from the warden that he's kind of straightened up in the pen." He shifted in his chair and looked across his desk. "A lot of men in jail get jailhouse religion. They just want out, so they're bein' good, but I know Warden Armstrong pretty well. We grew up together, and he tells me that's not the case with Stuart."

"Yes. I've talked with Warden Armstrong, and I've talked with Stuart. My family owes a lot to Richard and his wife. I'm gonna bust a gut trying to get Stuart out of there, so tell me everything you can."

"I'll do that. The first thing was that Richard made a big mistake hiring Mordecai Frasier to defend Stuart. I told him so, but he wouldn't listen to me. Mordecai's a great man, but he was really out of it. A sharp lawyer, I think, would have gotten Stuart off. . . ."

★　★　★　★

Tom's interview with the Reverend Charles Fields was short but convincing. He listened as Fields expressed his eagerness to help, and finally he said, "Leah Winslow's a member of your church."

"Yes. She has been ever since she came to Lewisville. Fine woman. Very fine!"

Feeling that he might be treading on shaky ground, Tom said carefully, "I've heard a rumor that she might marry another man."

"Mott Castleton. Yes, it's more than a rumor, I'm afraid." A worried look crossed Fields's features, and he shook his head. "The Bible's pretty plain about that. In Mark eleven, verse ten, Jesus said, 'Whosoever shall put away his wife, and marry another, committeth adultery against her. And if a woman shall put away her husband, and be married to another, she committeth adultery.' That's always been pretty plain to me, but this country's changing. More and more divorce all the time. I hate to see it."

"I think it's terrible," Tom said soberly.

This matter had apparently weighed hard on Charles Fields. He shook his head and said, "Do you know, Mr. Winslow, there are some kinds of physical problems that we can get over and some we can't? For example, if we get a case of the flu, we can recover and live just as if it had never happened. But if we have an auto wreck and lose a leg, we may live, but we'll have to limp around the rest of our lives. I think divorce is like that. From what I've seen, people never really get over it. It leaves a wound that just won't heal up. Don't get me wrong. They go on with life, but it's never the same."

"I agree, and I was a little surprised at Mrs. Winslow. I was expecting something else."

Reverend Fields put his hands together, squeezed them, and then shook his head. "I'm very concerned about her. She had such a wonderful, happy spirit, but after the tragedy, she seemed to lose some of her faith. Oh, she still comes to church and brings the children, but there's not any joy in it for her anymore." He got up, walked over to the window, and stared out for a moment, then turned back and locked his hands behind him. "I think she'll marry Mott Castleton for the children's sake. She's very concerned about them not having a father."

"But if we get Stuart out—"

"It wouldn't make any difference. She's adamant about that. She doesn't want him back. As a matter of fact, the last time I talked to her, she seemed more afraid of that than anything else."

"You've talked to her since I came to town?"

"Yes. She came to me last Tuesday. I can't reveal what she said, of course, but it's really nothing new. She's trying to make up her mind which way her life should go, and it's very hard for her. She's being pulled to pieces, I'm afraid."

Tom left shortly after that, and as soon as he was gone, Charles Fields sat down at his desk. He picked up his Bible, thumbed through it, then shook his head. "No one knows what Leah will do, not even she herself, but it'll be a tragedy if she can't open her heart to Stuart again and forgive him."

★   ★   ★   ★

When Tom Winslow came downstairs for breakfast, he found that his uncle had already left. He sat down and filled his plate with eggs and country ham and grits and some hot biscuits that Diane had just pulled out of the oven. He ate heartily as Diane sat across from him sipping her coffee but eating nothing.

"I ate with Richard. He's so busy," she said. She hesitated for a moment, then said, "You're not making much progress, are you, Tom?"

"Oh, it takes a while," Tom said evasively. He put a layer of apple butter on a fresh biscuit, bit into it, and said, "You just have to keep on turning over rocks and hoping you'll find something underneath. And I will. I don't care how long it takes."

"But your practice. What about that?"

"It'll be there when I get back, Diane. Don't worry about it. I got a letter from Dad yesterday, and I could tell he's very anxious for me to get this thing worked out."

"Bless his heart. I wish I could see him. He's such a fine man."

"The best one I know," Tom said.

The two sat there for a time, and finally Tom saw that something was troubling Diane. "What is it?" he asked. "Have you got something on your mind?"

"Well, you'll probably hear about it. Maybe you already have. Cora Simms came back to town. She's been gone to Europe, I think. Switzerland or somewhere. She's been traveling a lot since Carter was killed."

Instantly Tom sat up straight. "She's the one I need to see.

She's the only witness to what happened. I was about ready to leave the country and go run her down."

"You won't have any trouble. She lives in the big stone house out by the Old Military Road, just past the cotton gin."

"I'll go see her this morning," Tom said. He sat for a moment thinking, then he said, "Why don't you and I just pray that God opens a door?"

"I think that's exactly what we should do," Diane said.

The two did pray—Diane passionately—and Tom left feeling a stir of excitement. It was the last day of November and was very cold, and the car was hard to start. Finally he got it going, though he almost broke his arm getting it cranked. "I wish I could afford one of those new self-starters for these contraptions," he grumbled. Sailing down the road, he followed Diane's instructions and soon pulled up at an imposing stone house. A Cadillac sedan was parked outside, and he got out of the car, shook his shoulders against the cold, and advanced to the steps. When he rang the bell, the door was opened almost at once by a small young black woman.

"Yes, suh?"

"I'd like to see Mrs. Simms, if I might. My name is Tom Winslow."

"Yes, sir. Would you wait in the foyer? I'll see if Mrs. Simms will see you."

Tom stood looking around the foyer. It was an opulent house with the mark of wealth everywhere. The walls were painted a bright white with gold accents highlighting the trim, crystal chandeliers hung from the high ceilings, and the floor was made out of highly polished white marble with gold swirls running through it. Mahogany shelves and tables lined the walls and were covered with vases of fresh flowers, books with bright leather bindings, and crystal and gold knickknacks of all kinds.

Hearing footsteps, Tom turned to find a woman approaching him and was impressed by the beauty of Cora Simms. She was wearing a dark burgundy dress made of satin with an overlay of black lace that fell to her ankles. The neckline was low, the sleeves long and tight fitting, and the skirt had black beads along the edge of the hem.

"My name is Tom Winslow, Mrs. Simms. I apologize for calling without making an appointment."

"Are you related to Stuart?"

"Yes. He's a cousin of mine. You may not have heard, but I've come to see what I can do for Stuart. I'm a lawyer."

"Come into the drawing room, Mr. Winslow."

The two went into the drawing room, where a fire was blazing in the fireplace. A tall black man was putting logs on it, and Cora said, "That'll be fine, Ralph."

"Yes, Miz Simms."

As soon as the man was gone, Cora turned to Tom and said directly, "What have you done so far?"

It was a direct question, and Cora Simms was watching him carefully. Tom Winslow knew that he had to be very careful. This woman had been in the back of his mind ever since he had heard the story, and now he felt a sense of excitement growing in him. "I found out that there are elements in the trial that might lead to a new examination of the case."

"You mean another trial for Stuart?"

"Yes. I don't want to speak unkindly of anyone, but Mr. Frasier was in no condition to try that case, and he did not bring facts in that could have altered the verdict. I'm looking for all the evidence I can to prove that the trial was not fair for Stuart."

"And what do you want from me?"

Tom decided to take a chance. He had the spirit of a gambler deep in him, although his gamble was never with cards or dice. He gambled with people. Now something in Cora Simms's eyes and expression, her whole demeanor, in fact, compelled him to say, "I think you could do more than anyone else to help Stuart, Mrs. Simms."

"How can I help?" Cora said as she sat down.

He noticed that her hands were unsteady. Sitting down across from her, he said, "I read your testimony at the trial, but I'm afraid the district attorney twisted a few things."

"I was frightened," she said. "I'm usually not an easy woman to frighten, but I was worried about Stuart."

"How did it happen? Tell me exactly."

"Stuart never even had a gun," she said. She twisted her hands together, and words began to flow out of her. "Stuart and I had had an affair when he was first married but hadn't seen each other for four years. That night we were together again. Carter had always been suspicious of Stuart. He never believed our affair was really over. When he came through the door that night, I knew I was a dead woman. He had always said if he caught me with a man, he'd kill me."

"Did he ever threaten to kill the *man*?"

"Never," Cora said, and a bitter light touched her eyes. "He never loved me. I was nothing but a trophy to him. He always said he couldn't blame a man, because I used them, and he was right."

Cora's honesty took Tom aback, but he only said, "Can you tell me exactly what happened when your husband came home that night?"

"He had a gun in his hand, and he began to curse me, and he said, 'I'm going to kill you.' Then he simply raised the gun and shot me. I fell over backward and struck my head, but I didn't lose consciousness."

"What did Stuart do?"

"He jumped up and made for Carter. Carter shot at me twice more, and he missed both times. I think it was because Stuart knocked his arm up. The two started struggling for the gun, and then I heard another shot, and Carter fell down."

"This information is very important, Mrs. Simms. Did Stuart get the gun away from your husband?"

"No. He never did. He had a grip on his wrist, and he was twisting the gun away from him, trying to keep him from shooting me. He bent it all the way back, but it was Carter who pulled the trigger."

A great sense of relief came to Tom Winslow then. "This could change everything. Will you testify to this in court?"

Cora's eyes met Tom's. "Yes, I will," she said. "I don't have any reputation to uphold. I'll testify."

"I'll be getting back to you, Mrs. Simms," Tom said as he stood to leave.

When they reached the door, Tom held his hat in his hand and turned as Cora spoke again. "Get him out if you can, Mr. Winslow. He's not a killer. It was my fault he was here. I made him do it." Her lips twisted in a humorless smile, and she shook her head. "I can make men do things, you know."

Tom said briefly, "I'll be calling on you again once I attend to some matters, Mrs. Simms. I think we can do something with this new information." He turned then and left.

When Cora shut the door, she put her back against it. Her body began to tremble, and to her astonishment tears formed in her eyes. She had not cried over anything in so long she had forgotten she knew how.

★　★　★　★

"I think I've got enough new information to go ahead now and seek a retrial for Stuart, Richard."

"I can't believe it will do any good," Richard said. He looked weary but pulled himself up and said, "Do what you can."

Tom nodded. "I'm going to go see the governor in Little Rock."

Richard suddenly laughed. It was a harsh sound, and he said, "You don't know who the governor of Arkansas is, do you?"

"Why, no, I don't."

"The governor of Arkansas is Leonard Stokes."

Tom blinked with astonishment. "You mean the district attorney who prosecuted Stuart?"

"Yes. He got into office on a reform movement. The old governor was so corrupt that he had to go, and Stokes had a good record. But he's not going to be happy to see you."

"Happy or not, Mr. Stokes is going to see me in the morning," Tom said. His face was set in a determined mold, and he turned to Diane, saying, "You do the praying, and I'll talk to the governor."

CHAPTER TWELVE

ANCIENT HISTORY

★ ★ ★ ★

Tom arrived back in Little Rock a little before one o'clock. He took a room at the Marion Hotel, then asked for directions. The capitol was not hard to find. He simply turned west on Fifth Street, and off in the distance he saw the dome rising high in the air. Finding a parking place proved to be somewhat difficult, but after he had parked the Hudson, he made his way to the front door. The governor's office, he discovered, was in the east wing. When he entered he found a room full of people waiting. He stepped up to the desk and told the rather attractive young woman, "My name is Tom Winslow. I have an appointment with the governor."

"The governor's running a little late, I'm afraid, but if you'll have a seat, I'll work you in as quickly as I can, Mr. Winslow."

Tom took a seat, but it was an hour and a half before the young brunette spoke to him. "I'm sorry you had to wait so long, but the governor will see you now."

"Thank you," Tom said. He walked through the heavy walnut door and swept the room with a glance. The carpet was blue and thick, the walls were beautifully matched with walnut, and the desk was the most imposing one he had ever seen. Behind it the governor sat, but he rose at once.

"I'm Governor Stokes," he said pleasantly. "And you're Mr. Winslow, I take it."

"Yes, Governor." The two men shook hands, and the governor waved at a chair. "Sit down. Tell me what I can do for you. Sorry to have kept you so long."

"That's all right, Governor. You may recognize my name."

"Winslow? Yes. Tom Winslow," he murmured. "I don't quite remember—"

"But you do remember a relative of mine. Stuart Winslow."

Governor Stokes suddenly grew very still. He was a lean man with his hair growing gray at the temples, and his mind worked rapidly. "Yes, I do remember Stuart Winslow in Lewisville about seven years ago."

"Yes. You prosecuted him, Governor."

Stokes remained silent for a moment, studying his visitor. He never forgot a case, but the Winslow case had been particularly important to him. It had really launched his career. His victory there had aided him in pursuing his political aspirations, but somehow he had never felt proud of it. It had something to do with the fact that he had defeated an old man who had no business being in a courtroom.

"What can I do for you, sir?"

"I want you to pardon Stuart Winslow."

Stokes laughed abruptly. "Well, you don't mind asking big. Why should I?"

"Because he was innocent. He should never have been sentenced to the penitentiary. There was no malice. That's clear from the trial."

"He had a trial before a jury of his peers."

"And he was defended by a man who should not have been in that courtroom. I think you know that. You cut Mordecai Frasier to pieces, Governor."

Stokes's face grew flushed, for Tom had touched a nerve. No one had ever said this before, but over the years he had said it to himself. "He got a fair trial. I'm sorry, but this point is not debatable."

"Mrs. Simms doesn't think he got a fair trial," Tom said quietly.

Leonard Stokes turned quickly. "She testified that her husband was killed in his own bedroom by Stuart Winslow."

"But that's not what really happened, is it, Governor?"

"What do you mean that's not what happened? The man's dead! Winslow was in the room."

"But he never had the gun in his hands. You knew that, didn't you?"

Actually Stokes had known that. It was another one of those bits of evidence that Frasier had failed to turn over. Stokes had found it out simply by talking with Cora Simms, but since it would have weakened his case, he had never brought it up. If it had been brought up, he would, of course, have admitted it, but he had known in his heart that the verdict might have been very different. Carefully Stokes said, "What is your intention, Mr. Winslow?"

"I intend to get a retrial."

"That's impossible."

"No. I don't think so. I've been rather successful in matters like this if you'd care to check my record. I don't think it would be difficult at all when *all* the facts are presented."

"What facts?"

"The gun that killed Carter Simms was in his own hand. He pulled the trigger. Stuart never had the gun in his possession. Mrs. Simms will testify to this in open court."

"I can't pardon a man on that one piece of evidence."

Tom shrugged. "Then there'll have to be a retrial, and I'll get one. This time you won't be facing a tired old man, Governor. I don't lose many cases. . . ." Tom paused, and his voice was low, but there was a certainty in it. "And I won't lose this one."

Stokes turned and began to pace the floor. "I can't do it. He's a dangerous man."

"Warden Armstrong doesn't think so. He'll testify that Stuart's no danger to anyone." Suddenly Tom smiled and his eyes glinted. "He's a Republican, as I think you know. You came in to office on a very narrow margin, Governor Stokes. The election is coming up again. I don't know much about Arkansas politics, but Warden Armstrong would be happy to get this all over the front pages of the *Arkansas Gazette*. Indeed, in every paper in Arkansas with a Republican leaning. It'll make you look pretty bad, Governor."

Stokes chewed his lip. It was a bad time, and he did not need any fuel stirring the political fires. He turned and went and looked out the window, and Tom did not speak for what seemed like a long time. Finally, when Stokes did turn, he spread his hands out. "I've always felt bad about that trial. I didn't break any laws, you understand, Winslow, but I did take advantage of Mordecai. He's the best man I've ever known. He's dead now, so I can't tell him that I was wrong."

"You have a chance now to do something for him. If you pardon Stuart Winslow, you'll be vindicating Mordecai Frasier's memory."

Stokes was a political fanatic and did not want to lose the upcoming election. He weighed the situation and then made an instant decision. "There may be some trouble. I'll be criticized for pardoning a man, but I'll do it."

Tom Winslow took a deep breath. "Thank you, Governor. It's the right thing to do. Here's a copy of the warden's letter about Stuart. It ought to assure you, and it's better in your hands than on the front pages of the papers."

"Did me in, didn't you, Winslow?" Stokes said. "You're a pretty sharp lawyer. I'd hate to be crossing swords with you in court."

"I've got the right cause. That always helps."

★ ★ ★ ★

"What is it, Mr. Murphy?" Stuart asked.

"You got a visitor, Stuart."

Looking up from the guitar where he was working out a new song, Stuart rose and handed it to a tall, gangly young inmate. "You keep on practicing those runs, Sam. You'll be ready for the big time when you get out."

"Yeah, I'll do that, Stuart."

Stuart asked no questions as he walked behind Murphy to an office next to the warden's. When he went inside and the door closed, he said at once, "Hello, Tom."

"Stuart."

Stuart came over and shook hands, and Tom said at once, "I've got good news for you." There was excitement in his voice, and in a sudden burst of emotion, he put his arm around Stuart and hugged him. "You're going to be pardoned, Stuart."

At that moment, the world seemed to stop for Stuart Winslow. He thought he had misunderstood Tom. Tom had been back to visit him once but had never mentioned the possibility of a pardon. Now he swallowed hard and said, "You wouldn't fool me, would you?"

"No. It's real. I've just come from the governor's office."

"Stokes! Leonard Stokes said he'd pardon me? That's impossible!"

"I think he's a better man than I gave him credit for. His conscience has been bothering him all these years about the way he treated Frasier. Anyway, I laid enough before him to convince him."

"What could that be?"

"Basically, it was Cora's testimony. She'll testify in court that you didn't pull the trigger. She said that it was an accident."

The two men talked for some time, and after Tom left, Stuart left the office quickly. The first man he looked up was Pete Jennings, who was in the library shelving books. "Pete," Stuart said with his voice unsteady, "I've got something to tell you."

"It must be good." Jennings grinned. "What is it?"

"My lawyer just left. He tells me I'm getting a pardon from the governor."

Jennings suddenly threw the books in the air and shouted, "Hallelujah! Praise God!" He grabbed Stuart and the two did a little dance right there in the library.

Several of the inmates began to grin, and one of them whispered, "Jennings is having one of his religious fits again."

A guard came over quickly and said, "What are you doing, Pete?"

"Glory to God and the Lamb forever!" Jennings shouted. "Stuart's getting out. God done opened the prison doors, and Stuart's getting out."

The guard, a short, chunky man who was fond of both Jennings and Stuart, stared at the two. "This right, Stuart?"

"Yes. God's done a miracle, Daniel. I know you've been praying for me, and your prayers have finally been answered."

Word spread quickly throughout the library and up and down the halls. Soon everyone in whole prison knew about Stuart's pardon. Everywhere Stuart went he was slapped on the back. Almost everyone admired him, for he had been a friend to many of them.

Finally that night as he lay awake unable to sleep, he said, "Pete, you awake?"

"Sure."

"I wish you were getting out, Pete. I really do."

"Ah, that's all right. My place is in here. Yours is out there. After all," he said, "maybe I can do more good in here than I could outside."

"It's hard on you, but I'll never forget you," Stuart said. "If it hadn't been for you, I would never have found the Lord. I don't think I'd even be alive."

"You go out and serve Jesus. Get back with that family of yours."

"That may not be so easy," Stuart said.

"With God nothing is impossible. He opened the prison doors, didn't He? He can do anything."

Stuart nodded and took a deep breath. "You'll have to keep praying for me, Pete, every day. Just like I'll pray for you every day."

"It's a bargain, brother!"

* * * *

Zach awakened from one of his many catnaps and was surprised to see Tom sitting across from him. "Well, when did you sneak in?" He yawned and straightened up in his chair. He rubbed his hands through his hair, messing it up wildly, and said, "I must have dozed off."

"Yeah, you've been dozed off for over an hour."

"Why didn't you wake me up?" Zach saw something then in his son's face, and suddenly his eyes opened wide. "What is it, son?"

"Good news, Dad. Stuart's been pardoned by Governor Stokes. He'll be out in a week."

For a moment Tom did not think his father understood, for he did not move, and then he saw tears come into his father's eyes. "I did the same thing, Dad," he said, reaching over and squeezing his hand. "He's gonna have a tough time, but with

God's help he's going to try to get back with his family and put his life together."

"He'll do it. He'll do it," Zach said. His lips trembled and he shook his head. "You earned your keep this time, boy," he murmured. He stood up and reached out, and as Tom rose to his feet, the two men embraced. "God bless you, Tom."

"It was all your doing, Dad. I've got letters here from Richard and Diane. They'll tell you all about it."

"So he's free now?"

"Yes. He's free, but he's got some hard things to face."

Zach Winslow had faced some hard things himself, but now the good news had thrilled him, and he said with a rising tone of excitement in his voice, "He'll do it with God on his side. He'll do it, Tom!"

PART THREE

1917

★ ★ ★ ★

CHAPTER THIRTEEN

HOMECOMING

★　★　★　★

The two thin blankets offered scanty protection against the biting cold that gripped the cell. As Stuart Winslow came out of the black unconsciousness of sleep, he pulled the blankets closer and dreaded stepping out on the cold concrete. He slept fully dressed with two pair of socks, but the cold still numbed his face where it lay exposed.

Coming awake was like emerging foot by foot out of a deep well, at first total blackness, then unconsciousness, then his mind slowly seemed to come awake one cell at a time. Now the feeble rays of the electric light brought a flicker from the darkness, and he did what he had done every morning since he had been confined. Turning to his left, he opened his eyes and peered at the small calendar pinned to the wall with a broken nail. There had been a picture of some rabbits on it, but he had grown tired of it and had torn it off. Now just a simple rectangular page with the year 1916 at the top and the days of the months below, all checked. The month was December, and the first two days had been checked off by a firm X.

"December third," he murmured, and without meaning to, he went through the computation that had become a habit with him. "Three hundred and sixty-five days times seven years is 2,555 days. Add two days for two leap years, that's 2,557 days. I came in on November 20, 1909, and this is December the third.

That leaves thirteen days." He added them up easily and the figures seemed to loom in his mind. *I've awakened in this cell 2,570 times*, he thought. The number seemed enormous, but then he took a deep breath, and a sense of joy came to him. *But if I had to stay twenty years, think what that would be! Thank you, Lord, for getting me out of this place today!*

The familiar noises of the prison were beginning to sound now. The guards were rapping their sticks on the cells as they made their first count. From all the cells came the familiar snortings and sneezes and coughs, but Stuart had ceased to hear them years ago. But this morning they all seemed louder to him, and suddenly he sat up, threw the cover back, and swung his feet out over the bed. With one agile leap he came to the floor, and as he did, Pete Jennings said, "Getting out today. Bless your heart."

"I can't believe it, Pete. It still seems like a dream."

Jennings shivered and came out from under his covering. He, too, slept fully dressed, and he pulled the blankets around his thin shoulders. "The Lord sets the prisoners free. You'd better get shaved. You don't want to face the world with a five-o'clock shadow."

Stuart laughed and, moving over to the small washstand, shaved with cold water. It had been hard at first, especially during cold weather, but now as he drew the safety razor across his cheeks and then brushed his hair, he felt something inside that he could not express. The first three years in prison had almost killed him, and the last four had been hard. But now that was all over. He heard a voice say, "All right, Stuart. Come along. We're giving you an early start."

Stuart quickly reached out and grabbed Pete and pulled him to his feet. He gave the slight man a tremendous hug and then said, "You'll be hearing from me regular, Pete, and you'll be getting anything you need. Take all my stuff over there."

"God bless you, brother," Jennings said. "I couldn't be any happier if I was getting out myself."

There was no more time for Stuart to express the gratitude in his heart for all that Pete had done for him, for the guard said, "Snap it up! You've got things to do."

As Stuart stepped out and heard the doors clang shut behind him, it sent a thrill all the way down his backbone. He had heard that door clang shut thousands of times, shutting him out from life and liberty, but now he was walking away from it for the last time. Quickly he followed Donovan down the concrete walk. And as he went by cell after cell, hands reached out and voices called, "Have a party, Stuart." "Don't forget us." "Don't try to drink all the whiskey in the world, man."

These and more ribald comments followed him, but they were all good-natured. Strangely enough, none of the inmates seemed envious of Stuart, and he could not understand why.

Donovan guided him to a section of the prison where he had never been—a medium-sized room manned by an inmate. "Get him his going-away present, Slim." Donovan grinned.

The inmate, a tall, emaciated individual, grinned back and began to sort out the outfit that every inmate received on his release. "Would you like a Hart, Shaffner, and Marx suit, Stuart?"

"I'd go out of here naked if I had to, Slim."

Stuart put on the brown suit the guard handed him. It was ill fitting and shoddy. The shoes were cheap and poorly made, but at least he got a pair that seemed to fit his feet.

"Have a blast out there." Slim grinned.

"You trust in the Lord, Slim, just like I've been tellin' you."

Slim shook his head. "The Lord can't use no maverick like me."

"Sure He can. Jesus loves you just like He does me." He went over and shook Slim's hand and then quickly turned and left the room.

They made one more stop, and Stuart picked up his violin case. As he did, Donovan said, "I'm gonna miss all that music of yours." Then he said, "Come on. We'll go by the kitchen and get you a quick breakfast."

The men had not been called in for breakfast yet, but the cooks all knew Stuart. They gave him a plate piled high with grits, bacon, and four fried eggs along with a chunk of fresh bread. Stuart wolfed it all down, and when he finished, he bid good-bye to all the cooks.

"You're all set. Come along," Donovan said.

Following Donovan outside, Stuart passed through the inner gate, then approached the outer gate. He was surprised to see

Warden Armstrong standing there. "Good morning, Warden," he said.

"I got up early to say good-bye to you, Stuart. Here, the law says we give you ten dollars, and I've added twenty more of my own."

"You didn't have to do that, Warden."

"I know, but I wanted to. Now, I don't want to ever see you back here again."

"You won't. I can promise you that."

"Here, I brought these for you. It's cold as the Arctic out here today." The warden handed him an overcoat, saying that it was too large for him, and a hunting cap with earflaps. "It's gonna be freezing all day and even worse tonight, so there's a pair of gloves in the pocket, too."

It was unusually cold for central Arkansas, and the air was frigid. Stuart quickly put on the garment. He took the warden's hand before he put on the gloves and said, "I want to thank you for all you've done for me, Warden."

"God bless you, Stuart," Armstrong said simply. "Stick with Jesus and you'll be all right."

Armstrong stepped back and nodded, and the short, stocky gatekeeper threw the gate open. As Stuart stepped through and passed outside, he heard it clang behind him and he stopped for one moment. He looked up at the sky, which was gray and threatening to snow, but it was beautiful to him. He looked back, waved at the warden and the guard, then began trudging down the road.

As he moved along, he thought of all the things the warden had told him when he had called him to his office a few days earlier. Stuart could still hardly take it all in. The governor had pardoned him, with a strict condition that he never get into another fight or he'd be back in the slammer. That was no problem, Stuart thought. He had no intention of ever fighting anyone ever again. The warden had also revealed the shocking news that he had uncovered a conspiracy among some of the prison guards—headed up by Felix Munger—to confiscate all of Stuart's incoming and outgoing mail and to disallow all visits, with the intent that Stuart Winslow would be buried alive at Tucker Farm, never hearing from or being able to make contact with any family member or friend ever again. The warden was ashamed and deeply contrite that he had allowed such a plot to be carried out—never even suspecting that Munger would try to get even with Stuart when his authority over a new prisoner had been so humiliatingly stripped from him. The warden had assured Stuart that Munger and his accomplices had been found out, and all were now charged with fraud and mail tampering and were awaiting their own fate behind prison bars. Armstrong and Winslow had shed tears together over the evil that had so affected their lives and had prayed together, the warden asking for and receiving forgiveness from the prisoner.

Stuart shook his head as these thoughts tumbled through his mind and his feet carried him closer to home with each step. He wondered how his family would react to all this. Would they, too, be able to forgive him and let him start his life over again? He silently prayed a prayer of thanksgiving. *God, you're the one who got me out of there. Now I want to do nothing but serve you the rest of my life.*

★   ★   ★   ★

The snow began falling an hour after Stuart left the prison. It came down in tiny flakes. As it continued to fall, the old cotton fields were soon striped with a soft white carpet of snow. As Stuart moved forward down the road, he was aware that there was very little traffic, but then Tucker Farm had been built deliberately away from civilization as much as possible. He had hoped for a ride but none came. By noon his feet were frozen, for he had gotten them wet by crossing a ditch, and now he could hardly feel them. The snow was falling harder now, and although two vehicles had passed, they were both official cars of the penitentiary and had orders not to pick up any inmates.

He stumbled on his numb feet until finally he came to a crossroads and was glad to see a small general store. He stumbled inside, and the heat hit him almost like a fist. A large potbellied wood stove glowed a cherry color, and he moved over and stood beside it, soaking up the warmth.

"Just get out?"

Stuart turned to see an extremely fat man with several chins and a pair of careful gray eyes.

"Just this morning," he said.

"Thought so. Nobody much comes from your direction unless they're from Tucker. Sit down and warm yourself. Help yourself to that coffee. There's a mug over on that shelf."

Gratefully Stuart seized the cup and filled it from the pot. It was black as tar and stronger than any he had ever had, but it was the most delicious coffee he had ever tasted in his life.

The owner came over and plumped himself down in a cane-bottom rocker that threatened to give way under his weight. "I like my coffee strong. How about you?"

"Well, I like it any way I can get it on a day like this."

"Going far?"

"Pretty far. All the way to Lewisville."

"That's up north, ain't it? In the Ozarks?"

"Yes."

"Went there once trout fishin'. Close by, anyway. You got a long way to go. When you get over to Harrison, you can catch a bus."

"No money for that. I'll have to hoof it. Maybe I can catch a ride."

"Not likely. People around here are afraid of ex-cons."

"Then I'll just have a nice walk." Stuart got up and said, "Need to buy a few things."

"Sure. What will you have?"

Knowing that he needed provisions for camping out, he bought some sliced ham and had the storeowner slice up cheese for him. He picked up a bottle of pickles and a loaf of bread. He threw in some potted meat and cans of mixed fruit—two each of apples, oranges, and pears—as well as a can opener, small tin plate, and utensils. He walked over to the glass front of the counter and grinned. "I'd better have some of this candy. Just pick me out a dollar's worth."

The owner got all the groceries, totaled it up, and Stuart paid for it. "I got a canvas sack here. It's part of a cotton-pickin' sack. We'll put it all in there. You can put that fiddle in there if you want to. That way your case won't get wet."

"I'd appreciate that."

Stuart fixed himself two sandwiches, ate some of the pickles,

WELLS FARGO

Date: 05/15/14
Time: 12:05 AM
Location: SIERRA-LAKE(DU
ATM: 5913

Customer Card: XXXXXX0085
Transaction #:   1196
Transaction: Withdraw From Checking
Amount: $250.00
Account #:   Checking
Balance. $16.20

Thank you for using a Wells Fargo ATM

Over 12,000 ATMs from coast to coast.

Our ATMs offer 8 languages: English Spanish Chinese Korean Vietnamese Hmong French Russ

We'd love to hear about your experiences with our ATMs. Tweet and follow us at *@Ask_WellsFargo*

one of the apples, and then bundled everything up. "I'll be headin' on. Much obliged."

"Good luck to you," the man said. He hesitated, then said, "You probably had a pretty rough time, but there's a lot of young fellows like you havin' a bad time in France about now."

"Yes. I know. The war's a terrible thing."

"Don't look like it'll ever stop."

Stuart nodded and then left the warmth of the store. The cold hit him like an icy fist. He pulled his flaps down over his ears and was grateful for the cotton sack. It had a strap that he could put around his neck and carry it down to one side swung from his shoulder.

"Going to be a cold walk," he murmured, "but I've got plenty of time."

★ ★ ★ ★

The fat man had been right about rides. Several vehicles passed Stuart, mostly trucks and a few cars. None of them even slowed down. They all looked away, ignoring his glance. He did not ask for a ride. He simply stood there hoping someone would pick him up. But when none did, he shrugged and continued trudging along. He had dried his socks out at the store and managed to keep them dry, but still the cold penetrated his shoes.

The snow stopped for a while, and then about four o'clock it began coming down again in flakes as big as quarters. It was so thick that time and again he had to peer ahead and almost feel for the road.

He had no watch, but he knew that night was close, so he began looking for a barn or someplace to take refuge. Ten minutes later he saw a small house and heard a sound. As he moved closer he saw that it was a woman bundled up in an old coat trying to split wood. At once he left the road. The house sat back about fifty yards, and he saw a faint wisp of smoke coming out the chimney. The woman did not hear him, and he spoke so as not to alarm her. "Good evening, ma'am." When the woman looked up with a startled expression, he stopped immediately and touched the bill of his cap. "That's no work for a woman. Let me help you with it."

"I can't pay you."

"Not necessary. You go on in and get warm."

The woman's face was almost hidden. She had a wool scarf tied around her face. She was middle-aged, and her features were pinched with cold. "I ain't got much to eat, but I'll give you what I got if you'll split some wood for us."

"Sure thing. Just take this inside with you."

Handing the woman the canvas bag, Stuart picked up the ax and noted that the wood was white oak. He was glad of that, for it was the easiest wood to split. He turned one of the segments up that was about a foot and a half long, raised the ax, and hit it dead center. It fell apart in two matching chunks, each one's surface as smooth as frozen rock. Quickly he quartered these and moved on. He was toughened up from work in prison, for he had preferred to do outdoor work, for the most part. Now it was a pleasure to feel the ax in his hand, and as cold as it was, he enjoyed the exercise. It warmed him up, and soon the pile began to grow. He kept at it stubbornly, not knowing exactly why, until he had an enormous pile. He loaded his arms up, grasped the ax, and deposited it under the eaves of the house. Mounting the steps, he raised his hand to knock, but the door opened.

"Come in," she said. "You must be frozen solid."

"Fairly cold out." The room he saw was a kitchen, living, and dining area all in one. Three children with thin faces that were all bundled up stood there watching him. He moved across the room and dumped the wood in the woodbox next to the stove. Opening the door, he threw in two large sticks and said, "I'll fill the woodbox."

"Oh, I can do that."

"No trouble," he said as he filled the woodbox to overflowing and then took the seat that she offered him.

"My name's Allie Beal," the woman said. She still wore a heavy sweater, for she was thin and her face was marked with the scars that poverty always leaves.

"I'm Stuart Winslow," he said. "Fine young'uns you got there. What are your names, kids?"

The children seemed shy, but he kept talking to them as the woman stood at the stove cooking something. Soon he coaxed them to tell him their names. They were Harold, Martha, and Judy, and they were all under ten years old.

The woman turned to him, holding a spatula in her hand. "My husband got kilt in a sawmill accident last year."

"I'm sorry to hear that. Things been fairly hard since then, I guess."

"I can't complain."

Stuart thought she might have room to complain, for the poverty that had gripped her and her children was painful to see. He saw that she was cooking up cold-water corn bread on the stove, and a thought came to him.

"Hey, I know! I've got somethin' here that might go down good." He moved over to his sack and opened it up. He set the groceries out on the table and said, "Let's fry up some of this ham, and we got some of this fresh bread and pickles." He picked up a sack that contained the hard candy and winked at the kids. "Something in here for afterward."

"We couldn't eat your grub."

"We'll join together. You fix up that corn bread there, and we'll put it all on the table and eat until we can't move."

The meal was soon prepared, and the woman sat down after it was on the table. "Would you care to ask the blessing?"

Stuart nodded. He prayed a quick prayer, mostly for blessings on the house, and then they all began to eat. Stuart tried not to notice how the children ate like starving wolves. The woman tried to conceal her hunger but could not. Finally, when all the food was eaten, he reached out and picked up the sack and turned it out on the table. "There's dessert!" he said. "Does anybody here like candy?"

All three children looked with eyes so filled with longing that it hurt Stuart's heart. "Help yourself," he said. "It's that hard kind."

Each of the children looked at their mother, and when she nodded, they took one apiece.

Stuart took one himself and then nodded at Mrs. Beal. "Help yourself. I always had a sweet tooth."

The bright fire had warmed the cabin now, and the wind howled outside. Stuart finally moved his chair over to the stove. "You kids eat all the candy your mom will let you have. That's what it's for." He closed his eyes then and savored the heat of the stove. He did not know when he went to sleep, but he finally woke with a start. Looking up, he found Mrs. Beal sitting across from him watching him closely. "Must have dozed off," he said.

She smiled, and it revealed some of the prettiness that must have been hers when she was a young woman. "You slept for two hours. You were worn out."

"Well, I guess I'd better be getting on my way."

"You can't go out in that storm tonight. You stay here."

Stuart hesitated. "Might not look right," he said, "to the neighbors, I mean."

"It don't matter. I'll get you some cover. You'll have to sleep on the floor."

She disappeared back into what apparently was the bedroom area and soon returned with two blankets and a feather pillow. "Reckon you can make out with this."

"I sure can. I'll keep the fire up so it'll be warm in the morning."

He hesitated for a moment and then said, "Sorry you lost your husband. Don't you have people anywhere?"

"No. Just me and the kids."

The answer was simple and poignant, and Stuart longed to do something for her but could think of nothing. He watched her face and said, "Well, it's hard to face a Christmas without funds."

Mrs. Beal's hands twitched, and she dropped her head for a moment. "It is," she said. "I don't mind for myself, but I don't have a blessed thing to give my young'uns."

Stuart could not think of anything to say, and she eventually turned and left, closing the door behind her. He lay down on the floor and wrapped up in the blankets. It was not uncomfortable to him, and the heat from the stove warmed him thoroughly. He drifted off to sleep worrying about the woman and her kids, yet knowing there was little he could do about it.

★ ★ ★ ★

The sound of a pan clattering on the stove awakened Stuart, and he came out of the blankets and sat up at once. Seeing Mrs. Beal at the stove, he got up and said, "I meant to be gone before this."

"You've got to have breakfast. I've got a little coffee left."

"Save it for yourself," he said quickly.

"No. There's enough."

Stuart hated to eat the food and at that moment made a decision. He ate a small piece of the ham he had bought, a large portion of grits, and two buttered pieces of toast. When he had finished, he said, "Well, I've got to go." He turned and picked up the case that still contained the violin. "God bless you, Mrs. Beal." But she stopped him at once.

"You're forgettin' all your groceries."

"Those are for you and the kids. Merry Christmas."

Her eyes flew open, but he left before she could do more than say, "Why, thank you kindly!"

He had gone no more than twenty steps when suddenly he stopped. Something had come to him the night before, and he knew that the Lord was moving upon him. Pete Jennings had explained something about how God spoke to men, and he knew that this was one of those times. A rough grin crossed his face, and he turned around and retraced his steps. He knocked on the door, and when Mrs. Beal opened it, he reached into his pocket and got out the twenty-dollar bill the warden had given him. "Give the kids a good Christmas and buy something for yourself."

Tears came to the woman's eyes, and she reached out and took it with a trembling hand. "Look on it as a gift from Jesus, Allie." He reached out, squeezed her hand, nodded, and then left.

★   ★   ★   ★

Four days on the road in terrible weather had worn Stuart Winslow down. But now as he looked up and out over the landscape, he knew he was in his home country.

"Just ten more miles," he said.

He had spent all his money, except for some small change, just managing to stay alive. He had slept mostly in barns and spent one night in a railroad station. Now, however, he picked up his pace. Memories began to flood his thoughts as he made his way along the curving mountain road. The Ozarks lifted behind him, and he was headed down into the valley where he had lived all of his life. Almost every turn of the road held memories for him; some were painful, but he shoved those away at once.

Hearing a noise, he stepped over to the side of the road and did not look back. He had given up asking for rides and was surprised when a dilapidated pickup stopped. He hurried forward and came to the driver's side.

"Get in, buddy. It's too cold to be walking."

"Thanks a lot."

Stuart moved around the truck, opened the door, and sat down, careful to avoid the springs that were broken loose.

The driver said, "I'm Sam Pickens."

A shock went through Stuart, for he knew Sam Pickens. Stuart wore his cap pulled down as much as possible over his face, and he had not shaved since he left prison, so he was sure that Pickens did not recognize him. He didn't give his name but said, "Glad to know you, and I appreciate the ride."

Pickens ground the gears and headed down the road. He talked constantly, ending every sentence with, "Y'know," whether it was a question or not. Stuart chuckled inside. Sam was just as inquisitive, Stuart realized, as he had been years ago. He had always been the biggest gossip in the county.

Stuart rather enjoyed evading the man's questions. Finally he looked up and said, "You can let me out right there."

"Right there?"

"Yes, at the crossroads."

Pickens ground the truck to a halt and said, "Ain't nobody lives down that way except the Hayses and, of course, the Winslows."

"That's where I'm going."

Pickens leaned forward and shock ran through him. "Stuart! It's you, ain't it?"

"Yeah, it's me, Sam."

"Well, I'll be dogged. You didn't break out, did you?"

"Nope. Pardoned."

"Well, I'm mighty glad to hear it." Pickens watched as Stuart left, his eyes avid with curiosity.

"Thanks for the ride." Stuart shut the door firmly, and Pickens started off with a force that rattled every bolt in the old pickup.

"Wait'll the folks hear that! Stuart Winslow's back."

★ ★ ★ ★

Leah dried the last dish and put it on the shelf. She could hear the phonograph turned up as high as possible, the only volume that the children seemed to like. They were playing records, and now she glanced at the clock and saw that it was almost six. Dark came early this time of year, and now as she started down the hall toward the parlor to join the children, she was startled to hear a knock at the door. For one instant she stood still. Visitors were rare at this time of the night, but she knew it could not be Annie, for she never knocked. It could be Merle, however. She moved forward and opened the door expecting to see Merle—and then stood as still as if frozen into stone.

"Hello, Leah."

Leah could not think of a single word to say. She grasped the doorknob with such force that her fingers splayed and turned white. Stuart was wearing clothes she had never seen before, and they were all dusted with a white snow that still came down. There was no light on the porch, but she was able to see his familiar features by the light inside the house. Taking a deep breath, she forced herself to say, "Come in."

She stepped aside and noticed that he brushed the snow off before stepping in. When he was inside, she shut the door and turned to face him. Her lips were tight, and a riot of thoughts raced through her mind. He was watching her carefully, and she saw that he had changed little. When he removed his hat, she saw that his hair was as black as ever. His face was much thinner, but he did not look a day older than when he had left.

"You haven't changed, Leah."

Leah licked her lips and then said, "I heard you'd been pardoned."

At that moment she was aware of a noise behind her, and she turned and saw Raimey and Merry. They had come out of the parlor and were standing there staring at the man beside her. Leah thought with a start, *Merry's never seen him in her life!* And she knew she had to say something. Her eyes went to Raimey, and she saw that Raimey knew Stuart at once. She had told him that his father was getting out of prison, and he had said not one word in response. She could imagine what was going on in his mind, but could think of nothing to say. Then she heard Stuart say, "Hello, Raimey."

Raimey nodded, and his lips formed an answer, but nothing came out.

"I'll bet you're Merry."

"Yes. I'm Merry."

"This . . . this is your daddy, Merry," Leah managed to say.

Merry's eyes flew open with astonishment, and she came forward to look up into Stuart's face. "I thought you was in jail."

"I was . . . but I'm out now." Stuart suddenly knelt down so that he was on her level. "You're a very pretty girl."

Leah was watching him, and her heart seemed to close. She studied Merry's face and saw the girl smile.

"I'm glad you came home," Merry said.

Quickly Leah asked, "Have you eaten?"

Stuart came to his feet and shook his head. "Don't bother."

"There's plenty left. Come into the kitchen, and I'll warm you something."

Leah led the way and was glad that she had something to occupy her mind. She pulled out the leftovers from supper and began to warm them in the wood stove. From time to time she would steal a glance at Stuart. He was sitting in the chair, not looking at her at all but talking with Merry and Raimey.

"Raimey, you've grown up."

When the boy did not answer, he said, "How are you doing in school?"

"All right," Raimey said, not looking at his father.

This was the only answer he got. Raimey's face was fixed, and there was a light in his eyes that Leah had not seen before, and it disturbed her.

"I'm in the first grade," Merry announced. "Do you want to hear me read?"

Stuart suddenly grinned. "I sure do."

Merry ran away at once, and while she was gone, Leah put a plate on the table. As she did Stuart lifted his eyes and met hers. She did not say a word, nor did he, but of the two she was the more shaken. She could not get her mind pulled together, nor really believe that he was actually sitting there.

Merry came running back and put the book down on the

table and stood beside Stuart. "This is the one I like best. It's about a little dog named Rover."

"Well, let's hear you read."

" 'Once upon a time there was a dog named Rover. . . .' "

Stuart kept his eyes on the girl, marveling at her beauty. She had Leah's features, and he was glad of that. Her eyes were clear, large, and blue, and her hair was a light blond. He had not seen a child in years, and to be sitting here with his daughter for the first time overwhelmed him. He marveled now at the freshness and smoothness of her skin, and the fineness of her hands fascinated him. He had missed all the years of seeing her grow up, and strong feelings of regret rose up within him. He wanted to reach and touch her but knew that he must not.

Finally the meal was ready, and Stuart managed to eat something, although for some reason, he had lost his appetite. Merry talked constantly, and Raimey said absolutely nothing—nor did Leah. It was a rather one-sided conversation. Two-sided, really, with Merry chattering on and with Stuart speaking to her from time to time.

When he had finished, Leah said, "You children go back to the parlor. Go listen to your records."

"I'll read to you some more after a while," Merry said.

"All right, Merry."

Stuart got to his feet as soon as the children left, for Leah was standing with her back straight as a ramrod.

"When did you get out?" she asked.

"About a week ago. Took this long to walk."

By this time Leah had made up her mind. She was a woman of great gentleness, but this man had caused her more pain and heartache than she had imagined possible. She had been thinking about what to say and had it in her mind, but the sight of his face had driven it away. Now she braced herself and said in a clipped tone, "I don't want you here, Stuart."

Leah bit the words off and then waited, expecting an argument, anger, disappointment. Instead Stuart said nothing at all for a moment, then nodded.

"I thought you might not. I just came to ask you to forgive me, Leah."

His response shocked Leah, but somehow it brought anger,

too. She had lived this moment over in her mind often, and now she said, "It's so easy for you, isn't it, Stuart? It always was! You ruined my life and the lives of the children, and then you think all you have to do is say you're sorry! Well, it won't work this time!"

Stuart stood absolutely still for no more than ten seconds. He studied her face, thinking how pale she was and at the same time that she was more beautiful than ever. "All right, Leah." Without another word he turned and left the kitchen.

Leah stood there, almost paralyzed. She had braced herself for a blistering argument or shouting or incriminations, and now she did not know what to do. Finally she shook herself and ran out of the kitchen just in time to see him pull his cap down and leave. The door closed quietly, and she lifted her hand to her mouth, finding herself trembling all over.

The children came out at once, having heard the door close. Merry came running to her and said, "Where is he going?"

"He . . . he won't be staying here, Merry."

At her words Raimey stared at Leah, and suddenly she could not face them. "He's your father, but he left us a long time ago. He just came to say good-bye."

She could not say more, for her breath seemed to have left her body. She turned at once and went blindly past them to her bedroom and shut the door. She went to the window and tried to peer out, but there was nothing but the darkness of the night. She was aware that her hands were trembling, and her breath was coming very rapidly. She bowed her head and clasped her hands together, but all she could think of was Stuart out in the cold dark of the night.

★ ★ ★ ★

"Mistah Stuart!"

Stuart turned quickly and saw a big figure appear. "Why, Merle," he said, "it's you!"

"I seen you come in, Mistah Stuart." Merle came forward and put his hand out. "I'm glad to see you back. Welcome home."

Stuart took Merle's hard hand and felt a moment's grace. The scene with Leah had shaken him considerably, and only by a tremendous iron will had he kept from showing her what was in his heart. "I won't be staying, Merle, but I thank you for your welcome."

Merle did not answer for a moment. He was a wise man, and something he saw in Stuart's face kept him from asking questions. "Well, that's as may be, but you comin' in tonight. You can sleep in Wash's bed in the children's room. He done married up now."

Stuart would have protested, but Merle grabbed his arm and practically dragged him down the road to the small house where he still lived with Annie. As the two men went in, Annie was standing at the sink cleaning up. When she turned to him, her eyes narrowed at once, and her lips went together in a fine line.

Merle saw his wife's coolness, as did Stuart. "Mistah Stuart's gonna sleep in Wash's bed tonight, then he'll be goin' on."

"All right," Annie said briefly. "You need somethin' to eat?"

"Already eaten, Annie. Thank you. Coffee would be good, though."

"Sit down, Mistah Stuart."

Stuart found his legs were not steady. He could not remember a time when he was so shaken. He had known that Leah would not welcome him back, but the coldness of his wife's voice and what seemed to be hatred in her eyes had been like taking a bullet in the heart. He sat down, barely aware of his surroundings, but as he drank the coffee, he listened as Merle kept the conversation going. Merle told him about the farm, the animals, and the breeding program.

Finally Merle seemed to run down, and Stuart looked up at Annie, who was watching him steadily. "You don't have to worry, Annie. I won't be staying."

"What do you mean, Mistah Stuart?" she demanded.

"You hate me for what I did to my wife and family, but they won't be hurt anymore. Not by me." He stood up suddenly and turned to face her squarely. "I'd like to ask your forgiveness, Annie, and you, too, Merle, for all the things I did to you."

"You ain't done nothin' to me, Mistah Stuart!" Merle protested.

Annie said nothing for a moment, and then she nodded. "You won't be stayin'?"

"I just came back to ask for forgiveness. If you don't mind, I think I'd like to lie down."

"Sure, Mistah Stuart. Come on. I'll get you fixed up."

Annie sat down at the table and waited until Merle came back. When he sat down beside her, she said, "What happened?"

"I 'spect Miss Leah asked him to leave."

The two sat there, struck by the tragedy of it. Finally Merle said, "He's different now, ain't he?"

"He may be," Annie said. And then the bitterness that filled her heart came out, for she loved Leah and hated Stuart for what he had done to her. "A man reaps what he sows, and that's all there is to it."

CHAPTER FOURTEEN

"I'VE ALWAYS LOVED HIM!"

★ ★ ★ ★

A pale sun had risen in the east, shedding its beams but yielding no warmth. As Stuart trudged along the icy roads, he could not keep his mind free from thoughts of his wife and children. It was not what he had anticipated during the long years in prison, especially the last four. He had assumed that he would come home, ask for forgiveness, and then set about to prove himself a good husband and a good father. The coldness of the day seemed to match the condition of his heart, for despite his gratitude for being out of prison, he was still plagued with the question of what he would do with his life.

The sound of an automobile caught his attention, and he looked up to see a light blue car with white wheels and a canvas top shielding the driver. The car slammed to a stop, and a man jumped out and turned toward him.

"Well, you old codger!" The driver leaped at Stuart, wrapped him in a bear hug, and waltzed around.

"Hey!" Stuart cried. "What are you doing out here?"

Ace released Stuart and stepped back with a broad grin on his homely face. "I heard you were home. Sam Pickens has spread the word. I think everybody in the county knows about it by now."

"You could always depend on Sam to spread bad news."

"Bad news! None of that now. Hey, come on and get in."

"What kind of a car is this?" Stuart asked as he walked around to open the door.

"It's a Willis Knight. Just got it. Some pumpkins, huh?"

"You must be doin' pretty well to buy a new car like this."

"The surveyin' business is good. I've got three guys workin' for me now." As the car picked up speed, Ace turned and grinned at Stuart, saying, "You look good, man. When did you get in?"

"Just yesterday."

"Well, I've got all kinds of plans made for us. I see you still got your fiddle. We can do some fancy playin'."

Stuart hesitated for a long moment, then said, "I don't think I need to do much playing at dances. I'm out of the habit. We didn't do much dancing at Tucker."

"Well, nothin' wrong with gettin' some of the boys together and just havin' a little hoedown, is there? We can get Clyde and Ralph and Fatso any day."

"That would be good. Be glad to see the fellas. I guess they're all married and settled down now."

"Pretty much. Where you headed? I'll take you there."

"Going to my folks' house."

"I want to see your mom's face when she sees you." Ace nodded. "She's had everybody in the county prayin' for you." He hesitated, then said, "How did it go with Leah?"

Stuart turned and gave Ace a glance. "Not too well," he said finally. "I won't be staying there."

The car bumped over the rough road, slid on icy spots toward the edge, and Ace wrestled it back to the center. "One of these days we're going to get some of them paved roads out here." Not knowing what else to say, he murmured, "Well, Leah will come around. She's had a hard time. But how about those kids of yours? Aren't they somethin'?"

"I wouldn't have known Raimey, I don't think. He's gotten so tall."

"I'll bet he was glad to see you."

"No. He really wasn't, Ace. Merry was, but she's still just a baby really. All those years I missed, Ace . . ."

Stuart's voice choked at the thought of so much of his life wasted, and the men fell into an uncomfortable moment of silence. The conversation was difficult for Ace. He had known about the problems with Leah and had talked with Raimey enough to know that the boy seemed dead set against his father. Ace said quickly, "Well, I'll tell you what. You can stay with us. We can make room."

"I can't do that, Ace. I'll find a place."

"All right, if you say so, but one thing. If you want work, I've got that. I need a chain man. Not much money, but you and me could have some time together."

"I'll take you up on that."

Ace talked rapidly as he sped along the road, trying to be as cheerful as he could, but he was thinking, *Something's gone out of Stuart. He's not what he was. I'm afraid gettin' out of jail might be as big a shock as going into it.*

When he pulled up in front of the Winslow house, Stuart said, "I'll be ready to go to work tomorrow."

Ace fumbled in his pocket and came out with a wad of bills. Unfolding two of them, he said, "Here, you can't work in that outfit. Get yourself some stout boots and whatever else you need."

Stuart took the money and smiled. "Good to see you again, Ace. I thought about you a lot. As a matter of fact, some of the best memories I had were of you."

"Here, too, partner. Uh-oh, look out!"

Stuart turned to see his mother, who had opened the door and was flying down the walk. He turned to meet her and caught her up, clearing her feet from the ground and squeezing her. "Hello, Mom," he said huskily.

Diane clung to him, unable to speak for a time. She finally got control of herself, and when he put her down, she said, "Come on inside. It's cold." Turning to Ace, she said, "Come in, Ace."

"No. I've got to be getting along. Take care of this guy. He's gonna work for me, and I don't want anything but good men."

The car roared off, and Diane clung to Stuart's arm as the two went inside the house. "Come into the kitchen. I'll fix you some pancakes."

"I thought about your pancakes for a long time, Mom," Stuart said. He took a seat, and she fixed him a cup of coffee while she scurried around nervously throwing pancakes together. "Your father will be down soon. I'll make enough for all of us."

"Tell me about yourself, Mom. How are you?"

"Me? Why, I'm fine." She looked up from the mixing bowl long enough to study his face. "You look good, son," she said. "I was afraid—"

"I know. You were afraid I'd come out a skeleton."

Stuart had pulled off his cap and removed his coat on the way in, and now as he sat there, his mother saw that he did have a healthy look. His hair was as black as ever, his skin was tanned, and though he was thinner in some ways, he seemed very strong. "You did a lot of outdoor work at the—" She could not say the word and changed her expression. "For the last few years?"

"Yes. I did some janitorial work, too, but I liked being outside best. It was good for me."

The pancakes were just finished when they both turned to see Richard, who had entered the kitchen. He gave Stuart a quick look and nodded. "I heard voices. Good to see you, Stuart."

Stuart waited for his father to come across the room to shake hands, for he had hoped for a better welcome from him, but there was something very reserved in Richard Winslow's demeanor. "It's good to be home, Dad. You're looking well."

"So are you."

"Well, the two of you sit down. The pancakes are ready."

They moved into the dining room, and Diane set the table with pancakes, sausage, and a large pitcher of maple syrup. "I've got some of that sorghum you like so well, Stuart."

"I'll have some of that, Mom."

When the food was on the table, Richard bowed his head and said, "Lord, we thank you for this food and for every blessing." He hesitated, as though he would have said more but then cut the prayer off. "In Jesus' name. Amen."

"Here, eat all you can, son," Diane said, piling three plate-size pancakes on Stuart's plate.

"Mom, I can't eat all those!" Stuart protested.

"You eat all you can," she repeated.

Stuart cut the pancakes up and poured sorghum all over them, and at his first bite, he exclaimed, "Just like always! You're the best pancake maker in the world."

The meal was awkward and difficult for Stuart. Diane did almost all of the talking, with Stuart adding what he could. Since he had no news of his own to give, he mostly listened as his mother told him what had happened in the years that he had been gone. They had received a letter just that morning from Warden Armstrong, explaining about Stuart's release and with deepest apologies for the problems that had occurred with Munger. The warden had high praises for Stuart—for how far he had come in his time there—and high praises for God for the transforming work He had done in this man's life. For Diane, it was an answer to all her prayers to finally know that her son had not turned his back on them after all. She was torn between deep grief over all that had happened to separate them and joy over their reunion this momentous day.

Finally the meal was over, and Stuart sat back and held his hand up. "No more, Mom. I can't eat another bite. You're still the best cook in the world."

Richard had said little, but now he made an effort at small talk. "Well, we reelected Woodrow Wilson last month."

"Yes, and I'm so glad," Diane chimed in. "He's kept us out of the war in Europe, and I hope he continues to do so. At least that's what he campaigned on."

"I don't think he'll keep us out of it very long," Richard said solemnly. He looked over at Stuart, and after a moment's silence, he said, "What are your plans now, Stuart?"

Stuart met his father's eyes. He saw little welcome there, and when he spoke, his voice was very quiet. "I won't be staying at home," he said. "Leah would rather I go someplace else."

His parents exchanged a quick glance, and it was Diane who said quickly, "It'll work out, son. You'll just have to give her a little time."

"I'll be working for Ace surveying for a little while until I get some money together. Then I expect I'll move on."

"But, son, you can't do that. Where would you go?"

"I don't know, Mom." Stuart straightened up and looked into his father's eyes. "I hear that Leah is seeing another man and thinking about a divorce. I don't have any right to stop her if that's what she wants to do. But I had to come back and ask her forgiveness—and yours." Taking a deep breath, he said, "I was the world's worst son, I think. There was no reason for it. You were always good parents to me, so what's happened in my life is none of your fault. Never blame yourself for it. I do ask you to forgive me, Dad, and you, too, Mom."

Diane waited for Richard to speak, and when she saw that he was having difficulty, she at once got up and went around the table. Stuart rose and she put her arms around him. "Of course we do, son."

"Thank you, Mom. I never doubted that."

Richard said stiffly, "I'm glad you're out, Stuart. Let me know if I can do anything to help you." He did not mention forgiveness, and there was something foreboding about his tone.

"I'll do that. Well, I'd better get going. I have some things to do."

Diane went with him to the door and kissed him. "Give Leah and your father time," she said. "They'll come around."

"I thought about you every day, Mom. I know you prayed for me. Keep it up."

Diane watched him leave, and her heart seemed to break. She closed the door gently and then went back and stood for a moment at the window watching him go. Richard came over to stand beside her.

"I was disappointed that you didn't give Stuart a little more consideration, Richard."

"He's got to prove himself, Diane. This is an old pattern. Don't you remember?" Richard turned her around. His face was lined, and the years of shame of having a convict for a son disturbed him. It had eaten away at him, and he could not seem to find it in his heart to do other than he had. "He would always get in trouble and then come and confess. We'd forgive him, and then for a while he'd behave. And then he'd go back and do the same thing again. He's got to prove himself, Diane. I'd like to believe what Warden Armstrong has told us—nobody would like to see him change his life more than I would—but I'll have to see it for myself to believe it."

"Richard, I'm disappointed in you."

Richard Winslow's face revealed shock. He loved this woman and always wanted her approval. "What is it, Diane?"

"In the Scriptures, when the Prodigal Son came home, his father ran to greet him. When the son confessed he'd done wrong, he brought him to the house and put a ring on his finger and killed the fatted calf."

Richard Winslow dropped his head. The truth of his wife's words hurt, but the years of shame had marked him strongly. He muttered, "You may be right, Diane, but I've got to see honest change in him before I can do that."

*　*　*　*

Leah was listening to Merry as she read out of her reader. She did not read like a child, one halting word at a time, but fluently, and Leah thought, *She's so smart*.

When Merry was through reading, she looked up smiling and said, "Was that good, Mom?"

"Very good, Merry. You're a fine reader. Much better than I was at your age."

Merry closed the book and then stood up and came to stand beside her mother. "Mom, is Daddy coming to live with us?"

It was the question that Leah had dreaded. A week had passed since Stuart had appeared at the house, and during that time, Merry had said nothing about her father, nor had Raimey. Now she glanced quickly across to where Raimey was sitting in the light of the window working on a model ship that he had been building for some time. Something in his eyes troubled her, and she knew that he was waiting for her answer, as well.

"No. I don't think so."

"Why not, Mama?"

"I'm glad he's not coming here," Raimey said defiantly. "I don't want him here!"

"Why not?" Merry said, turning to face Raimey.

"Because he's nothing but an old jailbird!"

Leah was shocked to the bone at the hard edge of Raimey's voice and at the adamant glare in his eyes. Usually he was a gentle boy, and this cold fury shook her. "You mustn't say that, son."

"You don't want him here, Mom, do you? You sent him away."

Leah had tried to think of some way to explain the situation to her children, but now even as she spoke, her words sounded false and hollow. "Sometimes a man and a woman have difficulty. They start out loving each other, but then things happen." The more she tried to talk, the harder it got, and Leah found herself groping for words. "And that's what happened to your father and me. He's done things that have hurt us all, and so we think it's best that he not live here."

A silence filled the room, and then Merry said in a small voice, "Mama, if I do something wrong, will you not love me anymore like you don't love Daddy?"

The words cut Leah to the heart. She suddenly threw her arms around Merry and hugged her tightly. Tears rose in her eyes, and she blinked them away. "Don't even say that, honey," she said. "I'll always love you." Unable to continue, she got up and left the room.

Raimey stared down at his model and could say nothing. Merry came to stand by him and said, "Mama's crying."

"She'll get over it."

"I feel bad, Raimey. I want a daddy, and I liked him. He listened to me read."

"Well, he's not coming back here, and that's all there is to it. You'd better be glad of it, Merry. He's not a good man."

★   ★   ★   ★

The scene with her children had overwhelmed Leah emotionally. She avoided talking to them as much as possible, trying to get control of herself. About three o'clock that afternoon, she heard a car pull up and then a knock at the door. Desperately she hoped it was not Stuart. When she opened the door, she saw Reverend Charles Fields standing there and said at once, "Come in, Pastor."

"How are you, Leah?"

"Very well."

"The kids all right?"

"Yes, thank the Lord. They haven't got that flu that's going around."

"It's very bad. The whole family is down at the Hendersons'."

"I'll run over and take some food and see what I can do. Come into the parlor where it's warm."

The two moved into the parlor, and Fields took a seat across from the fire and waited until Leah seated herself. "I've come to get some of Stuart's clothes, Leah."

"Stuart's clothes!" Leah was taken aback. "What do you mean, Pastor?"

"Well, he's working with Ace now, but he doesn't have very many clothes. Ace asked me to pick up any winter clothes, including boots."

"Oh! Yes, of course."

"Did you know he was working with Ace?"

"No, I didn't."

Fields studied her carefully. He did not have the whole story, but enough of it had come to him, and he knew that things were not well. "He's staying with Luke Garrison."

Leah dropped her head and could not answer.

"I'm disappointed, Leah. After the miracle God worked to get him out of the penitentiary, I'd expected things to be a little bit . . . different."

Agitation stirred Leah, and she could not meet her pastor's gaze. "I . . . I just don't know what to do," she said faintly.

"I don't want to be judgmental, Leah, but Stuart's had a change of heart. I've talked to him. He knows the Lord now."

"I just can't forget all that's happened. I'm afraid he would do something again that would hurt the children."

Fields studied the woman across from him. Her face was flushed, and she could not look him in the eyes. He knew her well, for she was a woman he admired greatly. Her Christian character had always been one that he had held up as an example to others, and now he was troubled. "Did you know he was in church Sunday?"

Leah looked up with shock. "No. I didn't see him."

"He waited until the sermon started, and then he came into the balcony. He left during the benediction."

A silence filled the room, and Leah was conscious of the voices outside where the children were building a snowman. She sought for words to express the fear that was in her about Stuart and what accepting him back might truly mean, but she could think of nothing to say.

"What are you going to do, Leah?"

Leah understood that he was asking her what her intentions

were concerning Mott Castleton and what she would do about her husband. "I don't know," she said briefly. "I just don't know, Pastor."

Charles Fields saw the torment in Leah's eyes and knew that it would do no good to preach at her at this moment. *It's something*, he thought, *that she's got to work out for herself.* Aloud he said, "Well, will you let me pray with you?"

"Of course."

Fields prayed a brief but passionate prayer for Leah and the children—and for Stuart. He ended by saying, "Oh, God, it's your business to put things together, not break them apart, so I pray that you put this family together again in the name of Jesus."

When he left the house and got into his car, Fields was seized with a sense of depression. He had seen so many things go wrong with so many people. It seemed to him, sometimes, as if people engineered their own destruction. He was terribly disappointed in Leah Winslow, but as he started the car and moved out and headed toward his next stop, he said aloud, "You can't make people be something they aren't. They have to make their own decisions. Lord, you'll just have to help Leah and Stuart, for they've lost their way."

★　★　★　★

Luke Garrison admired the .33 Winchester for a long time, and now standing in the hardware section of the Winslows' store, he held it up and looked along the gleaming barrel. He pulled the trigger and enjoyed the satisfying *snap*.

"If that had been a deer, you would have got him, Luke."

Luke turned quickly to see Cora Simms watching him with a smile.

"Hello, Cora," he said. "Yes. I guess I would have. I can't make up my mind about this gun. It seems like seventy dollars is a lot to pay just for a rifle."

"You can afford it. You don't have any wife to throw your money away on. I guess I'm not the only one who wonders why you never married, Luke."

Garrison smiled. He was used to the teasing of the townspeople. He had come to the point in life when he wished he did have a wife and family, but somehow he had not found the right woman.

"Never know about those things, Cora. I might marry a widow with six kids tomorrow."

Cora smiled and laughed pleasantly. "I'd like to see that. Luke Garrison changing diapers."

"There are worse things, Cora."

The two stood there chatting for a time, and Garrison admired the beauty of the woman, as always. There was an aura about her that drew men, and momentarily Luke thought about making his own try. But he knew too much about Cora Simms for that.

"I hear Stuart's living with you now."

"Yes, he is. He's working with Ace."

"Separated from his wife, is he?"

"They'll work it out." Luke felt a sudden gust of caution go through him. "Cora," he warned, "stay out of it." When Cora did not answer, he said, "He's living on the razor's edge, Cora. His pardon comes with a condition—if he gets in any trouble he'll have to go back to prison."

"What kind of trouble?"

"A fight—anything like that. He can't use his fists on another man."

"What makes you think I would cause Stuart to do anything like that?"

Luke studied the woman carefully. Her blue silk dress fit her well, but somehow anything Cora Simms put on accentuated her appeal to men. Luke shook his head, unable to answer her question, but said, "You're just what you are, Cora. Men are going to fight over you. There are plenty of other men for you. Leave Stuart alone."

Something showed in her eyes at that moment. She was a woman who knew the ways of the world as well or better than Luke Garrison. Ordinarily she kept a reserve about her, but now, without meaning to, she let some words escape her lips. "I never loved Carter, Luke. It was always Stuart."

Cora's words shocked Luke. "Cora, it's too late. He's still married."

"Not for long, if what I hear is true. And I'll tell you this,

Luke. If Leah divorces him, I'll get him. I've got money enough for both of us."

Luke could find no answer to this, and Cora, after giving him a calculating look, turned and walked away.

Later on in the afternoon Luke encountered Ace and repeated the conversation. Ace stared at him and shook his head. His lips grew tight and anger flared in his eyes.

"Luke, if that woman hurts Stuart again, I'll break her neck."

"I might beat you to it, Ace. She's done enough damage to him. Surely he's got more sense than to get mixed up with her again."

Ace gave him an odd look and, after a moment, said, "Men are weak where women are concerned. You know that, Luke."

CHAPTER FIFTEEN

A Surprising Proposal

★ ★ ★ ★

"Leah, you shouldn't be doing this kind of work."

Mott Castleton had parked his car in the front, and not finding anyone in the house, he had gone around to the back. He had heard noises from the stable, and when he made his way across the lot and opened the door, he found Leah up in the loft shoveling down forkfuls of hay.

"Somebody has to do it, Mott. Merle is down sick. I don't mind."

"Here, let me help you with that."

"You'll get your clothes all dusty. I'm through anyway." Leah stuck the fork into the hay and came down the ladder, then dusted her hands off. The dust from the hay had coated her hair, and she took a handkerchief out of the pocket of the overalls she had donned and wiped her face with it. "I'm a sight, aren't I?" she said. "But the cows have to be fed."

"We'll have to get a man out here to help you," Mott said. "I don't like to see you doing this kind of work."

"Oh, it's just until Merle gets on his feet again. It was no trouble when Wash was here, but now there's really no one to do all of this."

Leaving the barn, she went into the house, where she washed her face at the kitchen sink and dried it off. She said, "Here, there's some coffee on the stove. It's still cold out there, isn't it?"

"Maybe more snow." Mott took the coffee absentmindedly and sipped it, studying Leah, who had moved across to cut a piece of cake. There was a grace about her, he noticed, even when she was wearing a pair of oversized, worn overalls. When she sat down, he tasted the cake and said, "This is good. Did you make it?"

"No. Annie did. She does cakes better than I do." Her eyes sparkled then, and she said, "But I can do pies better. What are you doing out here, Mott? I thought you'd be in Little Rock for a week."

"I got my business finished. Besides, I wanted to be back home for Christmas." He smiled, and putting his fork down, he reached over and took her hand. "What do you want? I can't get a word out of you."

"Oh, I don't know, Mott. Maybe one of those new vacuum cleaners."

"That's not very romantic."

For a moment a strange light flickered in Leah's eyes. "I guess," she said quietly, "I'm not too much on romance these days."

"Don't say that." Mott squeezed her hand and held it tightly. "That's not what I want to hear."

Leah let her hand lie in his and knew that he had something on his mind. He was a man who usually came straight out with things, but being a lawyer, he had some shrewd ways about him. Now she said, "What are you thinking? I can always tell when you're plotting something."

"I'm not plotting anything." Mott laughed shortly. "All lawyer tricks aside, Leah. I hate to keep hammering on this, but things have got to change." He put his other hand over hers and held it imprisoned between his two. "Get a divorce, Leah," he urged. "It's the only way." He saw her start to speak, then overrode her answer. "I know. It's not what you like. It's not what I like, either. Neither of us believes in divorce. It's just not acceptable, but this is a different kind of situation. You have to admit that."

"Brother Fields doesn't think so."

"Naturally not. He's a preacher. He has to be strict in such matters as this, but he's wrong in this case."

"I don't know, Mott." Leah freed her hand and shook her head briefly. "All my life I've seen people who got divorces, and they were never happy. Usually they got into a marriage even more unhappy than the one they were in."

"That may be true sometimes," Mott argued, "but not always. Look at what's happening. The kids need a father. You need a husband. You need to move back to Fort Smith. You like my house, don't you?"

"It's a beautiful house, but I'd miss the farm here."

"You wouldn't have to miss anything. If you want a place to get outside, we'll buy a little piece of land. We can go to it every weekend if you want to. The kids can have ponies. You can have your own horse."

Leah listened reluctantly as Mott painted a rosy picture, and finally she said, "Mott, I'm not sure I'm in love with you."

"Well, I love you, and I can make you love me. I know I can, Leah."

They had had this conversation before, but Mott was more persistent now. Leah listened to all his reasons why she should divorce Stuart and marry him soon. Finally she said, "Please, Mott, don't urge me anymore. Things are so hard right now."

Mott started to speak, then closed his mouth and nodded. He stood up and said, "Well, I'll be getting on. I'll be looking forward to our Christmas, though. I got the kids some surprises. They'll like them. I know they will."

Leah walked to the door with him and waved good-bye as he got into the car and drove away. She glanced at the clock and saw that it was almost time to go get the children, so she went upstairs and changed clothes. She ran into Annie, who had come in from the back where she had been gathering up the washing off the line and was folding it. "How's Merle?"

"I don't see he's no better. This flu is bad."

"I made some of that soup he likes so much. I'll take him a bowl of it while you do the folding."

"Try to make him get it down. He's gotta keep his strength up."

Putting a generous portion of soup into a large bowl, Leah covered it with a towel, then, putting on her coat and hat, she left the house. When she reached their home, she knocked on the door, then stepped in, for she knew Merle would be in bed. "Merle!" she called out. "I brought you some soup."

"Yes, ma'am. Come on in."

Leah moved on through the main room of the small house into one of the two bedrooms and found Merle flat on his back. His face was an ashen color, and his cheeks were drawn in. "Sit up there. You've got to eat some of this."

"I ain't real hungry, Miss Leah."

"I don't care whether you are or not. You're going to eat it one way or another." Leah fussed around helping Merle to sit up, then urged him along until he had eaten some of the soup.

Finally he said, "I can't eat no more. I just don't feel hungry."

"You'll feel better tomorrow. The doctor said you didn't have a bad case."

"Well, I don't know how he thinks he knows what I feels like."

Leah laughed suddenly. "I think you're right. Doctors always talk big, but they don't know what's going on inside of us, do they?"

She took the bowl and sat down for a moment, and Merle studied her. "You look tired, Miss Leah. I feel bad 'cause I can't do none of the work. I wish Wash was still here. You got to hire somebody soon."

"Well, we'll see about that later."

"Things ain't goin' too good, is they?"

Indeed Merle had hit on it, for it was not going well. The breeding farm had lost money last year. They had sold plenty of stock, but somehow the expenses had been higher or the prices had not been right. Leah could not figure it out. Night after night she had sat up going over the books, and she realized that this year was going to be even worse.

"You know what, Miss Leah?" Merle said. He coughed, and then turning his head away, he covered his mouth and said, "These tractors, they're gonna put folks like us out of business."

"I don't think so, Merle. A lot of people have tractors, but they cost a lot of money. The poor folks are still gonna have to have mules and horses."

"But the poor folks ain't got the money to pay prices for good stock. I been thinkin' about it a lot." He hesitated, then said,

"Why don't you go ask Mr. Stuart's daddy to help you? I know he wouldn't mind."

"It may come to that, Merle, but we've kept this place going, you and me, for years now. We can do it again."

"Annie said you was talkin' about lettin' Mr. Winslow sell it and gettin' a job."

"Oh, I was just feelin' down that day, Merle. It won't come to that."

Leah rose and patted Merle's shoulder. "You just lie there and take it easy. You'll be up by Christmas eating that turkey Annie and I are going to cook."

★ ★ ★ ★

Leah stopped dead still when she got a look at Raimey. His eye was discolored, and dried blood stained the front of his shirt. "What in the world happened to you?" she demanded.

"He got into a fight," Merry said.

"You shut up, Merry!" Raimey said through stiff lips.

"Got into a fight! What about?"

"Nothing! Just a fight."

Leah studied Raimey's ravaged features and knew well the stubborn cast that was set on his face. When he got like this, nothing in the world could change him. There was that much of Stuart in him. Now she said, "Well, get in the truck. We'll talk about it later."

She said no more about the fight, but she got the truth of it from Merry while Raimey was out doing his chores. Leah did not ask, but Merry said, "It was that old Samuels boy that did it."

"What was the fight about?"

"Burt Samuels called Daddy a jailbird, and he said bad things about you. Raimey jumped right onto him, but Burt Samuels is two years older than he is, and Raimey couldn't whip him. If I had had a stick, I would have beat him with it." Merry's face was flushed, and she said, "Why do people have to be so mean, Mama?"

"I don't know, sweetheart. They just are. Don't pay any attention to it."

"Raimey says he's going to beat Burt Samuels if he has to hit him with a baseball bat."

"No. He can't do that."

Later on, after supper, when Merry was in bed, Leah drew Raimey aside. "Merry told me what the fight was about."

"You just wait, Mom. I'm going to get that Burt Samuels."

"I know you'd like to. Nobody likes to hear their family abused, but it would be better if you didn't."

"I don't care what he said about Dad," Raimey said stubbornly. "But I won't put up with him talking about you."

Leah wondered what Burt Samuels could have said, but she knew that she could not pursue it. Reaching over, she hugged Raimey and said, "I'm proud of you that you'd take up for me and for your father."

"It wasn't for him."

"Maybe not, but you're going to hear more of it. Do you want to tell me what Burt said about me?"

"He said only a bad woman would get a divorce. That all divorced women were bad."

"Well, that's not true."

"I know it ain't, but I'll make him eat it. You see if I don't."

★ ★ ★ ★

"I hear that the Sanderson family has all got the flu," Annie announced as she came in with two tin buckets full of milk. "I expect we'd better take somethin' over there. I'll go after I get Merle taken care of."

"No. I've got to go that way, anyway, to pick up some feed at the mill. You just take care of Merle. Don't worry about supper tonight. We'll have leftovers."

"This flu's gonna kill half the population, it do seem like," Annie said mournfully.

"How is Merle this morning?"

"He's some better. He's settin' up now. I got him to eat a bowl of grits, but he's still gonna be a few days before he be back to his normal self. That flu just takes the strength right out of a body."

"I'll take plenty of food for the Sandersons," Leah said.

"How many young'uns they got now? Six?"

"Five, I think. Are Mr. and Mrs. Sanderson both down?"

"Both of 'em, from what Bessie tells me. You'd better let me go. They're bound to need some washin' done. You know how it is if you miss a washin' one day around here. And with them five kids and two adults, it don't take long to get a real mess on your hands."

"I'll take care of that. You just watch out for Merle."

★　★　★　★

Leah stopped the truck in front of the Sanderson place and saw fire curling up out of the chimney. "At least somebody's able to make a fire," she said. Getting out, she went to the back, picked up one of the two boxes she had brought packed with food, and walked up to the porch. She mounted it and knocked, but nobody answered. Opening the door cautiously she stepped inside. "They might all be asleep," she said.

Going on into the kitchen, she heard someone on the back porch, so she set the box down and stepped outside. She stopped at once, for there at one end of the porch she saw Stuart with his shirt sleeves rolled up and running clothes through a ringer. He did not see her and probably had not heard her over the chug of the noisy washing machine that was agitating the clothes. A huge mound of clothes rested on a table, and obviously he had been at the job for some time. Glancing out, she saw that the line was filled with clothes put out to dry.

Stuart turned suddenly to put a shirt on the pile and stopped abruptly. "Well, hello, Leah."

"Hello, Stuart." She had to speak louder to be understood. "What are you doing here?"

"Oh, I heard the Sandersons had some bad luck. Thought I'd come and see if I could help."

Leah hesitated, then said, "I brought some groceries for them. How are they?"

"Poor shape," he said. "Three of the kids are down, and the two youngest ones are over at the Porter place. Mrs. Porter said maybe she could keep them from getting it."

"What about Fred and Elsie?"

"About as sick as you can get, I guess. Dr. Morton was here. He's real concerned about Fred and Elsie." He laughed shortly and said, "I can get these things washed, but I declare I don't know how I'll get 'em ironed. I'll do my best."

"I'll go bring the rest of the food in."

"I'll get it. Is it outside?"

"Yes. Out in the truck."

Leah reentered the kitchen and saw that Stuart had built a fire. The kitchen was pretty much a mess with dirty dishes everywhere. She took off her coat and began to clean up.

When Stuart came back in a few moments and set the other box down, he said, "I was gonna try to cook something, but I guess you can do that better than I can."

"Yes. I'll take care of that."

"All right. I'll go out and take care of the stock as soon as I finish the washing."

Leah went at once to check on Fred and Elsie and found them both almost in a coma. The three children were restless, and she changed their clothes and bathed their faces, then put them back into bed.

She worked hard getting the kitchen cleaned up, made a meal, and saw to it that the children were fed. Elsie ate a little and thanked her profusely for coming, but Fred seemed to be almost past eating.

"I'm so worried about him, Leah. So many people have died."

"We're not going to let that happen. We're just going to take care of him and pray for him," Leah said quietly, "and trust God to help us."

Elsie lay back and said, "Thank God you came. And Stuart, he's been here working all day now. I don't know what we would have done if it wasn't for him and for you."

Going back into the kitchen, Leah cleaned up the dishes from the meal. It was almost dark now, and she had worked hard all afternoon. Stuart had not come back in, and now she went outside. The cold air hit her, and she saw him repairing a fence. "Stuart!" she called. "Come in. You've got to eat something."

He put down the hammer and started toward her. She went back into the kitchen, put a plate down, and filled it with the ham and beans she had warmed up on the stove. She had made fresh corn bread, too. Pulling off his coat and hat, he tossed them down. When he pulled off his gloves, she saw that his hands were callused and nicked by the barbed wire.

"Your hands look awful. You need to take care of them," she said.

"I guess so."

She put down a glass of fresh milk that she had brought and said, "That's not good for your playing."

"Well, I don't play much anymore."

The remark caught at Leah as nothing else that he had said. Music had always been a part of Stuart's life. He had not said it for pity. She was sure of that. It was as if that which he had valued so much was not at all important. "Did you play any at all while you were in prison?"

"Oh, I played a lot there. Taught a lot of fellas to play, and we had a concert every week. All of them said it was the best time of the whole week for them. I always was a little proud of that."

Leah sat down and watched as he ate. He commented on the work that needed doing around the farm, and finally she said, "What about your job with Ace?"

"He let me off. He's fond of Fred and Elsie. Everybody is. As a matter of fact, he's even going to pay me, but I won't let him."

When he finished, she gave him a cup of coffee, and he asked, "How are the kids?"

"All right."

"I got a shock when I got my first look at Merry. She looks just like you. Going to be a beauty. As bright as a button."

"She's so smart. Like you, I guess."

"Not like me. No one ever accused me of that."

Neither of them mentioned Raimey, and just as Leah was getting ready to rise, his voice caught her. "Leah, I want to tell you something."

Cautiously she sat back down. "What is it?" she asked guardedly.

He did not answer for a moment but stared down at the table. He lifted his eyes to her and, without expression, said, "If you want a divorce, Leah, I won't stand in your way."

Leah could not answer for a moment. She could not believe that she had heard him clearly, and as thoughts flew through her mind, she looked closely into his face. She saw a strength there that he had lacked before, and she could not identify it. He had been put through a crucible—she understood that well enough—but the firm set of his lips and the steady gaze he fixed on her with his dark blue eyes unsettled her.

"What makes you say that? Do you want a divorce?"

"No! Never in my life! But I want you to be happy, and I want the kids cared for."

Leah dropped her head and for one moment felt as if something was dreadfully wrong with the scene. She could not understand what was happening to her. Up until now she had not even considered Stuart's reaction, but she knew that if a man was determined, he could prevent a woman from getting a divorce. She finally lifted her head and said, "I . . . I don't know what to say."

Stuart shrugged his shoulders, then rose. "I'll be staying around a few days to be sure that the Sandersons are all right. Let me know what you decide."

★   ★   ★   ★

When Leah first awakened she knew something was wrong. Her throat was closed almost tight, and she was burning up. When she stood up a terrible pain shot through her head, and she suddenly knew the worst. "Oh no, I've got the flu!"

Getting out of bed was a struggle, but she managed to throw on a robe and a pair of worn leather slippers. She went down the hallway but became so dizzy she had to hang on for a moment. Finally she made it to the kitchen, and as soon as she did, Annie turned and stared at her. "You're as white as a sheet! What's wrong with you?"

"I don't . . . feel very well."

Annie came over at once and put her hand on Leah's forehead. "You got the flu! That's what's the matter with you."

"I can't be sick! I just can't!"

"You go right back to bed this minute!" Annie said. "I'm gonna call Doc Morton and get him over here right away."

Leah wanted to protest, but suddenly she felt so weak she was not sure she could walk. The fever turned into a chill, and by the time she got under the covers, she was shaking so violently that the bed creaked. "Oh, who's going to take care of Merry and Raimey? What if they get sick?" She huddled under the covers, holding herself and shivering. She tried to pray, but it seemed no use.

★ ★ ★ ★

Annie lifted her head wearily at the knock on the back door and managed to get up. She had exhausted herself for the past day taking care of Merle and Leah. The dreadful thought that came to her most often was, *What if I get sick? What will we do then?* Opening the door, she stared at Stuart, who stood there wearing his mackinaw and his billed cap. His face was flushed from the exercise. He had evidently walked from somewhere.

"I heard Leah was sick."

"Yes, she is. Real bad sick."

Stuart walked in, brushing by Annie, and suddenly he turned and looked at her closely. His eyes narrowed, and he said, "What's wrong with you, Annie?"

"Nothin'. Ain't nothin' wrong with me."

Stuart shook his head. "You're coming down with it, too, aren't you?"

"Ain't nothin' but a bad cold."

"I've heard that before. Annie, go home and go to bed."

"I ain't got no intention of goin' to bed!" Annie protested. Actually she had been feeling steadily worse since noon, and now there was a weakness in her limbs that she tried to hide. "What you doin' here?"

"I'm here to take care of my family. Now you go to bed. I'll call Doc Morton and have him come out again."

"He already been here yesterday with Miss Leah."

"Well, whatever he told her to do, you'll do the same."

"He said there wasn't much to do but stay in bed and drink all the fluids she could."

"How's Merle?"

"He's better, but to tell the truth, Mr. Stuart, I ain't feelin' too well."

Stuart moved forward and put his arm around Annie. "Go on, Annie," he said gently. "I'm not moving back in. I'm just here to see that you and Leah and the kids and Merle are all right. Now, you go on to bed."

Annie was too tired and weary to argue. She nodded and said, "I'll do what you say."

As she made her way back across the yard, it seemed to be a long way to her house. When she stepped inside, she said to Merle, who was sitting in a rocker by the fireplace, "I'm gettin' sick."

"I have to go take care of them chilluns," Merle said.

"No. You stay where you are. Mr. Stuart, he gonna take care of the kids and of us, too, I reckon. I pray our own babies stay well."

Merle stared at her for a moment and then dropped his head. "He's done come back at a mighty good time, I'd say."

CHAPTER SIXTEEN

AN OLD SONG

★　★　★　★

Leah could remember nothing but chills that seemed like iron bands freezing her bones. She would shake and tremble until the bed itself vibrated, hugging herself and trying to get some warmth out of the covers that lay piled over her. She had fallen through the ice once years ago while skating on a pond, and that had been a terrible shock, but the chills that shook her body now were far worse. No matter how much she bundled up, it seemed she could never get warm enough.

Always following the chills would come a fever, baking her flesh as if in an oven and drying her lips until they were like charred wood. She had never been one to perspire, but the terrible heat that rose up from somewhere deep inside and burned its way out of her caused her to soak the bed.

Sleep was a deadly coma that was not rest at all but merely a black hole of either freezing or burning as the chills or fever came. When she did wake up it was worse, for her eyes ached and her tongue seemed to be swollen no matter how much she drank. Once she tried to pour a drink from the pitcher beside the bed, but she trembled so violently that she dropped the glass and the pitcher both, soaking herself even worse.

Finally she felt hands on her, and she whispered, "Annie—?" Her eyes were swollen and the room was dark, but soon she felt her gown being stripped off and then a cool wet sheet put over her. "Oh, Annie, it feels so good," she whispered. She got no answer, but when the heat of her body warmed the wet sheet, it was changed and another cool one put on. Finally she felt her temperature going down, and then she felt herself suddenly being lifted and swung around and placed in a chair. She opened her eyes and saw a man stripping the sheets off. She tried to speak, but her lips were dry as toast. She knew it was Stuart, but yet it was all like a dream. Finally she felt herself being handled like a child as a dry gown was put on her and then a sheet put over her. A strong hand was holding her up and she heard a voice.

"You've got to drink, Leah."

Leah drank thirstily of the cool water and then whispered, "Merry—Raimey—"

"They're fine. Don't worry about anything."

Leah was too weak to argue. She felt herself slipping back into unconsciousness, and only once did she manage to open her eyes. By the yellow light of the lamp she saw Stuart sitting beside her silently. *It's all right*, she thought. *It's all right. He's with me. . . .* And then she drifted off to sleep.

★ ★ ★ ★

Raimey awoke out of a fitful sleep with a jerk and sat straight up in bed. He stared around and saw that morning had begun to lighten the world outside. His first thought was of his mother, and with it came a dreaded fear he had not been able to control. He had come home to find his mother in bed and his father waiting to tell him, "Your mother's got the flu, kids, but she's going to be all right."

Now Raimey rolled out of bed and began to pull on his clothes. He ignored the cold, and as soon as he had laced his boots, he left the room. He stopped once and looked into Merry's room and saw a mound of blankets and heard her steady, even breathing. Closing the door he went down to the kitchen, where he stopped as soon as he was inside. His father, he saw, was sitting at the table peeling potatoes.

"Hello, Raimey. Ready for some breakfast?"

"I've got to go do the milking."

"I've already done that. Sit down. How about bacon and eggs?"

Raimey swallowed hard and then said, "How . . . how's Mom?"

"Her fever got pretty high last night, but it's down now. We'll just have to be sure that it stays down. Here, you peel some of these potatoes while I fix up a breakfast."

Raimey sat down and began peeling the potatoes. He watched his father covertly as he moved around breaking eggs and frying bacon, and soon the aroma of fresh meat filled the room.

When the food was all ready, Stuart put it on a plate and set it in front of Raimey. Then he fixed one for himself and said, "You want to ask the blessing, or shall I do it?"

Raimey glanced down. "You, I guess," he muttered.

"Lord, I thank you for the food, and I thank you that you've given Leah strength for the night. I pray for her, for Annie, for Merle, and for all the others in the community who are stricken by this disease. In the name of Jesus."

Stuart deliberately paid no attention to the boy but began to eat hungrily. "I wanted to make biscuits, but I don't know how."

"I don't either. Mom always made them or Annie."

"I reckon I'll learn how. A man ought to learn how to cook a little bit."

"That's woman's work."

Stuart grinned at Raimey. "I'm not sure about that. I've known some men that could cook mighty well. One of them was as tough a fellow as you'd ever meet."

Raimey ate slowly, for his mind was primarily on his mother. He listened as his father went on talking about the farm and finally heard him say, "I'm right proud of you, Raimey. The farm's in good shape, and I know you put in a lot of work on it. I expect you've been a great help to your mother."

Raimey shrugged and shoved another forkful of eggs into his mouth. Something in him seemed to close in when he tried to speak, and he had been having many memories about the times just before his father had gone to prison. But he could not speak of them. It was Stuart who said, "You remember that big bass you caught? The one just before I went to prison."

Raimey nodded and looked up. "I remember. It never got mounted, though. You went off and it spoiled."

"That's too bad. I remember that day well. We had a good time, didn't we?"

Raimey once again stuffed his mouth full and would not answer. A stubbornness rose in him, and he refused to respond to Stuart.

"Well, I think your mother's going to be all right."

Raimey suddenly put his fork down and glared at his father. "You don't care a thing about her! You never did!"

"That's not true, Raimey."

"I heard about how you ran around with that other woman."

Stuart's jaw suddenly clenched, and Raimey saw his face grow pale.

"That's true," he said. "I wish it weren't. Your mother's the finest woman who ever lived. I was a fool for treating her as I did."

Raimey stood up suddenly and asked the question that had been burning in him. "Are you going to stay around here always?"

Stuart shook his head. "No. I don't think I will." He looked across at Raimey, and lines appeared at the corners of his mouth and his eyes as if he were under a strain. "Raimey, when I was in prison, for a time I didn't do anything but hate people. Mostly myself. Then I found the Lord, and things started changing. One thing I did after I found the Lord was to make a list."

"What kind of a list?" Raimey demanded despite his determination to remain silent.

"I made a list of people I wanted to look up to ask to forgive me. I'm working on that list, so right now I'm asking you to forgive me for all the things I did. I'm sorry for a lot of things, but most of all, I'm sorry for what I brought on you and on your mom and Merry."

Raimey stared at the tall man who sat there. He thought about how many years he had cried himself to sleep wishing his father could come home, and now that he was back, there was nothing inside Raimey but resentment. Without even answering the question, he turned and left the room.

Stuart Winslow watched his son go and knew there was nothing he could do. The thought came to him, *Prison was hard, but nothing has been as hard as this!*

★ ★ ★ ★

"Can I help you, Daddy?"

Stuart paused, the bucket in his hand, and grinned. "Sure you can. Here, go put this grain over in that trough right over there. Be careful, though. Don't let those little pigs nibble your fingers."

Merry laughed and took the bucket. She was wearing a long dress, black winter boots, and a wool coat. Her blond hair stuck out from underneath the white toboggan hat she was wearing, and as she poured the feed into the trough, she laughed and then reached down and pulled one of the tiny pig's ears. "Listen at 'em grunt, Daddy. They're so greedy."

"Well, I can't blame 'em there. When it comes to food, I guess I'm pretty greedy myself."

Stuart continued feeding the stock, listening with pleasure as Merry talked continually. She was like a fountain that gurgled endlessly, and no child had ever been better named, for she was merry indeed. Looking up at the sky, he studied it and then said, "It looks like we might get some snow for Christmas tomorrow."

"We can't have Christmas tomorrow. Mama's sick."

"Well, we're gonna do the best we can. Come along. I've got a chore for us, and I want Raimey to go along."

The two found Raimey splitting kindling in the backyard. He looked up as Stuart said, "We're going out and get a Christmas tree, Raimey. I'll need you to help."

"What do you want me for?"

"Well, I've got kind of a catch in my shoulder." Stuart moved his right arm around and made a face. "I guess I strained it trying to haul that ornery mule into the corral yesterday. I'd appreciate it if you would come and help me chop one down."

"Come on, Raimey!" Merry cried. "I get to pick it out. I know just the one."

"Guess I can go," Raimey muttered.

"Get the ax. I sharpened it. It's over by the grindstone in the barn."

Fifteen minutes later the three were standing in front of a

beautifully shaped cedar tree. "That's the one, Daddy!" Merry said. "Can we have that one?"

"I don't see why not. Raimey, think you can chop that one down?"

"Of course I can." Raimey began to swing the ax, and Stuart stepped back. Raimey did not wear a cap, and his hair was as black as a raven. Tiny flakes of snow had begun to fall, sprinkling the black crown.

Stuart grinned when the tree fell and said, "You ought to become a lumberjack. Tell you what. Tie this rope on it and drag it back, and I'll tote this here girl."

That was the way they went back to the house—Raimey pulling the tree and Stuart with Merry on his shoulders and the ax in his left hand. When they got to the house, he put her down carefully and turned to the boy. "Well, the next thing is to make some kind of a stand. Think I've about forgotten how, but I know we're going to need some lumber, nails, saw, and a hammer."

"I can do that," Raimey said at once.

"Can I help?" Merry asked.

"No, that's man's work. You can help decorate it," Raimey said.

The three went into the barn where the tools were kept, and Raimey pointed out some old boards that had been saved. "We can make it out of that," he said.

"Guess you'll have to boss the job. Don't think I remember how," Stuart said. He watched mostly as Raimey sawed the boards and then helped to hold them in place while he nailed them together.

"Now we've got to fasten it to the tree," Raimey said.

"Okay," Stuart said. "Merry, why don't you go into the house and figure out a place to put it while Raimey puts the base on. I'll have to hold the tree up, I guess."

Merry raced into the house while Raimey finished making the stand. Stuart held it up so that it would be easy. "This is a beautiful tree. Pine always smells good, doesn't it?"

"Guess so," Raimey said as he pounded another nail into the base.

It took some time to get the tree into the base and nailed together, and then Stuart said, "I'll tell you what. I'll take the bottom, and you take the other side. It's gonna be close getting it through the door."

The two climbed the steps bearing the tree, and Stuart pulled the storm door open and then opened the other. They went inside, and Merry was practically hopping up and down. "It's gonna go right there in front of the window. That's where we had it last year. I remember."

Stuart helped unobtrusively to straighten the tree up. "Why, that's a good job, Raimey. Look how steady it is."

"Not bad," Raimey said, trying not to show his satisfaction.

"I'm going to fix some supper. Do either one of you remember where the decorations are?"

"I do!" Merry said.

"Well, why don't you drag 'em out, and as soon as we have supper, we'll see what we can do."

Stuart fixed a quick supper by warming up some food. Merry could hardly wait to begin, and even Raimey seemed excited to decorate the tree. Stuart had to say, "No decorating until you eat!"

After they had eaten, Stuart hauled in a short stepladder so that Raimey could set the top decoration on the tree. As they started putting the rest of the ornaments on, he said, "I'll tell you what. Why don't I get my fiddle, and we'll have some Christmas music. You decorate and I'll play."

"Oh, that would be fun! I know all the words to the Christmas songs," Merry said with excitement in her large blue eyes.

Stuart had brought his violin, and bringing it back into the parlor, he sat down and began to play. He played some carols, then said, "Let's see if you know the words to 'We Three Kings.'"

"I know that, Daddy. I memorized it last year."

"Well, I've forgotten most of them, so you sing them, and I'll kind of join in. Raimey, maybe you could help with the words, too."

The room was filled with the mellow and full sound of the violin. Sometimes the hymns were slow, and other times they were fast, and Stuart was amazed that Merry did know most of the words.

Finally the tree was decorated, and Stuart shook his head with admiration. "Never saw a better-looking tree in my life."

"It's not bad, is it?" Raimey said. They turned the lights down and admired the tree for a time.

Merry said, "Could we go caroling?"

"It's too cold. It's startin' to snow," Raimey said. "Anyhow, there's nobody to sing to."

"Yes, there is. We can go sing to Merle and Annie and their children."

"That's a great idea," Stuart said. "Come along. Get your coats on."

Ten minutes later they were standing in front of the small house, and as soon as they began singing, the door opened and Merle stood there grinning. "Well, I'll be dipped!" he said. "If this ain't somethin! Carolin' on Christmas Eve. Come on in the house and have somethin' hot."

They went in and found Annie sitting up, playing a game of checkers with her children. The Winslows stayed for quite a while singing Christmas songs, but finally Stuart said, "We'd better get back. I've got to see to the patient."

Annie's eyes were bright, and her face was relaxed. "Thank you, Mr. Stuart," she said. "You done mighty fine of takin' care of these young'uns and Miss Leah. And the singin' was good."

"Glad you liked it, Annie. Merry Christmas."

They crossed back over to the house, and as they went, Stuart shielded the violin from the snow. "It ought to be pretty in the morning."

"It won't be Christmas without Mom there," Raimey said. "She always makes it fun."

"Well, we'll just pray that maybe she can come," Stuart said and noticed that the boy gave him a quick look of disbelief.

* * * *

Leah was sitting up in bed. She had awakened only a brief time before and had moistened her lips with water and drunk a little. When Stuart entered with a tray, she said, "How are the kids?"

"They're fine. Here, I want you to eat some of this."

"I don't really want any."

"You've got to eat."

Leah managed to eat some of the hot oatmeal and half a piece of buttered toast. "That's all I can eat." She hesitated, then as he took the tray and started to leave, she said, "I heard the singing downstairs. It was real nice."

"I'm amazed at Merry. She knows the words to more Christmas songs than I do. I can't get over how smart she is." He then added, "We went out and cut a tree and put it up. I let them decorate it. Then we went over and sang to Merle and Annie and their young'uns. They're doing a lot better."

"Stuart, I bought some presents for the kids. They're all wrapped up in the attic. Will you get them after they go to bed and put them under the tree?"

"Yes. I'll take care of it. How do you feel?"

"I can't complain."

"You never do," he said quietly. "Good night," he said, then left the room.

Leah was lonely and restless and tired of being confined to the room, but she felt so weak that she went to sleep almost at once. She slept well that night, and upon waking the next morning, she only had a little fever. *Getting better*, she thought. Even as the thought came, she heard the door open. She looked up to see Stuart enter.

"How are you?"

"Better. It's dawn. Are the kids up?"

"Yes. They're already down there at the tree. I put the presents under like you said, and I told them they couldn't open them until you got there."

"Why, I can't go down there!"

Stuart did not answer. He came over and turned the covers back and swung her feet over the bed. With the other hand he took her robe and said, "Here. Put your arms in this."

"Stuart, I just don't—"

"This is one time I'm going to have to insist, I'm afraid." He grinned at her and said, "It'll be good for you, and the kids say it's not Christmas without you."

Leah looked at him for a moment, then nodded. "All right. I'll try." She stood up and slipped her robe on, knotted the tie, then took a couple of steps. The room seemed to sway, and she cried out slightly and started falling. Instantly, she felt herself being picked up in the air.

"We've got a chair all fixed for you," Stuart said. "I'll carry you in."

"No, Stuart, don't!"

He stopped at the door and looked at her. Her face was wan, but the beauty that had drawn him the first time he had seen her was still there. "I carried you over a threshold once. I guess I can carry you to a chair."

As Leah was held in his arms, she laid her head against his shoulder. She was so weak, but he was strong, and she thought, *He's always been the strongest man I've ever known.* She felt the muscles of his chest and arms, and then they were in the living room. She heard the kids exclaiming excitedly as he moved over and gently put her into a chair.

"Grab a blanket for your mom, Raimey."

"Sure." Raimey dashed at once and was back with a blanket, which he spread out and put over her lap.

"Thank you, son. My, what a beautiful tree!"

"We did it all ourselves, me and Raimey."

"That's right," Stuart said. "They did a fine job, didn't they?"

"Can we open the presents now, Mama?" Merry begged. Her eyes were shining, and she was clinging to her mother's hand.

"I think so."

Stuart moved back and leaned against the wall, removing himself as far as possible from the scene. From time to time his eyes would go to Leah's face to see her response as the children opened the presents. She was pale, but obviously this was good for her, and he was glad that he had done it.

Finally all the presents were opened. The kids had gotten mostly clothes, but the prize for Stuart was the look of excitement when Raimey got a jackknife and Merry got a doll.

Merry hugged the doll and said, "I'm going to name her Missy."

"That's a beautiful name," Leah said.

"But you didn't get anything, and Daddy didn't get anything!"

"Well, Christmas is for children mostly," Leah said.

"I've got a present for each of you," Stuart said suddenly. "They're not wrapped up proper like. I didn't have time for that, but let me get them."

He disappeared and came back very quickly with three packages—two small boxes and one large long package. "This is for you, sweetheart." He gave a very small package to Merry and watched as she opened it. Merry ripped the brown paper off and then suddenly cried out with delight.

"It's a ring!" she cried. She put it on her finger, and the red stone glowed.

"That's a very old ring, Merry. It belonged to Nellie Winslow, your great-grandmother. Your great-grandfather Henry gave it to her when they married."

"Oh, it's so pretty, but it's too big."

"You'll have to grow into it, honey. I'm glad you like it."

"This is for you, Leah."

Leah looked at the small brown package and whispered, "You shouldn't have done it, Stuart."

He did not answer, and Merry was saying, "See what it is, Mama."

Unwrapping the paper, Leah found a small box. When she opened it she gasped. "How beautiful!"

"What is it, Mom?" Raimey said. He crowded in along with Merry on the other side as Leah took out a necklace with a fine gold chain and a beautiful opal.

"That necklace belonged to another Winslow. Harriet Winslow, my great-grandmother."

"It's so beautiful, Stuart."

"I'm glad you like it." Stuart took the long box and said, "This is for you, Raimey."

Raimey took the box and glanced at his mother, who nodded at him. He ripped the paper off and opened the box, and his eyes grew large. "Why, it's a sword!"

"Be careful. It's very sharp," Stuart said. He watched with pleasure as the boy took the sword and held it up. "Did it belong to one of the Winslows, too?" Raimey asked.

"Yes, it did. It belonged to Henry Winslow, your great-grandfather. You know about him?"

"Yes," Raimey said, his eyes fixed on the keen blade that still glistened after all the years. "He died fighting in the Battle of Gettysburg."

"That's right. And he fought his way with that very sword.

He died fighting for freedom for all men. He was a very good man, Raimey. Hope you'll grow up to be just like him."

Raimey could not seem to take his eyes off the sword. "Did he really use it to fight with?"

"Yes, he did. He was a very strong, courageous man, and there have been many Winslows just like him. I hope you'll always keep the name of Winslow clean and proud." He hesitated and said, "Not like me."

Leah turned her head quickly and saw that Stuart's face was tense, and there was a deep grief in his eyes. "Where did you get all these things, Stuart?"

"From my parents. I hope you like them."

"I'll wear this ring every day when I get big enough," Merry said. "Now, Daddy, play some more on your fiddle."

"Oh, your mother's too tired."

"No, I'm not," Leah said. "I'm tired of the bed."

"After breakfast," he said.

Stuart fixed a quick breakfast and fed the youngsters and brought a plate of soft-boiled eggs and buttered toast with jam for Leah. She ate it all and said, "Thank you, Stuart. That was good."

"Now play, Daddy," Merry said.

"All right, just a few. Then your mother's got to go back to bed."

Stuart took the fiddle out, ran the bow over the strings, and then began playing, "O Little Town of Bethlehem." He sang along with it, and his rich baritone voice filled the room. He did not strain and Leah thought, *He has the most beautiful voice of any man I've ever heard.* She sat there listening as he played many of the old carols, and finally the fiddle was silent. He looked at her and then played one more song. She listened and closed her eyes, and when it was over, Merry spoke up.

"I never heard that Christmas carol."

"It's not a Christmas carol," Stuart said.

"What is it, Daddy?"

"Just an old song. Now it's time to get your mother to bed."

Stuart stood up, put the fiddle down, then came over and without asking simply reached down and scooped Leah into his arms. The youngsters called after her, "Merry Christmas!" and she called back, "Merry Christmas."

When he reached the bed, he put her down carefully, turned the covers over her, and said, "You're tired."

"Yes, but it was wonderful." She looked up and said, "Thank you, Stuart—for everything."

He did not answer but turned and left without a word.

Leah lay there, and her mind was full of the song, the last one that he'd played. It was the one he had written for her the night they had married—the one he called "Leah's Song." He had played it for her often during the first few months of their marriage, and she had always loved it. Now as she lay there the thoughts of those happy times came to her, but it was mixed with sadness.

She thought of what it had been like to be young and in love with no doubt, and she blinked back the tears, wondering if she would ever know a time of happiness like that again.

CHAPTER SEVENTEEN

A NEW ARRANGEMENT

★　★　★　★

"You really shouldn't have brought all these presents, Mott," Leah protested. "It's really too much."

"Well, I don't think so." Mott was smiling broadly and watching as Merry paraded with a new doll buggy back and forth over the living room floor. The Christmas tree was still up, and over to one side, under the window where sunlight streamed in, Raimey was building a complicated construction out of something called "Tinker Toys." Mott had come in two hours earlier carrying a huge box.

Now as Leah sat smiling at the children totally engrossed in their presents, she repeated again, "You really did more than you should have."

Mott was wearing a navy blue suit with a pair of shiny patent leather shoes and a dark maroon bow tie. As always, he looked good in whatever he put on, and now he said, "I'm sorry you got sick over Christmas. If I had known that, I would have stayed."

"You had to go see your mother, Mott. You hadn't seen her in six months."

"Yes. She's not doing too well. I tried to persuade her to come and live with me, but she's too tied up with her life there in Atlanta."

"What all did you do in Atlanta?"

"Oh, just visited around. Took in a new movie there. It

starred that woman Theda Bara, the one they call 'The Vamp.' "

"I really don't like her much, Mott. She looks so awful."

"Well, a lot of people don't think so. The theater was packed. Anyway," he said, "I didn't enjoy myself as much as I would if I'd been here with you. Maybe I could have taken better care of you."

"We made out all right."

Mott studied her thoughtfully, and now there was a trace of jealousy in his tone as he said, "I understand Stuart did all the nursing. Was that necessary?"

"Why, Mott, somebody had to. I was absolutely helpless."

"You could have gotten a nurse."

"We couldn't afford that. And with Annie sick and Merle down, I was glad that Stuart was able to help."

Mott pulled a box out of his inner coat pocket and said quickly, "I haven't given you your gift yet. Here."

"Why, Mott, you shouldn't have spent money on me."

"Who else would I spend it on?"

Opening the box, Leah stared down at the glittering diamond that flashed with a thousand lights as the light overhead caught it. "Mott, I can't take this."

"It's an engagement ring."

Leah shook her head and closed the box. "Mott, I'm married. We've talked about this before."

Mott shook his head, refusing to take the box. "You've got to be reasonable, Leah. You don't have any life, and things are only going to get worse. You can't keep this place up by yourself. You've lost money the last two years. How long can that go on? And you won't let your father-in-law help you, so that doesn't leave you many options." Mott reached over and took her free hand. "I don't ask you to love me as I love you, but I can make you love me. I know I can. And we'd have a good life together."

Leah shook her head, but before she could answer, the back door opened and closed, and she drew her hand back quickly. "You've got to give me time, Mott."

Stuart suddenly appeared at the door and stopped abruptly. He was carrying a bucket and said quickly, "I gathered all the eggs, Leah. I'll leave some here and take some to Annie."

"All right, Stuart."

As soon as Stuart left, Mott said, "People are talking about you two."

Leah suddenly laughed. "How can they be talking about us? We're married."

"Everybody knows you're not really man and wife. He's living out in the barn. You won't let him in the house."

"Well, let them talk," Leah said. "Those who would say such things don't really matter."

Mott saw that he had pushed his case too far. He reluctantly took the box back and pushed it into his pocket. "This isn't the end, Leah. I'm a stubborn fellow." He rose and leaned forward, and when she stood up, he kissed her on the cheek. "I'll see you later." Turning, he said, "Kids, you have fun now."

"Thank you, sir. Thanks for the Tinker Toys," Raimey said. "Maybe you'll help me make some things with it."

"I'll do that next time." Turning to Merry, he said, "Good-bye, sweetheart. What are you going to name the doll?"

"Jezebel."

Mott laughed suddenly. "You can't name her that."

"Why not? It's in the Bible."

"Well, she's your doll." Mott winked at Leah, put on his overcoat, and, clamping his hat down, left the room.

"Come and play with me some, Mom," Raimey said. "Look. You can make a bridge or a castle or even an automobile with these Tinker Toys."

"I don't think I could ever get up once I sat on the floor," Leah smiled.

Even though Leah did not have her strength back completely, she spent all morning doing what she could around the house. As she sat down in the kitchen mixing dough for biscuits, she thought about Stuart and his tender care of her throughout her sickness. She had never seen that side of him before, and it had shocked her. Her mind flickered back to the times when he had brought her fever down covering her with cool wet sheets, how he had dressed her almost as if she were a doll, and had fed her soup when her hand trembled too much to hold the spoon. These thoughts troubled her, and from somewhere deep within, the thought rose, *Stuart always did well under pressure, but he always failed later. I still can't trust him.*

* * * *

Late afternoon had turned out to be warm, and Leah, for the first time, stepped outside and inhaled the rich air. It was not really cold, and the snow had all melted, so there was a clean, earthy smell in the air. She sat down on the rocker and gazed out the window, taking in the farm. Five minutes later she saw Stuart ride in on Thunder, dismount, and lead him into the barn. He was gone for some time, and she knew he was brushing the horse that had become his favorite. Finally he came out and headed toward the house. His head was down, but he was whistling a song. He always knew all the latest songs, for listening to the radio, she knew, was perhaps his only entertainment. The one he was whistling now was, "When You Wore a Tulip and I Wore a Big Red Rose." He would have passed by the house headed for the back when suddenly she called out, "Stuart!" whereupon he stopped and came over to the porch.

"Well, out for a little air. Good. It'll put some color in your cheeks."

"I haven't really felt well enough to ask how things are going."

Stuart sat down beside her and said, "Well, the stock is all healthy. The fences are getting pretty well mended. We'll be ready for spring plowing, I guess."

Leah sat there listening as he talked about the farm. She was thinking how little interest he had taken before, except for brief intervals, and finally without knowing why, she sighed deeply and spoke what was on her heart. "I don't know what's going to happen, Stuart. We've lost money for two years running. There's only one end to a thing like that."

Stuart lifted his head sharply and studied Leah. Her illness had planed her down, but he still admired the clean-running physical lines that had always been hers. He also was pleased with the structure of her face that made a definite, appealing contour. Even as he studied her, he noted that her features showed the quick, swift changes of her mind, and he could not help but notice the self-possessed curve of her mouth and the richness of her lips. "I've been thinking about something, Leah," he said finally.

She turned to him, and her lips made a small change at the corners. He thought again how she had a way that could charm a man or chill him to the bone.

"What is it?"

"Well, I've had a lot of time to think lately." He grinned wryly and said, "About seven years with nothing else to do, and a few things came to me about this place."

"What sort of things?"

"Horses and mules will be around for a long time, but the tractor and the automobile—that's where the future is."

"Well, we can't go into the tractor and automobile business."

"No, we can't, but we can, more or less, get out of the draft animal business."

Leah studied him carefully, noting the clearness of his eyes and the strength of his neck. He had always been a strong man and he still was. It troubled her that she would think of him in this way, and she said quickly, "What else could we do?"

"We could become pig farmers."

Leah suddenly laughed aloud. "Pig farmers! What an idea!"

"I'm serious." Stuart pulled his chair around so that he could face her. "Look, Leah, America's going to enter this war, and it's going to get in with both feet. President Wilson got reelected on the campaign promise that he would keep us out of the war, but he's not going to keep us out anymore."

"You really think so?"

"Yes. It's going to happen. Now, I've been studying the market reports, and there's going to be a tremendous call for meat for overseas as well as here at home. A lot of America will be going to work in factories. That's going to leave the farms shorthanded."

"But why pigs? Why not cattle?"

"Because it takes a long time to raise a beef critter," Stuart said quickly. "But you can raise pigs almost like they were rabbits. You know how fast they grow and how big the litters are."

"I hate pigs!"

"You don't have to eat them." He grinned. "You like bacon and pork chops and smoked ham and every other part except the chitterlings. I don't care for those myself."

"We don't know anything about it, Stuart."

"What's to know? Here's what it takes to raise pigs. You've got to raise corn to feed them, and you've got to keep them until they're big enough for market. Well, we've got enough acreage here that we're feeding these stubborn mules and expensive horses on to put in fifty acres of corn or more. What's more, we wouldn't have to buy a tractor. We have enough draft animals to do it easy."

Leah sat there listening as Stuart continued and found herself interested. "But what about a place to keep them?"

Stuart shrugged. "Merle and I will just have to build some pig pens. They wouldn't have to be very fancy. In this climate they don't even have to be indoors, except for the sows. We'll have to build some furrowing pens, but that's my idea. We grow the corn, we feed the pigs, we sell the pigs and turn a big profit."

"And get out of the horse and mule business?"

"We can keep breeding a few fine horses, but I think pigs are where the money is."

"It sounds terrible. Pig farmers."

Stuart laughed. "After you've been a convict, it doesn't sound too bad. Of course," he said quickly, "it might hurt your feelings, and the kids might be a little bit embarrassed by it. But I'm convinced it would get this place in the clear and be some security for the kids."

Leah said quickly, "It's too big a risk, Stuart. It would take so much work, and it's not a thing you can get into and then drop out of."

"Meant for me, I reckon," Stuart said slowly. "Well, I deserve it. But this is your place, Leah. If you want to keep working with the horses and mules, I'll stay with it. I've just thought about this a lot."

Leah rose and said, "I'm feeling a little tired. I think I'll lie down."

"Take care of yourself. You're still not strong yet."

★　★　★　★

For two days Leah thought about little else but the plan that Stuart had laid before her. At first it had sounded fantastic, but she had talked to a neighbor, Don Zimmerman, who had raised a considerable number of pigs. He had told her, "Anybody can raise a few pigs, but it takes a strong constitution to raise a lot of pigs. Don't think I'd care to get into it myself, but there is money to be made. If a cow lies down and dies, you've lost a heap of money, but with a pig there's always ten more behind him."

Leah did not discuss the plan with anyone else, but the more she thought of it, the more she was taken by the idea.

"I've got to do something," she said to herself firmly and made up her mind right then that raising pigs was the only door that was open. As for Stuart's character, whether or not he would stick with it, she could only hope.

Three days after Stuart had proposed changing their operation, Leah heard a knock at the front door. She had heard a car pull up and thought it might be Mott. Putting her book down, she went to the door and stood absolutely still, for Cora Simms stood there. She was wearing a dark green coat that came down almost to her ankles and a pair of buttoned boots that showed traces of mud left over from the thaw.

"Hello, Leah," she said, surprised.

"Cora. Won't you come in?"

"Just for a minute." Cora came in and slipped off her coat and hung it on the rack.

"Come in by the fire," Leah said.

"I can only stay a minute. I heard you've been sick."

"I'm about over it now."

"The flu's about to get this country down." Cora was entirely self-possessed, as always. After talking for a few minutes about the sick neighbors, she finally said, "Is Stuart around?"

"He's gone to town to deliver some stock to the railroad. If you want to talk about buying some stock, I can help you with that."

Cora smiled. There was a strange light in her eyes. "I guess I've been called a lot of things, Leah, but nobody ever accused me of being mealymouthed. No. I don't want to buy stock. I just want to see Stuart."

Anger suddenly ran along Leah's nerves. She rose and said, "I think you'd better leave, Cora. Haven't you done Stuart enough damage?"

Cora rose but stood there facing Leah. "I've heard you two are separated."

"You hear all kinds of rumors."

"I understand he's just a hired hand and sleeps out in a little house by the barn."

"That's none of your concern."

Cora had an enormous air of certainty about herself and a positive will. She was a woman of great vitality and imagination but of little restraint.

"Are you going to keep Stuart, Leah?"

"That's none of your business."

"I think it is," Cora said. "I want him if you don't."

The enormity of what Cora Simms said seemed to numb Leah. She could not answer for a moment, and a voice whispered in her mind, *What are you upset about? If you don't want him, let her have him.*

"I've heard you're going to marry Mott Castleton."

"I'm not responsible for what you hear, Cora. I think you'd better leave now."

"Leah, you know me for what I am. I've never made any secret of it. I've always cared for Stuart."

"Leave my house!"

"It's your house I'll leave, but I'll just say this. Stuart's a young man and he deserves a wife. You're not being one to him. From what I understand, you have no intentions of it. Turn him loose, Leah. If you don't want him, let him have something in this life. I know I'm partially responsible for his being in prison. It doesn't bother me that he's an ex-convict. I don't care a whit. I know your pride and your feelings are hurt, so let him go."

Without another word Cora turned and left. She plucked her coat off the peg, and Leah heard the door slam. She was trembling so hard, she clasped her hands together to keep them still. Finally she went over and sat down in the chair and tried to regain her composure. Nothing had upset her this much in a long time. The thought of Stuart and Cora being together was unthinkable. She shook her head angrily. "Why do you care?" she said to herself. "You won't have anything to do with him. You've told him that. She's no good, but you've convinced yourself he isn't any good, either. Let them have each other."

★   ★   ★   ★

Stuart looked up with surprise. He was eating supper, and as Annie opened the door, he saw Leah standing there. "I want to see you when you've finished," she said, then turned and left.

Stuart exchanged glances with Annie and then turned to face Merle. "She sounded pretty mad," he said. "I wonder what I've done now."

"She did talk funny. Maybe you'd better go find out," Merle said.

"Save some of that pie for me, Annie. I'll be back and get it unless she runs me off right away."

After Stuart closed the door behind him, Annie said, "What's she thinkin' now? I can't keep up with that woman."

"She better be careful. If it wasn't for Mistah Stuart, this place would go down quick."

As Stuart approached the house, he was puzzled but thought, *I'll never try to outguess Leah.* Going to the front door, he knocked and stepped inside. Leah was standing in the hallway.

"Come back in the kitchen," she said.

Stuart glanced into the parlor as they passed and called out, "Hey, what's that you're making, Raimey?"

"It's a castle."

Merry came running over holding up her doll. "Mama made me a new dress."

"My, that is a pretty dress. Jezebel doesn't deserve all these nice clothes." He gave the doll a look of approval, kissed it on the face, then winked. "You be sweet now like me." Then he turned and moved to the kitchen. He found Leah standing there before the table, and her face was tense.

"Cora came by to see you."

"Cora! What did she want to see me for?"

Leah had managed to calm her voice down. She said, "The same thing she always wanted to see you for, Stuart."

Stuart met her gaze and shook his head. "I haven't had a thing to do with her since I got out."

"She's after you. Why would she come here wanting to see you if you hadn't seen her?"

"You know Cora."

"No. *You* know Cora."

Stuart suddenly experienced a quick anger. "Look, Leah, I'm

not going to argue about this. That woman cost me seven years of my life. Of course, she didn't do it alone. It was my fault, but if you don't want me here, just say so."

Leah hesitated. "She upset me, Stuart. She's no good."

"No. She's not. Never was, but she might be someday. Nobody's past hope, I guess."

Leah studied Stuart's face and then said abruptly, "Sit down." She went to the stove, poured two cups of coffee, and seated herself opposite him. "If you want to see Cora, that's your business. I can't stop you, but I've been thinking about your suggestion of raising pigs."

Stuart studied her and saw that there was a determination in her features. "You want to try it?" he said.

"Yes. You can fix up that old room in the barn. You're not staying in this house."

Stuart did not hesitate. "If that's what you want, Leah."

"One more thing. You won't . . . bother me. I may be your wife legally, but don't ever touch me, Stuart."

"All right, Leah. Are there any other rules?"

"No. I'm doing this for Merry and Raimey."

"So am I," Stuart said. "And for you, too, Leah, though you don't believe that. I'll start tomorrow drawing up the plans. Anything else?"

"No," Leah said. "That's all."

"Good night, then."

"Good night," Leah said. She sat there after he left and forgot about the coffee until it grew cold. She was not happy about the situation with the farm, but she had come to a point in her life where she knew something had to be done. She thought of Mott and knew he would be upset about her new arrangements. She also thought of how Stuart had cared for her unselfishly and suddenly regretted that she had torn into him as she had. With a sigh she rose and went back to spend the evening with the children.

CHAPTER EIGHTEEN

"Will You Have Him Back As Your Husband?"

★ ★ ★ ★

The new year had brought beautiful weather to the Ozarks. Even though it was cold and dry, the sun shone every day, flooding the hills and the valleys with warmth. Although it was still weeks away from spring planting, the farmers were oiling their harnesses and walking over their lands imagining the fields as they would be when they were thick with the growing harvest.

Leah had built a protective shell around herself, and now she was less certain in her mind than ever about Mott Castleton. She had a genuine affection for Mott, for he had changed much in recent years. She thought often of the early days when he had wanted to marry her and wondered what sort of a life she would have had. But such thinking was futile, so she forced herself to put it out of her mind. Her attitude toward Stuart was curt, and she spoke to him only out of necessity.

Ellie Devainy had proved to be quite a trial to her, for although Ellie loved Leah, she had a short way about her and a very direct one. For over a month she had only given hints of the curiosity that seemed to boil within her, but one day it spilled over.

"Leah, where's Stuart?"

"He's gone, Ellie."

"For good?" Ellie demanded.

"No, just to Tucker Farm." Knowing that Ellie would never be satisfied with anything less than full details, she added, "He went to visit one of the prisoners, a man named Pete Jennings. He's the one who led him to the Lord."

"Oh, I see." Ellie hesitated, then said abruptly, "Leah, I've been quiet about it as long as I can, but everybody wants to know about you and Stuart."

"We've got a business arrangement. That's all."

"Oh, I know all about that pig-raising thing!" Ellie waved her hand impatiently. She had come rather early in the morning, and now the two women were sitting in the kitchen together drinking strong hot coffee. Ellie leaned forward and her eyes gleamed. "I hear he doesn't stay in the house with you at all."

"The gossip system is working well, as usual," Leah said shortly.

"Well, after all, Leah, you can't blame people for wondering."

"I do blame them. They could mind their own business." Taking a sip of the coffee, she tried to change the subject. "Stuart's working night and day, I'll tell you that much. I never saw a man work any harder. He's building fences, selling off stock, and buying pigs for this new business."

Ellie could retain her question no longer. She asked what everyone in the community was wondering. "Will you have him back as your husband?"

Although Leah well knew this was what was in the mind of nearly everyone, she could not help being angry. "Why don't you mind your own business, Ellie?"

Ellie was not offended, however. She had a genuine affection for Leah, and now she leaned forward and said, "It ain't right the way things are between you and Stuart, Leah, and you know it."

Leah's eyes flew open with anger, and she rose up, saying, "I've got to get to work, Ellie. You go ahead and finish your coffee, but keep your questions to yourself."

★ ★ ★ ★

Annie looked up as Leah entered the kitchen and said, "You

want me to fry up that ham for supper tonight?"

"I guess so. Have you seen Stuart?"

"Why, yes, ma'am. He come back a little while ago."

Merle, who had entered with an armload of wood and dumped it into the basket with a thunderous racket, nodded and said, "He's down at the south pasture finishin' up a pen."

Without another word Leah turned and left, and they heard the door slam. Merle went over and slumped into a chair and said, "I got to have some fixin's. That man's about to work me to death."

Annie went over to the stove and pulled out a plateful of bacon and put it on the table. "Here, have some bacon, and I'll fix you some eggs. That ought to do until suppertime."

"That'll go down mighty fine. What do you think about this business of Mistah Stuart and Miss Leah?"

Annie pulled a pail full of eggs off the shelf and cracked three of them swiftly and efficiently. "I seen the time when he wouldn't put in a day's work."

"Well, he's done changed from that." He would have said more, but at that moment Stuart walked in the door. "Mistah Stuart, I'm havin' up some eggs. You want some?"

"No. I'll just wait til suppertime. Would like some coffee, though."

Stuart sat down and drank two cups of strong coffee as Merle fell on the bacon and eggs and the warmed-over biscuits like a starved wolf. The two men talked for a while about the work, and finally Annie came and sat down across from the two.

"Mistah Stuart?"

"Yes, Annie?"

"Why you don't go to church? You ought to do that. If you done decided to follow Jesus, that's the only right thing to do."

Stuart stared at his cup, turning it around in a circle. He had spilled some coffee, and he set the cup down in the pool, then proceeded to make three little rings by lifting his cup and putting it down again. He finally shrugged and said, "It would embarrass Leah for me to be there."

"How you know that?" Merle said.

Stuart did not answer, and it was Annie who spoke up. She had been thinking about all this for some time, and it bothered her greatly. "Why don't you come to our church, Mistah Stuart? We got a fine preacher."

Stuart suddenly smiled. "Well, you know I've been thinking about that, Annie. You don't reckon the folks would mind having a white visitor?"

"No, sir, not at all," Merle said quickly.

"That's right. You come on tomorrow mornin' with us."

"And bring your fiddle," Merle said. "We likes good music!"

★   ★   ★   ★

Raimey and Merry walked through the woods, the dry leaves crackling under their feet. Overhead a gray squirrel suddenly sped across a limb, made a long dive, and landed on the branch of an adjoining tree. Raimey lifted an imaginary gun and yelled, "*Bang!*" He grinned and said, "I got you that time." He turned to Merry, saying, "I got to get me a squirrel gun. I'm gonna ask Ma to get me one."

"We don't have the money for that," Merry said.

"Well, I could put meat on the table. I could get enough squirrels to feed us for a year, I bet."

Merry was more thoughtful than usual and somewhat quieter. So much so that after a while Raimey said, "What are you thinking about?"

"I'm thinking about Mama and Daddy."

"What about them?" Raimey said shortly, glancing at her face.

"Why don't he live in the house with us? All the daddies of my friends live in the house with their wives."

"You know why."

"No, I don't. He doesn't have to live with Merle and Annie."

"Yes, he does. After what he did to Mama, he doesn't deserve to live in the same house with us. I wish he'd go on away and Mama would marry Mott."

Quickly Merry looked up at Raimey. "I don't want Mott for a daddy."

"What's wrong with him? Mott gives us presents every time he comes."

Merry had insight far beyond her years. "He just does that to get on the good side of Mama," she said.

Even though he knew she was right, Raimey still would not give in. "That's not so," he said. "He really likes us. He's got lots of money. We could get away from this place and go live in that big house in Fort Smith." He kicked at a bunch of leaves that had piled up and watched them scatter wildly, then he muttered, "People wouldn't make fun of us because our daddy's a jailbird."

It was an old argument between the two, and Raimey did not want to continue it. "Come on," he said. "Let's cut through the pasture." They had arrived at a fence with a path around the edge, but there was a stile to cross over.

Merry stopped and shook her head. "You know what Mama said. We're not supposed to get in that pasture where Brutus is."

"Ah, Brutus isn't there. Merle put him down in the south pasture. The grass was thicker there." Brutus was a fine bull used for breeding purposes. He was a monstrous animal with sweeping horns that should have been cut but had been neglected. He was also vicious, and the only person who could handle him was Merle.

"We'd better not," Merry said. "Come on. Let's go around."

"No. I'm going through."

"Well, I'm not going to, and I'm gonna tell Mama if you do."

"Go ahead and tell her! See if I care! I'll get home long before you do, so I'll tell her you wouldn't mind me."

Merry watched as Raimey leaped up, clearing the stile, and started walking across the field. There were nine head of beef cattle trying to find pasture among the dry winter grass but no sign of Brutus.

* * * *

"I'm gonna go huntin'. There's been deer tracks all around that spring, Annie."

"We got plenty of meat in the smokehouse."

"Well, I'm kinda hungry for some venison. The way you cook it, woman, is outstandin'!" Merle went over and grabbed Annie from behind and picked her up.

She tried to hit him, saying, "Put me down, you crazy ox!"

Merle set her down, turned her around, and gave her a loud, resounding kiss, then said, "I'll bring you back a nice fat deer. You can fix it the way you always do. That way you get on the good side of me, and I'll give you a reward."

"I ain't studyin' no reward," Annie said but could not help but laugh. "You go on and get out of here now."

Merle picked up the deer rifle, shoved a handful of shells in his pocket, and then left the house. Leaving the yard, he looked up, took a deep breath, and said, "Lord, it's always a good day, and I'd appreciate it if you would bring a big fat deer right up to me where I can't miss him."

Soon he reached the pasture and turned left toward the big thickets just north of the place where the deer often came to water at a spring. He had taken many there and was sure now that he would get another one. When he was no more than two hundred yards on his way, he heard a loud cry that startled him. Whirling around he saw a sight that seemed to freeze his blood.

There, running for all his might, was Raimey headed for the fence. Behind him the huge bull Brutus was kicking up turf as he made his charge.

With a hoarse cry Merle broke into a run, at the same time groping in his pocket for a shell. His fingers closed on one, but he knew he would never get the gun loaded, nor could he get to the boy in time to help him at all.

He struggled, trying to put the shell in, but could not do it. He came to a stop, threw the bolt, and shoved the shell in. But when he looked up, he saw that Stuart had suddenly appeared, and he yelled, "Mistah Stuart!" He ran forward, but even before he had taken six steps, he saw Stuart waving his arms as he got to Raimey. Stuart shoved Raimey to one side, and Merle saw the huge bull swerve, his attention taken by the man. Stuart tried to dodge but the bull was fast. To his horror, Merle saw the bull lower his head, then raise his horns, and Stuart was thrown high into the air. He hit the ground rolling, and the bull went after him, sweeping those wicked horns.

Suddenly Merle lifted the rifle to his shoulder. He knew the power of those horns, for he had seen another bull gored to death by them just two years earlier. It was too late for him to reach Stuart, and even if he could, he would be gored terribly by the time he got there. Even if he could reach him, what could he do with his bare hands against an animal like Brutus?

"Lord, make this shot true," he said. He was now a hundred

yards away from the animal, and he saw Stuart's body being tossed like a bundle of rags and dragged along the ground by the sweep of the horns. He waited until the bull raised his head and then with a desperate prayer pulled the trigger. The recoil of the rifle knocked him back, but when he looked he saw the bull beginning to collapse. "Caught him dead on!" Merle yelled and broke into a run. By the time he got to Stuart, Raimey was already there beside the bloodstained figure.

He lay there crumpled and crying. "Dad—Dad!"

★　★　★　★

Leah paused beside Annie and said, "Did you ask Stuart to come to your church?"

"I shore did." Annie looked up from the shirt she was ironing and nodded vigorously. "And it was a good thing, too."

Leah felt uncomfortable. "He could have come to our church."

Annie was a very direct woman. "He said it might make you feel bad. Kind of uncomfortable."

"I don't know why he'd say that."

"Well, I do. You make him feel bad enough around here."

It was a blunt statement, and Leah looked up for a moment, then dropped her eyes, unable to meet Annie's. "I can't see how he would fit in a Negro church."

"He fits in just fine. People was glad to see him, and he plays his fiddle every service and sings, too. You ought to hear him. Ain't ever heard nothin' like the way he play that fiddle. And he sings songs from the heart. Not like them old dancin' songs he used to sing. He really loves the Lord."

Leah picked up the ironing and began folding it. She was troubled about what Annie had said and, indeed, felt guilty about it.

Annie studied Leah's face for a moment and saw the troubled look in her eyes. In a more gentle voice, she said, "He's the only white man who ever come to our church and sang with us and cared about us."

She picked up the iron and was about to move the shirt when her eyes caught something through the window, and she screamed, "Good Lord, help us!"

Leah looked up startled at the scream and saw Annie slam the iron down and head for the porch. "What is it?" she said.

"Somebody hurt bad."

Leah's heart seemed to freeze. Her first thought was Raimey and Merry, for they were on their way home from school. She ran out on the porch right behind Annie and stopped dead still as she saw Merle bearing in his huge arms Stuart's limp body. She could not breathe for a moment, for Stuart's face was covered with blood, and the front of his shirt was ripped and torn and scarlet with blood.

"Oh, God, please help him!" she whispered.

"What is it? What done happened to him?" Annie asked.

"He done been hurt bad. Brutus done throwed him and gored him."

"Bring him in the house and put him on the bed," Leah gasped. She watched as Merle carried him by and could barely see his features for all the blood. Dirt was ground into his face, and she saw the gaping trench that had been gouged across his chest.

"It . . . it was my fault, Mama. My fault."

Leah looked down and said, "What happened, Raimey?"

"I went into the pasture. I thought Brutus was somewhere else, and the bull got after me. I don't know where he was. Dad came and got him away from me, but Brutus got him. Is he going to die, Mama?"

"I'll call Doc Morton," she said. She ran to the phone, and when the voice answered, "Number please," she said, "Quick, Stella, get me Doc Morton."

"Is there trouble, Miss Winslow?"

"Just get me Doc Morton, Stella. Quick, there's been an accident."

She waited impatiently while the phone rang—a long and two shorts—and then a voice said, "Dr. Morton's residence."

"Mrs. Morton, this is Leah Winslow. Stuart's been hurt in an accident. Dr. Morton's got to come at once."

"Oh my, Miss Winslow, he's gone over to the Grubmeyerses'. They don't have a phone. I can't call him."

"I'll send someone after him. Thank you."

Slamming the phone down, Leah ran into the bedroom. Stuart was lying on his back, his bloody visage still, and she said, "Is he . . . dead?"

"No. He's breathin', but he's cut up awful bad. I expect he's done broke somethin' inside. That bull tossed him and then gored him," Merle said.

"Go over to the Grubmeyerses' place, Merle. Doc Morton's there. Have him come quick as you can."

"Yes, 'um. I'll take Thunder."

By this time Merry had come into the room, and she began to cry.

Raimey stood beside the wall trembling, his face white as paste.

"Annie, you take the children out. I'll see what I can do for Stuart."

"Yes, ma'am. You chilluns come on with me now."

Leah was scarcely aware of Merry's shrill cry and Raimey's feeble protest. She heard the door close and at once went to stand beside Stuart. She placed her hand on his wrist and saw that his forearm was bleeding. "Got to get that bleeding stopped," she whispered and ran to get a basin of cold water. When she came back, she set the basin down and grabbed up a bunch of pillowcases and the scissors that lay on her dresser. She began to mop his face. She was afraid at first that his eyes had been gored out, but it was blood running down from a deep cut in his scalp. It was bleeding freely, but the cold water seemed to help coagulate it. There was no way to bind it, but she got the blood and dirt cleared away. She took the scissors and cut away the shirt. A long cut started at his ribs and went all the way on his left side and almost all the way to his neck. She could see the exposed bone of the ribs, and it nauseated her. Quickly she cleaned away the blood, and then ripping up the pillowcases, she improvised some sort of a bandage. The jagged cut on his left forearm was bleeding badly, and it took some time to get a bandage arranged that would soak it up and stop it.

Finally she had all the cuts cleaned and took a deep breath. "Oh, God," she said, "please don't let him die." Then she leaned forward and said, "Stuart, can you hear me?"

He did not respond, and she saw a huge bump just behind his right temple. She surmised it must have been where a sweeping horn caught him with a terrible blow and knocked him unconscious.

Time seemed to crawl, and Leah was in agony waiting for the doctor to arrive. She tried to pray but found herself unable to do more than come up with a childlike prayer. "God, don't let him die. Help him, God."

Finally she saw his eyes flutter, and she quickly put her hand on his cheek. "Stuart . . . Stuart, can you hear me?"

His eyes came open slowly. He tried to move, and she put her hand on his chest lightly. "Don't try to move. You've been badly hurt."

"Are . . . are the kids okay?" he gasped. The words came out in a hoarse whisper, and it was obvious it hurt him to talk.

"Yes. They're all right. They're fine."

"Thank God."

Leah stood there and kept her hand on his chest. "Don't try to move. I think you may have some broken ribs."

Stuart was in considerable pain. He kept his eyes closed for a time, breathing very shallowly, and finally he murmured, "It hurts when I breathe."

"It must be broken ribs. Doc Morton will be here soon." Leah hesitated, then said, "Merle said you threw yourself in front of Brutus to save Raimey. He said it was the bravest thing he ever saw."

Stuart opened his eyes, and the trace of a bitter smile touched his pale lips. "First thing I've ever done for them."

Leah took his hand and kissed it, something she had never done before. She saw him watching her and whispered, "It was a noble thing, Stuart."

"Well, they're my kids." And then he said in a whisper so faint she could barely catch it. "I wish I could do something for you, Leah."

Suddenly Leah leaned over and kissed his cheek and then lightly on the lips. Her hair was loose, and it fell over his face. She drew it back, and then she had to lean forward to catch what he was saying.

"In prison I thought about you. How pretty your hair was. Every night for seven years I thought about you. . . ."

And then his face grew still, and he lapsed into unconsciousness. Leah drew up a chair and sat down beside him. She held his hand, and now she pressed her face against it, crying out, "Oh, God, please don't let him die!"

PART FOUR

1917

★ ★ ★ ★

CHAPTER NINETEEN

SEIZE THE DAY

★ ★ ★ ★

Dr. Morton probed at Stuart's exposed upper body with strong, blunt fingers, ignoring the grunts of protest from the patient as he stitched up his wounds. The doctor was a weary man, for he had a busy schedule. With the flu epidemic affecting so many people, he was sleeping no more than five or six hours a night. Now he grunted and shook his head fiercely. "Any fool who doesn't have any better sense than to tackle a bull head-on has got to be crazy."

Leah had been standing beside the window, an anxious look in her eyes. "How is he, Doctor?"

"He ought to be dead."

"Sorry to disappoint you, Doc." Stuart grinned. He was sitting up in bed and now reached out for his pajama top, but when he tried to put it on, a grimace etched its way across his face.

Leah turned to Dr. Morton. "Does he need to be in the hospital?"

"What good would that do?" Morton said curtly. "It's full of people with the flu." He snapped the bag shut, jammed his battered black Stetson firmly on his head, and cocked his head to one side. "You can go outdoors after a few days, but no work until that rib heals." Turning to Leah, he nodded. "You make him mind, Leah, you hear me?"

"I will," Leah said.

When she started toward the door, Morton said, "I know my way out."

"Thank you, Doctor," Leah called, then she turned back to Stuart. "Do you feel like getting around a bit?"

"Anything to get out of this bed. Just give me my pants."

Leah moved over to the wardrobe, pulled out a fresh shirt, pair of pants, and socks and said, "You can wear these house shoes."

Stuart pulled back the cover and, moving very carefully, lifted his legs over. As Leah helped him with the clothes, he complained, "I'm just like a baby—have to be dressed and fed."

"You were badly hurt, Stuart. Be sensible."

When he was dressed, Stuart stood to his feet and hung on to the headboard of the massive walnut bed. "A little dizzy," he admitted.

"Why don't you go in the living room? Just sit down and look out the window."

Stuart navigated his way down the hall slowly. His ribs were tender, for they had been the most painful part of his accident. The stitches that Dr. Morton had put in his scalp and side smarted something fierce, but he didn't complain. The ribs were not broken but badly bruised and cracked, so he made no sudden moves.

Instead of turning into the parlor, he stepped out on the porch and closed the door behind him. There was no snow now, and the world seemed dead and brown. Overhead a pale sun sent down opaque beams that carried no heat, and the air was snappy. Stuart was glad to be out of the house and out of the bed. He swept his eyes across the farm. He took pleasure in the cattle that had gathered around and the horses and mules that were feeding now on what was left of the grass.

"February 1, 1917," Stuart mused, then the thought came to him. *All those years buried alive in a prison. Now here I am free.* He breathed a prayer of thanksgiving, then turned as Merle appeared from around the corner of the house carrying a basket of eggs.

He came over at once and grinned, saying, "Well, look at you! Ready to get back to work, I reckon."

"Not for a while, according to Doc Morton."

"You listen to that doctor. I can take care of this place whiles you heal up."

"Give me a report, Merle."

Merle stood there speaking quickly of all that had been accomplished on the farm in the last few weeks. The fences were now completed and all in place. One of the sows had produced a fine litter just the previous day, and the farm seemed to be turning around after such hard times.

"Merle, I wish you'd do me a favor."

"Yes, suh, Mistah Stuart. What is it?"

"Bring me my shavin' stuff." Stuart raked his hand across the sprouting whiskers and said, "I can't stand these whiskers."

"I'll bring it right away. I needs to put these eggs in the kitchen."

Stuart stayed until he saw Merle coming back from his small house, and then he went back inside. Leah was in the kitchen peeling potatoes, and when he picked up a kettle and moved to get water, she said, "What are you doing?"

"I'm going to heat water. I want to shave."

"I'll do that. You sit down here."

She filled the kettle, put it on to heat, and then turned to take the shaving things from Merle.

Merle winked and said, "I'll do that for you if you want me to, Mistah Stuart."

"No thanks. I'll do it myself."

As soon as the kettle was boiling, Leah said, "You can shave right here. I'll fix a basin of water for you."

"All right."

Leah quickly gathered a basin, filled it with hot water, and tempered it with cool water, then produced a towel and a washcloth. Then she got a small mirror and sat across from Stuart. "I'll hold this so you can see what you're doing." She watched him as he lathered up and waited for the beard to soften. "I always liked to watch you shave," she said suddenly.

He grinned at her, his lips seeming very red under the outline of the white froth. "You did, didn't you? I remember our first morning together. I had more romantic notions in mind, but you wanted to watch me shave."

Leah flushed. "And you got your way if I remember."

"I did, didn't I?" Picking up the razor, he studied it for a moment. "You gave me this on our first anniversary. It was one of the things I missed in prison."

Not knowing what to say, she simply watched as he shaved, noticing how carefully he moved. "Your side's still sore. I don't want you doing any work."

"I'll be all right soon."

He got up slowly and left the room, and she called out, "I'll fix some cocoa."

She quickly made some cocoa, and just as she was pouring it into the cup, he came back. She saw that he had put on a coat and a pair of boots.

"What are you doing?" she demanded.

"Well, I thought I'd go back to Merle and Annie's."

"Don't be silly!" She went over and took the sack from his hands that contained a few of the items he needed. "You're going to stay here."

Stuart looked somewhat embarrassed. "I can't take your bed, Leah."

"I don't mind sleeping with Merry."

For a moment Stuart stood looking at her. "If I stay in the house, it'll give the gossip mill a little extra to work with."

"Let them talk!" Leah said half angrily. "Now sit down and drink this cocoa."

He sat down, took the cocoa, and she sat down across from him. He said nothing, and somehow she wanted him to speak, to tell her what he was feeling. It was a strange experience for her, and she realized that the accident and having him in the house had changed everything. She leaned forward and said, "Tell me again about the pigs."

Stuart glanced up quickly, then grinned. "We'll be the pig kings of Arkansas," he said and went on speaking. There was a warmth in the scene that pleased him, and for the first time since arriving home, he felt the stirring of hope.

★　★　★　★

Philo March looked more like a professional fighter than a banker. A huge man, three inches over six feet and weighing two hundred fifty pounds, his countenance had a battered look, the results of some fights during his youth when he was less in control of himself. One of his depositors had said that March looked more like a bank robber than he did the president of the First National Bank of Lewisville, but under the rough exterior lurked a good heart. He was one of the deacons at the First Baptist Church along with Richard Winslow, and the two had been friends for many years.

Tilting back in his swivel chair, March studied the man opposite him and finally said, "Richard, I've been meaning to ask you about Stuart. How's he doing?"

The question startled Richard Winslow. He had come in the first of the month to do business at the bank and, as usual, had gone into March's office to talk for a while. The two men were close, but it was the first time since Stuart had returned that the banker had brought up the subject. "He's all right . . . or so I hear."

March's eyes narrowed. "You mean you haven't seen him?"

"Well, no. Not actually."

"Not actually! What in the world does that mean? You've seen him or you haven't."

"Well, I did see him once. He came by the house."

March leaned forward and, clasping his meaty hands, studied Richard Winslow. He was a shrewd man in the business world and even more astute when it came to reading people. He knew Richard Winslow was a man of honor and he trusted him completely. Still, there was a look of displeasure in his eyes, and he finally said, "That was a pretty fine thing he did, Richard, saving that grandson of yours."

Shifting in his chair uneasily, Richard Winslow said, "Yes, it was." He was uncomfortable with the subject and said, "Did you see where Buffalo Bill died?"

"Yes. I saw it in the paper."

"I saw him once," Winslow said. "He came to Fort Smith and brought his Wild West show."

"Yes. I was there. He gave his farewell address," March said, then wryly added, "For about the two hundredth time, I think. That man retired more often than any human that ever lived."

"Jack London died not long ago, too."

"I never liked his books," the banker said. "The man had no sense of God whatsoever."

Winslow chewed his lower lip thoughtfully. "He was only forty years old. Had everything a man could want it seems. Money and fame, and yet he killed himself."

"Well, Buffalo Bill didn't. He went out doing what he loved to do. I don't know whether he was a saved man or not. I hope he was."

Winslow got up suddenly and walked over and stared out the window. He was silent for a time, then he turned and said, "We've had three funerals down at our church the last month and four the month before that. Mostly old people."

"That's right. It looks like Mrs. Simpson isn't going to make it either."

Winslow sat down in his chair, and his face had a sober look. "This winter's done it. You know, I was thinking, Philo. Out in the woods trees age, and you think they're going to stand forever. You can't tell the healthy ones from those that are weakened by time, and then a blizzard comes along, and the ones that go are those that are worn out." Stroking his chin thoughtfully, Winslow added, "That's the way it is with us, isn't it? Hard times come and the weak go down."

"Well, I suppose so. But all of those funerals were for people who knew the Lord. Not like Jack London." March was not through with the subject. He said, "I heard that Stuart got pretty well demolished by that bull. Doc Morton said it was a wonder he wasn't killed." When Richard did not answer, March said, "You know, I've been hearing about that new venture of his raising pigs. Sounds like a pretty good idea to me. This country's going to need lots of pork. Needs it right now, as a matter of fact."

"I suppose it's a good venture."

"Are you in with him?"

"No!" Richard Winslow said stiffly. "He knows he can work with me if he wants to."

And then the banker asked the question that had been on his lips many times. "Have you asked him to come back and work with you since he got out of prison?"

A silence filled the room, and Richard got up and headed

toward the door without a word. But when he reached it and opened it, he turned and said, "No, I haven't." Then he left the room, leaving his friend to stare after him, a sad look in his eyes.

As Richard left the bank, he did not hear the teller's farewell remark. As he stepped outside, he almost ran into Charles Fields.

"Hello, Brother Winslow," Fields nodded.

"Hello, Preacher."

"I wanted to talk to you about that new addition we're thinking of building. When would be a good time?"

"Now is as good a time as any if you want to go to my office."

"Fine." The two men moved down the main street and turned into the store. There were a few customers, though not many. "Business is slow, isn't it?" Fields remarked.

"Always is this time of year. Come back to the office."

They adjourned to the office where a potbellied stove cast heat throughout the room. The two men went over the plans for building an addition to the church building, and finally Fields said, "I don't know what I'd do without you, Richard. You've been a great help to our church."

Waving his hand, Richard said, "It's little enough."

Fields hesitated, then said, "Maybe you heard about what Stuart's doing?"

"You mean the pig business? Yes. I've heard."

"I don't mean that. I mean he's going to the Negro church. The one where Cyrus Hawkins preaches."

Surprised, Winslow looked up. "No. I hadn't heard about that."

"I'm surprised you haven't. Everybody's talking about it."

"No one told me."

Fields wanted to remark, *Perhaps you aren't interested*, but he refrained as he studied Winslow's troubled face.

"What's the matter? Our church isn't good enough for him?"

"I don't think he feels welcome, Richard," Fields said, surprised to hear his friend speak grudgingly.

Instantly Richard Winslow looked up and met the minister's gaze. He did not see rebuke there but sensed some sort of reticence in Fields's attitude. "You think it's my fault, then?"

"No. I didn't say that at all, but I think probably he's embarrassed to come back."

"Diane asked him back. I know that."

"I think maybe he needs for all of us to encourage him. He went through a hard time."

"So did all of us."

Fields knew he had touched a sore spot with Richard, and he said, "I think it would be good if you would reach out and make a special effort toward Stuart."

"I'll think about it," Richard answered stiffly. His own answer sounded lame, and he felt convicted, for he was well aware that his attitude was bad. He had struggled with his feelings toward Stuart ever since he'd come back from prison, but Richard could not seem to overcome them. Now he said, "Well, I've got to go home for lunch. Would you care to join us?"

"No," Fields said. "Thanks for the help with this new addition. Tell Diane I said hello."

"I'll do that," Winslow said. He waited until Fields had left, then sat at his office staring at the wall for a time. Finally, sighing heavily, he got up and said to his chief clerk, "I'll be back at one."

"Yes, Mr. Winslow."

He made his way home, where Diane greeted him, then sat him down to a fine lunch. He found his appetite was gone, however, and said little until Diane spoke.

"I'm going out to see the grandchildren today. Why don't you come with me?"

Shifting uneasily in his chair, Richard said almost gruffly, "I've got to be at the store."

Diane Winslow was a patient woman, kind and generous, but at this answer an anger flared through her. "How long are you going to hold your son at arm's length, Richard?"

"Why, Diane—!"

"I've always admired you, Richard—until now. You're not the man I thought you were." She got up and without another word left the room.

Richard Winslow sat there, and when the door slammed, it was as if he had been struck. All their married life he and Diane had been close, but now this matter of Stuart had driven them apart. He sat staring at the plate before him, confused and angry, acutely aware of a tremendous sadness and frustration. "What's the matter with me?" He had no answer but got up and made his way back to the store, wondering if things would ever change.

★ ★ ★ ★

Diane stepped inside the door, and as she walked down the hall, she looked into the parlor. She saw Stuart sitting on a low stool with Merry across from him sitting on the floor. On a box sat Merry's tea set, an old one that she had given her to play with, and the two looked up as she entered the room. "Well, are we having a tea party?"

"Yes. Daddy and I would love to have you join us," Merry said primly. Then her face broke into a grin. "Come on, Grandma. You can sit on the floor beside me."

"No. My old bones are too fragile for that. I'll just sit over here, but I will join you."

She pulled up a chair and couldn't help smiling as she watched her granddaughter include her in the tea party. To watch Merry so happy was a delight. She was amazed at how Stuart had won the girl's heart completely. Merry, she could see, doted on her father, and as she stole glances at her son's face, Diane saw that he had a deep happiness inside. He kept his eyes fixed on Merry a great deal, but Diane could see the pride written on his features.

"Where's Raimey?" Diane asked.

"Oh, he's in his room," Merry said. "He wouldn't come and have a tea party with us."

"Well, I'll just check in on him."

Leaving the parlor, Diane went to Raimey's room and knocked on the door. When a muffled "Come in" reached her, she opened the door and found Raimey sitting on the bed with his feet drawn up and an unread book before him.

"Why, Raimey, how are you?"

"I'm all right, Grandma."

Diane sat down on his bed and tried to talk, but she saw that the young boy was troubled. "What is it? You having trouble at school?"

"No, ma'am."

"Well, what is it? You don't look happy."

Raimey looked up, and misery was reflected in his eyes. "He

saved my life, Grandma, and I've been so mean to him. Ever since he came home, I've been mean as a snake."

Her heart suddenly knew a joy, for the misery on Raimey's face was good news to her. Reaching out, she took one of his hands in both of hers. "Well, it's not too late to change, Raimey."

"I don't know what to do."

"I think your father would like for you to show that you love him."

"I can't say that."

"Well, you don't have to say it. Just smile at him and ask him to help you with something."

Diane talked for some time to Raimey and then patted his hand. "Your father's a Christian now. He's not like he was when he was home before. You just give him a chance, and you'll see how much he really loves you, Raimey."

Raimey said little, but after his grandmother left, he got to his feet and stood irresolutely for a moment in the middle of the floor. He had been unhappy for so long, and now he knew he had to do something. He had never stopped thinking of how his father had bravely charged into the face of Brutus to save him. He knew that as long as he lived that sight would be engraved in his memory. For days now he had struggled to find a way to say something to his father, but somehow his feelings were locked up. The years of bitterness had built a wall between the two of them, but now he suddenly left the room and went into the parlor.

"Did you come to play dolls with us?" Merry said quickly.

"No. I'm going to play with my Tinker Toys." Raimey walked over to the room and sat down and began putting the pieces together. He listened, however, to the conversation, envious that Merry had no bad memories of her father. *It's different for me*, he thought. *She wasn't even born yet when he left*. What his grandmother had said weighed on him, and finally he took a deep breath and looked over and said, "Dad, I can't make this castle. Would . . . would you help me, please?"

At once Stuart's head turned, and he saw something in his son's eyes that brought a pang to his own heart. Getting up at once, he came over and pulled his stool over next to Raimey.

"Well, I'm no engineer, son, but maybe between the two of us we can do it."

Fifteen minutes later Leah entered carrying a tray with hot cocoa and cookies. She stopped abruptly, for she saw Stuart flanked by Merry and Raimey. All three were laughing, and she heard Raimey say, "Aw, Dad, that's not the way it goes."

Leah suddenly felt tears rise in her eyes. She could see a joy in Raimey's face that had been missing for a long time. She simply said, "Thank you, God." And then she entered, calling out, "Does anyone want cocoa and cookies?"

CHAPTER TWENTY

"I NEED YOU!"

★ ★ ★ ★

Raimey turned suddenly, lifted the .410, and pulled the trigger. The sharp explosion of the weapon broke the silence, and Raimey cried out, "I got him, Dad! I got him!"

"You sure did." Stuart grinned. He watched as the boy scurried over and picked up the limp body of the gray squirrel. "That's a fat fellow. We'll have him with some dumplings tonight."

"It's your turn next time, Dad."

Stuart shook his head. "Nope, you're a better shot than I ever was, son. I missed that last one when I should have had him."

"Aw, he was already behind the tree when we spotted him. You take the next shot."

Stuart laughed and said, "I'll tell you what. When you miss one I'll try another, but we've almost got enough here. This bag's getting heavy."

The two had come out early on a March morning to hunt squirrels. The air was crisp, the sky was clear, and the two had good luck. Now as they tramped along, with Raimey talking excitedly, Stuart was amazed at how much had changed since that day when he had come in and asked for help with his Tinker Toys.

It's like a miracle, Stuart thought. *He's not the same boy at all.* Looking down at Raimey, he felt a surge of pride at his son's clear features, and he knew that something good had come his way.

As they walked along, Raimey suddenly asked, "Dad, what was it like in prison?"

It was the first reference Raimey had made to that time, and Stuart answered him honestly. "It was bad, son." He related some of the hard physical conditions, but then he said quietly, "But the worst part of it all was that I brought shame on you and your mother and your sister . . . and I couldn't do anything about it."

Raimey thought about this for a moment and then looked up and said quickly, "But it's all over now, Dad."

"Yep. All over. I'm home now with a son who can shoot better than I can."

Raimey tramped on for a time and then said, "Do you think you'll ever get over being in prison?"

"In a way I will, but look at this." Stuart held out his hand and said, "See that white scar there? I tore it on a fence when I was about your age. I can barely remember it now, but I bled like a stuck pig, and I was afraid I was going to die. It was a bad time, but now it doesn't hurt to even think of it. I guess prison's like that or any bad experience we have. We just ask the Lord to forgive us, and He does. Then I think He takes away most of the memory. Just a little scar is left."

The two walked on, and Raimey listened as Stuart spoke. He had been lonely all the years his father had been gone, and now he felt that something had been restored. A sense of belonging swelled within him, and he stole glances at the face of the tall man who walked beside him, thinking of how good life was to him now.

★　★　★　★

Leah had found Merry difficult to sleep with. The child sometimes muttered and, for whatever reason, would give a tremendous jump. Unable to decide if they were nightmares, since the girl never spoke of them, Leah finally decided it was simply growing pangs.

She had awakened when Merry had given a lunge, driving her elbow into her side, and now could not go back to sleep. She had lain there for some time when she heard a sound somewhere and stiffened in the bed, straining to hear. Finally she got up and put on her robe and slippers. The room was freezing, and she shivered as she left, closing the door quietly behind her. Moving down the hall, she came to the door of the parlor and saw Stuart putting wood on the fire. He had not heard her, and she watched him silently for a moment. He was wearing a worn wool robe that she had given him years before, and she noted that he still moved somewhat stiffly. Moving inside, she said, "What's the matter?"

Stuart, startled, turned, holding a stick of wood in his hand. "Couldn't sleep," he said. "Sorry I woke you up." He put the wood on, poked the fire with the poker, and then turned to her. The only light in the room was the pale flickering of the yellow-and-red flames. "Don't know what was the matter with me. I've been sleeping like a log."

"Would you like a cup of cocoa?"

"That would be fine."

"You stay here and build the fire up. I'll fix it."

"All right." Stuart put more logs on the fire until it was roaring, and by the time the sparks were flying up the chimney like fireworks, Leah was back.

"The fire was still warm in the oven," she said. "I used the big mugs."

"Here, let me drag this couch over. It's cold in here."

"You don't need to be moving furniture. Your ribs are still sore."

"It's not heavy."

Dragging the couch around to face the fire, Stuart took the mug and then sat down. He was surprised when Leah sat down beside him.

"I was looking at some of the pictures you made while I was in prison. I'm glad you took so many."

"I really wasn't very good with the camera, but some of them turned out well."

The two sat there talking about the children for a while, and the fire roared and then finally settled down to a steady burning. A strange feeling had come over Leah. She was sitting close to Stuart, and memories came back to her. "We used to sit before the fire like this a lot. Do you remember when we were first married?"

"I've never forgotten anything. Some things I'd like to forget, though."

Leah suddenly reached out and put her hand on his arm. "I wish you could forget all the bad things. I wish all of us could."

Conscious of the light touch of her hand on his arm, Stuart turned to face her. He kept his eyes fixed on her for a moment. The fragrance of her clothes and from her hair came powerfully to him, and he felt stirred by the same beauty that had drawn him to Leah at that Fourth of July dance so many years ago. And yet he knew the deep wound he had left on her heart would not be easily healed.

"What is it, Stuart?" Leah asked. "Why are you looking at me so strangely?"

"I guess I'm thinking about all I've missed."

"I think about that, too."

Startled by this confession, so unexpected and out of character with all that had gone on in the past, Stuart leaned closer. "Do you, Leah?"

Her lips made a small change, seeming somehow softer. She held her head straight, and yet as she looked at him, the hint of a smile appeared at the corners of her mouth. "Yes, of course, I think about it. Why wouldn't I?"

"I don't know," Stuart said quietly. "I guess it's been in my mind that you've forgotten me—or tried to." He could not pull away from her, for something about her provoked a challenge in him. She seemed to be complex and unfathomable, but he noticed that her breathing had quickened, and color had spread across her cheeks.

"I've been thinking of so many things, Stuart," she said. "I don't know how to speak of them, but I haven't forgotten the good things." Even as she spoke, Leah was conscious of the attractiveness of this man that had so captured her heart when she was but a girl. Without volition the thought came to her of all the love they had shared in their early days. He had the power to stir her that no other man did, and now she dropped her head for a moment and was still.

Stuart had always known she was a woman of great pride,

and now he saw that pride had softened, or so it seemed. She had a temper that rarely showed itself, but it occurred to him suddenly that she was the kind of woman who, if necessary, could shoot a man down and not go to pieces afterward. It was this strange mixture of gentleness and courage that attracted him to her, and now without thinking, he reached over and put his arm about her. She leaned against him, looked up, and he saw her eyes were enormous, and her lips were trembling. Moved deeply, he lowered his lips and kissed her. She wrapped both arms around his neck, and he felt the sweetness of her soft lips. The emotions he felt at that moment seemed to lift him beyond himself.

As for Leah, she could not pull away, though some distant warning, far off and feeble, sounded within her. The strength of his arms was the security she longer for, and the demands of his kiss reminded her of the love she had prayed for for years. Finally she pulled back and whispered, "I'm your wife, Stuart."

Stuart Winslow could hardly breathe for a moment, then he stood up and pulled her to her feet. He lifted her in his arms and took one step. The twisting motion aroused a fiery pain in his bruised ribs, and he gasped and took a step backward. The inside of his left leg hit the couch and threw him off balance. Still holding Leah, he fell to the floor, knocking over the lamp with a tremendous crash. The fall shocked him and drove the breath out of his body.

"Stuart, are you all right?"

Stuart tried to answer but could not for a moment. As he struggled to get up with Leah's help, a voice came.

"Are you all right, Mama?"

Leah straightened up, and her eyes, accustomed to the darkness, saw Merry standing in the doorway with her blanket tucked over her shoulder.

"Yes, we're all right, darling."

"What's wrong? I heard something."

Leah suddenly could not help giggling. "It's all right. Your father just . . . bumped over a lamp."

Stuart was getting up slowly, trying to catch his breath, and he was aware that Leah was laughing at him. For a moment his feelings were hurt, and then he saw the humor of it. "It's all right. I'm just a little clumsy."

"Come to bed, Mommy. I'm getting cold."

"All right, dear. I'm coming."

Leah left Stuart standing beside the fallen lamp. She gave him one look that he could not interpret and said demurely, "Good night, Stuart."

Why, she's laughing at me, Stuart thought, and then he said as they disappeared, "Good night—and sweet dreams."

Leah went at once back to Merry's bedroom, thankful that Raimey had not awakened. She got into bed with Merry, and almost immediately the child went to sleep without another word, clasping her favorite blanket.

But Leah could not sleep. Stuart's kisses had stirred her, and although she tried to ignore it, she knew she longed for love as she had not for many years. She wanted to put the thought away, but her lonely heart made demands that she could not ignore. She grew still and thought about what had happened. *I should have told him more. That I was sorry*, she thought. *I should have asked for his forgiveness. I never have, and I've never fully given him mine, which is wrong of me.*

These thoughts ran through her mind, and for the first time, she saw clearly what her unforgiveness and rejection had done. And in the silence of the room, with the warmth of Merry pressed against her, Leah began to pray, "Oh, God, I've sinned against you—and against my husband. . . ."

★   ★   ★   ★

Stuart heard the door open, saw the crack of light that issued forth, and suddenly stiffened in the bed. The door closed, and once again the room was only bathed by the silver moonlight that fell on the carpet from the single window. He felt the bed sag and then a warmth and a fullness pressed against him.

"Stuart," she said. "I want you to forgive me if you can. I've been horrible to you, and I'm so sorry."

Stuart turned and pulled her close, and as she pressed against him, she began to cry. He listened as she told him in broken sobs how she had failed as a wife, and when he kissed her, he found her cheeks were wet with tears.

"Can you ever forgive me for the shame I brought to you and the children?" Stuart said, and his voice cracked.

As the tears fell freely, Leah held him tighter and said, "I forgive you."

He began to speak about his love and how it had grown stronger, and finally he said, "You're the only woman I've ever loved, Leah, and I'll love you until the day I die."

The words were a healing balm to her heart, for they were what Leah had longed to hear. Her heart told her that she was hearing the truth from this man who had so hurt her, and as she rested in his arms, she knew without a doubt that his heart was now finally hers. And as she accepted him, she knew that she was a wife in a way that she had never been before. She moved against him then, holding him tightly and whispering, "I love you, husband. . . ."

CHAPTER TWENTY-ONE

A WOMAN SCORNED

★　★　★　★

A brisk spring breeze ruffled Raimey's hair, tossing it over into his eyes. He pushed it back and stared out at the mass of squealing, grunting, young pigs that bumped up against his legs, almost upsetting him. There seemed to be a sea of them as he held the bucket of feed high and made his way to the trough. Emptying the feed, he stepped back, and the pigs, grunting and shoving one another, pushed their snouts in and gobbled the grain down.

"Dad, I hate pigs!"

Stuart, who had carried two large buckets filled with feed, looked at Raimey and grinned. "I don't," he observed. "I think about what all these pigs are going to do, and I just about love them. As a matter of fact," he said with humor sparkling in his eyes, "it's all I can do to keep from picking these little rascals up and kissing them right on the snout."

Raimey looked up startled and saw the humorous light in his father's eyes. "Aw, Dad, you don't mean that! Nobody could love an old pig!"

"That's where you're wrong." Stuart moved over to another trough and emptied one bucket, then another until he had completed the job. "That's all you get for now, you greedy rascals!" He moved back, giving the suckling pigs plenty of room, but their attention was all on the feed. When he reached the fence and stepped outside, he waited for Raimey to exit, then closed the gate. Moving over to lean on the side of the rail fence, he fixed his eyes on the pigs, saying, "Just think about what all those pigs are going to do for us."

"What do you mean, Dad?"

"Well, you know your mother's been struggling with that old broken-down wood stove for a long time. The thing is about to fall apart. Those fellows out there"—Stuart pointed at the mass of pigs that fought and scrambled over the food—"are going to buy her the best stove made in the United States of America."

"What do you mean? How are they going to buy anything?"

Stuart, however, paid him no heed. "I'll tell you what else they're going to do. You know that saddle you've been looking at down at the store?"

"Sure, Dad. You mean the fancy one?"

"That's the one. Well, these pigs are going to buy you that saddle, Raimey."

Raimey's eyes grew large, and he said, "Really! When?"

"Well, they've got to grow up first. They're just little fellows. But they're going to do more than that. They're going to paint the house. They're going to buy us a new truck. And one of these days you're going to go off to college. And these young piglets are going to send you off in style."

Stuart turned and put his arm over Raimey's shoulder. It was an action he could not have done a few months earlier, but he had discovered that the young boy was starved for affection—especially for the affection of a father. He felt Raimey lean in slightly toward him and grinned. "I know you are embarrassed about being a pig farmer, but I'm not. As a matter of fact, pigs are a lot smarter than horses in a lot of ways."

"But they're so dirty and greedy."

"That's just the nature of a pig, son, to eat like that. As a matter of fact, I've seen you eat like that a few times."

"Ah, Dad, you didn't!"

"When you bucked into that blackberry pie last night, I expected you to start snorting and nosing into it just like those pigs are doing right now." Stuart laughed at the expression on Raimey's face and then squeezed his shoulder. "Anyway, these pigs are going to get your mother a lot of new things that she deserves."

The two continued talking as they walked around the farm, and Raimey stayed very close to his father. Finally a frown crossed his face. "Dad, what about this war over the water?"

"It's getting bad, son. The Germans have declared total submarine warfare."

"What does that mean?"

"It means they're going to sink every ship they see, and they're bound to sink ships with Americans on them. They've done it once and if they do it again, we'll have to fight."

They crossed the pig lot, and Raimey was silent for a moment. Finally he looked up, anxiety etching his features. "Will you have to go fight, Dad?"

Stuart shook his head, a glum expression on his face. "No. That's one of the penalties of being an ex-convict. You can't serve once you have a prison record. I'd go if I could, but I won't be able to."

Raimey considered his father's words, and then suddenly his attention was caught by a car speeding along the road in front of the house. "I don't know that car."

Stuart watched the car pull to a stop and shook his head. "I don't know it either."

They saw a man get out of the car, and Stuart's eyes narrowed. He said nothing, but when the man spotted him, he came toward him at once. He was a tall man with red hair and a pair of light blue eyes.

"Hello, Stuart," he said, and a grin crossed his lips. "Got a letter for you." Reaching into his pocket, he pulled out an envelope and handed it over. His eyes watched carefully as Stuart glanced at the handwriting, then he grinned loosely. "Want me to take an answer back?"

"No."

Raimey was surprised at the shortness of his father's reply. He knew something was wrong, but he would not ask. He watched as the man lifted a hand and laughed, saying, "Well, I've done my chore. Up to you now." He went back to the car. After the car disappeared and was on its way down the road, Raimey said, "Aren't you going to open it, Dad?"

It seemed that Stuart did not hear his son. He was staring at the handwriting, his face devoid now of humor and warmth. The sudden change in his father troubled Raimey, and he said no more.

Finally Stuart shook his shoulders together and said, "Son, would you go feed the cows? I've got to talk to your mother."

"All right, Dad."

Stuart stuck the envelope in his pocket, turned, and headed for the house. Raimey stood there watching him with a troubled expression as he walked off.

When Stuart entered the back door, he found Leah washing Merry's hair. He took a seat and watched them for a moment.

"Stuart, we're about out of rainwater, and the well water's just too hard."

"I'll see if I can't make it rain tomorrow."

Leah glanced up and smiled. "You men are lucky. You can wash your hair with lye soap. There's not enough of it to matter, but women are different. Aren't they, honey?"

"Yes, they are."

Merry was sitting on a tall stool in front of the kitchen sink. Now she laughed as she reached up and ran her hands through the suds. She had beautiful hair and loved to have it washed.

"Now bend over and let me rinse it, honey."

Stuart watched as Leah rinsed Merry's hair, then began to dry it with a fluffy towel.

"Why don't you go in the living room and sit down in front of the fire? It'll dry your hair quicker. Then I'll brush it out for you."

"All right, Mama," Merry said. Jumping off the stool, she went over to Stuart and said, "Will you have a tea party with me?"

"We'll have to see, honey. I've got a lot to do. Maybe so."

"All right."

Leah smiled fondly after the girl and said, "She's such a sweet child, isn't she?"

Stuart ordinarily would have responded, but now he did not answer. Leah looked up with surprise and saw something in his face that drew her attention. Drying her hands, she came over and sat down beside him. "Is something wrong? Don't you feel well?"

Without a word, Stuart reached into his pocket. He handed her the envelope and then fixed his eyes on her face. "This just came for me," he said.

Taking the envelope, Leah looked at it, and a chill ran through her. She did not know the handwriting, but something about Stuart's attitude told her that something was troubling him. "It's a woman's handwriting. Whose is it?"

"It's Cora's. I want you to open it."

His words startled Leah. She could not understand Stuart, but instantly memories began to come back. A hardness came into her, for it had been difficult for her to forgive Cora for what she had done to her family. Now she said, "Why do you want me to open it?"

"I don't want there to be any secrets between us, Leah."

The words warmed Leah's heart, and she reached over and took his hand. "You really want me to open it?"

"Yes."

Leah opened the envelope and pulled out a single sheet of paper. Her eyes scanned it quickly, and she said, "She wants to see you." She pushed the sheet of paper toward Stuart, who shook his head. "Don't you want to read it?"

"No."

The two sat there, and then Stuart suddenly put his arm around Leah. "I'm sorry I brought this trouble on you."

"Has she tried to see you before?"

"Yes. But I've kept away from her. If I never see that woman again, it'll be too soon!" He squeezed her and, reaching over, turned her face toward him. "You're my wife, Leah. You're all the woman I ever want. I don't care anything about Cora."

His look and his sincere words flooded her heart with love and helped to push back the dark feelings that tried to plague her with fear and doubt. She reached up, put her hand on his cheek, and for a moment the two sat there. Finally she whispered, "I'm glad you told me."

Stuart pulled her forward and kissed her and then was silent for a moment. Finally he said, "I've changed my mind. I will go see her."

Leah's heart sank. "You will?" she whispered.

Stuart grinned. "Yes. But I want you with me. We'll both go answer her note."

Leah straightened up, and her eyes glinted. "All right," she said. "Let's go."

★ ★ ★ ★

Cora was finishing up a letter when her maid, Ruth, came in and said, "There's somebody to see you."

"Who is it?"

"I don't know, ma'am. They just say they need to see you."

"All right, Ruth. I'll see them."

Putting down her pen, Cora rose and made her way out of the drawing room. She turned into the foyer and stopped dead still and for a moment could not think of a word to say.

Stuart Winslow stood beside Leah, feeling the pressure of her hand on his arm. "We got your note, Cora. So here we are."

Something in Stuart's tone was challenging, and Cora stared at Leah. She was not easily disturbed and shaken, but now rich color came up into her cheeks. She could not think of a single thing to say until finally she said lamely, "Well . . . won't you come in?"

"No. I don't think we need to do that, Cora," Leah said. "Your note came, and as soon as Stuart gave it to me, I knew we had to come over and get a few things straight."

Anger rushed through Cora, for she was not accustomed to situations where she was not in total control. When she had written the note, she had been sure that Stuart would come as he always had in the old days. Now she saw that he was watching her critically with a slight smile on his face. He was, she saw, enjoying her discomfort. "I don't know what you're talking about, Leah!"

"Yes, you do," Leah said quietly. And then she lifted her chin. She made an attractive picture as she stood there, for she had dressed carefully for this occasion. She wore a loose-fitting day dress made of a light peach-colored material and covered with a lightweight jacket that fell to hip level. The jacket had a V-shaped neckline, wide collar, and long sleeves all highlighted in a light tan, and the skirt hung down above her ankles where two-toned boots with buttons finished her look. On her head was a tan velvet hat with a high crown, an undulating brim, and a dark brown feather coming out of one side.

There was an assurance in her voice as she said, "You'll have to get another man, Cora. You can't have mine."

"I've had him before!"

"I know you have, but that's over now."

"We'll see about that," Cora said. "I can get any man I want!"

"Not this one, Cora," Stuart said easily. "I know I've been a fool over you in the past, but you can forget me. I learned some hard lessons while I was in prison for the mistakes I made, but God was merciful to give me another chance. When I had given up on Him, He did not give up on me. And He'll do the same for you if you give Him a chance. He's forgiven me and so has Leah. I'm not going to make that mistake again."

Cora's eyes flew open, and she began to scream. Curses streamed out of her mouth, and for a moment it seemed she would fly at the two to assault them physically.

Leah simply stood there and waited until the tirade was over. Then she said, "Good-bye, Cora. I don't think we'll be meeting again. Are you ready, Stuart?"

"Ready. Good-bye, Cora. Don't write any more notes. They're a waste of your time."

The two left, and Cora stood there, her hands trembling. She wanted to scream and throw herself against the door. Anger and jealousy raged through her like a turbulent river. She was a woman of deep emotions, but never had a man turned her aside so bluntly for another woman. Now she went back to her room, slammed the door, and for a long time walked the floor. She was shocked at the depth of anger that rose up in her. Finally she got control of herself, and going to the door, she called out to the maid. "Ruth!"

The maid appeared at once. "Yes, ma'am?"

"Pack a suitcase for me. I'm going to Fort Smith."

"Yes, 'um. How long you going to stay?"

Cora smiled and there was a cruelty in it. "As long as it takes," she said. "Pack that new blue dress I bought last week."

* * * *

"There's a lady to see you, Mr. Castleton."

Mott looked up from his desk where he was working on a mass of papers that were scattered all over it. It was an important case, and he did not want to be disturbed. "A woman? What's her name?"

"Mrs. Cora Simms."

"Cora Simms?" Mott sat for a moment with the pen in his hand, then he carefully put it in the inkwell and rose. "Have her come in, Simpson."

"Yes, sir."

Mott rose to his feet, and as Cora came to the door, he smiled. "Hello, Cora. I didn't expect to see you."

"Well, Mott. How are you? My, you're looking so well."

Cora was wearing the blue dress she had specifically ordered her maid to pack. It was tight-fitting, and she knew it made the most of her rich, full figure. Now she smiled and took his hand, holding on to it and squeezing it tightly. "I just came to Fort Smith to shop for a day or two, and I thought it might be nice to drop by and see what a rising young attorney does in his spare time. What are you doing? Foreclosing on some poor widow's house?"

"Nothing so exciting as that." Mott grinned. "Although I've been accused of doing worse things. Here, sit down, Cora." He waited until she was seated and drew another chair up across from her. She began to talk in a sprightly fashion, and Mott was pleased at the interruption. Several years ago he had thought she was interested in him, but it had come to nothing. Now he felt a stir of excitement within him. He knew she was not a virtuous woman, never had been, and he watched carefully for some sign of her intentions.

"I thought you might take me out to dinner, Mott."

"Why, it would be my pleasure! Where are you staying?"

"At the Majestic."

"Why don't I pick you up about six? There's a show in town. We might take it in and then have a late dinner."

"That sounds wonderful. I'll be waiting for you."

When she rose, she reached out her hand, and he took it as he escorted her to the door. When she paused at the door and squeezed it, Mott somehow knew that, for whatever reason,

Cora Simms had come to town for a purpose. He was a shrewd man, adept at reading the eyes of people, and there was a promise in Cora's expression that stirred him so that he said quickly, "I'll look forward to it."

"So will I, Mott."

★　★　★　★

The evening had been a success for Mott Castleton. He and Cora had attended a performance by a troupe of Shakespearean actors who had put on a rollicking performance of *A Midsummer Night's Dream*. The company had performed the play as a slapstick comedy, and Mott had found it highly amusing.

Afterward they had gone to the restaurant at the Majestic, which served the finest food in Fort Smith. The steaks had been delicious, and now as they sat there drinking coffee, Mott found himself more stirred by this woman than he had thought possible.

He listened as she spoke. Since she was a widely traveled woman, and a wealthy one as well, she had many amusing anecdotes to tell.

Finally Cora said, "Well, it's getting late, Mott."

"I'll take you to your room."

Paying the bill, Mott left the restaurant and took the elevator up to the fifth floor. When they got to the door, Cora removed her key from her purse, opened it, then turned and looked at him and said, "Would you care to come in for a drink?"

"Yes. Of course," Mott said quickly.

The drink turned out to be several drinks, and finally Mott reached forward and pulled her to him. They were sitting on a couch, and he kissed her passionately, but she suddenly pulled back.

"Mott—" she said and then hesitated as she held her hand on his chest, holding him away.

"What is it, Cora? What's the matter?"

"Mott, do you know what they're saying about you?"

"What who's saying?"

"Everyone," Cora said quickly. She looked up and held his eyes. "They're saying that you made a fool of yourself over Leah Winslow."

"They're saying that, are they?"

"They're laughing at you, Mott. I heard a man yesterday say that Stuart had made a fool out of you."

A flash of anger rose in Mott Castleton. Her words only enflamed a grudge that had never died out. For days after Leah had broken off with him long ago, he had been consumed by the same anger that now rose in him again. He had never liked Stuart Winslow, and now he said harshly, "That's what they're saying, is it?"

"Yes."

Despite the renewed anger that rushed through him, Mott suddenly caught something in Cora's expression. He thought quickly and then drew back. "What about you and Stuart?" He saw his question stirred something in Cora, and then he laughed. "Oh, so you made your try, and Stuart wouldn't have anything to do with you! Is that it?"

"Yes. That's it!" Cora said vehemently. "I don't like to be tossed aside, Mott."

"Well, it looks like there's nothing you can do about it."

"Yes, there is. There's got to be something."

Mott suddenly was struck with an idea. He had been hoping for some time that somehow Stuart would break the conditions of his pardon and go back to prison. And now he said slowly, "All he's got to do, Cora, is get involved in one fight. I'm sure we can find a judge only too ready to return Stuart to prison."

"He's too smart to get in a fight," Cora said quickly.

Mott shook his head. He had a vivid imagination and already was beginning to formulate a plan. "Leave it to me. I'll take care of it."

Cora stood to her feet and he followed. She reached up, pulled his head down, and kissed him. "That's my man," she whispered.

He held her tightly. He was smart enough to know that she was using him. Still, she was a desirable woman, and he was a man who took what was offered.

CHAPTER TWENTY-TWO

"YOU'RE A COWARD, WINSLOW!"

★　★　★　★

Hack Wilson leaned back in his chair and studied the face of the man in front of him. His dealings with Mott Castleton had been strictly professional, for Castleton had defended him more than once on charges. If there was one man whom Hack admired among the breed of attorneys, it was Mott Castleton, for despite Hack's contempt for men in general, Castleton had at least been able to keep him out of jail.

"You must want something, Counselor." Wilson grinned. He was a course and beefy man well over six feet with close-cropped fair hair and close-set blue eyes. He was one of those men who delight in using his physical prowess to intimidate other men and had killed one man in a brawl in New Orleans. He had crippled others so brutally that most men walked around him carefully, fearful of his massive fists and savage power.

Mott had found Wilson in a bar in Lewistown, and now he took a quick drink, then leaned forward. "I've got a job for you, Hack."

"That'll be a switch. What kind of a job is it?"

"An easy one."

"I've heard that before," Wilson said sourly. "You just tell me what it is, and I'll make up my mind whether it's easy or not."

"I want a man busted up."

"What man?"

"Stuart Winslow."

Wilson's smallish eyes opened wide with surprise. "Winslow!" He thought for a moment, then laughed. "Oh, you was all set to marry his woman when he got out of the pen. I guess that makes you look pretty foolish, don't it? I been hearin' talk about it."

"Never mind why I want it done. You don't have any cause for loving Winslow yourself, do you? I remember back in the old days he took you down a few cuts."

Wilson straightened up, and anger flared in his pale eyes. "That was a long time ago," he said. Castleton had referred to a fight that Wilson had once had with Stuart in which he had been beaten. It was one of the few times Wilson had lost, and for years it had gnawed away at him. Now he leaned forward and said, "It won't be any trouble. I can whip him, but if what I hear is true, he won't fight. If he does, he goes back to the pen. He won't be fool enough to fight."

"You'll have to find some way to make him fight. All he has to do is hit you one time. Now look, Hack. Do what you have to do, but there's a hundred dollars in it for you if you get him to strike a blow."

"Two hundred."

"That's too much."

"I meant to say two-fifty. I'm like you lawyers." Wilson grinned loosely. "My fees go up the more I argue."

"All right. Two-fifty, but he has to fight. This is not just for beating him up. That won't help me any."

"Don't worry. I'll make him fight."

"And keep my name out of it."

"I'll have half of that money now. I'm a little shy." Wilson waited until Mott produced some bills, stuck them in his pocket, and said, "I'll take care of it, Counselor."

★　★　★　★

"Okay, everybody get in," Stuart called. Stuart started the car, and as Leah put Merry in the front seat and then sat down beside her, he said, "Where's Raimey?"

"He had to go back and get his money. He's planning to buy that new pocketknife he's been saving for."

Raimey, at that moment, came bursting out of the house and jumped in the backseat of the Ford. "I'm ready," he said. "Let's go fast, Dad."

Stuart laughed and put the car in gear. Turning around, he left the yard and glanced over at Leah. "Be nice to have a day off," he suggested. "You've been working too hard."

"No, you've been working too hard. Those pigs take all of your time. I declare," she laughed, "I'm getting jealous of them."

"Well, if that don't take the rag off the bush!" Stuart grinned. He turned around and winked at Raimey. "There's a woman jealous of pigs. How about that!"

"Daddy, can we go to see a picture show?"

"I don't see why not," Stuart said. "I hear Mary Pickford's got a new one out. What do you say we get our shopping done, get that new knife for Raimey, get you a new bonnet, get your mama a new dress, and then we'll go."

"What about you, Dad? Don't you want anything?"

Stuart reached back and pulled Raimey's cap down over his eyes. "I've got you and your sister and your mama. What else could a fellow want?"

Stuart was feeling good. April had brought fine weather, and the pig venture was working out better than he had dared to hope. As he drove along waving at neighbors out the open window from time to time, the thought crossed his mind, *I never thought I'd be happy over a few pigs, but I am*. He glanced over at Leah, pleased with the serenity in her features. She turned to face him, and she seemed to grow prettier as he watched her. He was struck again at how her features were often a reflection of her thoughts. Laughter and a love of life these days seemed to lie behind her eyes waiting for release. The gray dress she wore set off her figure, and with one hand she reached up and caught her hat, which nearly blew off.

"That's a foolish hat," he said.

"Don't you be taking my hat in vain," Leah said. "I paid a dollar and a half for this hat at Montgomery Ward's."

"We'll get you a better one in town."

Her lips became soft. She shrugged slightly, then suddenly reached over and put her hand on his shoulder. The thought of a smile touched her lips, and everything about her pleased him.

She was looking at him silently, and he wondered what thoughts filled her mind. But Stuart Winslow knew that a miracle had come to him in these last days. The awe of it now filled his mind, and he felt a thrill of excitement at how God had delivered him from all that he had been and restored his family to him.

"Look, the town's full up!"

"Sure is," Stuart said as he drove slowly down the main street. "It's not Saturday, is it? I don't reckon they're having a cattle sale or anything."

Pulling up to the curb, Stuart got out and saw Luke Garrison leaning against the wall of the barbershop. "What's going on, Luke?"

Leaving his position, Luke came over and said, "You haven't heard? Congress has declared war."

Leah had come up, and she grabbed Stuart's arm. "War! Is it certain?"

"Yes. It's all set. Not gonna be nice, either. War never is."

"No, it isn't," Stuart said soberly. He turned and walked slowly along the Winslow Mercantile Company, his thoughts on the battlefields so far away. "There's gonna be some good Americans dying in that war," he said.

Leah did not speak. She could not tell him what was on her heart. More than once she had breathed a prayer of thanksgiving that out of all the trouble that Stuart had, at least he would not have to go to this war!

They entered the store, and Richard immediately came forward. He leaned over and picked up Merry with a laugh and said, "I know what you want. Candy."

"Yes! Lots of it, Grandpa!"

"Well, we'll have to see about that. What about you, Raimey?"

"I been savin' up the money for that deer knife, Grandpa. I got almost enough. If you'd just give me a little discount, I could take it home today."

Richard Winslow laughed. He doted on these grandchildren, and now he said, "A discount, is it? Well, I can see you're going to be a businessman. You go look at that knife, and I'll be right there."

Still holding Merry, Richard said, "You heard about the war?"

"Yes," Stuart said. "Too bad."

"Well, it had to come." Richard shook his head sadly, then turned to Leah. "Why don't you go pick out a nice new bonnet?"

"What's wrong with the one I've got?" Leah said.

"Every woman ought to have two bonnets."

"All right. Come along, Merry. We'll get you some candy, and then you can help me pick out a bonnet."

The two men stood there and, as usual, Stuart felt uneasy. His father had never completely relaxed in his attitude toward him, and Stuart was saddened by the wall he still sensed between them.

"How are things out at the farm?"

"Nothing much to raising pigs. I hope there's a good market for them."

"There will be. With this war going on, there'll be lots of salt pork shipped overseas."

The two men talked for a time, then Richard said, "Well, I've got to get back to work."

He left abruptly, which grieved Stuart. He longed to be closer to his father, but he did not know any way to heal the breach between them.

When they left the store an hour later, everyone had something. Raimey had the deer knife in a brand-new sheath on his belt. He would pull it out, admire the brightness of the metal until his mother said, "Put that thing away. You're going to hurt somebody."

Merry had candy and a new outfit for her doll, and Leah had a new hat and a dress to match. Stuart had bought a razor, and as they left the store, he said, "Let's go get some ice cream. I feel like chocolate. What about you, Merry?"

"Vanilla."

The four made their way along the sidewalk, the sun warm on their backs. They were nearly to Richardson's Drug Store when suddenly a voice drew them up shortly.

"Hey, Winslow!"

Stuart turned, and his eyes narrowed as he saw Hack Wilson approaching. Wilson's eyes glinted, and there was a cruel smile on his face. Instantly Stuart grew cautious. He had had trouble with this man long ago in the past. The two had never liked each other, and now he saw at a glance that Wilson was half drunk. "What do you want, Hack?"

"I just want to talk," Hack said. He came up and stood directly in front of Stuart, and the odor of alcohol, tobacco, and rank sweat burned Stuart's nostrils.

"We don't have anything to talk about."

"Wait a minute! You're not going to walk off and leave me!"

Stuart tried to edge by, but Hack had reached out and put his massive hand on his arm. "You think you're better than I am? You're nothing but a stinking jailbird!"

A crowd had begun to make a small circle, for Hack Wilson's reputation was well known. Leah said nervously, "Come on, Stuart. Don't pay any attention to him."

"Hey, lady, don't you want to know what kind of a man you're married to?"

Stuart knew at that moment that there was more to this than was apparent. Wilson's eyes were not those of a man completely drunk. He was crafty and vicious, and a coldness went over Stuart as he tried desperately to think of some way out. He had been strictly warned about getting in trouble with the law again, and if he had one fear in life, it was of going back to the penitentiary. Now that he had been restored to his family and things were going well, he determined at that instant that nothing would change that.

"We'll just move along, Hack," he said. "No trouble."

Hack reached out suddenly and grabbed Stuart by his shirtfront. He held him there and said, "No trouble! You're nothing but a yellow-bellied coward, Winslow! You always were!"

Stuart reached up and grabbed Hack's wrist and ripped it away, but at that moment a tremendous blow caught him in the temple. The world seemed to be full of rockets going off, and he had the taste of metal in his mouth. He heard Wilson's taunting as he fell to the ground.

"Get up! Show this kid of yours you're not a coward, Winslow!"

Stuart shook his head and got to his feet. "I won't fight you," he said, and even as he said it, he knew it was hopeless. Another blow came to him. He managed to slip it and could have at that moment delivered a killing punch into Wilson's face. When he did not take it, he suddenly was driven backward by a barrage of blows from the burly Wilson. They came from every direction, and Stuart barely kept his feet. He heard Leah crying out for Wilson to stop, but he knew now that Wilson never would. *I'll have to take a beating, but that's better than going to prison. . . .*

Wilson stopped and laughed at Winslow's bleeding face and bruised lips. "What's the matter with you? Ain't you any kind of a man at all? Come on. You were so tough a few years ago." He looked over and saw Raimey Winslow staring at his father, his face pale. "You don't want your kid there to think you're nothin' but a coward, do you?"

"You know I can't fight you, Hack."

"I don't know anything about that, but I know I'm going to beat you to a pulp if you don't."

Hack threw himself forward, and a blow caught Stuart in the chest. The force of the man's power was behind it, and Stuart fell over the curb, sprawling out headlong. He saw Hack draw his foot back and curled himself up. Wilson's boot struck him, and pain shot through him, making him gasp.

"You'll fight or I'll kick you to pieces!" Wilson roared. He drew back his foot, but the kick was never delivered.

Ace Devainy had come running when someone had told him that Winslow was into it with Hack Wilson. He arrived just as Wilson delivered his first kick. When the burly man drew back his boot again, Ace quickly reached out and picked up a heavy cane-bottomed chair from the outdoor café outside Richardson's. He raised it high in the air and brought it down with all of his force on Hack Wilson's head. The force of the blow drove the man to the ground and opened up a cut in his skull so that a gush of red blood flowed out. When Hack tried to get up, Ace raised the chair again and brought it down. This time he splintered the chair with the force of the blow. Wilson was driven down face first to the ground, and blood seeped into the street.

Breathing hard, Ace reached over and pulled Stuart to his feet. "Get your family out of here, Stuart."

Stuart took one look at his friend's face. "Thanks, Ace."

"Get out of here. Don't stop."

"This'll be trouble for you. You know Hack."

"I'll take care of it."

Ace watched as Stuart moved along with Leah clinging to his arm. He saw them get into the car, start it, and then leave town. Only then did he turn back to Wilson. The man was stirring, and Ace looked up to see Luke Garrison, who had joined the crowd. Luke did not say a word, but his eyes were watchful.

Hack rolled over, grunted, and got safely to his feet. Blood was running over his ear and left a crimson track down his face. He stared at Ace in confusion and then down at the remains of the chair. "Did you do that, Devainy?"

"Sure I did," Ace said. He stepped closer to Hack and had to look up at the other man. "Leave Stuart alone, Hack, or I'll rub you out."

Hack shook his head, sending drops of blood flying. He growled and said, "We'll see—" He suddenly halted, for Luke Garrison had come around his line of vision. Garrison did not say a word, but his eyes were fixed on Hack Wilson. Something in them gave Wilson pause. With a muttered curse he wheeled and turned and elbowed his way through the crowd.

"That'll be trouble for you, Ace."

"You know what he's doing, don't you, Luke?"

"I know, but there's not much I can do about it."

The two men stood considering each other, and finally Garrison said, "If I were you, I'd start carrying a gun. You know what Hack's like."

"Not a bad idea, Luke. I think I'll do it."

★   ★   ★   ★

The scene with Hack Wilson had shaken Leah. None of them had spoken on the way home. Merry had cried, but Raimey had sat bolt upright, his face pale, his lips drawn in a fine line.

When they had arrived home, Stuart had changed clothes and said, "I've got to go see about a little fence mending."

As soon as he was gone, Raimey turned to his mother and said, "He could have fought back, Mom."

Leah turned to Raimey, her face set in an angry mold. "You don't understand, Raimey. Your father's still considered an ex-convict by most people of the law."

"I know that."

"Do you know the conditions of his pardon? If he ever gets

into a fight with anybody, he'll for sure have to go back to prison. Can't you understand that?"

Even as she spoke, Leah saw the resentment and pain and grief in her son's eyes. She understood the code of honor that her son saw all around him constantly. Men who would not fight were cowards. Already there was no gray area. A man either fought or he didn't. If he did, even if he lost, he was a man. Leah knew this code existed even on the school grounds and that a boy who would not fight was a sissy by everyone's definition.

Now reaching forward, she put her arms around Raimey. "You've got to try to understand, son. Your father *can't* fight."

Raimey looked up in her face, then tore himself away. "He's a coward!" he said bitterly and then ran out.

★ ★ ★ ★

Stuart looked around and was surprised to see his father. It was almost dark now, and he had been walking in the woods for some time. Bitterness had taken over his spirit, and there had never been a time when he had felt less of a man. With one side of his mind he knew that he had done the right thing, but still it had taken every ounce of self-control not to fight back and defend himself in front of his family. But he knew it was better to have been beaten into the ground by Hack Wilson than to have fought back. The thought of prison was still a grim horror that never completely left his mind.

"Hello, son," Richard said softly. He came up to stand beside Stuart and was silent for a moment. He saw the grief in the eyes of this son who had given him so much trouble, and now for a minute he was uncertain how to go on. Finally he took a deep breath and said, "I heard about the trouble in town with Wilson."

"I guess everyone's heard about it."

Noting the bitterness in Stuart's tone, Richard said quickly, "Everybody understands that you couldn't fight him."

"Not everybody. Raimey doesn't."

"He's just a boy."

"That doesn't change it any. He still despises me."

Richard shook his head and was silent for a moment, and then he said, "Son, I was proud of you."

Stuart lifted his head quickly and stared at his father. "Proud of me?"

"Yes. And I want to tell you that you're the kind of son I've always wanted."

"You're proud of me for not fighting?"

"I'm proud of you for doing whatever was necessary in order to stay with your family and take care of them." Richard had struggled over this speech all the way out from town, and now he said quickly, "I've been wrong about you, son. I've waited to see you prove yourself. I should have greeted you with open arms, but I was too stubborn. I have to ask you to forgive me for that."

The words caught Stuart off guard. "Why, of course I will, Dad, but I'm the prodigal son. Not a very glorious prodigal, though."

"You are to me, Stuart. As soon as I heard how you had let yourself be beaten, I was proud of you. I knew you were a changed man. And I know you're not a coward. But I knew something had changed in you. All your life you were selfish, but you weren't selfish this afternoon. You let yourself be disgraced in your own eyes, although not in the eyes of others, for the sake of your family." Richard suddenly stepped forward and put his arm around Stuart's shoulder. "I'm very proud of you, my boy, and I hope to show it more as days go on."

The warmth of his father's arm across his shoulder was a marvelous thing to Stuart. He had longed for his acceptance and approval for years, all of his life perhaps, and now it had come almost like a gift from heaven. He stood there silently savoring the moment and said, "I wish Raimey could understand."

"He will understand. I promise you," Richard said. He stood there not removing his arm. "We'll show him, you and I and Leah."

The moment held deep meaning and healing for Stuart Winslow, and finally he turned and put his arms around his father. Huskily he said, "Thanks, Dad."

The two men stood there in the growing darkness. Both of them knew, somehow, that a bridge had been built—that never again would they be separated as they had been—and both of them understood that what had just happened was a miracle from God.

CHAPTER TWENTY-THREE

A MATTER OF FATE

★ ★ ★ ★

As soon as Raimey entered the door, Leah knew that something was wrong. Ordinarily he came in filling the house with his noise and demanding cookies or cake and milk. This day, however, was different, for she saw that he kept his face turned to one side and attempted to make his way to his room without stopping.

"What's the matter, Raimey?"

"Nothing!"

"Wait a minute." Leah saw that the boy did not intend to wait, so she followed him down the hall, took him by the shoulders, and turned him around. One side of his face caused her to draw a deep breath, and she put out her hand, exclaiming, "Who did this to you, son?"

"It don't make no difference," Raimey muttered.

"Go into the bathroom. I'm going to have to clean you up. That's a bad cut you've got there."

Raimey obeyed her silently. When she got to the bathroom, she dampened a cloth and wiped away the blood from a cut on his cheek. That side of his face was so puffy that his eye was half closed. Carefully she cleaned the wound, applied Mercurochrome, and then took him by the shoulders.

"What happened to you? Were you in a fight?" When he did

not answer, she said sternly, "Son, you've got to tell me about things like this. Who was it?"

"It was Ralph Cunningham. We got into it after school."

"What was the fight about?"

"What difference does it make?" Raimey shook his head. "He whipped me this time, but he's two years older. You just wait. I'll get him later!"

"What was the fight about, Raimey?"

Dropping his eyes for a moment, Raimey was silent. When he looked up there was pain in his expression, and he muttered, "He called Dad a bad name. Said he was a dirty, stinking, rotten coward and a jailbird."

Pain swept through Leah, but she knew she had to handle this. "People have been saying that for a long time, Raimey. I thought you had learned to deal with it."

"It's different now. Everybody knows that Dad wouldn't fight Hack Wilson. They're saying he's a coward."

"Well, he's not. He never was. Your father's one of the bravest men I've ever known."

"He didn't show it in town when he let Wilson beat up on him."

"We've talked about that, Raimey. Now let me make this clear to you. If your father fights, he'll go back to the penitentiary. Do you want that?"

Raimey shook his head and muttered. "No. No, ma'am. I don't want that—"

"Well, what would you have him do, then? He didn't have any other choice."

"I don't know, Mom. It's just so hard to have everybody talkin' about your dad like that."

"Not everybody's talking about him. Just those who don't have any judgment. How many times have I heard you say how dumb Ralph Cunningham is? He's just a bully, and that's all he's ever been."

Raimey gnawed on his lower lip. Ever since the fight he had been torn between two storms of emotion. One was the affection that had recently come into his life for his father. It was one of the most meaningful things he had ever known. For years he had felt deprived of something that other boys had. After his father had come home and they had made their peace, Raimey had been filled with a deep sense of satisfaction and belonging he had not dreamed possible.

But now that had been all taken from him. Although his mind could understand what his mother was saying, something in him would not accept it. Finally he simply said, "I don't know, Mom. It's just that I can't get it straight in my head."

Leah put her arm around Raimey's shoulder. "Son, part of growing up is learning to accept the limitations of those we love. When we find something lacking in our parents or brother or sister or even a friend, we have to accept it as part of who they are. Your father has a limitation. He's been in prison. He would be the first to tell you it was his own fault. You've heard him say so, haven't you?"

"Yes, ma'am."

"Well, then. That's his limitation, and part of that limitation is that he can't defend himself. You're going to have to accept that, and you're going to have to love him just as much, even though he has that limitation. No matter what people say, you're going to have to cling to him, and you're going to have to let him know that you do. He needs that right now."

Raimey felt a sense of shame, and the part of him that loved his father seemed very strong at the moment. "I know, Mom. I just don't know what's the matter with me."

"There's nothing the matter with you, Raimey," Leah said, squeezing his shoulders. "You're just learning how to become a man. Friendship and love are a matter of faith. I didn't always have that kind of faith in your father. I should have stood behind him all the time he was in prison, but I was weak and gave up. I failed God, Raimey. And I'm so ashamed of it. I can't go back and undo that now," she said, looking him directly in the eye. "All I can do is ask God to forgive me and to do all I can now to show your father that I've forgiven him and I love him and I trust him. I think you're going to have to learn how to do that, too."

Raimey considered all his mother's words and then nodded slightly. "I'll try, Mom. I'll really try hard."

After Raimey left to go to his room, Leah took off her apron and went out to the feed lot, where she found Stuart at the never-ending task of feeding the pigs. He turned at once and, seeing her, came to her. She took his hand and said, "Walk with me a little."

"Well, walking with you is better than feeding pigs."

Leah's eyes swept his face and saw that he was trying his best to hide his unhappiness. When they were past the pig lot, they walked along the edge of the woods, not speaking for a while, the tall pines towering over them. Finally she stopped and took his arm. When he turned around to face her, she said, "I need to tell you something. Raimey was in a fight today."

Instantly Stuart's mouth became a thin white line. "About me, I suppose."

"Yes, it was. That Cunningham boy started it, and Raimey couldn't take it, so they got into a fight."

Overhead, the wind stirred the evergreens, making a whispering sound. High in the sky a red-tailed hawk circled, looking for prey, and from far off came the yapping sound of a dog that had treed something.

"I don't know what to do, Leah," Stuart said simply. "If I fight back, I'll go back to prison."

"You did the right thing, Stuart. I was so proud of you. So was your father. So was everyone who understands. Raimey's just young, but he'll come around." She reached up, pulled his head down, and kissed him. "God has given us a second chance," she said quietly, and strength seemed to flow out of her as she held her hands behind his neck. "And we're going to make the most of it. No bully like Hack Wilson or that Cunningham boy is going to change that."

"It's going to be hard, Leah. Wilson's not going to give up. There'll be others."

"It doesn't matter. God is greater than any Hack Wilson, isn't He?"

A reluctant smile tugged at Stuart's lips. "You're right there. Thanks for reminding me." The two continued their walk, and as they did, he said, "You know. I want to do something, and I'd like to hear your idea about it."

"What is it?"

"I'd like to go to church Sunday and make a public confession of what I did, and then give a testimony of how God has delivered me."

"I think that would be wonderful, Stuart. And Brother Fields will be so happy. So will your family. Especially your dad."

"All right. I'll do it, then. I've been walking around making that speech up all day. I don't know if I can get through it."

"You can do it," Leah whispered. She squeezed his arm and added, "I know you can, Stuart."

★   ★   ★   ★

Brother Fields had finished his sermon and was about to pronounce the benediction. During the message his eye had gone often to Stuart Winslow, as had the eyes of others in the congregation. Stuart and Leah had come in with the children and taken Leah's customary seat in the front exactly behind Richard and Diane Winslow. Fields had ignored the stir and the whispers, but he was well aware that more attention was paid to Stuart Winslow than to his sermon. As a matter of fact, he himself had felt somewhat rattled. He had so often urged Stuart to come to church, and Stuart had always refused. But now he was here, and as he attempted to preach, Fields had been wondering whether to say a word about Stuart's appearance. He had finally decided not to, and now as he said the familiar words, "We'll have the benediction now—"

"Brother Fields, may I say a word?"

Fields stopped abruptly and saw that Stuart had risen. There was something in the tall man's eyes that gave the preacher a pause, but he said at once, "Of course, Brother Winslow. Take all the time you need."

Stuart stepped out of the pew and moved to the front of the church. He turned and let his eyes go over the congregation. An immense silence filled the room, and every eye was fixed on him as he said, "I won't take very long, but there's something that I need to say to all of you. I don't think I need to go over my story. But for those of you who may be new, I'm here to confess that as a young man I didn't serve God. I broke the law and went to prison. I failed my wife, my father and mother, my family. I failed the members of this church and the pastor by not being faithful to God."

Richard Winslow sat stiffly upright, and he felt Diane take his hand and squeeze it hard. He returned the pressure, and his heart seemed to beat very fast as he listened to his son's words.

"When I was in prison, through the witness of a godly man, I found Jesus Christ. Since that time I've tried to serve Him, and God miraculously delivered me from prison. When I came home I determined to serve the Lord with all of my heart, and I'm still determined to do that." Stuart looked down for a moment and did not go on. When he finally lifted his head, everyone in the congregation saw that there were tears in his eyes. "I want to ask every one of you to forgive me, for I need your forgiveness."

No one moved or spoke for what seemed like a very long time. And then suddenly a commotion caused everyone to turn. Richard Winslow had risen to his feet. He was in the center of the pew, and as he made his way out, he stumbled over the feet of his fellow worshipers. Reaching the aisle, he turned and moved forward, holding his arms out. "My son," he said and could get no more out. When he reached the front, he threw his arms around Stuart and sobbed. Diane had followed him, and Stuart stood there holding his parents, all three of them weeping.

And then there was what amounted to a stampede. It seemed as though everyone moved at the same time, crowding into the aisles. Stuart felt hands pounding his shoulder, touching his head, pulling at his arm. He could not believe what was happening.

Someone started singing "Amazing Grace," and the old church echoed with the joyful sounds.

Amazing grace, how sweet the sound
That saved a wretch like me;
I once was lost but now am found,
Was blind but now I see.

Leah finally managed to get to Stuart, although many were hugging her, and she could barely see through the tears. She held tightly to Merry's hand and was aware that Raimey was in front of her. By the time they had made their way through the throng, she saw that Stuart had seen Raimey and had dropped to one knee and thrown his arms around him. She heard Raimey, with his voice muffled and pressed against his father's chest, saying, "I love you, Dad. I always will."

Charles Fields had stepped back to watch as the entire congregation surged forward to forgive Stuart. His wife had come up to stand beside him, with tears running down her cheeks. He put his arm around her and said, "This is what being a Christian is about, isn't it, honey?"

"Yes, it is."

The two stood there and watched as seemingly every person in the church came by to shake Stuart's hands or embrace him and his wife. And as they did, Reverend Fields knew that God was still in the business of forgiving and changing people.

★   ★   ★   ★

"It looks good, Mistah Stuart. It shore do."

Stuart and Merle had made the rounds of the farm, and Stuart now grinned. "I never thought pigs would be so beautiful. Did you, Merle?"

"Well, they ain't exactly what you call beautiful," the older man said. "But iffen you think of them as cash money, I reckon they're right pretty. You done had a good idea here. We gonna have a fine crop ready for shippin' pretty soon. We ought to do even better next year."

"I've already got an offer, Merle. A lot better than I thought."

"Well, ain't that fine. Now I reckon you can buy Miss Leah a brand-new red dress."

"And you can get Annie one, too. Maybe with a red petticoat to match."

The two continued their stroll around the farm, speaking of the improvements to be made. It was Saturday, and Leah had taken Merry and Raimey over to the Devainys' for a visit while Stuart had stayed home to catch up on work.

He worked outside all morning and at noon had gone inside to fix a quick lunch—a bologna and cheese sandwich washed down with fresh milk. After lunch he had opened up the books and was going over the numbers when he heard a voice urgently calling his name. He went at once to the front of the house, where he saw Merle's son Wash dismounting from a horse lathered up from a hard gallup.

"What is it, Wash? Somebody hurt?"

"Not yet. But it's bad, Mistah Stuart." Wash's eyes were wide and his expression tense. "It's that Hack Wilson. You know I done been workin' for him some, and I was listenin' to him talk. He didn't know it, but I heard him. He said he's going over to beat up Mistah Devainy. I thought I better come and tell you right quick 'cause you might want to help."

Instantly Stuart ran toward the car. "Thanks, Wash."

"You better let me go with you, sir, and you get a gun. You know how he is. "

Ignoring this comment, Stuart started the car and left the driveway in a roar. He bent over the wheel, trying to urge more speed out of the Ford, and dodged a wagon that almost sent them into a ditch.

The Devainy place was only two miles away, and as he pulled up, he saw a strange car in the driveway along with a truck.

He shut the engine off, leaped out of the car, and ran up the front steps. As soon as he stepped inside, his eyes swept the room, and he saw Leah backed against the wall holding tightly to Merry and Raimey, one on each side. Ace was slumped against another wall, his face bloodied, and on the opposite side of the room, held strongly by two men, Ellie was crying and holding on to two of her children.

"Well, look who's here. If it ain't the jailbird," Wilson said with a cruel grin.

Hack Wilson's fists were bloodied, and cruelty glinted in his eyes. "What'd you do? Come to save your buddy?"

"Leave him alone, Hack."

Stuart's words were clipped, and he took in the three others who were with Hack. They were all roughnecks. He knew one of them, Zane Butler, a tall rawboned bully of a man who had been in trouble all of his life. He was grinning broadly as he held on to Ellie.

"Well, it looks like it's the fiddle player here. You gonna play us a little fiddle music?"

Ace was barely conscious. One of his eyes was swollen shut, and blood trickled down his chin. He gasped, "Don't let 'em make you fight. That's what they want, Stuart."

"Make him fight! Why, this yeller belly won't fight." Hack

moved over to where Raimey stood, held by his mother's arm. Reaching out, he took the boy's arm and jerked at it. "How's it feel to have a coward for a daddy, boy? He ain't much of a man, is he?"

"Leave the boy alone," Stuart said, keeping a tight rein on his temper. His mind was working quickly to find a solution. Though he could not see any good end to this, his one idea was to get Hack and his cohorts outside of the house. "Come on outside and leave Ace alone."

"You ain't givin' no orders here!" Hack growled. The muscles under his thin shirt rolled, and he gave Raimey a shake. "Come on. I'm mistreatin' your boy. Ain't you gonna do nothin' about it?"

"Don't do anything, Dad," Raimey pleaded. "He's just tryin' to get to you."

Stuart blinked at the boy's words. He could see that Raimey's face was pale, his lips set. "He ain't nothin' but a coward himself, son," Stuart said. "He wouldn't pick on anybody that could fight him back."

Wilson cursed and released the boy, but then a light leaped into his eye. His hands shot out, and he caught Leah by the arm. He pulled her over despite her cries and said, "Well, at least I'll get a little lovin' out of this good-lookin' woman here." He laughed at Leah's struggles and said, "Come on, now. You ain't had no real man. You and me might have some *real* lovin'."

At that moment Stuart realized there was no way out. A coldness overcame him, and he knew he was sealing his own doom. But these were his wife and son and daughter and friends, and he would fight for them no matter what penalty he might have to suffer.

Hack's eyes were averted, and his back was half turned. He heard Zane Butler cry out a warning, but even as he whirled around, it was too late. Stuart had lifted his right arm and pivoted his weight to bring his forearm down full force across Hack's neck. The impact drove him to the floor. It would have broken the neck of a smaller man, but Hack's thick muscles and heavy bones protected him.

Stuart spun in time to see Zane Butler release Ellie and lunge for him, yelling, "Get him! We'll beat the soup out of him!"

Zane was a wild and wicked fighter, the best in many a bar-room brawl, and his blow caught Stuart high on the head. Stuart half blocked it and at the same time grabbed Butler's neck. He swung him around, grinding until the man screamed out, then was forced to loosen his hold, for the other two were upon him now, throwing punches.

The room was filled with shouts, and Hack Wilson was getting to his feet and shaking his head. When he saw the three closing in on Stuart, he yelled, "Hold him!"

Hearing Hack's voice, Stuart picked up a chair, and as one of the men he did not know rushed at him, he shoved the chair legs at him. One of the legs caught the man in the mouth, shattering his teeth and ramming back into his throat. He fell back with a gurgling scream, and as he did so Stuart caught a tremendous blow in the mouth from Butler. He reeled backward and struck the wall. He doubled over to dodge a fresh onslaught of the two and was driven to the ground. The three began kicking and throwing blows, and Stuart knew he was no match for them. He struggled to his feet, but Hack was there and caught him with a blow that struck him in the chest. Again he was driven back against the wall.

He had no chance to move, for Butler and the other uninjured fighter had grabbed him by the arm.

"Well, y'all have seen it now—Stuart Winslow fightin'. You're going back to the pen, Winslow, but first I'm going to mark you up a little bit."

Stuart struggled but could not free himself from the grip of the others. He saw, as through a red haze, Hack Wilson drawing his hand back, and he knew it was over.

Suddenly Stuart caught the sound of footsteps, and everyone turned to see Merle come roaring into the room holding a pick-ax handle above his head.

"Get out of here!" Zane Butler snarled.

Without a word, Merle swung the pick ax with all of his force. Butler raised his arm, but the blow snapped it like a dry stick. His scream was cut off as the pick-ax handle came down on his head.

"Now, wait a minute—" the other man said, releasing Stuart's arm.

But there was no stopping Merle. He advanced, swung the pick ax, and caught the man on the shoulder. It drove him down, and he began scrambling to get away.

Shocked by this turn of events, Hack Wilson reached into his hip pocket and pulled out a revolver. "All right! I'm going to blow your brains out!" he snarled.

At the instant he raised the revolver, something crashed into his head.

He fell to the floor, dropping the pistol, and Stuart, who was now free, saw that Ellie Devainy had brought down a massive piece of her prized pottery on his head. It had shattered, driving Wilson to the floor.

Instantly Leah stepped forward, picked up the pistol, and pointed it at Wilson. Wilson's thick head was cut by the pottery, and he was dazed. But he got to his feet and saw the damage around him. Taking in the gun, he snarled, "You won't shoot!" He took a step forward, but no more, for Leah lowered the gun and deliberately shot him through the thigh.

The slug knocked Wilson's leg from under him, and he lay there with his eyes enormous. "She shot me!" he gasped. "She shot me!"

"Should have shot you in the head!" Ace said. "We'll have to have some law on this. Go get the sheriff, Merle. Better get a doctor, too," he added. "But if we have good luck, this bum will bleed to death before he gets here."

CHAPTER TWENTY-FOUR

LEAH'S SONG

★ ★ ★ ★

Richard Winslow looked up with a start, for Leah had come rushing into his office, her eyes wide with alarm. Her hair was mussed, and she cried. "Dad, you've got to help us!"

"What's wrong?" Richard said. "Is it one of the kids?"

"No!" Leah gasped, almost out of breath. Luke Garrison had arrived and taken charge, and Leah had come into town at once.

"It's Stuart," she said. "He's under arrest."

Richard blinked with surprise. "Under arrest! What for?" He listened as Leah told the story and then took a deep breath. "That's all right. Don't worry about it, Leah," he said grimly. "He was just defending his family. No jury would convict him for that."

"Luke hated to do it, but he said that the law was clear. You've got to do something."

"I will do something," Richard Winslow said, his jaw set. "Have you told Diane?"

"No. I wanted to come to you. I know you can help him. You've got to, Dad."

Richard Winslow, despite his agitation, felt pleased. "I'm glad you felt you could come to me, Leah. You haven't always been able to do that, but I'll tell you one thing. Before my son goes to jail again, there's going to be a lot of people made miserable! Now you go tell Diane, and I'll take care of this end."

Ten minutes later Richard stormed into the jail. He found Luke Garrison disturbed about the whole thing. "I didn't have any choice, Richard. I arrested those four thugs for assault and battery and anything else I could think of. Don't worry. They'll do some time."

"But what about Stuart?"

"Well," Garrison shrugged. "They all said he fought. You know what the condition of his pardon was."

"Forget the conditions, Luke! I'm not going to stand for this! You know as well as I do they set him up!"

Garrison stared at the older man and said, "I didn't think you would. Come on. You can see Stuart. Stay as long as you want."

Following the sheriff back, Richard waited until the cell door was open, then stepped inside. He found Stuart sitting on the cot looking despondent.

"Well, I guess I did it again, Dad."

"Don't talk like that, Stuart," Richard said sharply. "This won't amount to a thing."

"I think it might," Stuart said. Ever since the brawl he had been subdued. The governor had made it plain that one infraction would send him back to Tucker Farm. He had thought of little else, and now he shook his head. "I don't know, Dad. It looks pretty bad."

Sitting down beside Stuart, Richard put his arm around him and squeezed him. "I'm not worried a bit. God hasn't brought you this far to let you down. We've just found each other, son, and we'll get out of this bind. You see if we won't."

Stuart's heart warmed, and he felt the pressure of his father's arm. "I'm glad you're here, Dad," he said simply. "I need you."

"Don't worry about it. I'll get on the phone, and if I have to, I'll go all the way to Little Rock to see the governor. Stokes is up for reelection, you know. He's walking a mighty fine line. So if he wants my support and this county's, he'll listen to me."

Once again Stuart said, "I need you, Dad. I'm glad you're here."

★ ★ ★ ★

The courtroom of Judge Franklin Markham was packed. Every chair was filled, and spectators lined the walls. The bailiff had finally been forced to lock the doors. The air was full of the buzz of talking as the judge entered, and only when he slammed his gavel and said, "Order in the court!" did the noise mitigate.

Judge Markham was nervous, although he tried not to show it. He knew this case would be a hot potato. The district attorney, James Madigan, was a young man who wanted to get his name in the newspapers and was determined to press the charges against Stuart Winslow. Markham had argued with him that it was not right or just, but Madigan had simply grinned and said he was upholding the law and the conditions of Winslow's pardon.

"The governor got his seat by putting Winslow away once. I may get his seat by putting him away again."

What Madigan did not know was that Judge Markham had been under considerable pressure from many in the community. Every decent person despised Hack Wilson and those who had joined him in assaulting Ace Devainy and his family, and there was warm sentiment for Stuart Winslow everywhere. One of Markham's firmest supporters had said to him directly, "You send Winslow back to jail, Franklin, and it'll be open season on decent citizens. Put Hack and his bunch away as long as you want, but leave Winslow alone."

Now District Attorney Madigan rose and began addressing the judge. There would be no jury until later. "Your Honor," he said, "this is a clear case. I never hope to see a clearer one. The governor showed mercy on this man. He let him out of prison with only one condition—that he not get into a fight or trouble of any kind. The governor was very strict about that, and I trust he still is. I sympathize with the defendant, but he broke the condition of his pardon, and he must answer for it."

Madigan continued for some time, making a strong case against Stuart Winslow. When he finally sat down, Judge Markham said, "We will hear from the defense."

The lawyer that Richard had engaged, Dennis Cole, was a middle-aged man of good reputation. He had an excellent record of winning cases and now stood forward. A short man with quick motions of eye and hand, he said, "I will be as brief as my opponent. We at once admit that the condition of the pardon was fair and just. But there are mitigating circumstances here. The defendant's wife and family were being abused. A friend of his had been badly battered. Hack Wilson was carrying a gun, and I have no doubt he would have used it."

"Objection!" Madigan shouted. "Supposition!"

Judge Markham wanted to overrule, but there were no grounds to do so. "Sustained. You must not read the mind of anyone, Mr. Cole."

"Very well. I will not read his mind, but he *has* shot people in the past."

"Objection!" Madigan said. "No bearing on this case!"

Dennis Cole said quickly, "I withdraw the statement." He went on to state the record of Stuart Winslow, stressing the fact that he had at one point refused to defend himself when attacked by Hack Wilson. "In that case he kept the rules of his parole to the letter, but when his family was attacked, that was a different matter. I think Your Honor would not want any man to let his family be harmed while he stood idly by."

The duel between Madigan and Cole went on for some time, but finally the judge said, "The court will recess for one hour, at which time I will render my verdict."

Stuart was taken back to the small room by the bailiff. At once it was filled up with his parents and family, along with Ace and his family.

"Well, we've got to be prepared for the worst," Stuart said. "The judge doesn't have much choice."

"Yes, he does, Daddy," Merry insisted. "That judge has got to let you go." Merry had sat beside her mother in the courtroom and understood little of the proceedings, but she knew well enough that her father was in danger. Now she sat on his lap and held to his hand tightly. "God's not going to let anything happen to you. You're too good."

Stuart had to laugh. "I wish I agreed with you, honey. But we have to face the facts."

"Well, the fact is that God is going to help us," Leah said. "I know all the facts, but God's people never go on facts, do they? If the children of Israel had faced facts at the Red Sea, they would never have gotten across."

Richard nodded. "That's right, son. We're not going to give up. And no matter what that judge says, it's not over."

Ace, however, said, "I know the judge would like to let you go, but I don't think he can. The governor was pretty plain."

"Could you ever get in touch with the governor, Richard?" Diane asked.

"Yes. I talked to him on the phone. He said he didn't want to get involved. I put the matter as well as I could, but that was all I could get out of him. I got the feeling that he's sorry it all happened. But he's walking a tight rope these days trying to get re-elected, and I don't think he needs another touchy issue to muddy his political ambitions. His opponents would say he's soft on crime."

The door opened at that time, and the bailiff said, "The judge is coming in."

Leah put her arms around Stuart and hugged him. "It'll be all right," she said. "I know it will be."

It took some time to get the court settled down, but finally Judge Markham got the quiet that he asked for. He hesitated and shot a glance at Stuart Winslow and then around the room. His position was a lonely one, and in all his years on the bench, he had never had to face such a difficult case. He began quietly by saying, "It is a difficult thing to sit in this place. Many times I have had to give decisions that I regretted." He went on for some time explaining how it was the judge's responsibility to follow the law, no matter what his personal feelings. Everyone in the courtroom could see what was coming. He was leading up to a verdict against Stuart Winslow.

"And so it's incumbent upon me to render a verdict, and I must do so. No matter what my personal feelings are—"

At that moment the door opened, and a hubbub of voices made everyone in the courtroom turn around. Judge Markham sat up straighter and exclaimed, "Governor!"

Governor Leonard Stokes strode down the aisle. He smiled, speaking to those he knew and exuding confidence. When he got to Stuart, he stopped and looked at him and smiled crookedly. "Good afternoon, Mr. Winslow. It's good to see you again."

"It's good to see you again, Governor," Stuart returned. He felt Dennis Cole's elbow punch him, and he heard the attorney chuckle.

"Something's happening, boy. Something's happening!"

Planting himself before Judge Markham, Leonard Stokes said firmly, "I apologize, Your Honor, for invading your courtroom. It is unforgivable. And if such a thing had happened to me, I would have been very strict."

Markham knew something was in the air. He was a supporter of Leonard Stokes—as Stokes was his supporter. The two had been friends for years and knew each other well. Markham said smoothly, "You're very welcome in this courtroom anytime, Governor."

"Actually, I come as more than a spectator. I haven't had time to speak with the defense attorney, but I would like to ask him if he would call me as a witness."

"Certainly, Governor! Certainly!" Dennis Cole jumped up, smiling, beaming, and waving his hand freely. "I do call Governor Leonard Stokes as a witness."

Stokes took the witness stand, was sworn in, and then began by reviewing the case. He spoke rapidly at first as he reviewed the earlier history of his experience with Stuart Winslow. He then began to speak more slowly, and his face grew sober. "The law is about people," he said. His voice was quiet but powerful, and everyone leaned forward to hear. "In this case justice must take off her blindfold. Stuart Winslow proved he was aware of the limits of his pardon. He allowed himself to be publicly beaten rather than resort to using his fists or any other weapon to defend himself."

A murmur of agreement went over the courtroom, and Stokes, showman that he was, allowed the moment to go on. He turned to Stuart then and said in a firm voice, "But when this man's wife and family and friends were attacked, he did what any *good* man would do. He sacrificed himself. He knew well that he would sit in a courtroom like this before a judge. He understood what the consequences could be, but he sacrificed himself."

Again murmurs of affirmation and nods of agreement went around the courtroom. Stokes added, "In my judgment, we need men like Stuart Winslow out of prison serving their community, protecting their families. If the ruling goes against him," he said, turning at this point to look directly at Judge Markham, "I will do all in my power to see that he does not ever enter a prison again."

Judge Markham had noted a brace of reporters who had come in and knew that this story would be on the front page of the *Arkansas Gazette*. He had no doubt that the whole state would know! Even more important than that, his whole county would know what sort of a man he was. He also understood that if he ruled against Stuart, it would avail nothing, for the governor's power would prevail. With a smooth face but with a glad note in his voice, he said, "I find myself in total agreement with the governor. And thereby I dismiss all charges against the defendant. Mr. Winslow, you are free to go."

Cheers went up, and the governor left the witness chair and made his way to Stuart. The two shook hands, and Stokes said wryly, "I seem to have made a career of putting you in jail and getting you out. Let's have no more of it, if you please, Mr. Winslow."

"I'll do my part, sir. You may depend on that."

Stuart turned to his father, shook his hand, and said, "This is all your doing, Dad."

"No. It's the Lord's doing, and I rejoice in it. Welcome home, son. Really home at last."

★ ★ ★ ★

The day following the trial was a quiet one for the Winslows. They got up and did their chores as usual. That afternoon Stuart took Raimey out rabbit hunting, and they had poor luck, but they laughed a great deal. As they were on their way home with only two undersized rabbits, Stuart said, "We didn't do very well today, but you made two good shots."

"I don't care, Dad. We'll do better next time, won't we?"

"We sure will."

As the two trudged on, Stuart said, "Raimey, I hope you never get off the track like I did."

Raimey did not answer for a time, then finally he turned and gave his father a warm smile. "I won't, Dad. I promise. Can we go run the trotline tonight?"

"Maybe tomorrow night. I'm pretty worn out now."

The two reached home just in time for supper and ate hungrily. After supper Stuart played checkers with Raimey, allowing himself to be beaten once, but the next two games he was beaten not by accident. "You're getting too good for me, Raimey," he said. "We're going to have to find another game."

"Come on, Daddy. You promised to have a tea party with me," Merry said.

The tea party went on until bedtime, and finally the two children were sent off. While Leah was putting them to bed, Stuart got out his fiddle. He began to play very quietly, but the room was filled with the rich tones. He played for what seemed like a long time, then turned around to see Leah standing there watching him. She came to him and put her arms up, and he embraced her, still holding the fiddle and the bow.

"I know that song," she said. "You played it on our wedding night."

"It's 'Leah's Song,'" he said. "I've been putting words to it for quite a few years now."

"Let me hear them," Leah said. She was looking up, and the love in her eyes was obvious. But she saw Stuart shake his head.

"I can't tell you the words. Not here," he said, releasing her and laying down his fiddle and bow.

"Why not?" she asked puzzled.

"Well, you see they're such—well, *intimate* words that they can only be spoken in very *private* and intimate circumstances."

Leah suddenly giggled. She turned and took his hand. "Come along with me, Stuart Winslow. I think I can find us a very private and intimate place!"

He pulled her back then and took her in his arms. "You're the only woman in the world for me, Leah."

"And you're the only man for me."

Stuart bent and kissed her and felt complete and whole for the first time, perhaps, in his life. Then he lifted his head and said, "Come along and I'll tell you the words to 'Leah's Song.'"

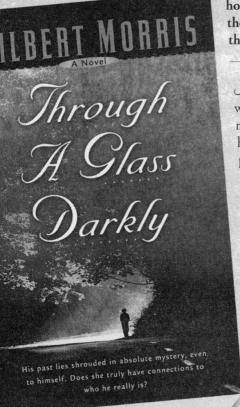